Wolves of Duty

Also by Charlotte Murphy

The EverVerse Series
The Antonides Legacy I
The Antonides Legacy II
The Antonides Legacy III
Genesis of Dragons

-

The Billionaire's Bribe

To Alexandra

Wolves of Duty

CHARLOTTE MURPHY

C Murphy xx

March 2022

First published 2022 in the United Kingdom Copyright by Charlotte Murphy via Amazon KDP.

Copyright © Charlotte Murphy

ISBN 979-8786-95400-6

The right of Charlotte Murphy to be identified as the author of this work has been asserted by her accordance with the Copyright, Designs and Patens Act 1988.

All rights reserved. No part of this publication may be reproduced, stored in a retrieval systems, or transmitted, in any form, or by any means (electronic, mechanical, photocopying, recording or otherwise) without prior written permission of the author.

Edited by Annelie Windholm
Map Design by Andres Aguirre
Formatted by Charlotte Murphy
Cover Design by Shashika2

DEDICATION

For readers and writers of colour who waited to be the receivers of magic, without oppression as a prerequisite. You are magical.

This novel features action that some readers may find disturbing, including emotional and physical abuse, questionable consent, violence and sexual acts.

LOVE, IS THE DEATH OF DUTY

Maester Aemon, Game of Thrones

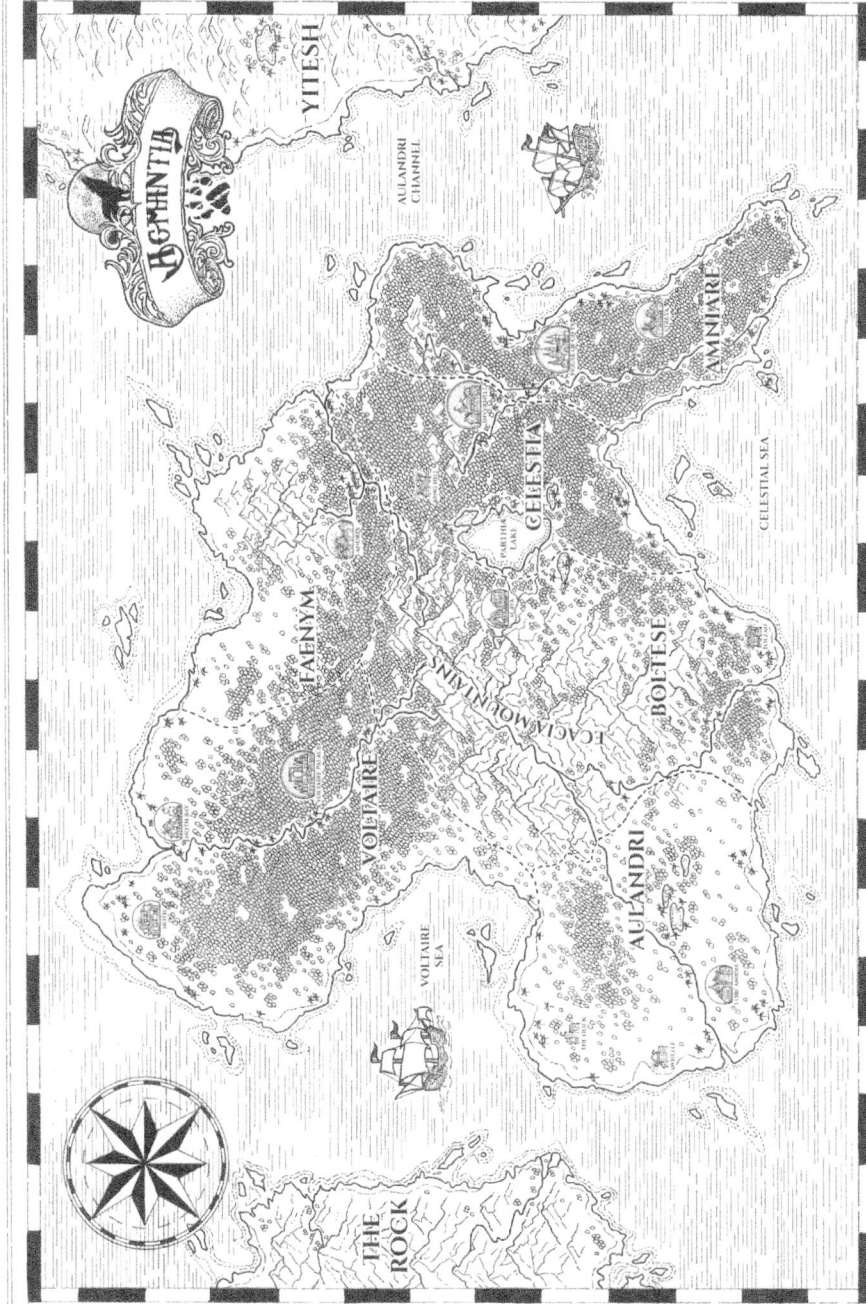

Princess
Part One

CHAPTER ONE

Thrills of potential danger coursed through my blood, as I raced through the shadowy Ecacian woods bordering my home. These woods always held the promise of adventure and after a last-minute decision to escape my rather annoying family, I ran through them on the hunt for it.

I'd been increasingly restless since the coronation two nights ago, where the Crown Prince, now King Ridian Voltaire III, had taken on the weight of the Agmantian crown. It seemed all Agmantia had turned out to witness the continued rise of the Voltaire dynasty, a dynasty that had ruled our now united nation since the end of the Dragon Age a hundred years ago. From the mountains of Faenym to the coasts of Amniare, many rejoiced in the advance of the Voltaire royals, but there were others—my family included—who did not. We weren't enthusiastic about our long-standing laws and magic being governed by *maejym*, since we kept a law onto ourselves.

The law of the *laecan*.

I continued running, wind blowing through my braided hair as I sped along, the air thick with the scents of *ceiba* giving way to towering *cecropia*. Since all of my senses were on high alert I took immediate notice when a new, distinctly familiar scent mingled with those of the surrounding nature, teasing my nostrils, making me stop.

My heart raced, but with a gentle roll I cracked the bones in my neck and edged toward the smell, my footsteps near silent in my current form. My travelling clothes clung to my body with perspiration in the substantial Agmantian heat, present even at this late hour.

The air suddenly congealed around me with potential threat.

My senses heightened, making the tiny hairs on my arms and back of my neck hum with energy. My body remained attentive to the sudden change in the wind and the odours that now blew with it. The familiar scent lingered, and my dark-painted lips twitched with the beginning of an amused smile.

I peered into the trees to my right and allowed my top lip to curl away from my teeth in a challenging snarl. My vision sharpened with an internal command and the night awakened, revealing two cunning eyes peering out at me from the darkness.

A large white wolf stalked out of the shadows towards me, its fur rich and thick from root to tip. Over eight feet tall, its piercing amber eyes studied me as it crouched on its front legs, its claws digging into the earth, ready to pounce.

I continued to stare at it with mild interest. My snarl remained on my lips until, the wolf sprung at me.

With preternatural speed, I flipped into the air. Reaching down into the ever-present magic inside me I morphed, *turned* into my wolf form just as the large paws of the white wolf connected with my chest. I spun from the impact, hitting the ground shoulder first, the white wolf relentless as it wrestled me. My paws, claws extended, wrapped around the wolf and I clamped my jaw into its shoulder. Not hard enough to draw blood, but definitely to bruise.

The wolf loosened its grip on me as we barrelled across the ground—then broke apart. There wasn't a moment of reprieve before the wolf sprung at me again. I wasn't fast enough to avoid the collision as it crashed into me, biting at a tender spot on my side. I yelped, backing away. It lunged again, its large jaws clamping around my neck.

I howled in pain.

Although the bite didn't pierce skin, it didn't stop it from hurting. I managed to wrestle free, but lost my grip on my hind legs and collapsed in a heap of fur and limbs at the base of a nearby tree. I lay panting, my large green eyes staring out at the wolf, who prowled toward me. I snarled and it snarled back, showing all its teeth in a display of dominance.

The wolf jumped as if to pounce, but instead *turned* and landed on the ground, now a man.

He was dressed entirely in white, matching his former wolf coat. A fitted sleeveless vest exposed his tanned and muscular arms. His tailored trousers and expensive boots complimented his toned, lean legs and I knew, hugged his tight backside. His hair was low cut with a dusting of black and gold curls on top. His honey toned face was clean shaven except for a small goatee and moustache. In that exquisite face, sat a pair of amber eyes that simmered like liquid gold as they observed me.

"You're getting better."

The pride with which he bestowed the compliment was like a caress.

I *turned* in response, my body morphing from paws to hands, fur to skin, in one fluid movement. My clothes mutating from where they had magically melded into my wolf form. I let his gaze caress my body—from the top of my neatly box braided head, over my breasts and curves, to the tips of my leather clad feet—as I lay on the ground before him. His look was a claim I didn't balk from.

Finally, he held out his hand to me, "There's the mother of my pups."

I took his hand and mustered all the swagger I could into my voice, "To the victor go the spoils."

He grinned with a knowing smile, as he helped me to my feet.

Sabre.

He was the heir of the Riadnak family, the current Alpha pack whose males had won the mantle of our prophetically charged Mating Games more often than any other.

He was also my boyfriend.

Sabre pulled me into his arms and stroked my side where he had bitten me. The pain was slowly subsiding: an advantage of our enhanced healing abilities. There wouldn't be a mark, especially since he hadn't bitten hard enough to puncture the flesh, but I let him soothe the spot anyway. Wolf on Wolf injuries would remain when we were in human form.

Our chests touched, all bravado gone as I fixed my eyes onto his beautiful face and invitingly licked my lips. I wanted Sabre with a visceral pulse that pounded through my veins every moment I was with him. It was hard to imagine a time where we weren't completely consumed by one another. I loved him completely.

Just three months until, with the communities blessing, we'd finally mate. After that, it would only be a few short months – *laecan* females gestate like wolves – before I would have his child.

Sabre reached up and stroked the side of my face with his index finger, "We still meeting up?"

I nodded. My long singular braids swayed with the movement, tickling my cheek. He licked his lips before lowering his head to place his mouth onto mine. My body tingled with the connection, my head light with the undiluted ecstasy of being with him. I protested against his mouth as he began to pull away, nibbling at my bottom lip as he did so.

"You shouldn't be out here alone, Aspen," he murmured, stroking my bottom lip with the pad of his thumb.

"I just needed some time away from my family," I admitted. "You know how my sister is."

Sabre nodded, "Still, you have to be careful. I was only testing your skills but I could have been anyone."

I poked my tongue out at him, "Who would dare mess with me, knowing that I'm with you?"

I wrapped my arms around his waist, pulling him further into me. Sabre smiled and kissed me again. When we eventually came apart, breathless, Sabre stepped away.

"I need to get in some more practice," he said and I nodded, knowing he meant training for the Games.

"I'll see you tomorrow," he said gently. "Please, don't stay out by yourself too long."

"I won't."

Sabre kissed me once more before he *turned* back into the white wolf and bound off into the woods.

Revitalised from my time with him, I grinned like a fool. The Agmantian night air was cool against my face, like the breath of home, welcome in my lungs. I felt elated, pondering how perfect my life with Sabre would soon be.

I *turned* into wolf form, my light grey fur shining under the distant moonlight, and took off through the trees, headed home.

CHAPTER TWO

I lounged in bed the following morning, comfortable in the cushioned pillows and warmth of my canopied bed. Iya, my maid, was bustling about my large room as usual, opening my curtains and readying my room for the approaching day. I threw my covers off, climbing out of bed barefoot, in just my underclothes and walked over to my connecting washroom where Iya had already laid out my training clothes. She bowed before leaving my bedroom, closing the door gently behind her.

The clothing reminded me I had training for Fight of the Female, a symbolic ritual fight that I'd perform with my younger sister and our friends at the Closing Ceremony of the Mating Games.

During our long and brutal history, the Riadnak family once ruled as Alphas with absolute power. As years went by, their increasing influence gave rise to resentment and jealousy from the other principal *laecan* families, each of them hungry for power and the chance to rule and soon, wars raged.

In an effort to stop the bloodshed, a shaman placed a spell on all *laecan:* when one child was born to each of the three dominant families—Riadnak, Anai or Caldoun—at the same date and time, these children would be known as the Triquetra. The two male Triquetrians would compete in challenges to secure the right to father a new Alpha generation with the Female. The family of the victorious male Triquetrian would rule—with the remaining noble families acting as their advisors and inner circle—until another Triquetra was born.

As it had given each family a chance to rule, the spell had kept everyone in line for the last two thousand years, with only one singular exception. The Triquetra prophecy was the law that guided wolf kind and now, *laecan* live in peace.

Almost twenty years ago, the current generation of Triquetra was born: myself the Female to the Anai family and Sabre as heir apparent to the Riadnaks. If Sabre won the Mating Games and secured the Riadnaks' rule, taking over from his father—the current Alpha—I would become the Alpha Consort and Sabre the reigning Alpha.

When he won the Mating Games.

There was no doubt in my mind that Sabre would win and we would finally be together.

I turned on the tap in the wash basin. Only the wealthiest families in Invernell had this type of water system. I washed and dried my face before popping a twig of *miswak* into my mouth and chewing. After a few moments, I spit it out and used a vial of mint-infused water to rinse out any residue, leaving the inside of my mouth feeling tingly and fresh.

Once dressed, I returned to my bedroom, where I found my morning tea set out. It was a concoction I'd been taking after I first *turned*. To avoid any conflict with my brilliant, though overbearing, mother, I drank it every morning before leaving the house. It helped calm my nerves, but I hated the lingering taste and smell.

Once I'd drained the dregs of my teacup, I rushed down the sweeping staircase of our manor house and out the back door, taking the short walk to the training ground.

Our home was large. It was remnant of the old days, when my forebears and those around them were lords and ladies. While the titles were gone, the money wasn't, and so we had an expanse of land behind the large, bricked structure of the main building. The training area lay at the back of the estate, separate to the gardens and entertaining lawns that my mother favoured.

Here, an armoury stood at the far end, along with a pit of sand for when we practiced hand to hand combat. The glorious Agmantian sun shone above, and as I walked into the training area I lifted my face to bask in its heat.

I found my friends already there and cursed myself for failing to keep better track of the time.

"So nice of you to join us, Miss Anai," Ulren commented as I took the spot next to my best friend Tala, giving the other girls a brief nod.

Ulren was as ancient as dust and he always wore beige. Beige pants, shirts, boots, everything the colour of boredom. I'd decided years ago that it was to match his wolf coat, but I'd never had it confirmed as I'd never seen him *turn*. He was old, much older than my father, and had the greying hair to match which lent a stark contrast to his rich umber skin.

"At least I'm not the last one here. Rogue hasn't arrived yet," I remarked, defiant at his tone.

I caught Tala's wince the second before I saw my sister's shapely figure step out of the armoury, a staff in each hand.

"I beg to differ," Ulren replied, voice droll.

I cleared my throat but found nothing to add as I watched my sister approach. Her long straight hair and makeup were as pristine as ever, even this early in the morning. She was wearing the same loose pants and bralette as me, in the ever-present stone grey shade of our House. The other girls—Rhea, Susi, Koda, Fern, Tala's little sister and Tala—all wore black.

When Rogue was close enough she threw one of the two white oak staffs at me and I caught it one-handed, twirling it to loosen my wrist. She smirked as if to say she'd expected me to duck, which made me shoot her a dirty look as she went to stand with Fern and Koda.

"Warm up, please, ladies. I do not have all morning," Ulren called out impatiently as we broke off into little groups, Tala and I separating ourselves immediately.

History told us that over eight hundred years ago, a Female named Erina Anai had not actually been born within the Triquetra. She was the sister of the Anai male Triquetrian, but had fallen in love with the Riadnak male, Jorah. When Jorah won two of the three challenges and therefore the role of Alpha Apparent he declared his love for Erina. My ancestor then killed the real Female Triquetrian, Orlagh Caldoun, so she and Jorah could be together.

What followed was a *laecan* war unlike any other. No one would support Erina and Jorah's rule, or their new born son's succession, stating his claim was invalid due to his mother's crime: only an Alpha child sired upon the true Female could rule.

Countless shaman stepped in, angered that Erina had defied the magic they put into play. Shaman, though not *laecan*, had magic of their own that had existed long before us. They held authority over our kind, even above Alphas, as all lines of succession had to be blessed by them. Their magic was mysterious and secretive, and we were taught from an early age to respect and fear them.

The shaman decreed that whoever could beat Erina in a battle would be blessed to take her place.

Dozens of female *laecan* descended upon Invernell to challenge Erina, but when the fighting was done, only she remained. As she had defeated all her challengers Erina insisted her victory proved her claim to the Female title.

She wasn't wrong, in my humble opinion, as our kind have always had a predisposition for settling matters through combat, but surprisingly, the shamans also conceded her right to rule as Alpha Consort beside Jorah. To stop any thoughts of other females repeating her action, however, the shamans declared interfering with the prophecy in such a way an act of treason, which carried with it a swift and merciless death sentence.

The tradition of commemorating Erina's fight began a few years after her death, when her son minted it to honour his mother as she had fought for, and secured his Alpha title. Perhaps I would understand it more completely once I had a son of my own. It was what my mother kept telling me, anyway. And I supposed the story had always come across as beautifully romantic… in a ruthless kind of way.

The fight would be harmlessly choreographed, since I would be newly pregnant when it came time to perform it. The thought of being pregnant with Sabre's child always excited me. It was my one purpose in life and I couldn't wait for the day to arrive and for my real life to begin.

During the fight, Rogue and I would be armed with the staffs, our friends playing the roles of the other females would attack me, and I would arise victorious after a final bout against Rogue, who would play the part of Orlagh.

We placed our staffs on the floor and began to stretch. It was barely six in the morning, and the day was already showing signs of how hot it would get in a few hours.

"What did you get up to last night?" Tala asked, rolling her neck out. She had short, dark brown curls that complimented the golden tone she shared with Sabre, her older brother. She was taller than me, with generous curves, thighs and hips and I'd always considered her incredibly beautiful, but her blue eyes, unusual among Agmantians, were her most striking feature.

"Nothing," I said pushing my arm over my head, bending it and pulling at my elbow to stretch my tricep. "I went for a run once we got back to Celestia. Just needed out of the house. Your brother caught up with me for a while, then I came home. I was too tired for anything else."

She agreed with a nod, "I would have fallen asleep earlier, but my father was going crazy when we got home."

"Crazy?" I dropped into a split on the gravel and stretched out my left leg.

Goliath Riadnak, our benevolent leader, was someone who deserved the highest respect and admiration. Of course, to Tala he was just her overbearing and annoying father but I knew it wasn't always easy bearing his name,

"He was at it for *hours*! Just going on about how much he despises *maejym* rule, hating the coronation and the pressure of invaders."

Maejym were humans who did not have *laecan* abilities and the reigning *maejym* monarchy, whose most recent king held the highest power in all of Agmantia. The Voltaires ruled the continent but didn't rule us, at least not directly. Province leaders still answered to them in all official political matters like taxes and trade. Tala rolled her eyes, but I only shrugged. The problems of the Alpha were none of my concern. As I looked over at my best friend, I watched as a brief smile graced her lips and her cheeks flushed.

"At least I got to see Sire. He came over with his father."

I laughed and moved to stretch out my right leg, "When are you two going to get together?"

As soon as the words left my mouth, I knew I'd said the wrong thing.

"How can we?" Tala murmured. "My father hates him."

I sucked my teeth dismissively, "Your father doesn't hate him, he's just… traditional."

Despite his prowess as a warrior and a leader, Goliath was a proud elitist. He loathed that Tala's only option for a suitable partner in his eyes was from the current Gamma pack—the Caldouns—since the Beta family—the Anais, my immediate family—had no sons. It didn't matter that Tala was all but in love with Sire Boltese who, although he didn't hail from a main family in the *laecan* world, came from a perfectly acceptable *maejym* one.

When the time came, Tala would be forced to marry a Caldoun, to honour tradition and keep the *laecan* aristocracy intact. She would have to marry someone she didn't love, while watching Sire do the same. Already set to marry the man I did love; I couldn't say I was particularly understanding of Tala's predicament. She knew what was expected of her, as did I.

I was just lucky enough that my want and my duty were one and the same.

Tala suddenly looked forlorn but her unhappiness made me uncomfortable.

"Things will work out," I said, standing up just as Ulren called out our names to re-join the group. "It always does."

"For *you* maybe," Tala mumbled.

Her words made me pause.

"Excuse me?"

Tala looked up at me, indecision on her face before she took a deep breath.

"Our world might turn itself inside and out for you, Aspen, but the rest of us aren't so lucky. Think before you make comments like that."

I scoffed, hands on my hips. "Comments like what? Optimistic ones?"

"*Selfish* ones!" she snapped before she recoiled, instantly regretful. "Forget it," she mumbled, marching ahead to join Ulren and the others.

I watched her walk away in disbelief, unsure where her unprovoked attack had come from. I wasn't to blame for our ways or how her father treated her. Tala's problems were her own and I wasn't about to feel guilty about them, just because I knew what was expected of me and accepted it wholeheartedly.

I shrugged off my annoyance and launched into training.

CHAPTER THREE

The following evening, I sat in front of my vanity table, my nimble fingers redoing a loose braid while making sure not to mess up my perfectly angled baby hairs. Once done, I dressed quickly, not bothering with too much make up since I'd be changing to meet Sabre later anyway. With the minimal amount of paint applied, I left my bedroom and headed down to dinner.

I'd had lessons with Ulren again today, because education in Invernell – whether theoretical or practical – was paramount, especially among the main families. As a Beta, I was obligated to attend, and Ulren claimed my sword training and tracking still needed work.

Well, so did his hairline.

I found the lessons pointless and stressed this to my parents when I finally joined them in the dining room.

"We're wolves!" I said for about the millionth time once our meal had been served. "Why do I need to learn to track anything in my human form!"

"Aspen." My father—Bracken Anai—was using his it-is-too-early-to-argue-with-my-teenaged-daughter voice. "We do not live as wolves so we must hone our human skills for when our wolf instincts fail us."

"Mine won't fail me."

I was being intentionally cocky because the truth was I was failing Ulren's classes because I didn't *care* about Ulren's classes. I simply had no incentive to actually try to succeed at something I knew, intrinsically, I didn't need practice in. My father just smiled in that way that said I had a lot to learn.

"I guess you think your wolf skills are as good as your untouchable puss—"

"*Rogue!*"

Ianthe Anai hissed at her youngest daughter from across the table. She hadn't even looked up from her jerked chicken thighs, but the bite in her tone told me she'd already had enough of my sister's shit this evening. Ever the lady I eagerly took after her in most things, and we both hated my sister's attitude. I was always happy at how I saw myself reflected in her face: the same nut brown skin, long elegant neck and shapely body beneath it. Our most prominent difference was that where my mother's eyes were the smoothest brown, mine were green.

"Have some decorum, won't you?" she continued to chastise my sister.

"Why should I? None of you care what I do anyway," Rogue remarked, despite everyone pointedly ignoring her noises of discontent. Or perhaps *because* they were ignoring her.

"If that were true, darling, we wouldn't be scolding you, would we?" my father asked.

Rogue was nineteen, same as me until my birthday in three months. She grumbled into her dinner plate, stabbing at the rice and peas. My own plate was running low on chicken and so clicked my fingers; signalling one of the servants who patiently attended us. I asked for more chicken and as my plate got whisked away I chuckled to myself at my father's use of words like *scold*.

"Aspen gets to mock me, but I get in trouble!" Rogue exclaimed at my mirth, spoon clattering against her bowl.

For once I hadn't been laughing at her, but now that the thought was in her head, I knew there was no point protesting it. Rogue had an almost obsessive jealousy of me. No matter what I did or said, she despised me simply because of the order we'd been born.

"Rogue," my mother said again, as she placed two fingers to her temple.

"Mother!" Rogue bit back, just as pissed off.

"Rogue." My father this time, a warning in his usually mild voice.

"Dad!" A whine now from my sister while I smartly remained silent.

Seeing she had lost this battle, Rogue growled at me. I looked over at her just as a ring of golden light flashed around her brown eyes—a signal of the rage that burned within her wolf form. My sister wanted my blood.

Bring it on, bitch.

I smirked at Rogue from under my eyelashes before she pushed her chair out from behind the table, and after throwing her napkin onto her chair, stormed out of the room, with a heated, "I'm going out!"

There was silence for a long moment before my father said, "You shouldn't rile her up like that, Aspen."

"That time, I wasn't even trying to." I held my hands up in surrender even as I couldn't stop a giggle. I dismissed the servant who'd been hovering by me with a fresh plate, no longer interested in the eating anymore.

"That's not the point. You know Rogue has her… issues about your position."

"Why is that my problem? I didn't ask to be the Female."

It was true. Sure, I could be nicer to my sister, but it didn't change our circumstances.

My mother chimed in once she'd slowly chewed and swallowed, "Just because you're happy with your position, Bracken, doesn't mean Rogue should be as content."

Ouch.

My mother never missed an opportunity to express her disappointment with my father's lack of political ambition. My mother was as refined as she was beautiful and had made the most of what the position of Mother of the Female had afforded her within the community. I knew that with her guidance I would be the best Alpha Consort who had ever lived.

"I endure the constant shame of my shortcomings, Ianthe."

I stifled a grin at my father's dry tone. He never let my mother distress him, no matter her endless attempts. I loved my father more than anything. He gave me everything I wanted and when my mother was being a little too imperious, he always saved me from her. My father had deep reddish-brown skin and kind green eyes, like mine. He was greying at the temples and his beard was speckled with white, but he had a youthfulness about him that age couldn't deny.

I reached out and put my hand on top of my father's.

"I'll try more with Rogue, Dad."

His appreciative smile made my face light up before my father requested that all our plats be cleared to bring on dessert.

After a spiced ginger cake with creamy custard, I pushed my chair out, while still chewing.

"*Ahfgotgo!*"

"Aspen," my mother said, impatience in her tone as she knew she'd taught me better, "do not talk with your mouth full."

I chewed a little and opened my mouth to show my mother the chomped contents before rushing out the door in another fit of giggles, her disapproving curses fading as I headed upstairs to my room to get ready for Sabre.

An hour or so later, I was dressed in a loose black dress that was able to hide the daring underclothes that Sabre liked me to wear. A variation of delicate lace that, though it covered my breasts, allowed my nipples to tease through. The thin barrier sent Sabre wild and I couldn't wait for his reaction. I slipped on some flat leather shoes and, as the night awakened, I left my room.

Laecan were nocturnal by nature and as I got older this fact had proven particularly useful. Our natural instinct coupled with being almost twenty years old, meant that my parents never questioned where I went most evenings.

Heading for the front door however, I ran into my sister as she returned home from her own nightly escapades. As she got closer to me, a strange scent brushed my senses and so I sniffed at her, taking it in.

"You smell weird."

Rogue came to a sharp stop beside me before sucking her teeth and narrowing her eyes.

"Hello to you too, big sister."

I started to roll my eyes, but then thought of my father's request this evening and offered clarification instead.

"I didn't mean it like that, it's just..." I looked at her disapproving expression. "You know what, —never mind."

I headed for the front door, already tired of her attitude, but I stopped at the sound of her husky voice.

"Aspen?"

When I looked back at my sister, for a brief moment, there was sadness in her expression. My sister was cynical, petty and jaded most of the time, but never down. It was disconcerting.

Rogue studied me for a long moment before turning her eyes on her feet, gently shaking her head. When her eyes returned to me, she looked completely indifferent.

"Nothing," she said. "Have a good night."

She turned on her heels and headed down the hallway and up the stairs to her room. I watched her go, a slight furrow between my brows.

Weird.

The Riadnak Manor sat within an impressive estate in northern Invernell. Along with the Alpha family, it housed a substantial workforce of servants, had a wing reserved for extended family, and boasted offices for our highest government officials, who all claimed they had to be as close to the Alpha as possible. Brown-nosing was a favourite pastime among Invernelli society and there was no better place to advance yourself among our kind than here.

Needless to say, I had been an official guest at the manor many times, and my mother brought me often, mostly to flaunt me in front of the other wives and mothers whose wombs hadn't been as socially fruitful as her own. My father only visited on official business and my sister less so. Even when our mother spent countless evenings at what was considered the *laecan* equivalent to the *maejym* royal court and Rogue was invited to attend, she usually found an excuse to go see Fern and Koda instead.

The guards who manned the front gates recognised me on sight. They bowed their heads, as was proper. I was the Female and—had the *laecan* main families not had their titles removed after the Voltaire occupation—I would have eventually been crowned their queen. While the title was no longer in existence, the privileges of the position were. They were what provided my mother with the reverence she received second hand—an attitude bestowed by others that had followed me my entire life.

Once past the large gates, I strolled purposefully towards the towering manor. Its tall glass windows shone with the light and activity within, while countless people and wolves roamed the front lawns.

There were many of us who enjoyed being in wolf form more than human form, but it was dangerous to stay so for too long. As children, we were told nightmarish tales of people who remained wolves after they lost themselves to the call of the night and forgot how to turn back. Wolves like that disappeared into the mountains and surrounding forests and were notoriously dangerous to come across. Fortunately, I'd never encountered one, and hoped I never would.

I continued through the estate, acknowledging those around me with a nod to the few whom I recognised. My former dancing tutor Altrix and his daughter Saelin were among them. I also spotted the ambassador to our neighbouring province Amniare, a wolf by the name of Kane Ryah who was a beady eyed whisper of a man who made my skin crawl whenever he looked at me. He smiled in my direction so I gave him a curt nod before holding my head high and directing my step toward the adjacent woods.

I left any prying eyes behind as I *turned* and darted off into the dark. My large paws bound heavily against the earth, the night blooming around me, my senses amplified. The evening air was balmy, the scent of wildflowers all around. It took me a handful of minutes to finally come upon the secluded cottage on the far edge of the estate. It was past the old buildings that few occupied unless necessary and the estate was at full capacity.

It boasted no more than one small bedroom, but it was where Sabre and I met for our too infrequent rendezvous and so it was especially beautiful to me. The intimacy of its tan timber, with thatched roofing and a wild-flower garden at the front door was a world all its own. Tucked away and utterly private, an Alpha's mate had built it many years ago for her own comforts. Once Sabre discovered it a few months back, he'd commandeered it for our own shared ... comforts.

Despite our pending mating and betrothal, it was still taboo for us to be alone together. I was the coveted Female and, as such, had to remain a virgin until Mating Day. It was an archaic way of treating the Female—none of my friends had a proverbial chastity belt strapped around their waists—but it was the only way to guarantee my purity before the conception, which was prophesied to occur on Mating Day. Not before and not after. I couldn't risk failing at my one task as the Female: to birth the next heir.

The shaman would surely blame me if I were impure in any way.

And worse—so would my mother.

I wasn't the only virgin left in our group as neither Tala nor Rogue had had sex, but we were the only female virgins left in our age group as far as I knew, which was progressive in and of itself. I bounded up to the cottage, my excitement triggering the adrenaline in my blood. Sabre was standing in the doorway waiting for me and so I leapt to him in my wolf form, but *turned* mid-air to fall into his arms, my mouth landing on his in a passionate and demanding kiss. With my arms around his neck, I wrapped my legs around his waist and he carried me into the cottage, kicking the door shut behind us.

I lay in bed with him hours later, both of us naked from the waist up. He circled a lazy finger over the smooth rise of my breast. I might have been a virgin but that didn't mean I'd never had an orgasm and I was suitably exhausted from the one I'd just experienced. I was content watching him watching me, but almost immediately the uncertainty set in.

Despite the intimacy of our current situation, I always felt shy once we'd finished our love making, left vulnerable and exposed in a way I couldn't explain. In an effort to quell my insecurity I studied the well-known lines of his face and the intense molten gold of his eyes. My gaze continued travelling down his neck, across his chest to where a tiny birthmark marred his skin. It looked like a tattoo, faint against his golden colouring, but if you looked hard enough, you could see an *A*. As dictated by the prophecy, all male children born to the Alpha Apparent bore the mark.

My own son would bear it someday, but any daughters would not.

"You feeling all right?" Sabre wondered, his voice lazy.

"Yeah. Was I... okay?"

I asked him this every time I pleasured him in the ways he had taught me. Sabre chuckled, looking at me in that adoring way I loved so much. He reached out, rubbing his thumb along my bottom lip.

"You were perfect, Aspen, stop worrying."

"I just... I don't know... I don't want you to be disappointed."

"I'm not disappointed. How could I be?" He suddenly looked sceptical, withdrawing his hand. "Is that why you do it...because we haven't had sex yet?"

"No, of course not!" I protested. I shuffled over to him beneath the covers, kissing him as he wrapped his strong arms around me. "I love this time with you. I just can't wait until we can go all the way." Heat flooded my face at expressing my desire. "I don't want to hide anymore."

The look he gave me in response wasn't pleasant. "We hardly hide, Aspen. Everyone knows we're together."

I'd annoyed him. I could tell from the steely look on his face. I swallowed, not wanting to push it, but needing to let him know how I felt. Everyone knew we were a couple, but until he won the Mating Games, I was still free for the taking by both male Triquetrians. It didn't matter that I had already chosen who I loved.

"It's not the same."

It came out as a mumble instead of the forceful declaration I'd intended. Whether it was my tone or what I'd said, it had the complete opposite effect and he shut me out. Sabre left the bed, his toned and muscular stomach on display as he began to get dressed. I cursed myself for breaking our peace and sat up in the bed, holding the sheet in place around my chest.

"Sabre."

He'd moved towards a vanity table in the corner of the room, getting his shoes from under the stool and putting them on, not looking at me and not replying before he marched out of the room.

I quickly scampered out of bed and got dressed. My body was still tender from his bites and kisses, my legs weak from the echoes of my orgasms, but once I was fully clothed and pulled my shoes on, I rushed out of the room after him.

I found him seated on one of the cushioned chairs that dominated the living area. Lounging was a more accurate description as he played with a dagger he'd found from who knew where.

"Sabre." His face was hard as marble. "Sabre, I'm sorry."

He sighed heavily, still not looking at me. "You know I don't like to be reminded."

I did know. He hated being reminded that he wasn't the Alpha and that the small decisions about our lives were not his to make.

My amazing man was a king with no crown.

I climbed onto the chair beside him, my legs folded underneath me as I leaned forward to kiss his cheek.

"I'm sorry," I said again, kissing him once more.

I leaned back, focusing intently on his profile, willing him to turn his head to me. He finally gave in and his eyes met mine. His fiery gaze burned through me, making my heartbeat quicken.

"I'm sorry."

He gave me a small smile before he finally kissed me back, his hands threading through my braids. I moaned against his mouth as he turned to lay me down on the chair. He pressed himself between my legs as his tongue wrestled with mine, both of our breathing growing heavy as we kissed.

I was losing myself in his warmth, his smell and his touch, when the front door suddenly opened, revealing an impressively tall figure in the doorway.

The mountain that was Goliath Riadnak stood peering down at us, his eyes carrying a sharp glare at his son before they fell onto me, and softened considerably.

Sabre straightened up, his back stiffening as he got to his feet. I rushed to stand beside him, smoothing down my dress to make myself presentable in front of our leader.

"Miss Anai."

I curtseyed, keeping my eyes respectfully to the ground, "Alpha."

The tips of his boots came into my vision and I took my cue to look up at him with a hesitant smile.

Goliath was gorgeous for an older man. He had long dark locs, intricately braided away from his dark-skinned face with a gold circlet adorning the top. While the title Chief of Celestia may have been defunct, Goliath remained every inch a king. The heavily embroidered white linen suit he wore, along with the circlet, showed he'd come from an important gathering. It was probably the reason it had been clear for Sabre to invite me over.

"How are you, sweet girl?"

I actually blushed as his deep voice swept over me, his amber eyes making my skin heat with excitement at being in his presence.

"I'm very well, Alpha. I hope it's okay that I stopped by?"

Although Sabre and I were destined to be together, there was still a level of propriety that needed to be maintained. Sabre on top of me, kissing me all over was definitely not part of that. My heart was pounding. How much had Goliath seen? My blush deepened and a tinge of fear rose with it. What would the punishment be? Goliath's eyes moved toward Sabre and a small smile graced his lips.

"Of course it's quite all right, my dear. Although, I suspect your mother will be expecting you home."

I nodded quickly, the dismissal and implication of my mother's disapproval clear. My heart fluttered with relief as the subtle rebuke seemed to be the only consequence for my recklessness. "Of course, Alpha. I was just on my way out."

I curtseyed before turning to Sabre, but at his stiff posture I decided even a chaste kiss on the cheek would be too much of a display of affection. Instead I gave him a small smile and waved goodbye. His jaws clenched and he kept his eyes facing forward, looking more like a soldier in his father's army than the soon-to-be heir to his mantle.

When I closed the door behind me, I exhaled an adrenaline filled breath, happy Goliath hadn't been too upset with me. With a giddy smile, I made to leave, but heard a menacing growl from behind the door.

"What the hell, do you think you're doing?" Goliath thundered, making me jump. I turned my head so I could hear better, invoking my lupine abilities to enhance my eavesdropping.

"Entertaining," I heard Sabre reply, his voice unhurried.

"Mind your tongue, boy. How *dare* you embarrass me?"

Goliath's voice was forceful enough to shake the glass in the window of the door. I'd never heard him speak to anyone like that before and I didn't wish to now. Desperate to get away from an uncomfortable situation, I turned and bounded off into the woods.

I ran for miles, my heart heavy for the trouble Sabre was in because of me. I was the one who kept pushing for more alone time and once Sabre found the cottage we knew it was the only place. He wouldn't have me in the dirt and underbrush of the woods, like others were prone to, and leaving Invernell would raise too many questions. He'd only wanted our time together to be special.

My heart pounded, not only from running, but from the fear of how this would affect me once my mother found out. And she would find out. Goliath would have to tell her.

I sighed, unsure why I cared when I knew I wouldn't get into any real trouble. She'd be mad at me for giving Celeste Riadnak something to gossip about her with, then in the same breath probably praise me for getting Sabre alone in the first place.

Either way, my mother would understand and life would continue just like it always did.

It had to.

When I finally came to a much-needed stop, I realised I didn't recognise where I was. Since we had all grown up in the woods, I stopped to get my bearings, my eyes and ears sharp and in tune with the nature around me. I padded into a slow walk, my upset weighing heavy on my conscience as I tried to establish the way home. They were as much a part of us as the snow and mountains were to the packs who lived in the north.

As I padded along, lost in thought, my senses heightened as I stopped to study the shadowy spaces between the trees. Suddenly, two amber eyes peered out at me from within the bushes and a black wolf stalked out of them to tower over me.

Caius Caldoun.

The third Triquetrian.

Caius and his brother Asher were the heirs of the Gamma pack. It was Caius who had been born to challenge Sabre on Mating Day and compete against him for the Alpha title.

And I absolutely despised him. Any time we spoke was a battle of insults. He was an insufferable, moody little nobody and I could not stand his self-righteousness.

His presence filled me with an intense dread, the root of which I couldn't seem to find. I knew he couldn't hurt me, not unless he wanted to be torn apart by the elders, but there was nothing in me that trusted this fact would deter him if he set his mind to it. He always unsettled me. His fur was so black; I could hardly tell the difference between him and the night sky. I got the thought in my head that if I were to touch him I might fall into that blackness and never come out again. His piercing eyes glowered at me, unyielding.

For a moment, I just stared back, then watched as he casually sat on his hind legs, not looking away. I hated that the same golden gaze that excited me from Sabre, gave me nothing but judgement and disdain from Caius.

His nose twitched,

...your tracking is incredibly shit...

As wolves, we spoke into each other's minds. Only other wolves around us would be able to hear as the connection was mute when we were in human form.

...*excuse me?*...

...*i've been watching you for a while and you didn't notice* ...

...*no...no, you weren't*...

...*yes, I was*...

...*no, you weren't*...

He didn't reply and even though we were wolves, I knew he'd rolled his eyes at me.

...*what are you doing out here grey?*...

Grey. His nickname for me from when we were children, back when we were friends. I should answer his question, but the truth was too raw. I couldn't admit that Sabre was in trouble, it was none of this silly gamma's business. I'd rather die than admit any vulnerability on our side to Caius Caldoun.

...*nothing. i need to get home. not being around gammas like you*...

I padded towards him, my strong grey shoulder brushing against his black one as I went past. I was a foot smaller than him, as most females to males.

...*are you okay?*...

The sincerity after my dismissal caught me off guard as the same words from a different time drifted into my head uninvited. A time when I was scared and alone and he'd asked me the same question...

...*you smell of him*...

I stopped. Caius stood and came to stand in front of me.

...*his scent is all over you*...

...*jealous?*...

It was a foolish thing to say, to even think, but the retort was all I had. There was mirth in his tone when he spoke next.

...*never*...

But his sombreness returned with the next sentence.

...*the riadnaks aren't admired everywhere, aspen. be careful who you allow to smell that on you*...

I was confused. Who would dare challenge the Alphas? And, by extension, me?

...*i can protect myself*...

...*i highly doubt that*... The amusement was back and so I growled at him.

...*i hate you*...

...*i know*...

...*i hope I don't ever have to mate with you*...

The truth felt good to admit but the elation was short lived as Caius chuckled, the reaction a feeling more than an actual sound.

...*you won't*...

...*excuse me?*...

...*we will never have to mate*...

My brain was taking a moment to catch up with the idiocy that had come out of his mouth. I might not want to mate with Caius, but the possibility was always there, no matter how I ignored it.

Caius turned his large head towards me and said, ...*because i won't be competing*

With a lasting study of me, Caius turned and took off into the night.

It was only after I'd left the clearing, I wondered what he had been doing in the woods.

CHAPTER FOUR

My life was over.

What would everyone think if Caius didn't compete in the Mating Games? I couldn't begin to imagine the outrage that would erupt through our society, or the effect it would have on me. What if I was blamed for it? No, it couldn't go that far. And yet, the possibility hung over my head like a guillotine.

Why would he *do* this?

Nothing would come from this but social leprosy for his entire family. Not to mention the complete destruction of our thousand-year-old traditions so what was he thinking?

I couldn't afford to think about it now so got ready for today's lesson.

There was never a more useless lesson than Tracking.

Why would I need to know how to track when I had wolf senses and could smell blood from over a mile away? I felt changes in the wind through the sensitive strands of fur over my body, and the change of weight in the ground beneath my paws.

The only perk to Tracking was that I spent that lesson with Sabre. After our disagreement, last night, I was anxious to spend some time with him, even if it was in the company of others. He looked gorgeous in navy blue pants and another sleeveless vest, sturdy black boots fitting snugly to his ankles and thick brown leather cuffs around his wrists, the top of them lined with silver, matching the buttons on his vest.

He looked extra glorious in the perfect summers day, but when you lived in a tropical climate, most things looked glorious. Invernell, our hometown, was nestled within the King Hill Forest of Celestia, southern Agmantia. While there were countless woods, forests and jungles that made up our country, the cecropia and intermittent palm trees that surrounded us would always be home. Colourful birds flew in the air while exotic creatures prowled the grassy terrain and mountainous regions of the neighbouring provinces. As wolves, we spent a lot of time in the woods and among the mountains—as at home there as we were in our manors.

Sabre and I stood with my back against a tree while the others waited for Ulren to arrive and start the lesson. He rested his arm against the tree behind me. He angled himself so no one could see me if they looked over and lowered his head. My breath shortened and my face heated in anticipation of his lips on mine.

"Are we okay...after last night?"

Sabre's eyes shuttered and became dark before a ring of gold light flashed. The gold happened when one of our emotions were especially heightened. He blinked, looked directly at me and the dark expression was gone.

"Yeah...we're good."

Sabre lowered his head without further comment until his lips were against my neck. The feather light touch of them would have sent me wild if the quick flick of his tongue hadn't done it first. My body jerked and sent a bolt of lightning skirting to the connection between my legs. I clenched my thighs together to stop the building ache between them.

"I'll arrange something again soon."

It was a promise of what he would do to me soon, a reminder of what he'd been doing to me for the past year. We'd been seeing each other for longer than that, but only in the past few months had we made our relationship more sexual. There hadn't been any point before, but now that our joint birthday was only months away, both of us were growing impatient about being together intimately.

I opened my mouth to respond, but was interrupted by Ulren's voice as he approached.

"Come now, children," he said sharply. Why Ulren continued to call us children never ceased to piss me off. "Gather around so I can arrange you into pairs."

"What?" I demanded, stalking over to him, but Ulren ignored me.

Our pairings were always the same, it's why Sabre and I got to spend so much time together. I was with Sabre, Fenrir and Susi paired, Koda and Asher and Tala and…

"Caius?" Ulren called into the crowd and Caius stepped forward. He removed his hands from his pockets as he walked to stand a little closer to me; listening to Ulren read off the other names.

In his human form, Caius was Sabre's antithesis in that he mostly always wore black, matching his fur. Or his mood. I'd never cared which. My heart beat rapidly at the rage from seeing him again and all the feelings about his intentions for the Mating Games came flooding back.

"Caius will be paired with…"

Don't say Aspen. Don't say Aspen. Don't say Aspen.

"…Aspen."

"*Why?*" I protested, stepping fiercely toward Ulren again. "We *always* have the same partners!"

"Things change, Miss Anai. I'm sure you of all people can appreciate that."

He was referring to the change in leadership that would come from my womb, but I didn't care. I didn't want to work with Caius. I narrowed my eyes at Ulren, "I'll tell my father about this!"

Ulren looked back at me with disinterest and laughed, "Go ahead. I'll be sure to tell him all the other classes you're failing."

I growled, my throat rumbling with the threat as I took a daring step toward him.

"Enough, Aspen!" Ulren snapped at me. It was so out of character for the geriatric tutor that I actually froze.

Ulren ignored me and continued down the list, putting everyone else together. Sabre ended up with Koda, Fenrir's younger sister of all people. She was pretty in her own way, but I'd never considered her a contender for Sabre's affections, so I never paid her much attention. I eyed her now, with her dark hair and dark eyes, and found her wanting. I growled, my frustration potent in the air as Ulren told us our assignment.

I gave Caius a sideways glance, once Sabre had kissed me and walked over to join Koda.

Caius had rich brown skin that darkened heavily in the constant sun. His hair was expertly cut, with dark waves on top. It shone with whatever product he added to it, maybe coconut oil. He had a serious and angled face, lined with dark stubble. He was well built, but that fact was currently hidden under his light wool shirt, gaping open at the neck, revealing his stark clavicle and a hint of hairless chest.

"Don't think I'm happy about this!" I hissed at him.

Caius finally looked over at me and his eyes, the colour of molten gold, shone with disdain and indifference.

"I didn't ask."

I turned to him, my hands on my hips, observing him through narrowed lids. Caius didn't spend a lot of his time in Invernell since his father—Maximus Caldoun—travelled a lot and Caius went with him. On the rare occasion when we did cross paths, it was never usually a great time for either of us. He was always rude to me and whenever he was around I just felt...nauseous. Having to deal with his attitude filled me with such apprehension that I felt ill enough to want to avoid him at all costs. I'd been preoccupied when I'd seen him last night but now every hateful thing I felt for him was in full effect.

"Just stay out of my way, Gamma."

He rolled his eyes with a contemptuous chuckle, "Gladly."

I wanted to say something else, to have a witty retort, but nothing came to mind. Frustrated, I turned back to Ulren, my anger coursing through my blood. I caught Tala's eye and she looked concerned, but I shook my head at her that I was fine and not to worry.

Once the dull sounds of Ulren's voice faded, Caius and I set off into the woods. Four Invernelli residents were being held somewhere among the trees and we simply had to find them. We'd been given an item of their clothing to catch the scent, then were sent on our way—no *turning* allowed.

Thirty minutes into our search, Caius spoke from where he strolled casually behind me, his hands still in his pockets.

"You're going the wrong way."

I didn't bother turning around, "Excuse me?"

"I think I was clear enough."

Still I didn't bother looking at him. "I know what I'm doing."

"Clearly not, since you're going the wrong way."

With a huff, I finally looked at him. He inclined his head in the direction behind him.

"The trail went that way about five yards ago."

I folded my arms across my chest, "You don't know that."

"I do know that," he said with finality. "Climb off that high horse of yours and you might know it too."

My skin prickled, the hairs all over my body standing to attention as my teeth ached. My canines wanted to extend and rip his throat out. I just wanted to get away from him and back to Sabre, where it was safe.

"High horse?"

Caius looked me up and down before turning to head the way he'd indicated, his walk unhurried as he lost himself among the trees.

"Don't walk away from me!" I ran up to him, grabbing his shoulder to make him face me. I didn't expect the anger that simmered in his gaze and instantly retracted my hand.

"Don't. *Touch* me."

I hated that I shrank from his tone, that I felt genuinely afraid. Still, I wasn't one to back down from a fight and definitely wasn't one to let him know he'd frightened me.

"Tell me what you meant," I demanded instead, trying to ignore the shiver of apprehension that crawled up my spine.

"Forget it." He walked away again,

"No, I won't forget it. What did you mean, Caius?"

He seemed triumphant as he stalked back toward me, but I had no idea why, "So you do know my name."

The sun caught his eyes in the most unusual way, making them look like they were on fire. I swallowed, annoyed that he looked almost handsome.

My eyebrows knotted at the stupidity of the question. We used to play together in the stream behind his house. I used to stay up late listening to stories his mother told, when my father defied Ianthe and let me stay over at Caius' house.

I'd known Caius forever.

"Of course I know your name."

"Then why do you never use it?" It was a challenge. "It's always *him* or *Gamma* or whatever colourful insult you cooked up that day."

He turned away, leaving me stunned, speechless.

"You're saying... I'm a snob."

The realisation hit me hard.

"If the fur fits," he called over his shoulder, walking away again.

I hurried after Caius and found him crouched on the ground with his fingertips lightly grazing a footprint in the dirt.

"If we *turn*, we can catch up. We *turn* back and no one will know you went the wrong way."

I started to say something, but decided against it. He wasn't even looking at me when he spoke. It angered me.

"I'm not a snob."

Why I cared what this *Gam*—... what Caius thought was beyond me, but I had an overwhelming need to stop him thinking that way.

A girl had a reputation to uphold.

"I don't care either way what you are, Grey," he straightened up from the ground and came to stand in front of me. "Do you want to *turn* or not?"

"Not," I said, folding my arms across my chest.

What was failing one class if it meant that he'd fail too? The idea delighted me.

"Look, I don't need Ulren on my back about this."

He was genuinely annoyed, the gold of his eyes practically sparking with it. Observing him I realised I hadn't been alone with him in years. Not since I was thirteen

I snorted, fiddling with one of my braids, "Ulren won't do anything."

"To you maybe."

I barely heard him, but his response irked something in me. Before I could reply, new smells joined us and seconds later, Sabre and Koda emerged into the clearing where we stood.

A smile erupted on my face as Sabre approached, but he took no notice of me as he marched up to Caius and gave him a harsh push.

"What are you doing with my girlfriend?"

Koda came up beside me, making no comment and instead giving me a small smile, which I briefly returned. One lesson with Sabre and now she apparently thought we were friends.

Highly unlikely.

Caius didn't bother responding to Sabre's taunt. Instead, he ignored him completely and headed into the woods. Sabre reached out to grab him just as I had done, and for a split second I found myself worried for Sabre.

"Don't walk away from me, Gamma!"

Caius turned his head and peered down at the hand on his shoulder. The same rage that he'd flung at me came through in his look and, shockingly, Sabre saw it, and let go. Caius still didn't say anything, but Sabre cleared his throat and continued.

"It's not enough your family fail at everything else, you fail at Tracking too. We all found our marks ages ago. Ulren sent us to find you."

A knowing smile curled onto Caius' lips, but there was no joy behind it, "Sure. That's exactly what happened."

"What did you do, Gamma? Go the wrong way?"

Koda laughed along with Sabre's jibe, but I took a step forward and opened my mouth to speak, to explain.

"Yeah," Caius said quietly, with a brief look in my direction. "I went the wrong way."

He walked away from us before I could say anything. I watched him leave, guilt softly blossoming in my chest as I let him go without another word.

CHAPTER FIVE

Caius and I came last in Tracking, and just as he said, Ulren blamed him.

Once the four rescues had returned to town, Ulren went on about Caius not meeting his full potential or some other bullshit. Everyone whispered between themselves or mocked Caius openly, but he remained silent, taking the ridicule and not telling anyone that it was my fault we'd failed.

I said nothing.

I didn't waste time dissecting the reasons why I stayed quiet, even as everyone harassed Caius but didn't extend me the same ridicule. My friends and I had always given the Gammas a hard time and I saw no reason to comment on it if Caius didn't. After all, it was only teasing.

Bullying.

The ugly word was like a bad smell but I ignored it, although it proved difficult, as difficult as trying to ignore that Caius calling me a snob had hurt my feelings. No one ever spoke to me that way, which was certainly enough reason for his words to linger, but his opinion didn't matter to me in the least, so why should I care?

Caius' treatment compared to mine had shown me for the second time that I was treated differently no matter what I did or who I got caught doing it with.

Maybe that did make me the snob Caius said I was. Despite my best efforts, his judgement stayed on my mind all day.

I hadn't heard anything from my mother, so it seemed my night with Sabre was a secret for now. Still, I drank endless cups of my mother's tea, determined to calm my erratic nerves. It helped enough for me to be able to get ready to meet my friends for a night out, pushing any pending trouble to the back of my mind. I changed into tight black leather pants and calf-high boots with an off the shoulder blouse, cinched in at the waist with an embroidered corset. I decided to wear my thick brown dagger belt that sat snugly on my hips, displaying the ornate dagger Goliath had given me for my eighteenth birthday. It was a beautiful weapon with gold forged into the intricately designed handle and a large blue gem in the pommel. Deciding I had no need for a jacket, I left the house, deciding to make the walk into Invernell.

My home town was one of obvious wealth. Within the wild terrain that dominated the united provinces, Invernell was an engineer's dream. Our roads were cobbled and our buildings and houses all made of strong taupe stone, with sturdy terracotta roofs and glassed windows. Invernell's citizens who were not as rich as myself and others, lived and worked the fertile lands that surrounded us. They traded with various towns and cities in all reaches of the kingdom and the Known World. Butchers and fishmongers sold their goods in neat little establishments, while market vendors yelled their deals from polished wooden stalls. In the market, you could find anything from plantain and green bananas to cow foot soup. Aloe Vera plants and stalks of sugar cane stood tall in the blinding sunlight.

Laecan lived in various areas all across the country however. Many of them had settled into communities that had both *laecan* and *maejym* where they stayed anonymous, but Celestia boasted the largest wolf population. Contrary to legend, and what many were eager to believe, there was nothing exceptionally special about being a wolf. Other than the obvious turn-into-an-animal thing and the strengths it provided, the ability to *turn* was just that—the ability to transform into majestic beasts; an ability that had been part of our world for as long as anyone could remember. We were taught there was a time when all Agmantians were *laecan*, but somewhere during our history this changed, and our numbers dwindled.

We lived as normal as most, with petty fights among the social hierarchy and the commotion that you would find within a bustling community. We loved, we laughed, we lived, and all with a sense of enchantment that, despite its secrecy, was never denied.

As I walked, hues of brown filled my vision. Skin tones that ranged from glistening gold, to warm umber and the darkest ebony were all around. Thanks to our proximity to them, Agmantia was also filled with Yiteshi. Their coal dark skin was radiant even in the dimming sunshine. The gleam of their inherent hazel eyes setting them apart from us, while their slightly broader noses and subtly coarser hair were differences few of our respective cultures would even consider.

There were a few porcelain-skinned, dark-haired Coznians among us, who made their living mostly from their extensive knowledge in herbal remedies and holistic medicines. There were several pale, blue-eyed Mortanians as well, the most popular of which was an old woman named Marla, who fancied herself a witch. She claimed to have supernatural powers, but considering most of us could turn into wolves, we didn't encourage her ramblings. The foreign *maejym* that were permitted to live here had signed agreements that they would not speak of the *laecan* they knew. They'd been tested by the local shaman and should any not be able to handle the truth, their memories were erased and they were compelled to seek out greener pastures. This practice kept our anonymity from the *maejym* and relegated us to mass superstition.

With a friendly smile to people I recognised and short conversations with people I knew well, I strolled through town before arriving at the Bane. Named after wolfsbane—one of two things that do us any real harm—the large tavern stood proudly in the centre of Invernell. It was flanked by a respectable and decorative inn on one side and a traveller's stable on the other. We were rarely in personal need of horses, but used them when travelling with supplies or *maejym,* or to important functions where they added a bit of visual flair.

The Bane held a sea of brown faces, with a multitude of hairstyles, head wraps and jewellery to go along with those hues. Afros, braids, dreadlocks, straightened or shaved heads were packed together as people mingled and entertained.

I thread expertly through and around tables and the people who occupied them before laying eyes on my usual booth at the back. The tantalising aroma of jerked chicken, cooking in the outhouse, wafted through the air, along with the smells of the side dishes that would accompany it. Fluffy white rice and kidney beans would undoubtedly be out there, along with cheesy baked pies and an abundance of sweet and savoury pastries.

Nights at the Bane were always bustling, packed for the food, drink and music. A four-man steel pan band were already chiming away in the corner, while patrons played heated games of cards and dominoes and others took over the dancefloor. The harmonious din of camaraderie and excitement sailed through the air, putting a smile on my face.

I approached the booth. It was a large open-ended square, with cushioned benches around it. A few of my friends already sat gathered: Tala, Fern, Olcan, Rhea, Susi and Sire.

Tala beamed when she saw me and I returned the gesture as she shuffled up to let me into the booth. I sat down and put my arm around her in a tight hug but while getting myself comfortable in the seat beside her, a weird yet vaguely familiar scent wafted from her.

"You okay?" she asked me. I hadn't realised I'd been staring.

"Yeah," I ignored the unusual smell. "What's going on?" I asked turning my attention to my friends.

Fern was in the middle of the booth, draped over the behemoth that was Olcan Salvaterre. He was built like a boulder, all rigid lines and muscles. He had a full dark beard and a neatly shaped afro that always had a wooden comb sticking out of it. The handle was shaped like a wolf's head, jaws open. He was twenty-one, the eldest of us, and was also the current love of seventeen-year-old Fern's life.

Sire Boltese, Tala's crush, sat at the far end of the booth slightly away from the rest of us, as was his way. He was twenty, quiet and reserved at the best of times, but we didn't judge him for it. He had close-shaven hair and a goatee on his otherwise smooth tawny-skinned face, and a pair of startling hazel eyes. Sire was an anomaly in that he had *maejym* parents and, as far as we knew, was the only *laecan* in his immediate family. His parents had moved to Invernell when Sire was thirteen and *turned* for the first time, as we all had. They wanted him to learn from and grow up around his own kind. Why he wasn't bullied for not being a pure blood, considering Goliath's view on his parentage, probably had something to do with Sire being rich. One of our provinces was even his namesake, but had been inherited through a different line. He was the oldest type of money, which in Goliath's world allowed all liberties. Except courting his daughter of course.

Rhea Lacoste and Susi Dune, who were nestled together beside Olcan and Fern, pulled themselves away from each other for a moment to giggle in response to my question.

"Nothing much, Female. Upset any more Alphas this morning?" Rhea asked with a smirk. Her head of tight curls were kept short, curling themselves behind her ears, which gave her angled and symmetrical face a wonderful frame. She wore her usual loose tunic and cropped pants with a multitude of bangles going up her right arm. Her mate, Susi, ran her elegant fingers up and down them as her other hand stroked the back of Rhea's head. Susi was bald. Bald, and tall like Tala. She had a gold ring through her nose with a delicate chain that led from it to a piercing in her ear. She was all thin lines and athletic muscle, and everything looked good on her.

Rhea and Susi were unique in that they were mates and actually a couple. Being mated was an unbreakable bond between wolves that predated marriage or the physical act of mating. Mating was one thing, but to be mated was quite another. It meant that a pair of wolves were literally born for one another. It didn't, however, mean that you automatically *wanted* to be with that person. You could know who your mate was and be completely in love with someone else, as could they.

I groaned, "Was Goliath mad?" Everyone nodded, Sire even raised an eyebrow and pursed his lips. "Does *everyone* know?" I asked.

"Of course," Susi laughed. "Why do you think we've been waiting for you?"

My eyes widened as I looked around the table, landing on Tala's guilty face. I understood: they wanted gossip.

"So, don't keep us in suspense," Olcan piped up this time, sipping from his overly large tankard. "What happened?"

I blushed, "Goliath caught us."

"Caught you... what?" Rhea needed the details apparently. I shook my head, dispelling any of *those* rumours.

"No, not that. He just caught us together, but he wasn't mad when I left."

I hated the lie but I didn't know how much my friends knew about Goliath's outburst, since his temper had been a new experience for me. I caught Olcan's eye and something about the way he avoided my gaze told me he might not be as clueless as I'd been.

"Well, Sabre was moodier than usual when they got home. My mother even cried from the shame of it all." Tala offered the statement rather dramatically and I hung my head in disgrace. If Sabre had got into real trouble, then my turn with my mother couldn't be far behind.

Fern surprised us by lifting her head from where it had been nuzzling Olcan's neck. Her hair was slicked into a ponytail, with her mass of curls coming out the back. She was petite, with slim hips and small breasts. She had the same amber eyes and honey gold skin as her brother, but, in my humble opinion, none of the personality.

"Sabre is *always* moody," she complained. "And don't get me started on the neurotic mess that is our mother!"

Okay, maybe there was some personality there.

She didn't bother waiting for a reply and went back to nuzzling Olcan.

"I think I need a drink for this one," I mumbled, making the rest of the table laugh while I looked at Tala expectantly. "I'll have a large wine to start, thank you!" Tala elbowed me in the side as I laughed, "What, it's not like you have to pay for it."

As a member of the Alpha pack, drinks at the Bane were put on a tab for Tala. Technically I had the same privilege, but I didn't want my father to see my bill.

"That's not the point," she giggled, caving to my request and climbing out of the booth to start our tab.

When she returned, Tala placed my glass on the table in front of me. I'd moved so there was no room for her to slide back into the booth. She now had no choice but to go sit next to Sire. With her own drink in hand, Tala approached the other end of the booth and asked Sire quietly if he would move up to let her in. He obliged without a response, barely even looking at her as she took a tentative seat beside him. It was like a continent lay between them.

Conversation soon returned to my indiscretion, but ceased once I explained that nothing else had happened. I'd seen Goliath's reaction to Sabre, but I was concerned at how angry the others claimed he was. I'd never seen him remotely hostile before last night so what had changed? It couldn't just be because he'd caught us together.

I remained at the Bane well into the evening. The drinks had begun to flow and by nightfall, we were more than a little drunk, taking complete advantage of the open Riadnak tab.

Music played on and soon Tala and I found ourselves on the dancefloor, swaying our hips to the infectious beat of steel pans. Onlookers around us beat the table tops in an infectious rhythm, smiling and laughing, enjoying their own liquor and merriment.

Tala and I danced and danced, our bodies warm with the heat of our sweat and intoxication. With one of my hands still in Tala's, I leant back towards a table top that held my wineglass. I lifted it to my lips and took a long drink, before slamming it back down. The two men sat on either side of the table looked up at me and I winked before Tala pulled me back into the sway of her dance.

"I need another drink!" I called over the music. Tala just nodded at me and continued to grind herself to the rhythm of the drums, her eyes closing as she swayed. It was only as I stumbled toward the bar, I realised that Sire had taken my place and was grinding with her. Sire was tall, much more so than Tala, who was the tallest of the girls. Her head fit comfortably in the crook of his shoulder as she reclined her head against him. His hands roamed her body, from her thighs and up to her waist before landing dangerously close to palming her breasts. I watched as Sire and Tala danced, grinding into one another, touching, but never speaking or looking at one another.

Somewhere, distant in my foggy inebriated mind, I was happy for my friend.

I spun toward the bar, excited for my next drink of rum, when I saw Sabre standing across from me. My entire body went rigid, the hairs on my arms standing on end at the sight of him. I tried to smile and lighten the steadily darkening mood, but the look on his face didn't broach for frivolity. He watched me for a moment, then turned and, strode out without a word. Somehow I knew he meant me to follow, but I also knew I didn't want to. Ignoring the unusual trepidation, I looked over to the booth where the rest of our friends sat, staring at me. I realised then that they'd held back what they thought they knew about the other night. They'd lulled me into a false sense of security, all of them already aware that Sabre was angry with me.

My face heated with embarrassment, but I quickly marched out after him, brushing past Sabre's best friend Fenrir in the process. He was fair-skinned like Sabre, with short dreadlocks close to his head. He had pretty grey eyes that when he turned, complimented his light brown fur. He had a smug grin on his face that told me everything I didn't want to know.

Sabre was standing outside in his wolf form and for some reason this worried me more. He took off into the trees that lined Invernell and with a fuzzy head, I *turned* and took off after him.

Sabre was a streak of white magic through the hushed dark-green tones of the forest. I struggled to keep up with him in my drunken state, so when he finally came to a sharp stop in the middle of a clearing, I was more than relieved.

He *turned* and stood before me with a horrific glower on his face. I *turned* to face him, but the splurge of magic it took to make the change rattled me. I swayed where I stood, the rum really kicking in.

"How *dare* you embarrass me like this, Aspen?"

I heard his father in his tone and I didn't like it, "What are you talk—?"

"Dancing with my sister in the middle of the Bane like a pair of whores, after spending time with that filth Caldoun!"

"Spending time? Sabre, what are you talking about? Nothing happened with me and Caius."

"Oh, *Caius* is it?" He spat the question at me, making me take a step back.

"Come on Sabre, that's his name. Why are you being like this?"

"Why am I being like this? Are you stupid?"

I blanched at his insult, "Sabre, don't talk to me like that."

Sabre marched up to me and grabbed hold of my arm, his eyes purposeful and aggressive as he pulled me towards him.

"I'll talk to you any way I please because you're mine. Do you hear me, Aspen? *Mine!*"

"Of course I'm yours, everyone knows that, even Cai—the Gamma. Nothing happened, Sabre."

He wasn't yelling anymore, but his temper hadn't waned. His hand still gripped my exposed arm, but I didn't want to cry, no matter how much it had begun to hurt. If I cried, I'd look guilty.

"I am the Alpha. Remember that."

"Not yet you're not."

I didn't know where it came from.

I didn't know why I said it, but the look that Sabre sent me was one I never wanted to see again.

It was murderous.

I watched as his canines extended and a gold ring blazed around his pupils.

"Sabre."

We both tensed at the sound of Sire's voice before both turning to face him. He stood behind me, with Tala beside him. She was glaring at her brother with a ferocity I'd never witnessed on her face before. Sabre let go of me and I was thankful when the pressure finally eased from my arm.

"Sabre, I—" I tried, but he stepped back to march over to Sire.

"This is *none* of your business," Sabre growled.

Sire simply stepped forward, clearly unimpressed with Sabre's attitude, not balking at his rage.

"You don't speak to or about women like that. I'm making it my business."

I realised he'd heard what Sabre said about Tala and he wasn't happy about it. Tala continued glaring at her brother, even as she came to stand by my side.

"You've had a long night," Sire continued, even while Sabre seethed at him. "Don't take it out on Aspen."

Don't take what out on Aspen?

Sabre kept his eyes in mine for a prolonged moment. Then the raging fires died in his eyes and he deflated before me. He cursed under his breath, looking between the three of us. He stepped forward, his eyes softening before he shook his head and backed away.

"I'm sorry, Aspen," he said gently. "I'm sorry."

Without another word, Sabre *turned* and bound off into the trees. I looked over at Tala and Sire, my eyes brimming with tears, but neither of them spoke. Sire's eyes rested longingly on Tala before he also *turned,* taking off.

"Nothing happened."

It was all I could think at that moment. Nothing happened between Caius and me and yet—somehow—it had become this.

Tala approached me tentatively and placed her hand gently on my shoulder, "He's just going through something… he'll come around."

Remembering the defeated look in Sabre's eyes, I wasn't entirely convinced that he would.

CHAPTER SIX

Tala and I went back to my house. She'd wanted us to go to the Riadnak Manor, but considering her brother's room was only a corridor away, I declined the invitation.

We lay wrapped up in my bed while she watched me bawl my eyes out. I'd been at it for almost an hour, and even though the alcohol had a lot to do with it, my heartbreak was deep and real.

"He's never looked at me like that before," I moaned, while Tala's hand stroked my arm comfortingly. "He's never hurt me like that before."

Tala didn't say anything. Even through my blurry vision and blocked nose I noticed how quiet she was being about the whole ordeal.

"Why aren't you defending him?" I demanded, suddenly annoyed that she wasn't even trying to help me get back into Sabre's good books.

Tala shrugged, "Should I be?"

"What? Of course you should be. I'm your best friend—he's your brother!"

"It doesn't mean he's not being an asshole, Aspen."

The way she'd looked at him in the woods fluttered through my mind.

"What has he ever done to you?" I accused.

"Nothing," she quickly protested. "He wouldn't dare. It doesn't mean I don't see when he has a bad attitude. You see how he speaks to Caius."

I tried not to react at the mention of Caius' name. I hadn't told Tala about the revelation he'd thrown at me about not competing in the Games. I wasn't sure I wanted to. I didn't know how to deal with him rejecting the prophecy, let alone how to deal with watching someone else react to the implications of that rejection. It had governed our entire lives since the day all three of us were born.

"I love my brother," Tala said as an afterthought, "And I know he's going through some things. But I don't like the way he treats people sometimes. I won't defend his behaviour just because you think you love him."

"Excuse me? What do you mean, I *think* I love him?" I wiped at my snotty nose and rubbed the tears away with a heavy hand, watching guilt creep onto Tala's face.

"Nothing." Tala sat up, and rather than have her looking down at me, I moved into a seated position as well, keeping us eye level. I was not going to be that easily dismissed.

"Tell me what you meant, Tala. *Now*."

"Look, you already had one fight with a Riadnak, I don't think you want another." She tried to play it off with humour but I wasn't in the mood.

"You tell me what you meant right now or I'll—" I paused mid-threat as there it was again. That peculiar smell. I leaned forward and took a big sniff of her scent. "What *is* that?"

"Hey!" She swatted at me, pushing me away. "What are you doing?"

"What is that smell?" I demanded.

"What smell?"

"*That* smell!" I sniffed her again, narrowing my eyes at her, annoyed with this game. I stared her out and she tried to hold her ground, before finally giving in.

"It's mimosa root," she mumbled, looking sheepish and uncertain. My head was still a little fuzzy from the liquor, the dancing and oh yeah, my world falling apart.

"Mimosa root? Why in the world would you ne—" My eyes widened as the answer came to me. Tala bit at her bottom lip, trying for an innocent expression that clearly didn't belong on her anymore. "You had *sex*!" I exclaimed.

Mimosa root was a well-known contraception.

Tala dived onto me and clasped her hand over my mouth, her face flushed red under her honey skin, blue eyes bright and wide.

"Tell the *whole house*, why don't you!"

I shook my head as I struggled to breathe, her strength cutting off my air supply. Tala was always better in combat training than me. We both knew she'd beat me in a fight without even blinking. She removed her hand with a mockingly suspicious glint in her eye, though there was a warning there. Finally, I drew in a much-needed breath, my chest pounding. When I could finally talk without coughing up a lung, I turned to her in disbelief.

"Who?" I coughed out, still catching my breath. It was all I could think to say, but when her face flushed a second time, I had my answer.

"Sire!" I yelled, not without triumph at the realisation. I placed both my hands over my mouth as an immediate show of contrition. Tala merely gave me a look and I relaxed, my hands dropping into my lap as I stared at her.

"How? *When*...? How?" I fumbled for the words. This was completely insane. Sire and Tala barely said two words to each other. I couldn't even think on it too hard, as Tala's face finally erupted into a beautiful and devastating smile. I couldn't help but smile back and interrupt her answer with another question,

"As wolf or woman?"

"Woman," she confessed and my heart swelled for her.

When a female mated for the first time, she could choose to do so as a wolf or as a woman. While both gave the same physical pleasure, there was a personal element to losing your virginity as a woman. It meant that the couple trusted each other to bear themselves in their weakest form. It meant, simply put, that Tala loved him.

"I don't know how I got so lucky," she finally answered. "We both wanted it to be special so we went into King Hill. He rented a cabin and there were flowers and Aspen, it was... it was everything I ever wished it would be!"

As I listened to Tala I suddenly felt a twinge in my chest that I initially couldn't explain. As she gushed about their night together in King Hill, I realised that Sire and Tala were a couple... and I hadn't known about it.

"Tala... how long has this been going on?"

Tala paused her reminiscing and looked at me incredulously before switching to annoyance.

"I tell you I lost my virginity to the guy I've been in love with for years, and the first thing you're worried about is why I never told you?"

"Tala, it's not like th—"

"No, Aspen. It's always like that!" she cut me off, scooting to the edge of the bed, putting on her shoes with quick movements.

"Tala. You're my best friend."

I didn't understand why she couldn't see how hurt I was.

"And you're mine, but for once this isn't about you."

I went quiet. Tala waited for me to say something, but I wouldn't give her the satisfaction. I raised my eyebrow at her and she raised both at me, irritated. She turned on her heels, "You think you'd grow up by now," she mumbled as she headed toward the door.

"Where are you going?"

"Home," came her gentle reply, but she didn't slow her step. "I'll see you at *Lunaveya*.

Lunaveya was the official opening event of the Mating Games, the three challenges to test endurance, strength and agility that would pit Sabre and Caius against each other.

"That's not until next week," I said, trying not to appear distressed at the clear rebuke.

"Yeah, well, I'm sorry... I just need some time."

I didn't want to give her time. I wanted my best friend to support me. I shouldn't have to ask. Why was she being so selfish? I stayed silent.

Tala shook her head with obvious disappointment, "I'll talk to you when you're feeling better, but just..."

"What?" I pounced, wanting her to apologise.

"Please, don't tell anyone."

Wait...did Tala not trust me? Enraged, I pursed my lips at her. Tala shook her head, opened my bedroom door and left. I fell back onto my pillows, overwhelmed and exhausted.

There was a light tap on my door. I sniffed, "Go away, Rogue!" I threw my arm over my head. "I'm not in the mood."

There was momentary silence before I heard her vacate the spot, her steps receding down the hallway. It wasn't until her lingering scent wafted into my room that I bolted upright in my bed and stared at the closed door.

I suddenly knew where else I had smelled mimosa root.

I didn't have any lessons the next morning, and after my drunken escapade I was glad for the lie in. I did, however, have training with Rogue for Fight of the Female. Since my sister was playing the part of Orlagh, she and I would clash at the very end of the staged fight and our choreography had an extended sequence. This meant our mother insisted we not only train with the others, but train privately as well.

My tea sat waiting for me on its tray, and after a quick drink I got changed into my training gear. When I arrived in our backyard, I found my sister already there, warming up. We didn't acknowledge one another. Instead, I warmed up a few paces away from her, trying to think of how to ask her about the mimosa root.

Once we were ready, Rogue stepped up to me, her eyes—so much like mine—revealing nothing.

"Mum knows. About you and Sabre. And Goliath finding you with him," she began, putting both hands in the middle of her staff and holding it out horizontally. I did the same. "The only reason she isn't kicking down your door is because she had an appointment for a facial."

I bowed before taking my first strike at her. Rogue blocked as expected, "What she doesn't know, is that you were seen leaving the Almani Woods… with Caius Caldoun."

I fought not to react and demand how she knew where I'd been? If I demanded she tell me, it would only pique her suspicions. It was clear by her expression that she believed I actually had been seen leaving the woods with Caius. Since I knew he'd left before me, where had the lie come from? Someone had seen me with Caius, put one and one together and come up with eleven.

I continued to watch my sister as she took one hit, then another, and I blocked the ones she directed back at me as we'd been shown. I kept my face just as unreadable as hers.

Okay, sister—game on.

"It wasn't like that."

Rogue smirked as she struck me with a two-hit combo and swiped me underfoot. I jumped and spun to hit her lightly on the back of her leg.

"Oh, yeah? Because I don't think Sabre would like the idea of you fooling around on him."

Was this nosey bitch threatening me?

"What I do or—in this case—*don't* do, is none of Sabre's business."

I struck again with a two-hit combo of my own, adding an impressive overhead strike, giving myself time to think of an appropriate lie. She ducked, avoiding the overhead strike, and we began to circle each other.

"Maybe, but what were you doing there?"

The Almani Woods were a small wood close to Caius' house so it made sense now why he was there. I hit out at her again. She blocked, our staffs crossed at the middle, and we looked into each other's eyes, brown into green, a challenge reverberating through the staffs, both of us determined to put pressure on the other.

"Last I checked, it wasn't any of your business either," I growled softly before pushing hard at her, using my wolf strength to send her staggering back. I advanced on her, spinning my staff until it was a twirl of brown in the air.

"What were you doing Aspen?"

She wouldn't let this go. I knew how stubborn she could be. We shared that delightful trait. I stopped the staff spin sharply and struck at her, but Rogue was fast, bringing her staff up to block the blow that would have – if we were fighting for real – cracked her skull open.

"I was talking to Caius about Mating Day," I relented, giving her the truth in sharp breaths as we cracked our staffs against one another in a quick succession of hits. I danced out of the hold Rogue's move would have placed me in, hitting her gently on her behind with the end of my staff. Well, not too gently as it made her stumble a little. She growled at me, the move not part of the routine.

"I went for a run after meeting Sabre," I elaborated, wiping the sweat from my brow with the back of one hand. "I ended up near Caius' house. When he saw me, he told me how much he wanted me, and that Mating Day was too long a wait."

Despite the absurdity of my lie, I saw that it hit the mark when Rogue scowled. The rage in my sister's eyes blazed as her lips pursed together, stopping herself from spewing the jealous acid she always had waiting for me.

We continued in our dance of unsaid hurtful words, daring the other to make the next move. Rogue said nothing for a long while, even as we slammed our staffs against one another in a flurry of defensive and offensive moves, each displaying our dexterity. When we stopped to catch our breaths, Rogue stood glaring at me, her chest heaving with the exertion it took to best my move, however un-fatal. When her look suddenly changed from anger to indifference, I knew I hadn't won this round, but wasn't entirely sure how I'd lost.

"Fine," she said, throwing her staff on the ground. "I'm done for today."

I didn't bother saying goodbye as my sister left the training ground, but I couldn't deny the long breath I exhaled when she did.

CHAPTER SEVEN

*L*unaveya had arrived.

The first in the line of social events that had been hanging over my head since birth. I was at the centre of the entire Mating Games as I was, quite literally, the prize. I'd anticipated this day with an eagerness that was unmatched. The opening ceremony was my debut, my first step into the role that had been laid down for me thousands of years before. I'd been so ready to formally step into my role in front of everyone but now, because of Caius Ruin-Everything-By-Being-Difficult Caldoun, I was terrified.

There was a ball that opened the celebrations, with food, drink, a formal dance for the Triquetra, and the announcement of the first challenge before the end of the night. In other words, I could look forward to suffering complete humiliation in front of the entire *laecan* elite if Caius didn't show up to do his duty.

What would everyone think of me?

What would the shaman do to me if I wasn't able to fulfil my destiny?

I stood in front of my bedroom mirror, looking at the glorious gown my mother had given me to wear. It had a stark white strapless bodice that dripped into silvery grey and ended in the darkest black I'd ever seen. The hem of the full billowing skirt had tiny diamonds sewn over it, so the black resembled the night sky littered with stars. The diamonds continued over the large grey portion of the dress and up to the snow white of the bust. The sparkling jewels made each perfectly blended section look like the nocturnal version of a monochrome sunrise.

The dress was a statement to all, that I was the link between the white wolf of House Riadnak and the black wolf of House Caldoun. I was the pivotal blend between two warring males, the peace we needed within their opposition.

It hugged my curvy frame, accentuating my waist and displaying the smooth rise of my breasts. I wore shimmering black high heels while my wrist and neck were adorned with an elegant diamond bracelet and delicate necklace, that rested coolly just below my throat.

My braids had been redone and wrapped intricately on top of my head so my crown could fit comfortably: The Crown of the Female.

It was usually kept safe at the Riadnak Manor, but my mother had it couriered over from there so I could get ready for the evening. It would be returned when the festivities were over. It was crafted out of silver, with a large crescent moon made of obsidian in the centre, surrounded by shards of diamonds. The look was finished with dark, sultry make-up that brought out the forest green of my eyes.

I looked more beautiful than I ever had, but what would all this matter if Caius wasn't going to compete? If he didn't cooperate, then this was the dress I was going to be embarrassed in, that I was going to fail in. No male Triquetrian had ever refused to participate in the challenges before, so I had no idea of the consequences. It was safe to assume the mantle would go to Sabre once his father passed, everyone wanted it that way and would assumingly give their blessings. I had to wonder though, what would the shaman do if our tradition and their magic was impeded in favour of the Riadnaks once again?

Our peace was held together by the shaman spell, it's very foundations in the condition that the wolves would compete. Now was the intended time for change and whether people were in support of a continued Riadnak reign or were out for new blood, the challenges had to be completed to maintain that order.

As I stressed over what would happen if Caius didn't comply, there was a knock at my door and, without waiting for an invitation to enter, my mother glided in.

Her eyes darted to the tea that had been laid out for me, but she said nothing about it.

"You look breath taking, Aspen."

My mother loved me, I knew she did, but I often questioned whether she loved *what* I was more than *who* I was. I saw it in her eyes as she appraised me now, as if she could already hear the words of validation that would be spoken at her during the opening ceremonies, all thanks to me. Tears pooled along the bottom of her perfectly adorned eyes. They wouldn't fall and mess up her make-up, of course. Even the laws of eye coal bowed to Ianthe Anai.

My mother stood behind me in the full-length mirror, her elegant satin gown the exact silvery grey of my own dress. Her dark brown hair had been pulled back into a tight ponytail that hung low down her back, longer than necessary, but this was my mother—the style was sleek and harsh, just like her, and exposed her wonderful cheekbones and smooth, brown skin.

She placed her hands on my shoulders and I flinched at her icy touch. Her voice was low as she spoke, but there was no mistaking her conviction. It bled into me. It always did.

"You will be perfect tonight, Aspen. Do you understand?"

I nodded. This was important to her and anything important to Ianthe was important to me and had to be respected.

She looked me directly in the eye in the mirror and said, "And you will stay away from that Gamma boy."

My breath caught with the shock that she would feel the need to say this to me.

"Mother, I told you nothing happened."

There weren't words to explain how angry Ianthe had been at me for being found alone with Caius. If it wasn't for Lunaveya, I probably wouldn't have been allowed out the house for the rest of my life. I'd thought about telling her what Caius had said, but was terrified of the consequences. She'd find some way to blame me for his decision not to compete.

"I know what you said," Ianthe squeezed my shoulders, her nails digging into my skin. "I also know what other people are saying and I will not have it any longer."

"It's not my fa—"

Her grip tightening was enough to silence me. I stared at her in the mirror, where she held my gaze. Whatever damage her nails were causing to my otherwise flawless skin would heal within a breath once she let go, but there was still pain in the moment. Any thought of telling her the whole truth about Caius instantly went out the window.

She'd kill me.

"There's a dance," I mumbled. "I have to dance with him."

Ianthe nodded, "The required performances are permitted."

Of course, they were.

"You are not allowed to speak to him at any other time. Do I make myself clear?"

"Mum, he—" Her eyes in the mirror steeled against me, cutting off any retort I had. "Yes, Mother."

She smiled then, a genuine smile before loosening her grip on me. "The carriage leaves in ten minutes. Make sure you drink your tea before you leave."

My family and I made the short carriage ride to the Riadnak Manor and it was lit up like a Full Moon Festival.

There were lights, decorations and banners in the colours of the most prominent *laecan* families, displaying their influence. The white wolf of House Riadnak, alongside the grey and black wolves of Houses Anai and Caldoun respectively, dominated the rest of the grounds.

While there was a variety of fur colours among *laecan*, the firstborn children of the three main families always had fur the colour of their father. Fur of the Father, as it was so inventively known, was announced when a child was born and a tiny patch of coloured fur could be seen on the top of one of their hands. The patch shed after a few weeks, but the firstborn was left with a birthmark in the place it had once been. I shared the silver grey of my father, while Rogue was a variation of brown and grey from both our parents.

Within minutes of arriving, my mother and I commandeered into the sea of high society in the Great Hall, where we mingled and crooned with whomever Ianthe thought worthy of our attention while my father and Rogue held back.

I hadn't had a chance to speak to my sister about me knowing she was having sex. Well, I'd had a chance, just not a reason. Who Rogue was sleeping with was technically none of my business. I was a little annoyed that I was the only virgin left in our unofficial group and neither Tala or Rogue had thought to share their experience with me. Not that Rogue would have done it for any other reason than to gloat, of course, but still. I was hurt that Tala felt she *couldn't* tell me.

Some best friend.

My mother and I continued to flutter from one social circle to another, like bees collecting pollen, eager for the sweetness it promised at every turn. The room was aglow with excitement and glamour. Wine and rum poured generously and music played as we mingled with ambassadors and other dignitaries.

After moving through the room on my mother's arm for close to an hour, my gracious smile not slipping for a moment, I kissed her cheek and excused myself to head towards the bar.

My path was cut short when a large figure stopped in front of me and I came face to face with the Alpha.

Goliath Riadnak smiled down at me, resplendent in his white formal attire, his heavy brocade coat dripping with accents of gold. He wore the Alpha circlet atop his brow, his amber eyes glowing as much as the gold on his clothing and the jewels in the rings on his fingers.

"Aspen," he said, his deep voice making my flesh tingle. Remembering my manners, I quickly bowed,

"Alpha."

He turned and gestured with a nod away from the crowd, "Walk with me."

I obeyed and followed him the short walk to a room just off the side of the Great Hall. There were guards outside the doors, dressed in starch pressed uniforms with swords at their hips. I could smell they were *laecan* and knew the swords were mainly for appearance, even if they did know how to use them. They opened the door for us and I could sense the multitude of prying eyes that followed us as I walked with my head held high behind the Alpha into the small room. The guards closed the door behind me and I jumped as the lock clicked.

We were in a small office. Not his main study I knew, just a room for quiet working. The Alpha turned to face me, resting himself against the edge of the small desk that sat at the back of the room. He took up the majority of the space and I swallowed, uncertain.

"You look beautiful," he finally said. "Every inch the queen you will someday be."

"Thank you, Alpha." I offered him a smile, unsure of what else I was expected to say.

"You appreciate that, considering the position you will one day hold in this community, you are to conduct yourself in the appropriate manner?"

Shit!

I thought I'd gotten away with no more reprimand than my mother's scolding earlier, but apparently, my meeting with Caius was enough of a scandal to have reached the Alpha. I'd been able to ignore my apprehension of Caius attending tonight but now it came roaring to the front of my thoughts.

"If I've caused any offense, Alpha, it was not my intention."

"Unfortunately, intention matters little in these circumstances," he was still smiling, but there was no warmth in it. "You have indeed offended me, and you've offended my family name."

I swallowed, fear creeping into my heart like frost over a window pane.

"Nothing is to get in the way of your mating with Sabre, not even that Gamma. Is that clear?"

I nodded, unable to speak. His choice of words perfectly indicated how little he thought of Caius, even though he had as much right to me as Sabre did. Goliath finally stood, approaching me and stopping so close I had to tilt my head back to be able to look up into his face, his amber eyes brewing with the hint of violence.

"You do not wish to make me your enemy," he said softly. "Make sure word of your indiscretions never reach me again."

I nodded, "Y-yes, Alpha."

Goliath stepped back and clapped his hands together, replacing his ferocious disappointment with a beaming smile before gesturing to the door. It immediately unlocked.

"Now that we understand each other, you may return to the party."

I didn't need to be told twice and quickly exited the room.

Shaken by my encounter with Goliath, and desperate to get the lingering discomfort of his eyes boring into me out of my system, I found the bar. In a gathering, such as this it was open to all and the bartender was there to immediately take my order. I practically inhaled my first three glasses of Yiteshi wine and was starting a fourth when I felt someone approach me.

It was Fenrir, in a rather fetching navy blue number. I made a point of ignoring him, but he came up beside me and leant his arm on the edge of the bar.

"Don't be like that, Aspen," he teased, as he reached out and touched my arm lazily with his index finger then drew it back. "He's my best friend."

I didn't bother looking at him as I spoke, "You knew he was mad at me and said nothing."

"No one else did, so how is that my problem?"

I didn't answer, because he was right—none of my friends had said anything. They'd let me get in trouble, they'd let me get hurt, however briefly. I hadn't spoken to Sabre about it at all.

"He wants to see you before the dance."

The command behind the statement was obvious, but I ignored it and took a casual sip of my wine.

"Then he should come and speak to me himself. I'm sure my mother would allow it."

I laughed at the hypocrisy of it all and drank again, aware of how quickly the cynic was revealing itself in me now that my boyfriend accused me of cheating and the person I had supposedly cheated with revealed he wasn't interested in seeing me fulfil the sole purpose of my natural born life. Pre-destination my ass.

Speaking of which—I hadn't seen Caius yet.

Panic threatened to rise into my throat at that realisation and I was glad of the alcohol coursing through my system. Something told me I would need it before this night was over. I didn't want to care what the elders and the shaman might do once Caius destroyed everything. It didn't bare thinking about what Goliath might do.

"Do you want to get back together or not?" Fenrir snapped and I finally looked at him.

"I wasn't aware we'd broken up!"

He rolled his eyes, "You know what I mean."

I said nothing.

"He's in the entrance room. I'll tell him I delivered the message."

So that he won't blame me if he doesn't get his way, were the unspoken words.

"I—"

"Attention!"

The booming voice of the Riadnak House Steward Balton Asvid came tearing through the hall.

"Can you all make your way to the ballroom for the Mating Dance!"

That was our cue and still no sign of Caius.

I didn't bother saying goodbye to Fenrir as I searched for my mother. She found me almost instantly and ushered me through the crowd of people in the Great Hall, then through a side door that led to the other side of the manor. She held my forearm as she practically dragged me through the dimly lit hallway towards another set of doors.

"You will dance with the Gamma first," she repeated what I already knew. "You will smile and you will dance perfectly and when the first dance is over, you will curtsy before saying your line and being handed to Sabre."

"Am I a baton now too?"

My mother's grip tightened on my arm.

"I'll bruise if you keep doing that."

Her grip loosened just as we came to the doors. She spun me to face her, her hand still clamped around my arm.

"Do not mess this up, young lady, or you won't like how nasty I can be."

My heart raced as my head cleared and fear finally engulfed me. Caius wasn't here, my family would be shamed and everyone would blame me. My mother would be furious and I didn't have it in me to confess that our world was going to crumble around us, so I swallowed any response and simply nodded.

Ianthe turned me to the doors, knocked once and they sprung open, letting in a burst of unexpected bright light. The room beyond was the entrance room, a holding chamber before we were to enter the ballroom. The source of the bright light was found in the countless candles placed in holders all around the room, reflecting themselves in the gold that coated the walls.

I blinked through the glare of the place, but was soon enough able to take in the people around me.

The Riadnak family were there of course, waiting by the double doors that would lead into the ballroom. Goliath was talking to Sabre, who stood by his side; Celeste was talking to Fern. It was only Tala who turned to see who had entered. She smiled at me, a little unsure of my attitude, and at seeing that I smiled back. My dad and sister were already there, servants milling around them and the Riadnaks, but standing in a far corner of the room were the Caldouns. Dressed entirely in black, the Caldoun family looked both regal and terrifying. Maximus Caldoun stood talking with Asher, while his wife Regina looked on.

Maximus was a quiet man who I only ever saw on formal occasions. He was scholarly and loved to talk of our history and traditions. I found him good natured and kind and he seemed to have a good relationship with both his sons, despite spending so much time away from home. When I'd played at the Caldoun Manor as a child, he always had a treat for us in his pocket or a kind word of encouragement. He had made me feel seen and heard at a time when I'd felt suffocated by what was expected of me.

The random memory hit me with its forgotten truth, of that stifling need I'd had back then, to get out of my house and escape to Caius' backyard. How odd that I'd never once longed to go back.

I continued to watch Maximus until finally, Caius moved into view. He stood next to his father, angled so I could only see the left side of him. He wore a long double breasted black coat in the sherwani style of Cotai. It hung low past his knees over black pants and shoes. There was gold stitching along the hem and the cuffs of his coat and he'd recently cut his hair, if the perfect hairline was anything to go by.

The breath I'd been holding escaped me and I physically shook with relief.

He was here.

As if he felt me watching, Caius looked over and his golden eyes made my heart stop. He held my gaze for a fraction of a second before turning back to his father.

I didn't know why I felt deflated. What had I expected?

I felt my mother place her hand on the small of my back and lead me into the procession behind the Riadnaks. The Caldouns eventually took their place behind us.

The room echoed with a sudden and deeply resounding banging outside the door. It drew the attention of the gathered crowd and everything went quiet for a drawn out second before the large double doors swung outward, revealing the ballroom beyond.

"The Alpha, Goliath Riadnak, and his family: Lady Celeste, Lord Sabre, Lady Tala and Lady Fern," I heard Balton call.

The Riadnaks filed into the ballroom as new music filled the air. It was the Agmantian national anthem. The tune was probably the only thing that all the tribes had agreed upon while they were still divided.

The Riadnaks were all dressed in white and gold, Goliath heading the procession with his wife walking graciously by his side. She was a stunning woman, all creamy honey hues and dark hair flowing in soft curls around her petite face. Fern looked the most like her, entering behind Tala in a long sultry silk gown that exposed her flawlessly curved back.

I couldn't help glancing at my mother as Celeste Riadnak glided through the ballroom. Ianthe's face was a picture of loveliness, but her eyes told a different story. I saw the festering jealousy that lived under her skin like a disease.

Once Balton announced us and my family finally entered, I was breathless at the sight of the decorations chosen for the already enchanting ballroom. It was large enough to fit nearly five hundred people and did so comfortably. The room itself was inlaid with gold but the emblems and banners in blatant favour of the Alpha family were everywhere.

When the Alphas were seated at the front of the ballroom—with my family on their right and the Caldouns on their left—Balton announced that the Mating Dance would begin. As instructed, I rose from my seat, walking as gracefully as I could to the centre of the ballroom.

"Who will compete for the right to my hand?"

I said the words, both terrified and hopeful at the response. Caius was here, so perhaps he'd changed his mind or maybe, he was waiting for this moment to humiliate me in front everyone. I don't know how long I stood there, eyes on me, but it felt like an eternity before I heard a deep rumble that said, "I will."

Caius stood from his chair and walked towards me. He looked handsome and confident and completely in control and I hated him for it. I hated him for making me worry that he wouldn't be here, that he would let me be shamed.

I extended my hand. He took it and delicately kissed the top of it, even as it shook with nerves. I ignored the tingle that went up my arm when his lips grazed my skin. My body thrummed disconcertingly at his touch. I actually swayed, beginning to feel lightheaded and blaming the alcohol, the stress, the excitement—blaming *him*—but he steadied me, even just by holding my hand.

Once he'd straightened, he pulled me into him, placing his hand delicately on my lower back as his right hand lifted my left one. I placed my free hand gently on his shoulder and as the music began to play, we danced. We moved expertly among the sea of well-known faces before they blurred into the background and I focused on not tripping on my dress.

We had nothing to say to each other. Not anymore. I briefly remembered a time when everything I had to say, I said to Caius.

That was all a memory now. Dead and buried under my hatred for the boy who took every opportunity to put me down when he was nothing but a stupid Gamma who would never amount to anything.

I looked up at Caius then, hoping that the rage I had for him showed through my scrutiny. Instead, I found myself sharply looking away from the fire in his eyes and the unusual feeling that erupted in my stomach. The nausea reared its ugly head but I managed to keep my stomach in.

"Did your mother tell you not to speak to me?" he suddenly asked and I looked up at him, shocked as we continued to glide around the floor.

"How did yo—"

"My mother told me the same thing. Something about not upsetting the order of things."

"Order of Ianthe, you mean," I muttered, making him laugh. It was more like a chuckle in the base of his throat because his face didn't change. We spoke quietly, our lips barely moving.

"You find my overbearing mother amusing?"

Caius continued to look down at me, still in control of the dance. "I find everyone in this room amusing."

"Including me?" I didn't know why the idea bothered me. Everything about Caius bothered me and I felt it in every fibre of my being.

"Especially you."

I could have imagined it, but his voice lowered, taking on a dark tone that I didn't understand.

"Why?"

He thought about his answer for a long moment. He let go of my waist to twirl me out of our embrace, then pull me back into his arms. I hadn't even realised how far along we were in the song. Thankfully my dancing lessons had paid off.

"I find you amusing," he finally said, "because you think this is real. You think any of this means anything."

"Don't talk in riddles, intelligence doesn't suit you."

His hand was on my back again and my body sung at the connection before actively trying to repel the feeling.

"What does suit me, Aspen?"

The way my name rolled off his tongue did... something. For the first time, I actually wished he'd call me Grey instead.

"Lies," I said. "You said you weren't competing."

"I'm not."

"Then why are you here?"

He was quiet again, contemplative before answering.

"We all have obligations. Mine are to my mother and not having her lose face in front of the other families."

I could understand that. The Mating Games were important not only for myself and inaugurating the new Alpha, but for establishing the new power order of the *laecan* elite. The runner up of the Mating Games would become the Beta family—second in command—and the remaining family would be Gamma.

"She'll lose face if you don't compete in the games, even after coming here. She'll be a laughing stock. She'll never survive it."

"My mother will be fine. You and yours... I'm not so sure."

He was right of course, but I hated that he knew. He was always so self-righteous and condescending, like he was so much smarter than everyone else.

"Why aren't you competing, Caius? Tell me now." My demand took him so much off guard that his eyebrows raised, but he answered,

"I'm not competing because I have no interest in the prize."

"But..."

Caius twirled me around and pulled me into him so our chests were touching as the dance came to an end. Our faces were inches apart, our breaths short from excessive movement. I could smell the mint on his breath and the coconut oil in his hair. I could feel the sudden pulse between my thighs as my face heated up.

"But the prize is... me."

"Exactly."

He let go of me and stepped back so quickly I almost stumbled, catching myself at the last moment. Caius bowed, his eyes cold as I curtseyed.

He didn't want me.

He didn't want... *me?*

"W-who will challenge him for my hand?" I spoke without realising. I had to stay focused on the task at hand. Sabre stood from his seat beside his father,

"I will."

He walked over to me and bowed. I curtseyed and held my hand out for him to take. He lowered his head to kiss it, but as his smooth lips touched my hand he lifted his eyes to look at me.

At the fire that blazed there, a tremble of fear crawled its way up my spine.

CHAPTER EIGHT

As Sabre and I danced, I felt the hostility between us as firmly as I felt his body beneath my fingertips. We twirled and dipped when required, but were nearly at the end of the dance before he said a word to me.

"Meet me in my bedroom in twenty minutes."

"Your bedroom?"

Even if he was the Riadnak heir, I didn't think my mother would approve of this deviance from what was very much expected of both of us for the remainder of the evening.

"It's the only place we can be alone."

I didn't tell him that was the problem. I nodded instead, and when the dance finished and we bowed and curtseyed, Sabre sauntered back to his father and *Lunaveya* was officially open.

A more upbeat song floated in from the orchestra hidden somewhere in the room. The remaining guests flooded onto the dancefloor. The ballroom was heaving with people and most of them wanted to speak to me. They complimented my dress, my hair and my jewels and asked a stream of questions. I answered what I could and politely evaded responses I couldn't. I narrowly avoided a conversation with Ambassador Ryah, his lecherous gaze following me any time I was near him. By the time I found Tala in the middle of the Great Hall, talking to Olcan and Asher Caldoun, I was exhausted.

"How's it going, Aspen?" Asher asked me politely. We rarely spoke, but when we did it was always painfully stilted.

Asher was seventeen and had the good looks and charm of most males I knew. He was the leader of the colour brown and his skin, eyes and fur were all varying shades of it. Tala was expected to marry him when the time came.

"I'm fine, thank you. Can I steal my best friend for a moment, please?"

I smiled, acknowledging Olcan, before I took hold of Tala's hand and led her away. I noticed that once Tala left, Olcan didn't continue talking to Asher. They had less in common than a fish had with a lion, but I found it concerning.

"So I am still your best friend?" Tala asked while we graciously ignored the throng of people trying to get our attention. We made our way through the ballroom to the main foyer, where I lead Tala toward the grand staircase.

"You will always be my best friend, Tala," I smiled at her as we walked. "I was hurt you didn't tell me, that's all."

She at least had the decency to look guilty, "I couldn't risk telling anyone. You might have told Sabre."

I stopped in the middle of the staircase and looked Tala in her gorgeous blue eyes. Her curly hair framed her innocent face, her dark make-up beautiful against her golden skin and white gown.

"I would never betray you. You should know that."

Tala shrugged, "I do. I was just… being cautious."

I nodded in agreement.

"A lot like you are being right now, I guess?" I cocked one eyebrow, quizzical and she elaborated with: "Using me to get upstairs so people won't think you went off to see Sabre."

A faint blush bloomed on my cheeks, "I didn't think you would mind."

Once at the top of the stairs, we continued through the hallways that led to the Riadnak family suites. The house was even more grand than mine, with no expense spared throughout. Golden fixtures and crystal chandeliers helped spread a soft glow in every space, and plush, expensive carpets lined the floors, hushing our steps.

"I don't mind," Tala assured. "Just ask me first, okay?"

I nodded, happy that our friendship was mended. It didn't happen often, but I hated when Tala and I fought.

We approached Tala's bedroom door and she opened it, "I'll come get you in a bit so we can go back down together."

I thanked her, then continued down the hall to Sabre's room.

When I knocked, he answered instantly. I walked unhurried into his room. I'd been in there a handful of times so I was familiar with the varying tones of grey, white and accents of silver. His large bed dominated the centre of the room against a plain white wall that had the Riadnak white wolf stencilled onto it.

I approached the foot of the bed, waiting for him to join me. Sabre stood across from me, leaning casually against his desk, much as Goliath had done; his writing materials scattered all over it. There were a few books and some empty glasses but nothing overtly interesting. He continued staring at me, his right index finger casually stroking his bottom lip. He wore white tailored pants and shirt, with a silver embroidered waistcoat. He looked delicious and I wondered how I could have ever let Caius even threaten to come between us.

Sabre finally stopped caressing his lip and straightened up. He walked over, stopping inches from me so I had to tilt my head back to look up at him.

"Is something going on with you and the Gamma?"

"No!" I exclaimed. "How can you ask me that?"

"That's what people are saying. What am I supposed to think?"

"What people?"

"Does it matter?"

It didn't, except now I had confirmation that the people downstairs who had laughed and smiled in my face with good wishes were most likely saying disgusting things about me behind my back. What bothered me more than knowing for sure was the fact that I'd not seen it coming... and no one had told me. Not even Tala.

How had one conversation with Caius turned into this nightmare?

"It doesn't matter, but I want to know who's telling lies behind my back," I said.

Sabre started to turn away from me, but I pulled him back before I raised my hands and put them either side of his face, imploring him to really look at me.

"Sabre, baby... nothing is going on between me and that Gamma. Why would I ruin myself with him when I'm meant for you, for the Alpha?"

"You said I wasn't the Alpha."

He was hurt. His eyes imploring me to take my words back.

"I wanted to hurt you," I admitted. "You embarrassed me in front of everyone at the Bane and I... I'm sorry. I shouldn't have said it."

Sabre kept his gaze in mine, the hurt I'd caused him clearly showing and unyielding in its torture of my heart. I was mad at him for how he'd spoken to me at the Bane; I was mad at him now for believing such wretched things about me and Caius, but damn it, I loved him, and wanted us to be okay again.

"Please, baby. Please, believe me." I raised on my tiptoes for my lips to reach his. I kissed him once, twice and went for a third but he pulled his head back.

"You looked like you enjoyed your dance with him tonight."

It dawned on me that he was jealous, that he needed reassurance, because he loved me.

"I didn't," I said. "My mother said I had to play the part, so I did what was expected."

He was happy with that answer, knowing my mother would expect nothing less than perfection.

"I know all about doing what's expected." He said it so quietly I realised something was wrong.

"What happened?"

Sabre looked up at me, his eyes tortured, "My dad, he... I wasn't..." he cut himself off twice before shaking his head, defeated.

Instead of pushing himself to find the words, he lowered his head and kissed me, stopping anymore questions between us. I melted into his arms as his mouth plundered mine. My fingers gripped at the firm muscle beneath his clothes before he finally pulled away,

"I just..." he seemed unsure of himself.

"What is it?"

Sabre poured his gorgeous golden gaze into mine, "I just don't want people talking about my wife like that."

My entire body froze, "Wife?"

"One day," he murmured. "One day you'll be mine and I won't have to be jealous of anyone."

Sabre lowered his head again and kissed the space behind my ear, making a tingle travel from the spot all the way down to my toes.

"I'm sorry about the other night," he finally said and my heart swelled. "My father and I had a…disagreement. I was angry and I shouldn't have taken it out on you."

"It's okay," I whispered. Sabre lowered his hand and gathered my skirts up until he was able to get his hand underneath it. I tried to concentrate, but his lips and hands were doing unexplainable things to my nervous system.

"One day," his hand was safely underneath my skirt and his fingers grazed my underclothes, "this will be mine."

Sabre slowly began to stroke me through the material. I took a barely detectable step with my right leg, so he could get between them and feel the moisture building there.

"Mine," he whispered again as he lowered his head and kissed the top of my breast.

"Y-yours," I fumbled as his fingers moved to pull my underclothes to the side. His finger brushed against my folds and just as he was about to…

KNOCK KNOCK!

Our actions came to a screeching halt as I rushed my skirt down and rearranged my dress.

"Who is it?" Sabre growled at the door.

It opened and Tala appeared, sniffing the air she made a face, "Sorry to… interrupt… but Aspen should get back."

Sabre clearly didn't agree but had no reason to stop me, so stepped back, clearing his throat. When I felt presentable, I quickly went over to kiss him.

"Soon," I promised, then left the room with Tala.

The ball continued and I remained in Sabre's good graces. The rest of our friends were there, including Sire, but Tala kept a safe distance from him. I respected their ability to stay away from one another if they were in love.

We danced, we drank and ate in abundance the delicious Agmantian delicacies on offer. There were fried dumplings with jerked chicken baked inside. There was curried goat dripping in hot, spicy sauce that I lapped up with thick slices of hard dough bread. There were salt fish fritters and slices of sticky plantain and an endless amount of rice. I felt myself begin to sway from the effects of the strong rum punch—an exotic mix of Agmantian rum mixed with sugar and fruit juices— taking care not to spill anything on my dress. I handed Sabre another glass of it, my brows furrowing as the music suddenly died down.

"Honoured guests!" Balton's voice rang again throughout the hall and we all turned to him. "Your Alpha, Goliath Riadnak, would like to address you."

We bustled towards the stage where Goliath stood, looking not unlike a holy man about to preach to his adoring congregation, exuding an air of power and dominance.

"Dear friends," he boomed over the crowd. "It is my pleasure to announce that the first challenge for the Mating Games will be held in seven days."

I turned involuntarily to look at Sabre, who had gone completely rigid as he looked over at his father.

"The first challenge will be a test of endurance. The competing males will race from Invernell to Lorcanion and back."

Lorcanion was the capital of Aulandri. It was over a hundred miles away, over a week by carriage, depending on the route. There was no telling how long it would take the wolves.

"The males will have the month to complete the challenge. The first to return will be the winner."

The room applauded, soft murmuring erupting while people speculated how the males would fare. Fenrir came up beside Sabre and slapped him heavily on the back in some display of manly encouragement. Though he smiled, Sabre didn't look happy.

"And now," Goliath continued and the whole ballroom fell silent. "As some of you know, there has been some civil unrest between our beloved Celestia and Faenym in the north. It has put a strain on our export and has caused a number of *laecan* injuries."

There was a murmur through the crowd that I couldn't work out. Whether it was because they were speculating who was financially effected or they didn't know about the altercations, I wasn't sure. I personally didn't know anything about either issue, but subconsciously looked for my dad in the crowd. He was staring straight ahead at Goliath, the expression on his face betraying nothing. I assumed that meant whatever harm our export had suffered; it hadn't affected our family in any major way. It pleased me. I was sure to get the emerald earrings I'd requested for my birthday.

"The Faenymese, after an arduous discussion with Barbas Akando, have now aligned with us."

The murmurs grew as confusion spread through the crowd. Even I was a little lost. While I didn't pay much attention to court politics, I knew Faenym were notoriously against Goliath's exclusive rule. Despite the shaman's conditions about the Triquetra, the Faenymese *laecan* still thought it biased that only three families could compete for the Alpha mantle. They wanted all *laecan* to compete and, as I understood it, they weren't the only ones.

Adding to my confusion, the leader of the Faenymese *laecan*—Barbas Akando—had publicly denounced Goliath, claiming he would never break figurative bread with him. I'd heard my father complain about Barbas' disrespect more than once, so this apparent change of heart was shocking to say the least.

"Eat and drink well, knowing that your coffers will increase and you can sleep soundly in your beds."

The crowd erupted into applause as they all moved forward to praise Goliath for putting an end to the political and financial strife. Sabre kissed my cheek, mumbling something about wanting to stand by his father's side, before going over to him, taking that very position.

I watched him, delighted that I was witnessing him become the man he was born to be, when the moment was interrupted by a tingling across my skin. My eyes wandered to the other side of the room, though I was unsure why, until I noticed the Caldoun family.

They were standing closest to the door that lead to the hallway and were quietly observing the exalting of Goliath, not moving an inch before Maximus turned away and swiftly exited. Regina and Asher followed, but Caius stayed put. I watched him watching Goliath and an intense look of hatred flashed in his eyes. It was gone almost as quickly as I'd caught it. Caius turned to follow his family; when he got to the door, he stopped and looked back, straight at me.

We eyed each other for a breath—Caius unblinking, but pensive—before he slipped through the doorway and gently closed the door behind him.

Seven days went by in a blur of parties, dinners and day drinking, all of which Caius did not attend. He'd told me outright he had no interest in me, that he would not compete, and so, for the last week, I'd stressed about whether he'd show up for the first challenge.

Sure, I partied and danced and drank copious amounts of alcohol with the rest of my friends, but it didn't stop the feeling of impending doom looming aggressively over my head. If he didn't compete, our family would be ruined. Not has heavily as the Gammas for being rebels to tradition, of course, but without fulfilling my destiny as the Female, what purpose did my family serve? We could be cast out, made destitute, or worse—made to work.

Although most Celestians wanted Sabre to win, it was always on the basis that he competes for the victory. My only saving grace was that there was still the possibility no one would think it was my fault if Caius didn't show up. I'd danced, curtseyed and behaved as perfectly as was expected. No one could say I'd done anything to destroy the future political stability of our kind.

Coupled with the internal turmoil that Caius' lack of participation brought me was the undeniable hurt that he didn't want me. I didn't want him either, but the fact he had no interest in me was completely unthinkable. I was beautiful, I was rich and I was fairly intelligent. And that wasn't even counting how being with me would make him the Alpha. Surely I represented what every male wanted. He should be worshipping me the way every other male did.

The fact that he wasn't angered me.

As the start of the endurance test drew closer, I became steadily more convinced that Caius wouldn't show. The thought of it kept me awake the night before the race, tossing and turning in my bed.

Thinking a hot drink would help settle me, I put on my robe and slippers and crept out of my bedroom into the dark hallway. Candles weren't left burning overnight so I *turned* my eyes to see better in the dark.

Our bedrooms were all on the top floor of the manor. Rogue's bedroom was next door to mine while my mother's and father's suites were at the far end. They hadn't slept in the same room for years and I didn't care enough to ask why. My bedroom was closest to the stairs, giving me easy access to the rest of the house. I made my way down the thick carpeted steps.

The ground floor housed all of our rooms for socialising: dining and breakfast room, library and the like. The kitchens and laundry rooms were all below. I'd been down there on many occasions when I was younger, stealing treats from our cook and playing with her son. The memory shocked me—I hadn't thought of him in forever. My mother had put a stop to those shenanigans once I got older. Around the same time, she stopped me visiting the Caldouns.

Soon after, I *turned* for the first time.

I found our cook in the kitchen and she curtseyed as best as her old bones would allow, surprised at my intrusion. Her name failed me, so I smiled, but said nothing.

"Is everything all right, Miss?"

"Everything's fine…"

"Lydia," she offered with an understanding smile that made me feel guilty.

"Lydia," I returned her smile. "I just wanted to get something to drink."

Lydia went to dust what looked like flour off her hands, "I can get it for you miss."

Thank God she offered. I had no clue how to make a warm drink. I'd never had to do anything remotely domestic for myself. I'd only recently started doing my own hair.

I smiled appreciatively and took a seat on a stool by the wooden island that stood in the middle of the kitchen. The room was warm, a small fire crackling away at the far end, while large metal ovens simmered with heat behind them. The ovens were iron and so most of our working class were *maejym,* since the metal wouldn't harm them. My mother said it proved that *laecan* weren't meant to do manual labour.

"Your usual tea?"

I opened my mouth to say yes, but something stopped me, "No," the word came out softly. "No tea tonight."

"As you wish, Miss."

I was content watching Lydia go about making my drink, but as the silence stretched, I found myself asking, "Why are you up so late?"

Lydia chuckled to herself as she poured milk into a small pot, hanging it from a hook on a chain that was attached to a metal arm. It allowed her to swing the small pot and position it over the fire without the heat burning her fingers. "Late?" she echoed. "It's early to me, Miss. Someone has to get the bread kneaded and baked in time for breakfast."

I was humbled by my stupidity, "I'm sorry," I mumbled. "I didn't mean to interrupt."

Lydia chuckled again as she reached toward some shelves that were built into the stonework beside the hearth. She added whatever she took from there into the milk and continued to stir it.

"It's no trouble, Miss." She hesitated, but added: "It's good to see you down here again."

The comment made me feel embarrassed, but I didn't quite know why. I stopped further questions and soon enough Lydia placed a large mug of sweetened milk in front of me. I cupped my hands around it and lifted it to my lips. It tasted just like she used to make when I was little and I told her as much.

"I'm glad you still like it, Miss." Lydia's eyes lit up, then almost instantly saddened. I was jarred by the fact I wanted to know why, it dawning on me how little notice I took of the servants of our household, even those that had been part of it since before I was born.

"What is it?" I pressed gently.

"Just thinking about my Jacob is all. He loves sweet milk too."

"Your son. Where is he?"

At that moment, I realised I hadn't seen Jacob in years. I used to play with him almost every day.

"He went home—back to Mortania."

Lydia and her husband Jon—wait…Jeff…maybe Jack—were Mortanian and vague memories resurfaced of them talking about their homeland. From what I could recall, life wasn't great for them there.

"When… why would he go back?"

Lydia looked like she would burst into tears, "Two years now, Miss. He left to avoid the fighting."

Two years! How could I not have noticed a member of my household wasn't around for *two years?*

"Fighting?"

At my question, Lydia looked confused. She stared at me as though I'd grown an extra head, but when I didn't offer anything more, she whispered, as though the walls would betray what she told me:

"The *laecan* troubles, Miss. My Jacob left so he wouldn't have to fight alongside the wolves."

I didn't understand. Lydia seemed deathly afraid, looking as though she wanted to swallow the words she'd just spoken right back down again.

But why would a *maejym* boy be required to fight in *laecan* troubles? He wouldn't be half as powerful as the wolves were. He'd be like a lamb to the...

Oh.

"How long has this been going on?"

"For almost three years now, Miss." Still, she whispered. "Faenym won't back down and until they do, it won't be safe for young men who can fight back to be here."

But Goliath had declared to everyone that the countrymen of Faenym had come into the fold. He'd made peace with them. Lydia had to have it wrong.

I took another sip of my milk and tried to piece things together. In seconds, my head began to hurt and I'd completely ruined any chance of getting back to sleep.

"I'm sorry," I finally said as Lydia got back to her dough. "I'm sorry Jacob had to leave and that... I didn't say goodbye."

"It's not your fault, Miss," Lydia said kindly, her light brown eyes so warm and loving. "You're the Female, you're special. You've got more important things to worry about than Jacob. Or little old me."

Lydia turned back to kneading her dough and I put my emptied mug on the countertop.

For the first time in my life, in that moment, I felt like being the Female wasn't such a great thing.

CHAPTER NINE

The following evening, we gathered in the King Hill woods of northern Celestia, for the opening of the endurance challenge. The moon shone gloriously in the sky, clear and white against the navy and black expanse of the night. The stars twinkled like diamonds, the clouds hung low, thin and wispy like smoke.

Tradition dictated we attend this challenge as wolves, so the hundred or so guests permitted to bear witness at the starting line of the race, stood proudly in their lupine form. We prowled the clearing, finding comfortable spots to lounge, conversing while we waited for the challenge to begin.

The mighty white wolf that was Goliath, had positioned himself atop a mighty boulder, purposefully raised to allow him the optimal vantage point. He was a slightly larger version of Sabre, with ink black on the tips of his ears, which was the only physical mark that distinguished him from his son. Sabre was behind him on his right and Ambassador Ryah to his left. Ryah's straggly mottled black fur looked dirty in comparison to the pure Riadnak white.

Tala, with her mother and sister showing off white and grey furs, all stood proudly in their designated place behind the Alpha. The Caldouns stood yet another row behind the reigning Alpha Consort, in an array of their black and brown coats.

Caius was nowhere to be seen.

We would begin once the moon was highest in the sky, and so all wasn't lost, but still I worried. How my family would react was one thing, but how the shaman would take it was entirely another. We didn't have much interaction with them other than for formal blessings and religious events, but they'd put a price on the head of the last Female who defied them. I might not be Erina Anai but there was nothing to say they wouldn't do the same to me for failing to execute their magic.

I'd be the first Female in history to turn off one of the males.

It didn't bear thinking about.

I waited with my family, listening insentiently to the countless conversations that hummed through the crowds. Most were placing bets on who would win, others condemned them for even contemplating that Sabre wouldn't. Others simply placed bets on the length of time the winner would take to make it back.

Even though it was only the first challenge, the stakes were high. The first winner set the precedent for the remaining games as he would only have to win one more before being able to claim me.

I yawned, my jaws wide, exposing my sharp teeth. My mother growled softly from her place beside me. I clamped my jaw shut immediately. Despite catching up with various naps throughout the day, I was tired from my interrupted sleep the night before. I'd grown weary of trying to make sense of what Lydia had said about *laecan* fighting, but as I caught pieces of conversation between some wolves, the questions came barrelling to the forefront of my mind.

...slit his throat. they said one of his own did it...

...why would someone do that?...

...beats me. goliath had just brokered peace and now this...

...will they uphold their trade? my son is training at the house of gifts. i can't afford his tuition without some of those investments...

...goliath will handle it. barbas was an odd man, but he didn't deserve to die like that...

...his son must be devastated...

My mind reeled with this information: *Barbas Akando was dead?*

The Faenymese leader had been described as a formidable force whenever I'd heard my father talk about him. A military man and powerful *laecan* who disliked Goliath immensely.

When did this happen?

I wasn't given the time to think about it because Goliath finally addressed the crowd and all talking ceased.

...i, goliath of house riadnak, alpha of all laecan tribes of agmantia, hereby declare the first challenge of the mating games... open...

Almost at once, every wolf lifted their heads to the sky and howled. Gloriously, triumphantly, dangerously, we howled into the night, letting all the world know our strength. When the echo of the howls faded into the wind, Sabre dismounted the rock from his father's side and stood on the designated marker. He looked magnificent, the white of his fur like newly dropped snow against the dark of the night and shadowed trees behind him. His golden eyes shone from his pale face, a look of cunning and determination in his lupine gaze.

He looked so beautiful that, for a split second, I forgot I was afraid that Caius wouldn't show.

The crowd slowly reminded me, as they we were still waiting. I turned my great furry head to my mother.

...where is he?...

...shut up...

I didn't expect the harsh retort but I stayed quiet, my mother's brown coat gleaming beside me. My heart beat faster, threatening to burst out of my chest. I couldn't breathe and I could suddenly smell every little emotion around me. The anger from my mother and the impatience from those closest to me, but also the smugness from others I couldn't quite see.

The wait teetered between suspense and outrage when a pair of golden eyes finally peered out from between the nearby trees. I felt a tremor go through me as I watched the black wolf stalk out of the woods behind Sabre, his mighty paws clawing into dirt. I stifled the stirring need to howl with triumph and sudden gratitude.

He was here!

His fur was so black I could barely tell where the shadows ended and Caius began. He moved into the light of the moon and seemed to gleam silver as he padded up, unhurried. As Caius took his place beside Sabre without acknowledging anyone, I felt my mother's relief and for the first time, wondered why she would have even been worried?

Goliath surprisingly didn't comment on Caius' tardiness and instead addressed both challengers.

...you have thirty days to travel to lorcanion and return to this very spot. a guard will be here night and day to know who returns first and how long they took to do so...

The journey would take them through jungles and forests, over hills and mountains and under varying climates. There would be baking sunlight, harsh winds and snow both there and back again. Not to mention jaguars, tigers and wild wolves.

They could get hurt, superficially or mortally, and if the former, they would have to survive and make it back. I suddenly wished I'd said a better farewell to Sabre than the orgasm-filled fondle we'd had in the woods a few nights ago. While we hadn't gone the whole way, I suddenly felt ashamed of how I'd been on my knees pleasuring him.

Balton, in his speckled brown wolf form, stepped up beside Goliath, lifted his head and howled once more; the signal to take off. When appropriate, we had the ability to relay content in our howls. Calls for help, orders to treat or calling for a mate for example.

Sabre took off like a blur of white, leaving nothing but trampled earth in his path, while Caius merely plodded towards the trees.

Everyone saw it for what it was: a slight. A big fuck you to this competition and everything it stood for.

Caius finally took off into the woods, leaving the crowd behind to gossip among themselves.

It was at that moment that for the first-time, I questioned Caius' true motives. He said he wasn't competing because he had no interest in the prize, but his defiance just now was to the community— not to me. Caius had something against the wolves and I suddenly had the most curious inclination to find out what that was.

Sabre won.

He returned two and a half weeks later and the guard's howl of his triumphant return, from the return post, echoed through Invernell like a parade. Hundreds of wolves heard the call and raced through the woods to see who had returned victorious.

Sabre was filthy, his white coat caked with dirt. I stood on all fours, waiting for my chance to speak to him, and could see a few superficial cuts on his face and on the tops of his paws, but otherwise he seemed okay. When the fame whores and adoring fans of the Riadnak name had finally dispersed, Sabre came over and kissed me. Well, we were wolves, so technically he licked me, but the reaction from our audience was the same: he had all but claimed me as his in front of the town. I was elated.

I stood by his side as Goliath entered the clearing. All the wolves parted for the Alpha to gain access to his son and Goliath padded deliberately toward us, so tall that he cast a dark looming shadow over those closest to us. Sabre straightened up imperceptibly and looked his father in the eyes.

...*well done my son. you have made me and your family proud*...

...*thank you, father*...

Goliath turned so he was facing the gathered crowd and his voice carried through our minds as clearly as if he were in human form.

...*my son sabre has made me a proud father and an even prouder alpha. he is now one step closer to being your new rightful leader*...

The howling was deafening. I joined in, mixing my howls with that of my kind as we praised Sabre and his achievement.

...*come*... Goliath said, looking back down at his son. ...*you must rest*...

Sabre bowed his large white head and as his father took off, he turned to me. He came close so his head was inches from mine and his wolf voice wouldn't carry to any prying ears.

...*come to see me tonight?*... He sounded exhausted

...*send a messenger to let me know when. you might need a lot more rest*...

...*it won't matter. i want to see you. please come*...

I didn't have it in me to refuse him when he spoke like that.

...*of course. i'll come over after dinner*...

He licked me again before setting off rather labouredly toward his house.

Now that Sabre was gone, the rest of the wolves headed back into town, ready to praise his victory and gossip about Caius' loss. I stood in the clearing for a while, just myself and the guard. He remained beside a large torch that had been lit, waiting for Caius to return.

I shouldn't care where he was, but the most peculiar feeling took over and I couldn't stop thinking about what he'd said and how he'd looked during *Lunaveya*.

...are you all right, miss anai... the guard asked and I bowed my head,

...i'm fine, thank you...

I turned from him, but didn't head back towards town, deciding instead to make my way into the King Hill woods behind me. I walked aimlessly, random thoughts fighting desperately to find some kind of pattern in everything I had learned in the last few weeks.

Caius didn't want to compete and had something against the wolves, but he'd showed up anyway.

My sister was having sex.

Lydia said her son had fled Agmantia to avoid fighting in some skirmish that Goliath implied had stopped.

My best friend had a star-crossed lover.

And my boyfriend was one step closer to being my husband.

While the last part of that had always been true, now that things were hurtling towards that end, my certainty about it was faltering and I didn't understand why. I loved Sabre. I wanted nothing more than to be with him forever, but something was off and I needed to figure out what, so I could get rid of it and return to my life the way it had been. The way it should be.

As I continued to lament, a familiar scent tickled my nostrils and I quickly turned towards it. I snarled instantly as a pair of eyes stared out from the shadows at me, but within seconds I saw who they belonged to.

...caius?...

Caius stalked out of the surrounding trees and slowly began to circle me.

...*what are you **doing** here?*... I demanded.

...*I could ask you the same thing. congratulations by the way*...

I was momentarily distracted, ...*for what?*...

...*i'd only been following you for five minutes before you smelled me*...

So much was running through my mind as I turned this way and that, following his movements. He was taunting me but something was bugging me about him being here...

...*you never left*...

Caius didn't say anything but stopped circling, looking down his dark nose at me. I wasn't that much shorter than him in wolf form, but the intense black of his hide made him all the more intimidating.

...*answer me*...

...*why? you know the answer*...

He had thrown the first challenge.

...*why would you do that?*...

...*why do you care? your boyfriend is now one step closer to winning your sweet spot. everyone gets what they want*...

I lunged for him.

I bit at his throat, but he dodged at the last second. I didn't let it deter me and once again, lunged at him, my lips peeled back from my sharp teeth.

Frustratingly, Caius didn't fight back but instead went on the defence. He dodged every bite and outstretched claw until I began to tire.

...*grey. relax*...

...*don't tell me to relax! and don't talk to me like i'm some kind of easy bitch*...

I snarled the last word at him and he stepped back, suddenly contrite.

...fine. i apologise. happy now?...
...no! why didn't you compete?
...i told you i wasn't going to...
*...then why let Sabre race? you let him run halfway across the country for **nothing**...*

In an instant, Caius *turned* and stood in front of me in a pair of ink black loose fitting trousers and shirt. The clothes didn't look rough or worn, so either he'd remained a wolf the entire time he'd been in the woods, or he'd gone home to change. The rage that seethed through me was a living, breathing thing. I *turned* and marched up to him, ramming my index finger into the solid wall of his chest.

"How could you embarrass Sabre like this?"

"Hey!" he snapped at me, slapping my hand away. "Does it look like I give a shit about Sabre?"

He took the wind out of my sails, "No, but—"

"But what?"

I had nothing and he knew it. I just didn't understand. I didn't understand any of this.

"There's a guard in Lorcanion to make sure you get there. How are you going to explain not turning up?"

He shrugged, "I'll rough myself up a bit and come back claiming I couldn't make it. No one will care anyway." He was so nonchalant about it but I knew he was right. The community had their victor, they wouldn't care what Caius did now.

"You said you weren't competing," I tried a different tactic, ignoring the bias of our community. "Why go through the trouble of making everyone think you were?"

He didn't say anything, but continued staring at me with those eyes made of fire. I realised belatedly that he didn't smell unclean. He actually smelled good. Like sugar and coconut.

Focus, Aspen!

"Answer me, Caius. Why the theatrics?"

"Did you listen to anything I said at *Lunaveya?*"

I had. Too much, actually, but now his meaning was clear. He was doing this for Regina—for his mother.

"What is losing one challenge going to do when you'll be observed during the other two? You can still win."

Caius chuckled, "There is such a thing as throwing a match." He widened his arms in a meaningful as-you-can-see gesture.

My eyes widened, "That's breaking the law!"

"Call it what you want."

My heart sank at his blatant disregard for our traditions, at how our history meant nothing to him. And neither did I.

"You really hate me that much?"

This time he laughed. He outright laughed in my face before taking a sharp step toward me, bringing us mere inches apart. Just like when we danced. When I'd felt his warm breath on my skin and his strong body beneath my fingers…

A growl escaped his throat as a ring of golden light flashed around his pupils. He was containing some emotion inside him, keeping it back like a dog on a chain. I hazily noted how, for once, I didn't feel sick at his proximity, but the rage buried deep in him was palpable.

"Did it ever occur to you that none of this is about you?"

"I-I—"

"No, because in your perfect little world, *everything* is about you, isn't it, Grey? Everything is about the Female and who gets to win her like a trophy instead of an actual person!"

I remained quiet, unsure what to say. I suddenly wasn't sure why this whole scenario, or his motivations, bothered me so much. I'd thought Caius not competing in the games meant that he wouldn't show up, but he had. My fears had been unfounded as no one was any the wiser about his intentions. Why did it matter if he handed Sabre the win?

It's what I wanted anyway.

Wasn't it?

"Aren't you bothered by everyone running your life?" Caius cut into my internal battle, but then didn't actually let me answer. "Aren't you bothered that you have no choice in who you'll let *inside* you?"

I swallowed, embarrassed at the reality of his words. My mouth suddenly dry, "I want Sabre. I love him."

"You *think* you love him."

He looked at me like I disgusted him and he didn't know how to deal with it. I vaguely acknowledged that Tala had said the same thing. I didn't like it then and I didn't like it now. His anger was mellowing. It emboldened me somewhat.

"So you didn't compete, fine. But you wanted everyone to see you disrespect the race," I remarked, adding. "Is this about the fighting?"

Caius' eyes narrowed to slits but he crossed his arms over his chest, resting his weight on his right foot.

"It seems the princess knows a little something after all."

I didn't know shit about anything but I couldn't let him know that.

"Goliath said the war with Faenym was over, but my cook said her son escaped to Mortania to avoid conscription. One of them has to be lying."

Caius continued to study me, "Who do you think is lying?"

That didn't even need thinking about, "Goliath is our leader. Why would he lie to us?"

"Why would your cook lie about her son fleeing possible death?"

I had nothing to say to that and he nodded, as though I had confirmed something for him, "You'll never be ready," he said.

"Ready for what?"

"For what's coming."

"Stop talking in riddles, Caius, *please*. If you're going to push my entire world into turmoil, I need to know why!"

Caius looked defensive and stood straighter to look down at me, "Anything I tell you could risk your life and mine."

"From what?"

"From *Goliath*," he finally snapped, shocking me into silence. "He can't be trusted, Grey. None of them can. When you learn that, maybe I can tell you what's really going on. Until then you're one of them, and I can't trust you. I can't trust that you'd do what needs to be done."

I growled my frustration, realising that Tala had said almost the same thing. Caius didn't trust me with whatever information he had on Goliath and she hadn't trusted me not to tell Sabre about her and Sire.

None of them thought I was strong. None of them had any faith in me.

I hated that somewhere, deep down, I agreed with them. I'd never had or taken any real responsibility for anything in my life. My almost twenty years had been an amalgamation of privilege and wealth and, most importantly, of ignorance. I saw that now. And it didn't feel good.

"Just forget it," Caius continued, defeated. "It'll be over soon and you won't have to worry about any of it."

It will be over soon.

The words came to me in a whisper. They echoed from a time Caius had said them to me, when he had been my friend.

Caius stepped back from me and shook his head, "It's better if you stay ignorant, Grey. For both of us."

He *turned* and once again disappeared into the trees.

I was beginning to despise the feelings he left with me after we spoke. The feeling that I was missing something, that I was heading towards something dangerous and ultimately, that he pitied me for it.

CHAPTER TEN

Considering he'd spent weeks travelling across mountainous and treacherous terrain, Sabre looked pretty good. He was exhausted, that much was obvious, but by the time I arrived at his home, most of his cuts and bruises had healed.

I lay on his bed with him, his head resting on my lap as he told me about his journey across the country. He explained how he'd encountered wild wolves, ones with no human form, and how they'd attacked him. He also showed me some scars that wouldn't fade because they'd been given by those wolf claws. When his tale was done, he lay contemplative as I stroked his golden curls.

"My father said I should have been back sooner," he said.

"What?" I scrunched up my face in disgust. No matter Caius' actions, Sabre had made it back in record time. How much faster had Goliath wanted him to be?

"He said that if I was stronger, I would have returned in a week."

"A *week*!" I scoffed as I continued stroking his head tenderly. "No one could have made that journey in a week."

There was a moment in which he didn't reply, but then he said, "He would have."

I rolled my eyes—at his words, not at him. The idea that anyone could have made that trip in that time was laughable. The fact that Sabre believed it showed me the effect his father had on him.

I pulled gently at Sabre's face, forcing him to shift onto his back. His expression showed his deep misery and my heart suddenly went out to him. His eyes held mine with a longing in them that heated my body for the first time in a while.

Automatically, I lowered my head to kiss him gently. A warm flush went over me as I remembered all the ways I'd loved him before all these complications. Seeing the hurt on his face from his father's words...

If Sabre ever found out that Caius had let him go through that for nothing, he'd be crushed.

"No one could have made that journey in such a short time, Sabre. Not even Goliath."

He nodded, choosing to believe me and I lowered my head and kissed. Soon enough, we lost ourselves in each other's bodies, he neither of us had to worry about anything.

Dinner with my parents the following evening lacked its usual monotony, as my mother was ecstatic about Sabre's win. She went on endlessly about how it clearly meant that soon enough we would mate and the Anais would be elevated to become members of the first family.

Once Sabre and I married, this elevation would cement Ianthe as a power behind the figurative throne. As Alpha Apparent, Sabre would receive counsel from his father, but as Lady of the Manor, I'd get my counsel from her. Considering my mother was an expert on all things court life, it had always been an unspoken assumption that she would handle the running of the court for me.

As I watched her now, I realised the idea didn't fill me with relief as it once did. Now, I wondered what other parts of my life Ianthe would always control.

"I've already spoken to Celeste about the gown," Ianthe was saying. "There is some glorious silk left over from the very first Alpha wedding that we might be able to include. Nothing but the best for my daughter."

She went on about the wedding that, so far, I'd had nothing to do with,

"Oh!" I cut in, my excitement dry and superficial. "So you do know it's me getting married? God forbid I have a say in what I wear on my wedding day."

Even my sister laughed at that, and she was never on my side. I lifted my eyes to hers over my rice filled fork and for a brief moment we were allies. Ianthe lowered her cutlery to stare over at me.

"Do you have something to say, Aspen?"

I should have dropped it at the sharpness I detected in her tone, but I didn't have anything else to do this evening, so why not give my mother a burst blood vessel. I never spoke out of turn with her, but I felt restless and unsure—no, I felt out of place, with no apparent way of righting myself, and I needed an outlet.

"Quite a lot of things actually," I said putting my fork down and graciously wiping my mouth with my napkin. My curried mutton, rice and coleslaw would have to wait.

"Aspen," my father warned. I didn't even look at him. I'd started this and now I couldn't stop.

"You realise that Sabre is marrying *me*—not *you*."

Ianthe laughed politely in a way that was anything but polite, "Don't be ridiculous, Aspen. Of course, I'm not marrying Sabre."

"Then why are you taking over like this is about you? You haven't included me in any of these preparations, not once."

My mother told me where to be and what to wear, what to say and how to say it, but she never included me. It had never bothered me before but things were changing drastically for me and I didn't like it.

"Would you like to be included?"

"Would it matter?" I fired back.

Of course, I wanted to be included. After *turning* and mating, a female's wedding day was one of the most important days of her life, but my mother didn't see fit to include me in any of it. Despite being her favourite, I realised, she didn't use my being the Female as a way for us to bond, but only to flaunt herself at the Riadnak Manor. I wanted nothing more than to please my mother, but at moments like this, my need to be as she expected was beginning to feel extremely misguided.

"There is a meeting tomorrow afternoon for the wedding council. If you would like to attend, be my guest," Ianthe said, her voice saccharine.

"No. You'll be *my* guest."

"Aspen. Don't." Rogue attempted to intervene this time, but I ignored her.

"When I finally marry, you won't be a Riadnak, mother—*I* will."

The table went silent. The servants who stood waiting to attend us tried to sink into the richly painted walls to escape the tension.

My mother stared at me from across the table and the familiar gold ring of magic flashed before me. I refused to back down. I didn't know where my outburst came from, but it was the only ammunition I could use against her. While my family would become akin to the Alphas and part of the tight inner circle, it was only me who would become a Riadnak.

I was special.

Not her.

My mother pushed her chair back and stood gracefully. An attendant rushed to pull her chair out further and stepping around it she stalked determinedly from the dining room.

"That was cruel, Aspen," Rogue said. She stood from her seat beside mother's and left, assumingly to go and comfort her.

I was left alone with my father.

I resumed eating before casually taking a sip of orange juice from the crystal glass on the table. When the silence went on too long, I turned my head to look at my father. His green eyes met mine. Bracken Anai was a lovely man and an even better father, but when he looked at me like this, which wasn't often, I knew I had gone too far. My anger and resentment deflated but I didn't know how to take it back.

"Aspen, that was unnecessary."

"It was the truth."

"You should have more respect for your mother."

"Like she has for you?"

It was clear I'd shocked him, but like me, he refused to back down.

"Our relationship is complicated, but it serves its purpose."

"Like I'm supposed to serve mine without question?"

The room was getting uncomfortable, but I couldn't find it in me to stop. The last few days had made me question everything I knew about myself and my family. Everything used to be so perfect and now there were questions and uncertainty and I hated how it made me feel.

"I don't have any say in anything I do. I'm told who I'm meant to marry, who I'll have sex with!"

"Aspen, I'm your father!"

"That doesn't stop you letting her parade me around here like a pig ready for the slaughter."

"You never had a problem with it before," my father remarked coolly. "I never heard you complaining when you were spending my money and using your last name for your frivolous ends."

Shame exploded within me— unfiltered and raging—but I refused to look away from him. I stared my father down, emerald green glaring into emerald green as I blew out my nostrils.

"I want a say in how I run my life!"

Caius' words coming out of my mouth, but it didn't make them any less true. I couldn't allow him to guilt trip me into ignoring that my mother was trying to live my life. Caius' words were opening doors in my mind that I didn't want closing.

"What do you want, Aspen?"

I sighed. I'd already gone over this. I was about to reply that I didn't want anything, that it wasn't about wanting, when an idea struck me.

"I want to be included," I said simply. "I want to know what's going on in Faenym."

My father sat a little straighter in his chair, "What exactly are you talking about?"

"I'm talking about the fighting, Dad. I'm talking about the fact that Barbas Akando agreed to a truce with Celestia, and now he's dead."

My father looked confused, "Where did you hear that?"

"Does it matter? It's odd, don't you think?"

"Aspen,"

"Everyone knows he hated Goliath, so why agree to peace just before his death?"

"Aspen, stop."

"Lydia said Jacob had to fight," I was on a roll now.

"Aspen, stop it."

"Why would *maejym* boys have to fight in *laecan* battles if the fighting is over anyway?"

"ASPEN, ENOUGH!"

My father had never yelled at me before.

Never.

He was the mild mannered one. He was the one who saved me from my mother's gruelling etiquette and horse riding lessons when I wanted to play in the creek with Caius and Asher. Against my better judgement and complete embarrassment, tears pooled in my eyes. I was nineteen years old and crying because my father yelled at me? What was the world coming to?

Tala's mumbled comment about needing to grow up already echoed in my head.

"You will not talk about this anymore, do you understand me?"

I didn't say anything and just continued staring at him in utter disbelief.

"Aspen, I need you to promise me that you will not discuss political matters with me or anyone else."

"Why?" It came out like a plea. What was so terrible that my father would scream at me like that. Plenty of people had strict parents, I had one in Ianthe, but my father... my father was my friend.

Bracken Anai reached out across the table and took my hand into his. His large, calloused fingers felt warm against mine and when he looked into my eyes, I saw the tenderness and love that he always had for me. Yet, there was something else. Something I hadn't seen before, if ever, in my father's eyes—fear.

My father squeezed my hand lovingly and said, "I would never forgive myself if anything happened to you. Please, enough with the questions."

Still I said nothing,

"Please," my father said. "For me?"

There was a tense moment of silence before I said softly, "For you."

I lay in the hazy place between sleep and awake later that night when I heard noises coming from outside my window. Invernell was heavily wooded, and so any multitude of bird calls and animal cries could be heard on a normal evening, but this was something different.

Sleepily, I got out of bed and walked up to my window, forcefully pulling back the curtains, ready to curse out whoever had chosen to disturb my slumber. But as I lifted my hand to bang on the window, I saw my father and Goliath in wolf form standing on the lawn grass.

My father and the Alpha talking in the middle of the night wasn't a weird sight—nocturnal meetings were the norm, after all—but what was strange was the fact they were clearly trying to hide it. Only someone in my room and maybe my sister's next door would be able to see them on this side of the building.

I briefly scanned my room and saw that where I stood, was clear of anything important so I *turned* so I'd be able to hear them. Simply *turning* the inner workings of my ear would simply amplify my hearing but I couldn't hear wolves speaking, even I wasn't a wolf myself.

...and i'll tell you again... my father was saying *...there is nothing to be worried about...*

...you better be right, bracken. i wouldn't want things to get ugly between us...

...funny, that sounds like a threat...

Goliath chuckled at that, *...i wouldn't dream of stooping to those levels...*

...no... my father said ...you have more dangerous qualities than making threats...

Goliath was quiet for a long while.

I held my breath, desperate to keep any scent as dormant as possible, even from my window.

...do you need reminding that your daughter is the protected one... not you...

...leave aspen out of this...

...i will...as long as the little princess keeps her mouth shut about whatever idiocy she's heard...

...she won't be speaking of it again...

I felt sick. Goliath was here because of me, because of what I'd said to my father at dinner.

...the cook...

...lydia has been with our family for many years. i won't just throw her out...

...she must be punished...

...i will not get rid of her, goliath...

There was another long pause and in that moment, I was terrified for my dad.

...you make an example of her, bracken... or I will...

I hear Goliath's departure and long after they'd both gone, even after returning to my human form; I stood by my window, shaking before climbing back into bed. I lay on my back for the rest of the night, trembling, wondering what I had got myself into and whether or not Lydia would be safe.

The following morning at breakfast, my father announced that Lydia would no longer be working for us. Rogue and my mother barely acknowledged him, but I did. I also saw the tears in the eyes of the maids who stood around the dining room. I saw the bloodshot eyes of our butler Noa, as he handed my father his mail.

I saw everything for the very first time.

I saw they had lost their friend and colleague.

And I saw that it was all my fault.

CHAPTER ELEVEN

I found my mother in her sitting room, reading.

She was dressed in an elaborate gown that had no place seeing the inside of these walls in the middle of the afternoon, but it did make for a striking impression. She looked like a queen. The wide skirt of the gown fanned out dramatically around her legs where she had placed herself on a window seat, the window framing the gardens behind her. Her finger was going along the page she was reading and obediently the sun created a soft halo around her head, as if nature itself was affording her a crown.

One of the maids admitted me before she softly closed the door behind me. I approached my mother in a much simpler pale yellow gown that only just brushed the carpeted floors, showing the tips of my satin sandals. Fashion in Invernell was a fluid concept, but I hoped dressing more traditionally would make Ianthe more prone to forgiveness. I knew I needed to make amends. The thought of what I'd said to her, how I'd voiced so many grievous thoughts and made her privy to them, made me feel ill. I'd thought about taking it all back, but this was as good as it would get.

She didn't lift her head to look at me and so with a deep breath, I started my apology,

"Mother, I apologise for what I said yesterday. I was …angry and upset and I had no right speaking to you that way."

Ianthe remained silent so I stepped forward and continued, "Getting close to Mating Day is putting me on edge and I just haven't been able to deal with it all."

I couldn't tell her what was really upsetting me. She would never want to hear about Caius' intentions, especially if I had no idea of how to stop them. I couldn't implicate myself in his machinations in the same breath I was trying to get her to forgive me.

"I'm so sorry, Mother," I collapsed to my knees, now inches away from her, and hung my head low.

Finally, she moved from her position at the window and came to stand in front of me.

"Up," she instructed and I got to my feet. "Look at me," my mother commanded and so I lifted my eyes to hers. She studied me for a long time, "Have you been taking your tea?"

I hadn't.

Since not taking it from Lydia the other evening, I'd poured my tea into the flower pots in my room when the maids weren't looking.

"Yes." The lie came easily. I was surprised at myself. "Every morning."

The visible relief that showed on my mother's face was hard to ignore.

Ianthe reached out and placed her delicate hands on my shoulders, continuing to look at me intensely. I eventually had to look away from the scrutiny. She lifted my tucked chin so I would meet her gaze, "You will never speak to me that way again, Aspen. Do you understand?"

"Yes, Mother."

"You will continue to drink your tea and do as you're told until Sabre wins the challenges and you conceive with him. Nothing can get in the way of that. Do you understand?"

"Yes, Mother."

My mother lowered her head to place a delicate but cold lipped kiss on my forehead, "I love you more than anything in this world," she whispered against my head and my heart warmed at her words, "but if you jeopardise the future we've worked so hard for, I will never forgive you."

My heart plunged into an icy hole as I stared wide-eyed at my mother, registering the truth that rested in her eyes.

"Yes, Mother."

She patted my cheek gently, giving me a smile at last. "I'll see you at dinner," she said.

I nodded with a thankful smile before leaving her presence.

When I closed my mother's door behind me, I knew, that if I had any hope finding out what was going on, I could never drink my mother's tea again.

I needed some time to myself so decided to go shopping. I walked the crowded cobbled streets of Invernell, basking in the overhead sun. I strolled in and out of shops and boutiques, my arms growing laden with bags. A myriad of smells surrounded me: oils for food, hair and body teased the senses as vendors displayed their wares. An amalgamation of colour and sunlight burst before my eyes as I lost myself in the wonder of my hometown. I passed familiar faces, people I'd known my whole life that now I wondered whether I knew at all.

Being the Female was a blessing, a gift bestowed on me since the day I came screaming into this world and now, every day, I felt closer to steering away from my duty. Recognising many around me sought to abuse the positions that my own position would give them, I contemplated my calling with a heavy heart.

Still, the more I thought about things, the more I reassured myself that there was no real problem. Even if Caius wasn't actively trying to win, he was competing and that was all that mattered, because Invernell got a show of compliance, and Sabre and I were joined at the end of it.

Still, no matter what I told myself, the simple fact that Caius didn't want to try for me was driving me insane. What was so wrong with me that he would jeopardise our ancient and glorious tradition and evoke the wrath of the shaman if he were found out?

I strolled, not taking in anything around me as I accepted there was nothing I could or needed to do as long as Caius showed up for the challenges. It was the fallout of all the things I'd learned since his bold revelation that were destroying my life now—the realisation that I couldn't completely trust my family and friends and that I was very much alone.

I found myself beside Marla's stall of trinkets, baubles and vials of sweetened rat piss when I heard someone call my name. I stopped abruptly in my confident stride, all self-assurance gone from my stance as I turned to the owner of the voice.

"Aspen Anai," she said firmly. "Come speak with me, child."

I wanted to do the opposite of what she was asking, turn and run, but you didn't go against the request of a shaman. You didn't go against the request of *this* shaman.

"Lady Xana," I approached on hesitant legs. She stood between Marla's stall and that of a jeweller I'd bought countless jewellery from, completely unbothered as she waited for me.

Lady Xana was old, though not decrepit. She had a head of thick white hair that hung around her head in loose bouncy curls. Her face was a warm brown, etched with the thin lines of age at the corners of her eyes and mouth. She had bright green eyes that observed me so deeply I couldn't hold her gaze for too long. She wore a long, dusky orange embroidered kaftan that matched the headband on her head, and wooden hoop earrings in her ears. Beads hung from her neck in colourful strands that sat comfortably on her generous bosom. She held a large ornate staff that curved into the head of an open-mouthed wolf with eyes of blue gems that glistened in the sunlight. It was said the spirits of previous shamans who blessed and supernaturally watched over Invernell were inside. Whether that was myth or truth, we all knew that Lady Xana was the real thing, along with the shamans who lived at the Laecan Temple. Lady Xana was a direct descendant of Lord Assim, the shaman who put the Triquetra spell on our kind.

I stopped a few steps from her and waited as she eyed me from head to toe.

"Beautiful," she mused and I shuddered under her scrutiny. She chuckled, amused by my discomfort. "You're afraid of me child?"

"Shouldn't I be?"

Lady Xana laughed out loud this time, her green eyes twinkling with amusement. She flexed her hand around her staff.

"Not just yet."

My heart raced, "What do you mean?"

Lady Xana smirked once more and licked her lips, readying herself to speak, "Your ascension will not be easy, Aspen Anai, but the fate of our kind rests with you."

"Ascension?"

"Your choice will affect us all since your blood is key." She looked at me then, really looked at me, and almost as an afterthought she said, "The poison now eludes you."

"Poison?" I asked her.

"Something has changed and it is why I am able to approach you now. What have you done differently?"

The words left her lips and the first thing that came to mind was… "The tea."

I looked up at the shaman, but she'd disappeared. Right in front of me, she simply vanished. I blinked, bewildered as I stepped back, looking around for her.

Scared, I backed away before heading into the congested market and losing myself in the crowd.

I went to visit Tala.

After arranging for my shopping bags to be delivered home, I ran to the Riadnak Manor in wolf form but *turned* when I got to the main gates. I was admitted without question and taken to Tala's room. I found her sitting at her writing desk and when she looked up, a beaming smile erupted on her face. She got out of the chair and ran to pull me into a hug. In minutes, we were lounging on her bed, gossiping about the ball and Sabre's win.

"Where is he anyway?" I finally asked.

Tala shrugged, "Out with Fenrir, Olcan and Sire."

I hesitated, "How are things with you two?" I popped a grape in my mouth – one of her maids had brought them in – as Tala fell back onto her bed with a soft sigh. Her curls fanned delicately on the pillow behind her head as she looked up at the ceiling.

"On the one hand, everything's perfect." Her voice sounded so tender. "We find moments to meet up whenever we can, and when we do, it's just… perfect."

"And the other hand?"

We both knew the other hand was the law of the Alpha that stood between them. Tala sat up again and looked me dead in the eye, "Aspen, I love him so much. How could I ever end it?"

I didn't have the answers.

"I won't marry Asher," she said, more to herself than me before she slammed her clenched fist into the duvet covers. "I won't."

She seemed to remember I was there and turned to me with a cheeky grin, "Could you imagine? Me and Asher?"

We both giggled at the thought until her eyes widened, "Oh God, or me and Caius!" Tala fell onto the bed again, giggling to herself, but I suddenly didn't find the idea so funny.

"All he does is brood," she added, then scowled at me in a mocking imitation of Caius, "Hi, I'm Caius. I hate everyone and everything!"

That time, I did laugh. Her attempt at his deep voice was completely ridiculous.

"Maybe he has a reason to be so moody?" I tested the water.

"Like what?" Tala reached for a grape, bit off the top and lazily sucked out the juice.

"I don't know, maybe the way we tease him…"

Tala sat up again, she was like a see-saw. This time she rested on her elbows as she peered over at me, "We? You mean you and Sabre. I have never said a bad word to Caius or Asher."

I opened my mouth to rebuke that statement, but realised I couldn't. I had always been the leader of that bitch parade.

"Exactly," Tala laughed. "You, my brother, Fenrir and my sister's dumb ass boyfriend Olcan, are the ones always getting at them. It's your fault if he's such a boring little shit."

I knew she was joking but it didn't stop her being right. I took a deep breath and Tala looked concerned, "Aspen are you all right?"

"I'm fine, I just…I think Caius is…" I trailed off. My big mouth had gotten Lydia in trouble before. What if me telling Tala got her in trouble too?

"Caius is what?"

"Nothing. Forget it."

"No," Tala was suddenly more concerned as she placed her hand on my shoulder and turned me to face her, her blue eyes intense with her concern. "Tell me."

"Caius didn't actually compete in the challenge," I whispered,

"What?"

Tears suddenly gathered in my eyes and I couldn't have told her why, "He didn't go to Lorcanion at all. I found him in the woods after Sabre's win and he admitted it."

"Oh, God," Tala held her hand to her mouth.

"That's not all."

I told Tala about my conversations with Caius, what he'd said about her family and the fact that Barbas Akando was dead. I told her what Lydia said about the *Iaecans* fighting and that her father had been at my house last night.

Tala said nothing for a long time but when she did finally speak, it wasn't what I expected her to say.

"Aspen, promise me you won't talk about this with anyone else."

"…What?"

Tala scratched her cheek uncomfortably, "My father, he's very powerful and I wouldn't want you to get in trouble by talking about this with someone who might tell him."

"Who would tell him? You!"

"Of course not me, but…" she lowered her voice, "You did say that you were talking to your father about the fighting, so how would my father know, if someone in your house hadn't told him. Anyone could be listening."

Shit! I hadn't thought about *how* Goliath had found out when he wasn't even there. My father wouldn't have told him, especially as he'd fought to keep Lydia in our employ. Eyes and ears were seemingly on us in our own home.

"You need to be careful. My father doesn't like being questioned or challenged."

"I'm not trying to challenge him, but I—"

"Aspen... please. Just let it go."

My heart chilled as I looked into Tala's worried eyes. She had the same look as my father had last night. She knew something and was trying to keep me from it.

"I should go," I murmured, pushing myself off her bed.

"Where are you going?" Her worry deepened, but I made myself smile and look agreeable as always.

"Home. Maybe I'll have a nap or something. It's been a long morning. I'll see you later at the Bane?"

Tala nodded, a warm smile spreading on her face, my casual attitude calming her, "Aspen?"

"Yeah?" I turned to her as I held the handle to her door. "You know I love you, right?"

I smiled genuinely at that, "I love you too." I left her room and headed towards the staircase.

Once I left the manor, I *turned* and headed towards Caius' house. If my father and my best friend could lie to my face, then maybe someone who cared nothing for me would tell me the truth.

CHAPTER TWELVE

It didn't occur to me until I was on the Caldoun's grounds that Caius might not be home. And, it wasn't until a gardener on the front lawn greeted me, that the possibility of someone spotting me and reporting back to my mother was a very real thing.

Or Goliath.

Since he'd cornered me at *Lunaveya*, together with Tala's comment about spies, I couldn't get over the suspicion that he would find out my every move.

Right now, I wasn't of a mind to care. I needed to get some answers, and if Caius was the only way to get them then so be it.

I put aside my fear and smiled politely at the gardener as a return greeting, hoping that if someone did tell my mother and Goliath I'd been seen at the Caldoun manor, they would at least say my manners remained impeccable while disobeying them.

The stately manor was similar in size to mine, but as I approached I couldn't help but notice how empty of people it was. In comparison with the life and constant movement of my own home, from servants and visitors alike, it struck me how it wasn't just the sons of the Caldoun family that suffered the brunt end of the social stick. The whole family was evidently snubbed at every turn and though I'd been aware of it, it had always seemed normal to me.

I battled back a wave of anger at myself, at my mother's voice in my head, telling me the Caldoun's were lesser and me simply agreeing without questioning why or how.

Vines grew up the brickwork of the house walls, climbing over the door and front windows like green lace. I couldn't see any activity behind the windows at the front and so, with an uncertain hand, knocked the front door. There was a long moment before anyone answered. In fact, it was so long that I'd decided to leave when the door finally opened and Regina Caldoun stood in the doorway. I was shocked, to say the least. My mother would never dream of answering her own door, and I knew from experience that Celeste barely spent enough time at the Riadnak Manor to know when anyone came by.

"Aspen?"

Her confusion was evident, but she saved herself with a polite smile.

"Hello." Now that I was face-to-face with Caius' mother, I felt myself completely at a loss for words.

"It's been a long time. How are you, Aspen?"

Regina Caldoun was cordial as ever. She stood elegantly in a formal gown, with a large skirt that had lace on the three-quarter length sleeves and along the bust. The yellow complimented her warm brown skin and further accentuated the radiant smile she was directing at me. Her dark hair was pulled up and away from her face in an intricate braid, her face was heart-shaped face and her brown eyes were bright and welcoming.

"I'm fine, thank you, Mrs Caldoun. I just…" What could I say? "I…"

"Mama, who is it?"

Mama.

I'd never heard anything so cute in all my life.

The door widened and Caius appeared behind her in the doorway, his hand hooking itself over the top of the door and he leaned on it, holding it open. To his credit, the only reaction he gave to being surprised to see me was an almost undetectable widening of his eyes. His gaze returned to normal as he lowered his head and kissed his mother on the cheek.

It was the most loving I'd ever seen him. It appeared his crappier attitude was reserved solely for me.

"It's okay, Mama. Aspen came over for some help with Tracking." He looked up at me. "She sucks at it."

I wanted to kick his face in. Instead, I smiled at Mrs Caldoun and nodded, "Exactly. I suck."

Regina chuckled to herself as she stepped back, throwing one arm out in a gesture to Caius, before heading back into the house.

"It was nice to see you, Aspen," she said over her shoulder.

"You too," I called as she disappeared behind the door.

When Regina was gone, all amusement on Caius' face disappeared. He looked especially good today, in loose-fitting maroon pants, black shirt and black boots. He lazily let go of his grip on the door, to instead lean the crook of his shoulder heavily against the doorframe, observing me, clearly irritated. The nauseating feeling, I usually got around him was faint now, teasing the edges of my senses, but without being intrusive.

"What are you doing here, Grey?"

"I need to talk to you."

"About what?"

I started to answer, but paused, looking around at the open space behind me. I heard him laugh to himself, "Afraid you'll be seen with me?"

"No!"

He smiled, reading the lie for what it was, but I got the feeling he was somehow impressed by it. I was too annoyed with myself and having to come to him for answers that I folded my arms across my chest, defensively. Caius didn't reply, but I refused to speak. I knew what game he was playing and I wanted no part of it. I just had a few simple questions. I shouldn't have to beg to get the answers.

Finally, with a heavy sigh, he pushed off the door and stepped outside, joining me on the front steps as he closed the door behind him. I had to move out of the way to avoid his foot landing on my toes. Then he *turned* and the black wolf took off down the front lawn so I *turned* and followed him.

We ran in the direction of the King Hill Forest. We ran for what felt like miles, with me close at Caius' heels. The greens and browns of the trees of our community flew by in a blur. We pounded heavily through trees and bush, dodging and leaping over the natural obstacles that came up before us.

The air rushed through the strands of my fur, the forest coming alive in my ears, on my tongue and under my paws. The sun shone heavily overhead, beaming through the canopy above us as we splintered fallen hollow logs under our weight and disturbed the earth with our claws.

When I was running, I felt free. There were no mating dances, overbearing mothers or demanding boyfriends. Just the call of the wild, the freedom of being *laecan*, in a world that seemed made for us.

I kept pace beside Caius, his black hide darting through the trees effortlessly. He had incredible speed and stamina and soon, though I tried my hardest and despite the excitement that pumped through me, I began to tire.

Not wanting to give Caius anything to tease me about, I did my best to keep up, but by the time he came to a stop, I was ready to keel over and die. I might have skills with a sword and staff but running was not my thing: sweat wasn't attractive.

We stopped at the partially hidden mouth of what looked like a cave. On closer inspection, it was, in fact, a den. There was evidence of constant traffic from the entrance, but Caius stopped in front of me before I could look all the way inside.

...*what did you want to talk about?*...

...*where are we?*...

...*somewhere safe from prying eyes or ears. what did you want to talk about?*...

I tried to go around him, but he blocked my path once more.

...*why won't you let me see?*...

...*because it's none of your business. there are some things in this world that aren't*...

That stung, but I kept my retort to myself. I just needed answers from him, it wasn't like we had to be friends. I glanced forlornly at the cave, wondering what was in it and how long he'd had it. How had he even found it? Wrong questions. I refocused on my actual reason for being here.

Now that he saw I wasn't going to try and get past him, Caius settled. Lying down on the ground he rolled onto his back and, in a short moment, *turned*. Still on his back, his arms moved to interlock his fingers behind his head, perfectly at ease on the leafy dirt. He closed his eyes,

"What do you want, Grey? I haven't got all day."

I snarled at him, but *turned* and stood staring down at him. With his face so unmoving, I could see the perfect arch of his eyebrows and the smoothness of his skin. His eyelashes were thick and his lips were full and moist from having been freshly licked.

I cleared my throat, "I want to know about the fighting with Faenym. I heard that Barbas Akando is dead and I think it's a big coincidence that he died right after Goliath told us we had peace with him. To be honest..." I trailed off as the thought really took root. "I don't think he was dead after granting peace... I think we only have peace because he's dead."

Finally putting it into words sent a thrill through me, as though I knew I was right and all I needed from Caius was his confirmation, but he lay silent on the ground. He lay there so long I kicked his ankle to make sure he was awake.

"What?" he didn't even open his eyes.

"Did you hear what I said?"

"Yes, but I didn't hear a question." Caius finally opened his amber eyes. "What is it you're asking me, Grey?"

The way he was looking at me made me feel stupid, but I held my ground. I had to know if what I was piecing together was even a puzzle.

"You told me that not everyone likes the Alphas. Who did you mean?"

"His enemies."

I rolled my eyes, exasperated, "Yes, but who are Goliath's enemies?"

"How should I know?"

"If you don't know, then how do you even know he has them?"

Caius smiled, impressed, but I was not amused. I knew he was being difficult, but I was also quickly learning that I couldn't get the right answers from him if I didn't ask the right questions. I took a seat on the floor, slightly deflated, and Caius finally sat up. He bent his knees and rested his folded arms on them.

"I need to understand," I said. "I told my father what I thought and he forbade me to talk about it." It came out quieter than I'd intended, but shame would do that to you. "Someone told Goliath

I'd been asking questions. He came to my house, spoke with my father, and then my father fired our cook—Lydia."

My eyes filled with tears at the memory of Lydia heating milk for me, always smiling, always kind. Still, I was surprised tears appeared. I'd barely spoken two words to her for years before the other night. I was beginning to see how I'd barely spoken two words to many people for years, and for no good reason.

"She used to make me sugar cookies when I was little, even when my mother said I couldn't have any… She lost her livelihood because of me."

I lifted my now glassy eyes to Caius, who simply stared back at me. The confession of what consequences had come of my actions hadn't been an easy one to make, and yet he said nothing.

"I need to know why what I said got an innocent woman fired," I offered. "I need to know why Tala would be the second person to tell me to keep my mouth shut."

I finally seemed to have his interest at the mention of Tala's name, "You spoke to Tala about this?"

I nodded.

"What did she say?"

"I just told you what she said," I growled at him. "I don't think that's really the point here."

"Look, what do you want from me, Grey?"

"I want *answers*, Caius!"

"Why do you think I can give them to you?"

"Because no one else will," I snapped at him and he looked taken aback as I raised my voice in frustration, adding: "My dad and my best friend—the two most important people in my life—looked me in the eye and told me to stay quiet, forget I ever saw or heard anything, forget *Lydia*, when I know there's something more going on here."

Caius studied me, "Then why not forget? Why let this bother you?"

It was a fair enough question. I would have to give an honest reply.

"You asked me whether it bothers me that people run my life; that I have no say."

"Yeah, so?"

My brows furrowed at his dismissive attitude and my tone sharpened, "Well it does now! It bothers me that Lydia lost her job because I couldn't keep my big mouth shut. It bothers me that you've made me think about things that I never would have thought about before. I wish I could just forget and move on like nothing's happened, but I *can't*."

I stood up, filled with energy now that my thoughts were all tumbling out of my mouth.

"You and your little riddles and your defiance, and now I have to deal with *this*. All of it! People gossiping and my mother and Sabre being mad at me because he thinks there's something going on between you and me which is just—"

I hadn't meant to confess that part and stopped myself short, but I couldn't take it back now. Caius had heard and as I paced, he finally got to his feet.

"That's all this is to you, isn't it?"

"What?"

"An inconvenience," he practically spat the word at me. "You don't actually care that your cook got fired. You care that you feel guilty about it and you can't ignore the feeling as easily as you did before."

The denial was immediate, "That's not true."

It was true.

It was as true as my name was Aspen Anai.

Caius looked me up and down, utterly disgusted. I shrunk away from his scrutiny, knowing I deserved it, but hating it all the same. How did he have the power to make me feel so accountable for everything?

Ashamed, I wrapped my arms around myself, suddenly feeling cold and alone.

"Lady Xana cornered me in the market today," I said and I could tell I had his full attention. "I don't know what's going on with you, but when she called my name, I was so scared it had something to do with the Mating… with my part in it."

"Your part is set, Grey."

"What if it isn't?" I fired back at him, finally looking him in the eye. "How do you know that what you're refusing to do isn't going to have an effect on me that you can't take back?"

He didn't seem to have a smart answer for that.

"We have a duty to our kind; to do what's expected of us. Why can't you see that?"

"I see it. My duty is just a little different to yours, Grey."

"How?"

"It just is. You wouldn't understand."

"I'll never understand if you don't tell me!"

I was angry and frustrated and terrified that he was meddling with things beyond our control. I didn't want to be known as the Female that toppled a dynasty just because Caius couldn't get his act together. I didn't want to find out what the shaman could do if we didn't comply.

Caius eyed me for a long while before giving in to some internal battle.

"Look, I might not agree with your motives for asking questions, but yes, there is something going on."

My eyes shot up from where I'd been staring at his feet, "What is it?"

"It doesn't matter, because you can't do anything about it."

I was immediately indignant, "I could if I—"

"No, Grey, you couldn't. You aren't ready."

He prepared to walk away from me but I rushed towards him, reaching out and grabbing him by the shoulder. I expected him to snarl at me the way he did during Tracking, but he just stopped and looked back at me expectantly. I lowered my hand, terrified at the heat that shot through it the moment it touched the light fabric of his clothes and felt the hard muscle of his shoulder beneath it.

"How-how can I be ready?" I stammered.

I didn't know why proving myself to him meant so much to me, but the more he spoke, the more I understood, I couldn't ignore what was happening around me anymore.

Caius shook his head, "It's not that easy, Grey. You can't just wake up one morning and decide you're going to go against everything you've ever known. You have to find the truth, for yourself, and you have to decide that you believe it, not to rid yourself of guilt, but because it's the right thing, the only thing you can do."

"I can't believe in something I know nothing about."

"I'm sorry, but I can't be the one to tell you. I won't put countless other Lydias in danger because you aren't able to make the hard choices."

"What hard choices?" I practically screamed my frustration at him but he just shook his head in pity.

"When it's time to make one, you'll understand."

He went to walk away from me again but I dragged him back once more, "*Please*. Please, don't walk away."

"I'm sorry, Grey, but you have to do this part alone… I can't hold your hand this time."

I'm here with you.

The words jumped into my head alongside screaming and the distinct sounds of breaking bones. Like watching someone through fog, I saw a girl on grassy ground, crying, as a boy lay beside her and told her that she wasn't alone.

I scrunched my eyes up tight, trying to block out the image.

When I opened them—my breath sharp as I panted, suddenly scared—Caius was gone.

CHAPTER THIRTEEN

Sabre returned from Lorcanion two weeks earlier than given, which left just over a month until the second challenge. The agility challenge was announced during a soiree at the Riadnak Manor, and, as ever, the glamourous event saw my family and I dressed to impress.

Sabre and Caius would be required to compete as wolves like before, but we didn't know how their agility would be tested. Considering what I knew about Caius' plans to throw the competition, I wasn't particularly excited about having to watch Sabre achieve another false win. It shouldn't matter that Caius was allowing Sabre to succeed, but knowing Sabre had prepared his entire life for a win that was being handed to him, left a bitter taste in my mouth.

Part of me wanted to tell Sabre the truth, simply to ensure he was prepared. It would spur him on and he could still prove himself fit to be Alpha. What stopped me was knowing that he would rightly demand to know *how* I knew, and I couldn't confess my conversations with Caius. There was no way that would go down well. I wanted to tell him, but my self-preservation was stronger than my need to protect his ego.

I stood with Rhea and Susi at the reception bar, throwing back shots of tequila. The strong liquor came from the southern regions of Cotai, and while indulging in small amounts of the lethal liquid sounded like a great idea on nights out at the Bane, it didn't feel that way the next morning.

It didn't stop us from drinking it, though.

"Okay," Rhea chuckled as we removed thin slices of lemon from our mouths to dull the hit of the alcohol. "If you didn't have to lose your virginity to Sabre—who would it be?"

"Ergh," I wiped my finger tips on a napkin by the bar and waved the bartender over for some more shots. "None of these pathetic dogs."

Susi fell into fits of laughter. Candlelight from the chandelier above us shone off her bald head and she looked stunning in her tight-fitting outfit, an embroidered cropped jacket tastefully draped over her shoulders. She had never balked at wearing heels and tonight she towered over most women in the room.

"'Dogs!' she giggled.

Why the word was so hilarious to her, I would never know but I suddenly found it funny too. The three of us stood cackling at our wit until Rhea fanned the air in front of her, trying to get us to stop.

"I'm serious!" she said.

"So am I!" I squealed.

"Come on!" Rhea would not let it go. "I might not like what they're offering, but I can still browse."

"Browsing better be all you're doing," Susi remarked in her sassiest tone. Rhea simply stood on her toes for a kiss, and Susi happily obliged her.

I rolled my eyes even as I laughed, "Fine, if I have to pick, you go first. Who would you pick if you went that way?"

Before I could even blink, they both said, "Olcan!"

Rhea and Susi twisted their heads to look at each other and burst into another fit of laughter. Susi was clutching her sides as tears spilled down her cheeks. She held onto Rhea to keep herself upright, but Rhea wasn't faring any better. She was bent over the bar, practically screeching at the hilarity of it all.

"I see you've both discussed this," I chuckled,

"Discussed it? We've *done* it!" Susi blurted out and Rhea was suddenly stone cold sober. Susi seemed to realise what she said and the joke immediately died as her eyes widened with terror.

"You two…slept with Olcan?"

Their eyes darted to one another before looking back at me and the guilt was almost a tangible thing.

"While he was with Fern?"

Their lack of response was answer enough.

"It's not what you think." Rhea said sharply and I shot a look at her that could have curdled milk.

"What could I possibly be thinking, Rhea?" I hissed at her, my fists clenched with rage.

"I have some idea, but you have no right to judge on things you know nothing about."

"Rhea," Susi cut in, trying to calm her mate down, but Rhea shrugged her off as she closed the space between us and got into my face.

"Susi and I did what was needed to help our kind. It's no different to you doing your duty."

"Rhea."

There it was again, our duty, our obligations to our kind. It seemed I wasn't the only one fighting this battle, but that I was the only one on my side. Was everyone I thought I knew going to turn out to harbour secrets?

"What do you know about duty?" I asked, voice low.

Rhea scoffed knowingly, as though my words offended her.

"Do you know the things I've done for this community?" she bit back. "If you paid attention to the world around you, Aspen, you would know that Olcan is all but leading *Iaecan* forces into battle. Getting information from him wasn't easy, but *we* did it."

"Rhea. Stop. *Now*."

Susi was practically pushing Rhea away from me, and as her mate finally got her to look at her, the anger that had taken Rhea seemed to dissipate and she looked at me fearfully.

"Aspen…"

"What are you two involved in?"

"Nothing," Susi said. "Absolutely nothing."

She pulled Rhea off into the crowd and I was too stunned to go after them. Once I'd digested the information they'd unwillingly given, I tried to ignore Caius' voice in my head murmuring about finding out the truth for myself and I knew I had to get Susi to tell me more. I left the bar, about to head into the crowd when I was side-tracked by a horrific bang at the other end of the room.

The doors had been thrown open, the sound arising as they crashed against the walls. There was a collective gasp and then the crowd hastily parted as a handful of Riadnak guards made their way through it. Amidst the clatter of armour and weapons banging against metal was the blood-curdling sound of a woman screaming.

"Tala?"

I tried standing on my tip toes to get a look above the sea of heads and brightly coloured head wraps, but I didn't have the height, even in my heels. The screams continued and I forced my way through the tightly packed people to get to my best friend. The crowd thickened, full of dresses, feathers and drunken revellers.

"Get out of my way!" I hissed at the people in front of me, and when they saw who I was, they instantly parted.

At last I stumbled into the front row of the crowd, and to my horror it was Tala being held between two armed guards, her hair and clothes in disarray. I watched in shock as the guards marched her toward the end of the room where Goliath, Celeste, Sabre and Fern were standing. The guards threw Tala to the ground and she landed hard on her knees. The palms of her hands skid across the marble floor with a sickening squeak.

Her family looked down at her. Goliath did so with an expression of pure hatred as she tried to compose herself. Once she was upright, but still kneeling, Tala pulled her clothing around her in an attempt to cover her modesty. As I watched in confusion and growing terror, I realised her clothes weren't torn, just dishevelled, as though she'd put them on hurriedly. I stepped to go to her when someone grabbed my wrist. I turned to see my father.

"Dad, what's going on?"

My father didn't bother looking at me or respond. Instead, he set his gaze to the front of the room, where Tala knelt crying.

"Where is he?" Goliath's deep voice echoed through the silence. He stepped down from the stage, standing over his daughter, broad and foreboding. As if in answer, the doors banged open for a second time and another set of guards marched in with someone else between them.

"Sire," I whispered.

Oh, God...

The guards threw Sire to the floor beside Tala and he crashed to his knees just as she had. His shirt was open, revealing the fresh bruises and shallow cuts that covered his sculpted abs and muscled chest. He'd been beaten, his light brown skin was marred with rising bruises and scratches of blood. I could see, as the guards violently wretched his arms behind his back, that his fly was undone.

Oh, no… oh, no…

Sire tried to turn his head to look at Tala, but the grip of the guard who held him didn't allow him much movement. He reached out to take her hand instead and just as she reached for him, one of the guards kicked him in the stomach. Sire crouched over in pain as Tala cried out,

"Stop them, Daddy, *please!*"

Sire groaned in agony. From the kick the guards just gave him and the fresh blood I could see in what must be old cuts by *laecan* standards, I realised with trepidation that the guards must have laced their weapons with wolfsbane. His healing would be slow and it was possible he might die from blood loss if his wounds weren't treated.

Goliath stepped toward the couple, looking down his nose at them,

"Daddy, please don't do this."

"SILENCE!"

There were times when in human form you could project your voice as if you were a wolf. The resulting sound was a word that was laced with a growl so animalistic it could shake the foundations of where you stood. Goliath used this tone with Tala and the room was instantly silent. Tala held back her sobs, even as she looked fearfully at where Sire now lay.

Goliath reached down, grabbed Sire by his neck and pulled him to his feet. I surged forward again, shocked at the savagery with which Goliath dragged him into the air, but my father continued to hold me tight. Goliath punched Sire in the side and the air exploded from him along with spittle and blood.

Absentmindedly, I saw my sister across the room, staring at the spectacle before us and she looked ill. Somewhere, faintly, I registered how pleased I was at the evidence that my sister had a heart.

"You thought you could defile my daughter and get away with it?"

Sire clawed at his throat, trying to loosen the grip Goliath had on him, but we all knew it was pointless.

No one was stronger than the Alpha.

"You disgusting piece of half-breed filth!"

Goliath punched Sire repeatedly in his side and the entire room heard the cracking of ribs. The sound that escaped Sire was torture. I barely heard him speak on a good day, so to hear that mewl of agony from him was heart breaking. Tears pooled in my eyes as I watched Tala watching Sire, seemingly unable to look away, even when there was nothing she could do to intervene. I couldn't see Sire's parents in the crowd and that didn't bode well.

After another punch to his broken side, Goliath finally dropped Sire to the ground. Tala rushed over, falling to her knees as she reached out and tenderly stroked Sire's face. He looked at her, all of his love gathered there, but his face scrunched into a grimace as he winced, hand going to his side. Tala turned her icy blue gaze onto Goliath.

"How could you?" she screamed at her father. "I'll *kill* you for this!"

The gasp that went through the crowd was so thick I was surprised people didn't choke on the inhale. Goliath looked down at his eldest daughter and smiled unpleasantly. It made my skin crawl.

"For the sake of the blood that flows through your veins and the name you bear, I will not kill you for that insult against your Alpha."

"Fuck you!" Tala shot, clearly meaning it.

The smile disappeared from Goliath's face and from where I stood I saw the golden light flash in his eyes. He was furious and I knew that if it hadn't been for the hundreds of people in this room,

Goliath would have killed Tala for her insolence. It wouldn't matter that she was his daughter, his blood.

"I hereby declare," Goliath raised his voice, "that Sire Boltese and Tala Riadnak are both banished from Invernell."

The crowd erupted into shouts of shock and confusion.

My heart sank. I wanted to step between Goliath and Tala, but I stayed by my father, the fear of facing the same declaration myself keeping me in my place. Still, I wondered how Goliath had found out. Who had told him? Where had Tala and Sire been when they'd been caught?

"Furthermore, they are banished from Celestia and all lands that fall—"

"For what crime?" Tala demanded, voice loud enough to echo through the room. "For being in love? For not following your stupid rules?"

"—under my rule and jurisdiction," he continued, ignoring her. "Any who assist this whore and her mongrel lover will suffer the same treatment."

The murmuring continued through the gathered and hundreds of people took a collective step back, as though merely being close to the couple would contaminate them with their punishment.

"Tala Riadnak, you are no longer my daughter. I strip you of any and all rights to my name and the privilege it entails."

"*Take it!*" Tala screamed at him. "I want no part of your legacy and I hope it kills you. It's more than you deserve for everything you've done!"

Goliath was unfazed, "Take them away."

Two guards moved towards Sire and, quicker than I had ever seen it done, Tala *turned,* placing herself protectively over Sire. Her seven-foot height dwarfed his broken body on the floor. Her lips curled back from her teeth in a snarl and even though we were all in human form we knew what that meant.

If any one of those guards tried to touch him, she'd kill them.

They would not *turn* to combat her, there wasn't enough space; but that wouldn't deter them for long. Tala continued to snarl, warning them away, just as Sire struggled to crawl out from under her and staggered painfully to his feet. He reached out and took hold of Tala's lustrous white and grey coat, stroking her lovingly. She stopped snarling and calmly walked forward, the crowd hurriedly parting for her. The couple exited down the pathway they'd previously been dragged.

I took a step forward, about to ignore my trepidation and go after her, but my father's hand wrapped tightly around my arm. I tugged, trying to wrestle myself free, but when I looked back I found my mother standing there with him. She shook her head at me, just once.

I was not to embarrass her.

I was not to make a spectacle of myself and follow a pronounced traitor in front of the entire town. If I did, I would doom us all to the same fate and, God help me, I knew I didn't want that.

Who would I be if not Aspen Anai, the eldest Beta daughter, the Female Triquetrian, born to be the Mother of Alphas?

I was nothing without those titles.

I looked away from my mother and back to the devastating scene before me as Sire and Tala disappeared out the front door. Tears flooded down my cheeks as I looked to the Riadnak family, where Fern and Celeste were also in tears, the mother holding her remaining daughter close. Sabre stood stoic beside his father, his face unreadable as he stared after his sister.

I searched the sea of faces for some pity, some upset at what had just happened, but everyone remained silent, though already braised for gossip. When my eyes settled on Caius among the crowd, his golden eyes stared back at me from across the room and I understood everything he said to me in that one look: I had shown my true colours—I couldn't make the hard choices.

Not when it mattered the most.

I may have thought myself nothing without all those fancy titles, but in that moment, looking into Caius' damning eyes, I knew I was less than nothing with them.

Pawn
Part Two

CHAPTER FOURTEEN

My father finally loosened his hold on me and I immediately ran over to Sabre. Goliath and Celeste had left the exposure that came with holding court from the Great Hall stage, disappearing through a side door. Olcan was comforting Fern as she wept into his chest. I didn't dwell on that mockery of a relationship, taking Sabre's hand and leading him out of the room and away from prying eyes. He followed me without question until I found a room that offered us some privacy and locked the door behind me.

I spun around, gripping his shirt as I cried, "Do something!"

"Like what?"

"*Anything.*" My guilty tears spilled over as I pleaded with him. "Get your father to take it back, get Tala to come home."

He took hold of my hands and held them, giving my forehead a kiss before meeting my gaze.

"I can't do that. My father's word is law. You know that."

"That's why you have to change his mind. Get him to take it back."

I knew I should calm down, or at least stop yelling at him, but I felt the desperation of my own inability to do anything. Sabre looked down at me, but didn't reply. Something cold crept through me as I took in the lack of emotion on his face.

"Unless…" I said slowly as the ugly thought took root. I took a step back, letting my hands fall from his grip, "You agree with him."

"Tala sullied herself." His reply was instant.

"She's your sister."

"Sire isn't pure."

"He's our *friend*, Sabre."

"That doesn't mean I want him breeding with my sister!" Sabre snapped with such intensity I took a step back. "Tala knows what father is like, she knows the rules. She never should have let this happen."

I couldn't believe what I was hearing. It didn't matter what I knew and thought about purebloods. Sire was one of us and Tala was *family*.

"Sabre. She loves him. They love each other, doesn't that count for anything?"

Hi eyes narrowed, "Did you know about them?"

I realised my mistake and quickly shook my head, "N-no. I just assumed…"

He looked relieved, "Well no, it doesn't count for us. Not for Alphas."

My head snapped back as though he'd hit me, my eyes narrowing into slits as I sassily brushed my braids over my shoulder and crossed my arms over my chest.

"What if you loved me, but I wasn't the Female?"

"What?"

"You heard me," I challenged. "What if you loved me but I wasn't *pure*, as you say?"

"That's ridiculous."

"Why?"

"Because I *couldn't* love you if you weren't the Female."

The way my heart plummeted into my stomach, you'd have thought somebody died. My eyes never left Sabre's face as I tried to find some evidence of the boy I thought I was in love with.

Thought...

I uncrossed my arms and retreated from him, "Sabre. Do you love me...*because* I'm the Female?"

He rolled his eyes and laughed as though the idea was ludicrous, "Come on Aspen, don't do this."

"It's a simple question"

"It doesn't matter", he exclaimed, losing his patience, "You *are* the Female."

"It matters to *me*," I yelled back, tears threatening to fall all over again. The silence between us was telling: a void of all the things I needed him to say and all the things he wasn't.

"I have a duty to my family and to all *laecan*—"

Again with the duty.

"Answer the question, Sabre."

"No, I don't love you because you're the Female."

He was lying.

As surely as I knew grass was green, Sabre was lying.

He believed he loved me, but I could see in the way his admission fell routinely from his lips that my being the Female made me more desirable. It might not be the entire reason he loved me, but it was a big part of it and, maybe, that was even worse. I had been trained into one role—so had he. It was suddenly the only thing we had in common. The irony was stifling.

"This isn't about us," he said, reaching out to pull me into his arms. "This is about Tala and the fact that she broke the rules."

I allowed myself to fold into his arms, even though my startling realisation was making me feel sick.

"Sire was never going to be good enough. He didn't have a place here. You're not like that. *We're* not like that. Soon we'll be the Alphas and everything will be the way it should be."

"And what way is that?" I breathed against his chest, terrified of the answer that I knew would follow.

"With me as Alpha and you dutifully by my side. Isn't that what you want?"

I'd thought it was.

Nothing was turning out the way I thought it would. Our obligations to our kind were popping up in every conversation I had, but they didn't all align. Our priorities were all different. Mine, Sabre's, Caius'—even Rhea and Susi's—our destinations were the same, but the journey wasn't.

Sabre took hold of my bare shoulders and for the first time I wanted to recoil from him, but I didn't dare show my feelings as he held me out at arm's length to peer into my face.

"Isn't it?"

"Yes," I couldn't find it in me to embellish any more than that. I'd heard all I needed to hear.

Sabre came toward me again and lowered his head to kiss me, but I kept my mouth closed, trying to deny him the full kiss I knew he wanted. My infinitesimal resistance didn't deter him and he forced my mouth open with his tongue as he pulled me into him.

I kissed him back. As soon as the memory of his kisses registered in my core and heated my blood, there was no stopping my response. He kissed me harder, more passionately, and I threw my arms around his neck and succumbed.

This was the Sabre I knew—this was the Sabre I loved and who loved me. Not because of *what* I was, but *who* I was. He loved my laugh and my smile and the beauty marks shaped like a star on my hip bone. This was the Sabre who had me calling his name through waves of multiple orgasms and told me I was the most special thing in his world.

I moaned into his mouth and he growled into mine as he backed me toward the door. I slammed into it and let out a cry as he moved his lips from my mouth to my neck and down over the top of my breasts. I panted as I slowly lost my mind to the adrenaline running through me.

He reached down, grasping the fabric of my skirt and with a sharp ripping sound he tore it all down the side before he gripped my now exposed thigh and lifted it around his waist, pressing his erection into me.

No. This couldn't happen. Not like this.

Sabre continued kissing me, sucking me along my tender and exposed skin until I felt him fumbling between us. The pressure of his manhood momentarily stopped teasing against the soft pulse between my legs and it gave me the clarity I so desperately needed. He was struggling to undo the tie on his pants, but I stopped his movements by pushing him away.

"Sabre, stop."

His eyes were glazed with the heat between us, "Why? We're going to be together anyway, so why wait?"

"The rules," I said, the certainty that had eluded me recently coming back with a vengeance.

Our first time together was destined to sire the Alpha Apparent. We couldn't anger the shaman or risk the conception by doing anything before our birthday. He knew this.

"What?" he looked confused. I straightened up and placed my hand on the door handle, I was ready to leave.

"Tala broke the rules remember? I won't be caught doing the same…not even to be with you."

His eyes widened as his own words came back to haunt him. I stepped forward and he retreated to let me unlock the door. I closed it gently behind me and made my way to the front of the house. When I was safely at the front door, I turned and ran to the comfort of home.

I didn't leave my house for a week after Tala's exile.

My father didn't push me to attend classes and even Ianthe didn't pressure me to do anything, knowing how distressed I was. So long as I wasn't embarrassing her, she was fine with whatever I did.

After my talk with Sabre, I'd cried for what felt like forever but when I was finished, I was done with trying to figure everything out. My best friend was gone, Barbas Akando was dead, I still knew next to nothing about the fighting and Caius, Rhea and Susi were somehow all a part of it. so the only sensible course of action was to accept that there was nothing I could do, and move on.

My duty was to my family. I was to obey my father, to honour my mother, and play the part of the Female. I only strayed further from that path trying to impress Caius with my new moral compass and intuition. If he and others like Rhea and Susi didn't care about how their actions affected me and the community, then I wouldn't care how my actions affected them.

I'd managed to get to a point where I could meet my eyes in the mirror and keep my smile on for longer than a few seconds, so decided to leave my room. Not wanting to see my family, I went to the kitchen. I was amazed and pleased to see Lydia. She was less talkative than usual, and didn't offer me much by way of information. She'd been in King Hill looking for work when my father reached out to her again and so she returned to the only home she'd known for the last thirty years. When I asked my father why she had returned, he didn't offer any explanation. I didn't press for one. It wasn't my place.

To work off my guilt and anger, I went to the training ground. With my Agmantian steel sword, I sliced at my invisible enemies. I slashed, swiped and manoeuvred the blade, cutting through wind as if it were against me. I was so caught up in my internal fight, I didn't notice someone behind me until it was too late. I turned and struck my sword but it was met by another blade.

"F-Fenrir!" my chest pounded as Fenrir's grey eyes peered back at me, a smirk on his lips.

"If I knew you could fight like this, I would have challenged you more in class."

He grunted against the pressure I put onto our crossed swords before I pushed out of the hold and stepped back, chest heaving with exertion. I had no time for his shenanigans, my prowess with a sword was none of his business. Fenrir eyed me as I stabbed the tip of the sword into the floor. The hilt swayed with the force of my action. I was coated with sweat and didn't give a damn about my appearance. He was intruding.

"What are you doing here?"

He stabbed his own sword into the ground, my family crest on the pommel, and I realised he must've gotten it from the sword rack in the weapon's shed. He'd been here longer than I realised.

"I came to deliver a message."

"Is courier your main profession or does Sabre keep you around for other things too?"

To his credit, Fenrir didn't rise to my insult but I couldn't find the energy to care. Fenrir's feelings or lack thereof, were completely unimportant.

"He wants to see you." He offered instead. "He misses you."

I lifted the bottom of my sweat drenched tunic to wipe my face, revealing the brown taut skin of my stomach.

"So he sent his lapdog to tell me that? How romantic."

I rolled my eyes and pulled my sword from the ground, intent on putting it back on the rack. One of the servants would make sure it was sharpened again.

I wanted a hot bath and rest. It was too late in the evening to receive any visitors, least of all annoying little shits like Fenrir.

"He's been busy with Goliath and Olcan." Fenrir continued, as though I'd asked or shown interest, but, his mention of Olcan did pique my interest. "He wanted me to let you know that he was still thinking of you. He's really sorry for what happened, Aspen."

"He told you?"

Fenrir shrugged, "He's my best friend."

"Well, Tala was mine," I replied, choking on her name. I didn't even know where she was or if she was okay.

Sire was in bad shape when they left and I hadn't had the chance to say goodbye. Sire's parents had also conveniently disappeared from society and no one had questioned it. I remembered the fear on Susi's face when she realised what she and Rhea had confessed; her and Rhea's words of being as duty bound as I was; and the worry on Tala's face when she told me not to ask questions about her father...

I would never see her again. "What is Sabre up to anyway?" I asked, brushing up against that buried need to see the bigger picture. "Why is Olcan with him?"

Fenrir visibly tensed, "Olcan is serving his Alpha. That's all you need to know."

"Fine. Then tell Sabre I have nothing to say to him until he can speak to me himself."

Fenrir regarded me with new interest, "He won't like that."

"Does it look like I care?" I snapped, taking a menacing step toward him, but when he didn't move, I turned spiteful, "Doesn't it bother you?"

"What?"

"That your so called best friend thinks you're a piece of shit?"

"Excuse me?" his eyes went cold.

"Sabre is just like Goliath. He doesn't respect you because you're not from a main family. You're trash to him."

Finally, it seemed I hit a nerve as Fenrir straightened up and looked over at me vengefully, "Sabre respects me because I know my place. You should try it sometime, *Female*."

My stare could've cut through iron, but Fenrir didn't immediately take the words back, his eyes frosty. As we stood glaring at one another, I couldn't understand how I'd never known how much Fenrir hated me. I saw it clear as day that he detested everything about me. I'd been so sure about my position, my friends, family and my feelings for Sabre, but here Fenrir stood, glaring right at me like I was dirt. It was clear how different everything was now or maybe, it had always been this way and I'd just not seen it. I didn't trust anyone as wholeheartedly as before, and even if I were to do nothing but obediently bow to what was expected of me, considering Fenrir was someone who was meant to protect me one day, my reservations were a little concerning.

"I'll catch you later, Aspen." He didn't bother waiting for my reply and turned to head back into the house.

When I'd calmed myself down enough that I knew I wouldn't snap at anyone I might run into on the way to my room, I made my way back into the house. After a hot bath and changing into some warm pants and a thick wool jumper, I decided it was finally time to leave my self-assigned confines and head to the Bane. Only problem was that there was no one there I really wanted to see. I wanted someone to confide in, not drink with, and Tala was no longer an option.

The truth was, there was only one other person who I could possibly talk to, but how did I find him?

Track him.

It was as simple as that. All I had to do was pick up Caius' scent and find him.

I headed for his home and followed my wolf nose around the outside of the house until I stopped below a window that had his scent: coconut oil and sugar. Using the basis of this scent, I *turned* and followed my instincts into the woods.

It was a long time before I found him.

I'd barrelled through the woods on the hunt for him, splintering fallen trees and trampling dirt. A few wrong turns had me doubling back on myself, but the weight of his paws in the dirt and the scratch of his claws on exposed wood led me straight to him.

I heard voices before I saw anyone. Deep, familiar voices, but I couldn't make out the words. I edged closer, careful to keep my own scent down wind and avoid being detected. I only knew I'd succeeded when I finally laid eyes on two wolves in a clearing, and neither of them turned to acknowledge me. It was only when I edged closer to the pair that I realised who the other wolf was.

...sire?...

Sire's back was to me, but both he and Caius lifted their heads to look in my direction. Sire's rich beige fur looked almost golden as he stood in a beam of moonlight, but there was no mistaking him.

...i thought you said this place was secure!... Sire growled at Caius as he returned to facing the black wolf.

...it is...

...i have to get out of here... Sire backed away from Caius as I leapt from the rocks I'd been perched on, and landed beside him.

...*sire, please, wait. what are you doing here? is tala okay?...*

...*she's fine*... he replied, but I knew he was reluctant to tell me anything. He continued to back away and I acknowledged faintly that he was moving well, our healing abilities obviously effective after a week.

...*i must go...*

...*wait! what's going on?...*

He turned his attention to Caius, who said nothing. When Sire turned his large head back to me, his glowing hazel eyes were finally sympathetic.

...*i'm sorry, aspen, but i don't know if i can trust you. i can't risk tala's life...*

I wouldn't do anything to hurt Tala, surely Sire knew that. Then again, why would he? He knew practically nothing about me or my recent revelations. I'd always been Team Riadnak and there was nothing to show that my allegiance had changed, no matter what I now felt about myself.

...*please...* I didn't have all the words so I went with the simplest ones. ...*tell her i love her and i miss her. tell her...tell her i'm sorry...*

Sire bent his head in agreement.

He took one last look at Caius, who bent his head as well before Sire disappeared into the woods.

I turned to Caius, ...*start talking. now...*

CHAPTER FIFTEEN

Caius *turned* and stood before me, dressed entirely in black. I hated that my first thought was how delicious he looked. I didn't even like him, so why did I care that his black shirt fit so perfectly across his broad shoulders, or that his trousers fit snugly against his powerful thighs. I shouldn't be bothered that his hair gleamed in the sunlight, or that his eyes looked at me like they could burn my clothes away.

"What the *hell* are you doing here?"

I knew I was in the way, that I shouldn't be here, but I couldn't bring myself to say sorry, not after discovering that Tala was okay and that he and Sire were meeting in secret. In true Aspen Anai nature, I ignored the part of the conversation I didn't like and just asked another question.

"Why was Sire here?"

"You really don't listen, do you?"

I stared at him. He stared back, before finally relenting, "He doesn't trust you, Grey. I'm not telling you anything he's not willing to tell you himself."

"Can I... help?" I knew how weak it sounded.

I felt weak. I'd given up. After one bump in the road—even though it had been a big bump—I'd sounded my retreat and decided it was all too hard.

"You couldn't handle it if I said you could. Didn't Tala's banishment prove that?"

"Yes," I conceded, my shame bubbling inside me. Why couldn't he see how hard this was for me? "But I don't want to be that girl who stands by while her best friend gets kicked out of her life and there's nothing she can do about it."

The harsh edge went out of Caius' glare.

I took it as my opening to continue, "Sabre didn't even care. Tala said all those things, about Goliath and his legacy and I want to know why. I want to know why I have this feeling you're in the middle of it."

"I'm not in the middle of anything."

"Stop lying to me!" I yelled at him, tears flooding into my eyes, but I bit back against them running over.

For the last few weeks, all I'd done was cry. I cried over Tala, over Sabre, and over the end of my life, the way it used to be. I wanted to be done. When Caius still didn't answer me, I confessed.

"I hate who I am now," I whispered, afraid to utter what had been taking up space in my head for days. "I hate who I've always been and I need your help."

I choked on my tears, "They took her and I did...nothing. Her family did nothing and I don't want to be like them."

Caius remained quiet for a long time, but when he spoke, his voice was dark and unforgiving, "And yet you're going to marry Sabre. There's no changing that, Grey."

There was a way to change it. He was standing right in front of me, but I couldn't say that. He'd know it was just to save my own skin. I sighed, defeated. If baring my soul wasn't enough, then I had nothing else to offer.

"That may be true, but I want to change who I am before that happens. I just need you to tell me the truth. Please, trust me."

Caius remained silent, taking me in, until finally he said, "Goliath killed Barbas Akando."

I had been looking down at the floor, ashamed of my confession and the reassurance that failed to come from him. My eyes shot up as soon as Caius continued.

"Goliath's been trying to get control of the Faenymese, Amniari and Boltesian lands for some time, but they're resisting. Aulandri are slightly less important because of their small *laecan* population, but Boltese stands between us and them anyway. Unless Goliath can get the Boltesians on side, he can't do much."

My mind whirled. Sire was Boltesian. His family owned the land, rich through their cultivation of the diamond mines that populated the area. His family were also kin to the royals in some way. I hadn't bothered to find out how. Goliath's hate for Sire wasn't only because of his *maejym* parents and Tala being with him, but because his countrymen were resisting his conquest.

"He can't go through Voltaire either," Caius was saying, "considering it's the royal province, but now that he has Faenym and Amniare, he controls the entire Eastern half of Agmantia's *laecan* territories."

"He's trying to take over Agmantia." I could hardly believe it, terrified to even speak the words. This was the truth I'd been pining for. "He's creating an army to overthrow the monarchy."

Caius gave a short nod.

I stared as it dawned on me that this was so much bigger than me. Everything was just so much…*bigger*…than me.

"Tala and Sire are going against Goliath… with *you*."

"I can't—and won't—tell you anymore. It's not safe."

"Is it safe for Tala?"

"Tala has given up everything to be with the man she loves. Safety is an afterthought at this point."

He chuckled at the simple statement and I felt childish for even questioning Tala's involvement,

"I could help," I said quietly. "If you just tell me how, I'll help you." Finally, I'd be on the inside, to have a purpose that was real and not indoctrinated.

Caius looked at me questioningly, "Would you be willing to spy on Sabre?"

"Wait, what?"

"You know, espionage? Infiltrate, eavesdrop, gather information. Any of those things mean anything to you?"

"Hey, you just threw this at me out of the blue, okay? Stop being mean," I snapped.

The laughter was gone from his face and he cleared his throat, the change in attitude making me chuckle, feeling myself relax.

"Now who's mocking?" he asked, eyebrow cocked.

A smile twitched at the corner of his mouth and the anger began to simmer out between us as we stopped hating one another for two seconds and just... looked. Caius cleared his throat again and I realised he was uncomfortable.

We both looked away from each other.

"I think Rhea and Susi are involved with something." His head shot back as I continued, "They admitted they seduced Olcan for information and I know that Olcan's with Sabre and Goliath somewhere right now."

"What are you saying, Grey?" he asked after a moment of tense silence.

"I'm saying I'll spy on Sabre when I can. I want to help, but I don't want to get anyone in trouble. Lydia was enough."

Caius chuckled again and I stood watching him, the breeze of the night air cooling, the scents of the woods surrounding us.

"Fine," he conceded and my heart leapt at his words. "This isn't a game, so I expect you to do what I say regarding this and back off if I tell you to." I nodded enthusiastically. "Goliath has everyone fooled into thinking he's a saint, but everything he does is for personal gain. We can't allow him to amass any more power or influence. The *Iaecan* who oppose him won't stay quiet forever and you need to be ready."

I nodded, then looked past his head and as I sharpened my eyes so I could see better in the dark, I realised we were at his mysterious cave.

"What is that place?" I made to step toward the opening to the cave, but he stepped in front of me, "Still not allowed to see your little den, am I?"

"No. You're not." He was serious.

He looked down at me and I peered up at him, suddenly very aware of the way his eyes seemed to glow. He licked his lips, and dear God above, butterflies erupted in my stomach. It differed from anything I'd ever felt with Sabre, but I didn't immediately understand if that was good or bad.

"You really want me to trust you?"

"Yes."

I didn't hesitate, desperate to redeem myself in his eyes. Caius reached up and pushed one of my braids away from my face and put it over my shoulder. It was so unexpected that I stiffened just before a shiver erupted across my skin. His finger grazed my face and it sent fire searing all over me. I swallowed, my mouth suddenly dry with anticipation.

"It's going to be very lonely for you without Tala around, so if you ever need some place to think or just be alone, you can come here," he murmured, "but you can't go inside."

"What if I come here because I don't want to be alone?" The words left my lips before I could stop them. I knew what it sounded like. "I need a friend, Caius," I tried to cover the implication.

"If you want us to be friends, then don't go inside. Agreed?"

"Yes," I replied, my heart pounding as he took a step away from me. I immediately missed his warmth and unconsciously swayed into him.

"Good," he said. "Bring me some dirt on Sabre, don't go into the cave—then we can talk."

I nodded, unable to find the words, as simple as they were. He turned to leave, trusting me not to run into that cave as soon as he left, but I called out after him,

"Caius!"

He turned, expectantly and without realising I was going to do it, I blinked at him.

One slow blink and nothing more.

He was silent for a very long time until he softly said, "You're welcome, Grey."

I lay in the middle of the jungle, screaming until it felt like my lungs would catch fire.

The raw heat from the ferocity of my screams tore through me as I turned for the very first time.

My heart pounded in my chest as it pumped blood to my body, my entire system suddenly working overtime, but my laecan *blood prepared me for this, knew what I needed to do, to finally take my place within my family.*

I was thirteen and had only recently had my monthly bleed. My mother had been ecstatic; my father had been worried and my sister wanted to know what all the fuss was about.

I told Caius. I told him first as I did everything else. Mother said I was a woman now but she hadn't said that this would follow the bleeding.

That my skin would shred and my bones would break and my teeth would fall from my mouth, replacing them with the new, more powerful set I would need for the rest of my life.

No one spoke of the turn and now I knew why.

No one told you how excruciating the pain was, perhaps because they had no way to truly describe it. How does one retell the moment of torture, when your spine breaks to accommodate its new form. How do you explain how claws as sharp as blades, rip through your fingertips and your eyes go blind as they adjust to their new, superior level of vision?

There were no words to define the agonizing torture that took place while you lay in the jungle alone.

The first and only time you went through this physical change, it had to be alone—a rite of passage toward being a true laecan.

I'd been brought here during the full moon, when my turn started. The moon did not dictate when we turned, but heightened our abilities. Our magic was born within us, not gifted, like the power that now ran through the veins of the Antonides bloodline of Mortania. We revered the moon, but worshipped one God.

It started as stomach cramps. Soon, they escalated into daggers that stabbed me relentlessly for what felt like hours. I didn't know how much time had passed, but the full moon was high in the sky, watching me.

It built character, my father said, to make the turn alone. To go through this pain and come out the other side unscathed was what made us true laecan. The solitary change gave us our strength.

I didn't want it.

I didn't want strength or purpose or any of the lessons my father had taught me.

I just wanted this to end.

Tears streamed down my cheeks as my lower half finished changing. My hind legs were massive, the paws at the end of them large and grey. Even in the midst of my pain, I acknowledged how beautiful my new coat was.

I lay on my front, fingers clenching fistfuls of dirt. From the waist down, I was wolf, but I still had the rest to go. My mouth was bleeding from the teeth pushing through, my jaw broken in preparation for my head to elongate and stretch.

I cried.

Dear God, I cried until I thought I'd used all my tears and then I cried some more.

Please, help me.

I couldn't say the words, and even if I could have, no one would have come. All I knew was that I didn't want to be by myself. I didn't want to be here, in the dirt, on the ground... alone.

"It will be over soon, Grey."

Even at thirteen, his voice was deep, husky. He sounded wiser than his years. He'd turned days after our birthday, the first of the three of us.

I was the second.

I hiccupped and slowly moved my aching head, my right cheek now on the cooling ground.

"It will be over soon," he said again. "I'm here with you, Grey... I'm here with you."

I tried to smile, but I couldn't. I tried to show him how thankful I was that he was here with me.

I blinked instead.

One slow blink to thank him for being my best friend, and for never leaving me alone.

CHAPTER SIXTEEN

A few days later I lay on my bed, staring at the ceiling. I'd just had a shower and rubbed myself down with coconut oil and because of the afternoon heat, making me feel too lazy to reach for my underwear, I just lay naked, lost in my thoughts.

I'd agreed to spy on Sabre.

I'd never done anything remotely like it. A week ago, such a betrayal would have been unthinkable and in the cold light of day, I had to wonder what I'd gotten myself into. I'd meant what I said to Caius: I wanted to help. I couldn't stand the person I now saw in the mirror, but what would my being involved turn me into?

I wasn't a spy or a rebel, I was just me; Aspen the Female. No matter what I wanted, that would always be the bottom line. That I had a duty to myself and my kind to see this thing through; it shouldn't matter what I'd learned. The community, the shaman, my mother; none of them cared what I wanted for myself because I had a responsibility to my family. Helping Caius would serve to clear my conscience about Lydia, about the part I'd played in treating Caius terribly, but it wouldn't change who I was and had to continue to be.

I adjusted myself on my bed, restless even though my mind was going a mile a minute. I understood now that Sabre saw me as a prize, a reward for all he would do with his power as Alpha. He didn't love me, not really, and he probably never had. I could barely stand to think how my love for him had been just as superficial, but now that I saw the lie I'd been telling myself for years, I couldn't *un* see it.

I had given myself to him in so many ways, physically and mentally; handing myself over to him without ever questioning it, but as I lay on my bed, thinking, I knew I had never really shared my heart with him.

Until recently I hadn't had a heart to share.

Everything was always about him and his needs and I'd let it happen. I'd convinced myself that he was what I wanted, that he cared for me. Now I remembered how someone else had shown me real affection, many years before.

Caius had stayed with me during my first *turn*, even when he shouldn't have. He'd made sure I wasn't alone through that pain and after that I'd never spoken to him again.

My mother hadn't allowed it.

My mother had purposefully stopped it.

She'd told me I was a woman, the flowering Female, and I had no business playing with Gamma scum, because I was destined for bigger and better things.

The intensity of old conversations came flooding back and with them came the clarity of how I'd repressed memories of my best friend, of sleepovers and races through the woods, because my mother told me I should.

I remembered Ianthe slapping me so hard across the face when I'd snuck out a few days after my first *turn* to try meet with Caius and Sabre. We'd all been so close back then and I didn't understand why we couldn't play together anymore; why only Caius was considered somehow unclean.

"I can smell it," my mother had screamed at me as I held my hand to my stinging face. "I can *smell* your intent all over you!"

I shut my eyes, trying to squeeze out the bad memory and replace it with a new one.

Fiery amber eyes peered out of the darkness and my breath caught, my fingers twitching where they lay on my stomach. The eyes watched me watching them, the intent carnal and brutal. Slowly my hand slid down. I lightly grazed the plump smooth mound between my legs, licking my lips as a black wolf stepped out of the shadows of my mind and dissolved into a man.

Into Caius.

"No!"

I snatched my hand away from myself and quickly sat up on my bed, my heart racing.

Despite my current feelings towards Sabre, he remained the Riadnak heir, he would win the Mating Games and I would birth his heir. Sabre was strong, and he would be good to me. All I knew was that I could not break with tradition—not for anything. Or *anyone*.

My growing feelings towards Caius didn't matter.

The way his touch had felt, like it stopped time against my skin, didn't matter.

The way my heart raced when he smiled that rare smile, did *not* matter.

I wouldn't let it.

Quickly, I dressed. Just because I couldn't let myself think about my hand reaching for Caius' shoulder, feeling hard muscle beneath thin fabric, didn't mean I couldn't do what I'd promised him I would. I was going to spy on Sabre and if I learned something useful, it meant I'd have a legitimate reason to see Caius. An all-round win.

I bent forward, collecting my braids together and with a long stretch of material from my vanity table I tied my braids on top of my head so they fell down my back and framed my face. A few quick brushes with my make-up and I was out my bedroom feeling determined.

I was at the bottom of the stairs when I suddenly heard my parents in my father's study. My mother rarely went in there, so for want of anything better to do, I eavesdropped. Standing by the door, I caught the end of one of my mother's rants.

"...that doesn't mean it's enough, Bracken!"

"It will have to be enough," my father replied calmly. He had his I-can't-be-asked-to-deal-with-this-woman voice and I stifled my laughter behind one hand. What my mother said next, killed any amusement altogether.

"So he's forgiven us?"

"Lydia's back, isn't she?" my father replied. "Goliath saved face with the Council once I told him about Tala and we got to avoid any scandal with Aspen. Isn't that what you wanted?"

There was a moment of silence from my mother and I was glad of it. I didn't know how to process that it was my wonderful, understanding, supportive father who had told Goliath about Tala and Sire.

"We are so close," my mother finally said. "We can't have Aspen messing up anymore."

"Aspen will do what is required of her."

"She'd better," my mother said in that hard tone she reserved only for my father. And me. "Why couldn't Rogue have been the Female? At least she knows how the game is played. I blame you."

"How is that different to any other day, Ianthe?"

"You spoiled Aspen with her games and sleepovers and letting her befriend that Gamma boy."

"She was a child. With what is expected of her, we owed her a childhood."

"Well she's not a child anymore, even though she's almost twenty and acts like one! Look what's happening now. Months away from being the Mother of Alphas and she's making an enemy of Goliath. She should not be interfering in Alpha business or politics or anything of that nature. Goliath is not impressed that she doesn't seem to know her place."

"Aspen knows her place," my father replied with a heavy sigh. "We all have our parts to play. Although I would have thought that yours would be a little more influential."

My mother was silent for a beat too long.

"I won't stand for anymore disruptions, Bracken," my mother insisted. "Talk to your daughter and do it *now*."

Realising my mother was at the end of her speech, I sped away from the door and didn't slow until I was out of the house.

Thankfully, Sabre was home, but I'd caught him getting ready to head out. Olcan and Fenrir were lounging on the small couches in his bedroom, waiting patiently for him to finish dressing. I couldn't immediately tell from his outfit where he was going, so I asked.

"Nowhere you need to worry your little head about, babe," Sabre said with a wink.

I kept my heating face away from Olcan and Fenrir's sniggering. Sabre eyed me, detached, making annoyance flare in pure retaliation.

"I didn't ask if I should worry about it," I replied smartly, "I asked where you were going."

Once he'd pulled a shirt over his head, he marched over to me, "We're going with my father into Faenym. We have a meeting."

"A meeting about what?"

His eyebrow arched, "When did you become so interested in politics?"

"When did you get so secretive about it?"

There was a standoff as neither of us deigned to answer the other. It might not have been the best way to get information out of him, but it irked me that he had no inclination to tell me in the first place. I'd always imagined us as equal partners once we were married. I'd thought he'd respect me enough to consider my counsel and that I'd have influence over how Celestia was run, even if I knew I would be leaving the bigger issues to be sorted by him. Here he was already digging his heels, in against me asking a simple question.

Sabre blew heavily out of his nostrils, turning away to thread a gold ring on his little finger which reminded me briefly of his father.

"Alpha business does not concern you, Aspen," he confirmed my misgivings, making the statement in that bored tone I'd grown to dislike.

The phrase was almost a mirror of what I'd heard my mother say only minutes before, but I couldn't stop myself.

"But it concerns *them*?" I gestured toward Olcan and Fenrir who had risen from the couch, ready to leave. Fenrir watched me with obvious disdain, while Olcan eyed me with curiosity.

"Yes," Sabre snarled at me, a ring of gold igniting in his eyes. "Olcan and Fenrir are my warriors, it will *always* concern them"

At least she knows how the game is played.

No matter how my mother's words had hurt, maybe I could take a page from Rogue's manipulative book.

"What concerns me then? If not things that could get you killed?"

I watched his face soften at my supposed care for his wellbeing. His ego would always get the better of him. Perhaps another thing we had in common, but I disliked that thought too much to linger on it.

"Just worry about keeping your ass tight for me until the time comes for me to claim you."

The comment was such blatant disrespect that I had to keep myself from slapping him.

My eyes darted to Olcan, who looked away, embarrassed.

"I'm done talking about this," Sabre said. "You can see yourself out."

He brushed a chaste kiss on my cheek before leaving the room with the others on his heels. Fenrir was actively laughing at me while Olcan looked almost pitying. Shame tore through me. If this was how he could speak to me in front of our friends, I could only imagine how he spoke about me behind my back.

Where had this new Sabre come from? Since revealing his views on Tala and Sire's relationship, it was like I didn't know him.

When I was finally out of the manor and saw the boys nowhere in sight, I *turned* and headed into the woods.

I lay on my belly in wolf form outside the mouth of Caius' cave. Night crept its shadows between the trees, but the woods were already alive with the nocturnal creatures who inhabited it. These woods and forests surrounded Invernell on all sides, the city nestled within them, like the large seed in an avocado. The trees further south would blend into jungles with sweltering heats and the exotic birds to match. Agmantia had a tropical climate on any good day and so I was thankful for Invernell's close proximity to the mountains in Boltese, that allowed us some cooler days. Other predators rarely came near the town, since the scent of so many wolves deterred them.

Coupled with lupine speed, strength, sight, taste and smell, the world was open to me in ways it never would be as a human. I took a deep breath, taking in the wondrous scents around me before laying my head on the floor between my paws. Soon the days would grow shorter, the nights longer and the winter chill would set in. Until then, I was content to laze in the heat.

I knew I'd failed today. Sabre didn't respect me enough to tell me anything worthwhile so how was I meant to help Caius? I'd thought for hours how I was going to tell him that I couldn't do this, but I didn't want to admit defeat. He'd just started to trust me, to believe there could be more to me, and I didn't want to lose that feeling.

...is this going to become a habit?...

I loved that wolves couldn't smile so he wouldn't be able to tell how pleased I was to hear his voice.

...you told me you didn't mind, so most likely... I said, not lifting my head to look at him approaching. *...i spoke with sabre...*

Caius was silent for a moment, *...and?...*

I told him that Sabre and his friends were going to Faenym and that it was all I'd managed to find out.

...you were right. i'm not cut out for this... I said quietly. *...i'm not built like you...*

...you don't have to be built like me but you do have to keep trying. you can't give up when things are hard...

I still wasn't looking at him and I couldn't bring myself to. I knew he was just being nice. I didn't deserve it. For the second time a slight bump in the road had landed me in a pit of self-doubt.

My mother wasn't even on my side anymore, thinking my sister better than me. And sadly, I was starting to believe her.

...*why don't you go home, get some rest? try again another day*...

I took a deep breath and stretched my large body before exhaling, sending dust particles spiralling into the air.

...*home is getting a little suffocating these days*...

Caius appeared before me, his hide as black as the approaching night and joined me on the floor, laying his head in front of mine so our noses were inches apart, our claws barely touching.

...*do you want to talk about it?*...

Desperately.

...*my mother doesn't think i'm good enough and my father was the one who told goliath about tala and sire*...

He took a moment to respond, ...*how do you know?*...

...*i overheard my parents talking in his study*...

Caius was silent for a moment, ...*i know what that feels like*...*to be betrayed by your family*...*by your father*...

I was intrigued at that, ...*what did maximus ever do to you? i always thought you got on well*...

...*we do but*...*not everyone's perfect, as i'm sure you've discovered*...

I couldn't deny that. I had learned a lot of things lately, about my family and myself, and none of it was good. People were not always what they seemed and it never seemed to be for the better.

Except with Caius.

...*i never got to thank you*... I said, once again ignoring the uncomfortable path of the previous conversation.

...*thank me for what?*...

...*staying with me during my first* turn...

...*oh*...

...*my mother wouldn't let me see you anymore and i never thanked you*...*i never would have got through it without you*...

...that's not true...

...it is true because...because i'm not strong enough...i never have been...

I *turned* into myself and Caius followed. He stood before me dressed in a thick-necked white sweater, tan pants and black boots. Those eyes of his peered back at me with knowing, but not judgement.

"You were right," I said again, my voice was barely above a whisper as I fought back tears. "Tala was right...I couldn't have been trusted with your secrets." I shook my head at myself, at having to confess it, turning my back to him to cover the emotion all over, saying, "I'm Sabre's little pet, right? Who doesn't ask questions and believes in him even when he treats me like shit. I'm meant to smile and look pretty and do as I'm told?"

"I take it you don't want that anymore?"

When I spun around to face him, angry at my vulnerability, Caius was much closer to me than I had anticipated. I was so close, I had to brace my hands against his chest to stop my face from smashing into his. I peered up into his eyes as he looked down at me and I didn't immediately pull my hands away. He didn't push them away either.

"No," I said, breathless, as air struggled to reach my brain.

Coconut and sugar. Coconut and sugar.

I licked my lips, "No... I don't want that anymore."

I wanted him to ask me what I did want. I needed a reason to force me to answer what was steadily growing inside me. My hands were still on his chest and Caius still wasn't moving them. I felt his heart beating beneath my fingertips, I felt the heat of him through his sweater and the flush rapidly rising up my neck.

"You don't have to be with him, Grey. Not if you don't want to."

It was the complete opposite of what he'd said last time, so what had changed?

"What will I do otherwise? Mating with Sabre is my purpose…it's my duty."

"And if I won the challenges, would your duty be to me?"

My eyebrows knotted together, "Of course it would."

Unexpectedly, Caius ripped my arms away from his chest and my body went cold, "Then why does it matter how you feel, Grey? If mine and Sabre's actions decide who gets to breed you, why bother having a conscience about it at all?"

"I—I…"

Caius growled in frustration, "You're still going to do what's expected of you? You're still going to give yourself to him? To them?"

"I don't have a *choice*."

"We all have a choice, Aspen," he raised his voice in frustration. "I've made mine—I chose not to compete. You can do the same."

"Exactly," I turned vicious, hating that he was making me feel guilty for things I had no control over. "You made your choice and now *I'm* stuck with it."

"Come on, don't put it all on me."

"Why shouldn't I? Your choice makes it impossible for me to have one." He didn't have anything to say to that. "Did you even think to include me in your little mutiny?"

It was clear he hadn't.

"We used to be friends. I know the reason we aren't is my fault, but you never, not once, tried to fight for that friendship or explain to me what was really going on."

He sucked his teeth at me, "It's not my responsibility to fight for you, Grey. Why would I include you in a plan that involves us being together, when I don't even want you like that?"

I tried not to let his words burn me, I tried so fucking hard but the poison bled into my chest anyway. I swallowed the pain and embarrassment down, even as tears threatened to fall.

He didn't want me but I knew, with the force that his words threatened to suffocate me, that I desperately wanted him to.

"Y-you don't have to want me," I said quietly, trying and failing to keep my voice strong. "It's not about wanting each other. It's about the fact that if you wanted to fight Goliath, then maybe having me on your side would give you a chance to actually beat him."

He looked disbelieving, "How?"

"By *winning*," my chest was pounding. "If you won the Games, you would be Alpha and all this would stop."

He shook his head, "I can't do that."

"Why not?"

"The entire country sees the Riadnaks as their rightful leaders—prophecy be damned. Goliath has friends all over Agmantia, in every city. He has access to rooms of power I wouldn't be accepted in. If I won, it would mean all-out war, not just for Celestia—for everywhere."

"According to you, war is already coming, so what's the difference?"

I knew he didn't have an answer. For a moment, I thought he'd see reason but he shook his head.

"You wouldn't understand."

Defeated, I looked into his honey coloured eyes. "I just want to help. Is that so bad?"

"No," he replied gently. "It's not."

I turned away from him and angrily wiped at my tears. I didn't care that he didn't find me attractive.

I didn't care.

I didn't.

"Hey," I felt his hand on my shoulder and I jumped. He turned me to face him and when I looked down, trying to avoid looking at him with my reddening eyes, he tilted my head up to face him; his index finger under my chin.

"I didn't mean it like that… about not wanting you."

"I don't ca—"

"I didn't mean it."

He spoke over me, cancelling my attempt to save face.

"Think about this. If you were raised to think your shit doesn't stink because you're the Female and Sabre was raised to believe he was the most important thing to *laecan* kind, then what do you think I was told?"

The clarity of it, hit me like a brick.

"You know you're beautiful, Grey," he murmured looking down at me. "Just because I was told I would never have you, doesn't make me blind."

My heart warmed at his words.

He thought I was beautiful.

A brief moment of silence went by before Caius playfully tapped the tip of my nose with his finger,

"You're all right, Aspen Anai," he chuckled. "Now that we've got your head out of the clouds, I think we could be friends."

I smiled back at him, broadly, a weight of loneliness lifted off my shoulders, "I think so too."

CHAPTER SEVENTEEN

As it became increasingly clear that Caius was my only friend genuine in Invernell, I naturally gravitated to him. We talked, we laughed and joked together, and I felt more free with him in those moments then I had in a very long time.

We ran together in the mountains, hunting and exploring, and gradually his trust in me grew to the point where he felt comfortable sharing the details of what he knew about Goliath's plans.

As he'd mentioned before, Goliath wanted to take over Agmantia, and he needed to control the *laecan* communities of neighbouring provinces to secure the power to do so. He'd killed Barbas Akando to forcibly take leadership of the wolves following him, but they were resisting with the help of Barbas' son Isaac. Caius also shared that Ambassador Ryah of Amniare, the old man who liked to stare at me lecherously, had brokered an alliance between Celestia and Amniare. How their leader Porvi Belau felt about that, Caius was unsure. Caius' contact said they had not heard from Porvi Belau or her daughter—and rightful heir—in months. The silence didn't bode well for anyone's plans. Sire, living on his parent's estate in Boltese, was keeping up the Boltesian resistance, but until Goliath made an official play for them, they couldn't make any move that risked painting them as the aggressors.

As Caius and I ran along the base of the Ecacian Mountains on our way home from a hunt, my lungs were bursting with energy and the crisp winds that whipped around the mountainous region of our beautiful country. Chilling gusts brushed heavily through my fur as the air faded from pale dusk into the dark of night. My eyes adjusted to take in the wonder of the nature around me, and I listened as night awakened. Nocturnal birds and woodland creatures escaped from their burrows as we ravaged through their homes on the way to our own. My large paws barrelled against the earth, a feeling of exhilaration at the sense of freedom that filled me. I never wanted to risk the safety of my home. I wanted it to remain as it always had been, so that my children would be running these paths themselves, and their children after them.

I panted with wondrous exertion, snipping playfully at Caius who came up sharply beside me. His black coat faded into the night, his golden eyes the only thing visible as we tore through the trees at incredible speeds. I had the blood of a small kill on my nose and teeth and as we raced through the woods, I smelt water.

...follow me...

I called the words to him and veered to my right. Soon enough, we came upon the body of water and after a quick scan of our surroundings, I realised we were at Parthia Lake. A large expanse of water that toed the border between Celestia and Boltese. Once I could easily drink from it, I would be on Celestian soil.

I came to a stop at the water's edge and lowered my large head to take a much-needed drink. We mainly hunted as a form of training and exercise but I hated the smell of drying blood on my fur, metallic and intrusive. I washed it as best I could, while Caius did the same beside me. Once done, we stood there quietly in our wolf forms, lapping up the water, listening to the sounds of the surrounding night and content in one another's company.

...*you're really fast...* he said once he'd finished drinking.
...*i am?...*
...*you kept up with me well enough...*
...*and i guess you're the bar to meet, right?...*
...*of course...*

Caius' playful side was one I still didn't see often, but ever since he opened up to me about Goliath, it seemed it was coming up more frequently. I finished with the water and stalked over to take a seat in front of him, so close our noses were almost touching, as was the *laecan* way.

...*modesty is a virtue you know...* I teased.
...*so is honesty...*
...*well, then i honestly think you have a big head...*

I felt the laugh escape from him rather than heard it as he continued to stare at me. I never got over the feeling of looking into Caius' eyes. A feeling of internal warmth that spread all over my body in ways I'd never really experienced before. It wasn't arousal, more a feeling of utter safety and completion. I shifted my eyes away from him, embarrassed by my own thoughts, even if he couldn't hear them.

...*how are things at home?...*

I sighed, not wanting to get into that right now.

...*as tense as ever but I don't want to talk about that. what's going on with you?...*
...*you mean what's going on with the fighting?...*
...*that too...*

In an instant, he was standing in front of me as a man and so I followed his incentive. We sat down next to each other on the cold ground. He pulled his hands over his head in distress and I watched him, keeping quiet, wanting to show respect by being patient and letting him take his time. I'd learned this was something Caius appreciated a lot: patience.

"Goliath has been buying weapons," he finally said. "Swords, arrows. He's preparing for an attack, but we don't know where."

I marvelled at the reality of it all. While it would ultimately be a *laecan* war, fought as wolves, Goliath was taking no chances by including *maejym* weapons as well. He might not want his precious congregation to know that he was provoking war with his machinations, but it was clear he was preparing for one. Any news of an uprising in the country would have to be looked into, whether the Voltaires thought they were the target or not since they ruled the entire country. The Voltaire royals were *maejym* and so was their army, so if for any reason *laecan* were unable to fight in their wolf form, they would need weapons to fight against the Voltaires. As far as I knew, the royals knew nothing about us, we didn't technically exist to them so they had no cause to interfere.

I suddenly thought of Lydia's son, Jacob. *Maejym* were being recruited into the *laecan* forces as additional arms against the *maejym* warriors on the other side. The weapons were to equip them as well as our backup strength considering *maejym* outnumbered us considerably.

I could see Caius was angry and frustrated.

"We know he's trying to take out the main leaders first, but we don't know when or where he plans to strike next. He doesn't trust people and only tells his closest allies."

"Can't you get through to anyone? I mean, they don't know you're against Goliath so why wouldn't they share information with you."

"Sorry, Grey, but I don't think one hand of men twice my age and the other hand of men that don't like me are going to be very forthcoming."

I sat quietly, but he added for clarification, "Sabre, Fenrir, Olcan and their parents are the closest to Goliath, but there's no love lost between us. His other allies...well, if my father can't get them to speak to him, there's no way I can get anything out of them."

I nodded, understanding his predicament.

"Kade Lacoste has made his upset with Goliath's choices known, but he has to play his cards close to his chest. He went against Goliath once before about some shipping profit and it didn't end well."

Rhea's father was almost as terrifying as Goliath. He'd always been nice to me, but there was something so powerful and intimidating about him that you always knew to be on your best behaviour.

"Goliath needs to be weakened somehow," Caius mused. "But he has almost everyone in his pocket."

Even before realising his sinister nature, I knew Goliath's control over everyone. Whether you were aware of it or not, you wanted to please him, make him happy, and if that meant doing exactly what he told you to do, when he told you to do it, then so be it. Invernell had been a province of peace since he came into power, but now I had to wonder if that was thanks to his political prowess, or because he killed anyone who dared oppose him.

"Except you," I said finally, looking up at Caius. My hands lay in my lap, my fingers twirling idly as my face heated with nerves.

"You're not in his pocket and that's why you're going to get through whatever this is."

Caius' honey gold eyes lit up as he chuckled, "Whatever this is?"

I shrugged, "I can't pretend to fully understand why you're doing this. Your reasons are your own, but I can respect them...like I respect you."

Caius eyed me for a long time before he stood up and held out his hand, not to help me up, but for me to take. It felt like a silent question. I got to my feet and looked down at his outstretched hand. Before I started lingering too hard on why I was so afraid to touch him, I reached out and put my hand into his. His palm was warm, so were his fingers. They were strong and slightly calloused but slowly, our fingers interlaced as he took a long look at me and said, "Care to take a walk?"

I smiled. A large toothy smile that hurt my face, "I'd love to."

Caius squeezed my hand and we strolled into the night.

We walked like that, hand in hand, for a long while in companionable silence when Caius' voice drifted through the darkness,

"Tala says hi."

I stopped and turned to him, eyes wide and threatening to fill with tears, "What?"

Caius continued to hold my hand, but turned to look down at me, "She said to tell you that she's fine and that she misses you. She says to be brave and to believe in yourself."

"When?" I asked. "When did she say this?"

"Yesterday. She came with Sire when I met with him. I didn't know she'd be with him or…"

My heart warmed even though he didn't finish the words. He knew how much it would mean to me to have seen her and he would have let that happen for me. I couldn't stop the tears that fell but for the first time in too long, they were happy tears.

"Thank you," I said, voice almost cracking from the emotion. I missed my best friend so much.

Caius finally let go of my hand, reaching up to wipe my tears away with the pad of his thumb. I closed my eyes, leaning into his touch, the strength of his large but soft fingers as they grazed the skin of my cheek.

"You're welcome, Grey."

I felt him take a step closer to me but I didn't open my eyes. I could feel his warm breath on my forehead, the heat of his body on my chest.

Not ready to look into what was unfolding between us, I retreated out of his reach. I opened my eyes and hardened my face against him, shutting off any possibility of questions I didn't want to answer. Caius saw the change in me and his expression shuttered.

"We should get back," I mumbled, looking away from him again, my resolve leaving me. I regretted my rejection of his closeness and so I *turned* and took off into the trees, hoping to outrun the confusion and uncertainty, that Caius had been about to kiss me and I'd desperately wanted him to.

CHAPTER EIGHTEEN

The weeks leading up to the second challenge were the best I'd had in a long time because I spent them with Caius. With a better understanding of what he was dealing with outside of Invernell, I felt so much closer to him. I felt him in my heart, on my skin and through my veins. I spent so much time with him now, I had to constantly dodge endless questions from my friends and Sabre about how I spent my time.

I found myself bounding through the woods every day that I wasn't in lessons to claim my spot outside Caius' cave that I was still forbidden to enter. We hadn't seen Ulren in weeks and it had been easier to ditch the lessons since he hadn't been teaching them. Since it gave me my much-wanted freedom, I saw no reason to question it.

More than once, I'd asked Caius to go inside, and as he continued to deny me, the more annoyed I became. I'd rarely been denied anything, so this was more than a little frustrating.

Our escapades grew more dangerous with every passing day and I had to excuse why I was constantly bathing—there was only so much repressing of scents one could do in the day so before anyone caught whiff of Caius on me, I had to get rid of him. It was exhausting, but unless I wanted my mother or Sabre to catch on to who I was spending my time with, it had to be done.

It was the beginning of another week and the second challenge would be at the end of it. While the endless events of *Lunaveya* continued throughout the months, the intensity had died down. A party here, an outdoor dance there, was all it took to keep the momentum going, until the major events put on at the Riadnak Manor. During them all, Caius and I kept our distance from each other, but there was a solidarity in his gaze whenever he looked at me. Our meetings were a secret between us and I felt special that I shared something with him, no matter how risky it could be.

I continued my attempts to spy on Sabre, but that tree hadn't born much fruit.

I was in town before my afternoon classes, looking for something to wear to the agility challenge. Since the sharp words with my mother about not being included, I'd asked if I could collect the clothes myself and, as a peace offering, she'd agreed. I left the local seamstress' shop, the bell on the door jingling behind me as I walked out. All I needed now were shoes, and so made my way to Mr. Wren, the best cobbler in Invernell.

I strolled casually through town, smiling politely at those who smiled at me. Knowing that every move I made had a habit of getting back to my parents, was weird in itself. Now, knowing I actually had something to hide, it was terrifying.

I soon arrived at Mr Wren's store and as I approached the door to head inside, Asher Caldoun stepped out. Asher looked a lot like Caius in many ways, but a little more boyish, being two years younger. He smiled at me once he realised who was in his way, and for the first time, I smiled back, uninhibited. I wasn't sure if Asher knew what his brother got up to, so I wouldn't say anything, but he was no longer the enemy. He never was, and I needed to make amends for having treated him as such.

"Hey, Aspen, how are you doing?"

"Great. Just here to pick up some new shoes."

He nodded but didn't move to leave.

"How about you?" I asked.

"Just getting some boots re-heeled for the challenge. Mum said I had to."

"Mothers, right?" We both laughed softly.

"Well... bye," he said gently, turning to leave.

"Umm, Asher, wait here for a minute?"

"Sure..."

I rushed into the shop and over to the counter where Mr. Wren lifted his head from his work and smiled at me. Mr Wren was a sweet Coznian *maejym* I'd known all my life. He'd made countless shoes for me over the years. My father often joked that I'd bankrupt him from being in this store alone.

"Good morning, Aspen. How are you today?"

"I'm great, Mr. Wren. Do you have a pencil, paper by any chance?" I asked and he rummaged through some of his things to hand it to me. Quickly, I scribbled on the paper and rushed outside to hand it to Asher.

"Could you umm... give this to your brother for me?"

"Uh... sure."

I could see he wanted to ask me what it said, but when I didn't offer an explanation, he simply nodded.

"Thank you," I murmured, turning and heading back into the shop with a smile and chit chat for Mr. Wren.

After lessons, I went home to change before heading out to meet Caius. I'd asked him to meet me at his cave in my note for no other reason than wanting to see him. The times we'd spent together these past few weeks had only occurred because I went to the cave under some pretence of needing time alone and he turned up to the cave while I was there.

My note was a legitimate request to see him on purpose, and despite trying to tell myself that I hadn't, I took care getting myself ready. I wore a dark blue summer dress with thin straps over my shoulders. The skirt swished around my thighs as I walked but hugged my small waist and chest and made me feel sexy. I'd not worn a bra and as I stepped into the cooling night, my nipples hardened, poking through the light material. My chest tightened at the prospect of Caius noticing and I smiled to myself as I walked down to the front gate. Dusk bloomed around me as I revelled in my new-found freedom when in Caius' company. It was a freedom of the mind, of my spirit. Of not feeling like a pawn in everyone else's game.

I'd redone my braids and spent almost an hour in the bathroom so I was smelling fresh and sweet. Maybe it was the smell of my own bath soaps that disguised Sabre's smell because I was startled when he approached me in front of my house.

The white wolf stood at the gate of my house, honey coloured eyes staring out at me. I stopped in front of him. The fact I wasn't *turning* told him I didn't want to talk to him. I waited, staring up at the large beast until he *turned* and stood on lean legs in front of me.

"Where are you going?"

"Out," I started to walk past him but he blocked my path. He had on a white shirt and pants with a white leather vest over the top. Out of nowhere, I was mad at his outfit.

What idiot wore so much white in the woods?

"Aspen, don't irritate me. Where are, you going?"

"I told you, I'm going out."

"Where?"

"It *doesn't* concern you."

"When you're my girlfriend, it does concern me."

"Well, maybe I don't want to *be* your girlfriend anymore!"

Two surprises occurred at that moment. The first was that the words had left my mouth in the first place.

The second?

I didn't regret them.

It was drastic, sure, but I had never felt so sure of anything in that moment. I didn't want the rigidity that being with him would give me. Now I knew how he really felt about people and how he felt about me, and I didn't want any part of it. I didn't want this for myself anymore.

"Aspen. I'm going to give you a second to think about what you're saying."

He peered down at me, so confident in his position in my life. His face wore a soft expression that told me he was waiting for me to come to my senses and take it back. How had I ever thought that look was caring when really it was pacifying?

I wanted to smack him.

Then, I wanted to smack myself.

I took a deep breath to compile myself and thought of a better tactic. If I wanted to get information out of him, I couldn't alienate him.

"I don't like the way you treat or speak to me."

"Excuse me?"

"At your house, in front of Olcan and Fenrir. You embarrassed me, Sabre. My father doesn't talk to my mother that way and I shouldn't expect to be spoken to like that either."

He watched me, seemingly unsure of how he should respond so I continued, attempting to push the right buttons.

"If I'm going to be your girlfriend and your wife, then things have to change," I lowered my lashes and wrung my hands together. "I need you to respect me. And trust me."

He looked thoughtful, then with a resolute sigh, he smiled. He took me into his arms and kissed me on the forehead, "I do respect you and I do trust you."

I made my face look elated, "Really?"

He nodded, "You've seen that Ulren hasn't been teaching lessons lately?"

"Yeah…"

"My father's been using him to get rid of a rebellion attack in Andrix."

Andrix was the capital of Faenym, the seat of Barbas Akando.

"Used him?" I didn't understand and when Sabre laughed, I knew I wouldn't like what that word meant.

"Ulren is an Addict. My father used him to get rid of the attack so he wouldn't have to sacrifice any extra *laecan*. One hundred Faenymese wolves taken out so those mutts couldn't get onto our land."

My eyes widened. Addicts were *laecan* who were susceptible to going wild, never returning from their wolf form and becoming feral killers. There were ways to bring them around again but it was extremely hard to do and required a shaman. When they did, they were so weakened, they lay on the brink of death for days even weeks at a time. Knowing you could be an Addict, a laecan would rarely turn. It opened them to the need to hunt and an Addict chose to hunt and kill for sport.

Thinking about it now, I should have realised Ulren was one, considering we never saw him *turn* and when we had events where being in wolf form was required, Ulren was never present.

"Is that enough for you?"

It would have to be enough. Goliath was using an Addict to eradicate enemy *laecan*. I'd have to tell Caius. I nodded.

"Good," he lowered his head and kissed me this time on the mouth. I closed my eyes endured. Sabre lifted his head a little bit so our lips were barely touching,

"Can we go inside now?"

I made myself smile. I made myself try to accept this.

"But my mu—"

"Is at the manor with my mother and the other *Lunaveya* council members."

"My da—"

"Is out hunting with my dad," he jerked his head back. "What's wrong, don't you want me to come in?"

"Of course I do," I rushed out. "I just don't want to get in trouble again."

He smiled, instantly reassured, "You won't. I'll protect you."

I didn't mention that I didn't know how he could protect anyone from anything when his sister was exiled and his girlfriend was spying on him for a rebel group who planned his demise. He couldn't protect his own interests, let alone me.

Sabre turned to lead me back into my house and all I could think about was not being able to tell Caius that I wouldn't be able to make it. I had to hope that what I'd learned would be enough for him to forgive me.

CHAPTER NINETEEN

During the rest of the week, I tried to find Caius to explain why I didn't show, but I wasn't able to. In the last three days leading up to the agility challenge, classes had been cancelled and so I had no legitimate reason to see him. I'd gone to the cave, but he'd not been there. I went to his home, but he was out. When I finally saw Asher in town, I learned Caius had left with their father, but would be back for the next challenge. I couldn't risk writing down what I knew, unsure if Asher was in the know or not.

Now, the morning of the challenge, I still hadn't laid eyes on Caius. The news about the Addicts would have to wait.

I was washed, primped, pruned and dressed in a fitting one piece. Once again, it was strapless and grey, but had pants rather than a skirt. It also had pockets! I didn't have anything specific to put in them, but a girl does love pockets. On my feet were steel grey high heeled filigree shoes, on my wrist a mixture of grey and silver bangles gleamed; I'd let my braids hang free, but woven grey feathers, beads and ribbon into them. To top the look off my make-up was flawless. My outfit was titillating, the perfect combination to accentuate my body: the main prize.

As I looked in the mirror, I felt like a garnished pig.

"Aspen!"

I jumped at the sound of my mother's voice and headed out of my bedroom to find her. She stood at the foot of the stairs in a glorious outfit of her own, looking up at me with a rare smile. Her beautiful brown skin practically glowed with pride.

"You look perfect."

"Thank you," I didn't know what else to say. My stomach was in knots and I needed to speak to Caius. He probably didn't care that I hadn't shown, focused more on the conflict than me, but I needed to explain. I needed to let him know that I could be trusted and hadn't meant to let him down. Our newly acquired friendship was too fresh, his trust of me too fragile for me to go back on my word.

"The carriage is here for you."

I would be heading to the challenge alone in a special carriage while my mother organised other affairs for the day. I made to step around her and head out the front door, but she stopped me with a firm grip on my arm.

"I need you on your best behaviour today."

Why couldn't Rogue have been the Female?

My mother's words stung, but I smiled demurely with a polite nod, "Of course, Mother."

Ianthe looked at me for a moment, trying to gauge if I was mocking her, but when she saw whatever confirmation she needed, she smiled and pulled me into a hug. I was shocked, not expecting her to touch me so lovingly, but I found myself relaxing into the embrace. She smelled like pineapples on a fresh summer day. No matter what she did, she was my mother and I loved her.

"I knew you'd come around," she whispered softly into my ear. "I knew you wouldn't disappoint me."

I didn't bother responding. I smiled and nodded. She let go and I headed out to the carriage to make my way to the Arena.

My carriage rode steadily through the woods lining our manor, through Invernell until the driver turned the horses north. If we continued on, out of the town and further for another few hundred miles we'd reach the Aulandri Channel—the strip of water that separated us from the enigmatic continent of Yitesh. I had played in these trees as a child with Tala. Thinking of her brought the pain of missing her to the forefront, but I wished the feelings away.

The Arena was a colossal structure built hundreds of years ago. It was where we held many of our province-wide sporting and large scale social events.

After an hours-long ride, the carriage pulled up to the front of the Arena, I lifted the sheer curtain hanging in front of the carriage window and caught sight of the spectators approaching.

I spied my usual band of friends: Fern, Fenrir, Olcan, Rhea and Susi. Koda was also there, walking with a girl I knew by face but not by name. There were countless other dignitaries and ambassadors that I recognised and a fair amount that I didn't, along with regular attendees. They were filing through different entrances, all depending on their social position and for the non-aristocracy, on the admission price.

The looming entrance that my carriage went through had no resistance and soon, I was out from under the beating Agmantian sun and in a cool stone covered entrance yard. The carriage rocked as the driver brought the horses to a stop. Moments later, the footman had opened the door, extended the foot bar and, placing my hand in his, I stepped out.

I had been to the Arena before, but had never given much thought or attention to my surroundings. My sister and I would usually follow our parents to our box, where food and beverages would be ready for us until the games began. We would fuss and fight, my mother would complain about it, my father would ignore her until he lost himself in betting on the participants.

He would give me a gold coin to bet on my favourites and whether I won or not, my father would give me two gold coins in return.

Simpler times.

"Welcome, Miss Anai, to the Arena!"

An older gentleman appeared out of the cooling shadows of the entrance and bowed to me.

"I am Arlo, Head Steward here. If you would please follow me." I inclined my head then and followed Arlo without question. I looked up and around at the ornately carved marble ceiling of the entrance arch as I walked. It had carvings of wolves and trees and various moon phases, some more weathered than others depending on their age. The Arena had fallen into disrepair over the years and so there were some newer additions to the architecture in various places.

Massive unlit braziers lined the marble columns that held the ceiling up. In the walls between the columns, on my right were carved openings where I could only just see the heads of people entering. On the left was what I remembered used to be an open area that went around the perimeter of the main arena. The wall to the left was a little lower so you could see the feet of lower tier spectators. Now, it was covered by…

"Excuse me?"

"Yes, Miss?" Arlo turned to me. He wore a traditional large flowing robe that covered his hands and sandaled feet. It was plain but a deep, sea green with embroidered sleeves, hem and collar.

"Are those hedges?"

Arlo smiled, excitedly.

"Why yes, we've been growing them for a while. We had some help from Lady Xana of course, for it to be ready for today."

"What had to be ready for today?" he looked at me quizzically, but when Arlo realised I had no idea what he was talking about, he added,

"The maze, of course."

I smiled my thanks, but didn't reveal any further ignorance as we finally came to the door I knew would lead to the highest boxes. Through the door was a pulley system that would take us to the top. When I'd once asked my father how the box got us all the way up there, he'd said it was magic. I'd giggled in wonder until my mother simply cleared her throat and pointed to the outside of the shaft we'd rode in. I'd looked down and seen the faces of *maejym* workers, rotating a large crank that turned thick rope in a loop. As they turned we ascended, and for a moment I wished the reality wasn't quite so harsh.

We reached the highest tier a few moments later, passing the lower tier seats on level one and the middle and upper tier seats on levels two and three. As I stepped out of the pulley box, I took a deep breath of the refreshing jungle air. The platform went all the way around the highest level of the arena where individual boxes were closed off with thick drapes and as I stepped through the curtain of the Beta family box, I finally understood the nature of the challenge.

The Arena floor was square shaped, even though the Arena was oval. An oval of marble and limestone with four tiered rows of flat bench seats and held almost ten thousand people. While a handful of those actually lived in Invernell, others had travelled for the challenge and while the seats were relatively empty now, they would be filled to bursting in a few hours.

I peered over the edge of the box where, what used to be a sand filled space where horses could run and people battled and competed, there was the maze.

Well, a quick look over the layout, told me there was one direct path to the exit at the other end, so not quite a maze but something akin to it. On my left, the entrance path went straight ahead then banked right, while the path on the other side of the hedge went left. The paths were exactly the same, but mirrored, and it dawned on me why it had been arranged this way.

"Refreshments, Miss Anai?"

I was startled by an attendant's voice who was standing beside Arlo. I shook my head in decline and gestured to the maze instead,

"You built this with Lady Xana?"

Arlo was excited again. It seemed the prospect of getting to explain this was a delight for him. Since I was ignorant to the event, I let him.

"Oh yes. The Council designed it but I, as Head Steward of the Arena, made sure all the intricacies could be accommodated. Lady Xana will be the one orchestrating them."

"What kind of intricacies?"

Arlo smiled conspiratorially, "That would spoil all the fun, wouldn't it?"

I smiled politely, although it was clear I wasn't pleased. He quickly reasserted himself,

"Apologies Miss, I was told not to divulge the details of the maze, t-to anyone."

The stutter made me give him a reassuring smile, "That's fine, Arlo. Thank you."

He bowed graciously, happy that he had not offended me.

"Do you know if the competitors have arrived yet?"

"Why, yes. Lord Sabre and Master Caius are in the competitor's rooms in the lower levels."

I turned back to the maze and realised it had been built deeper into the ground than the usual arena floor. They had to accommodate the growth of the hedges so the lower levels could see in but also whatever intricacies Arlo had mentioned. The greenery between the mirrored paths were huge and I was unsure what to make of them, but knew a lot of magic had gone into this construction.

"I wish to see them."

"See, miss?"

"The competitors. I wish to see them before we begin."

I could see he didn't want to go against protocol, but propriety compelled him. More likely he didn't want to go against my mother, but he didn't want to risk offending me again.

"When I return, I wish for some iced pineapple juice and banana fritters. Warm, not cold."

"Y-yes, Miss Anai. Right this way." Arlo clicked at the attendant who scurried off to do my bidding. I didn't need the refreshment but let them think me bossy so they wouldn't question me.

I followed Arlo out of the curtained box and back into the pulley. We made our way down, past the lower levels until we emerged into the basement, where sconces held torches along the walls, dimly lighting the hallway.

I knew from my history lessons, that the depths of the arena were where they once held wild beasts or enslaved fighters when the events held here were a little more, shall we say, barbaric. Since then, the large chambers had been renovated to little more than gilded cells for the competitors to reside in. Arlo led me now toward a room with a large door and told me, Sabre was inside. Caius was in the same room further down the hall but it was obvious

Arlo expected me to see the almighty Alpha heir first. I couldn't risk any misdemeanour getting back to my mother. Better to get this over quickly since it was only Caius I wanted to see.

"Come back for me in twenty minutes, Arlo. I will need to be prepped and back upstairs before my mother arrives. Is that understood?"

I know I shouldn't be down here. You know I shouldn't be down here. If you don't come and get me in good time, we'll both be in trouble, so do what I say with no questions asked.

He seemed to get the message as he bowed quickly and exited the hall. I knocked and stepped into Sabre's room. I found him pacing the floor as I entered, his eyes wide with what looked like fear. When he realised it was me, his shoulders relaxed and an uneasy smile graced his lips. Sabre came towards me, pulling me into his arms, before kissing me firmly on the mouth. I pushed at him and laughed my rebuff off,

"If you mess up my make-up, my mother will kill me."

"Oh, sorry," he chuckled, and I knew I was free from any suspicion. I hadn't been able to get away from his affections the other night. Days later, I still had his bite marks on my inner thighs, a constant reminder of what I'd allowed him to do, even while I couldn't stand the sight of him. If not for the additional knowledge he'd let slip after a few drinks about a march on Boltese, it wouldn't have been worth it. I just needed to be able to tell Caius.

"What are you doing here?"

"I have to prep for the speech I give before you begin. They said you'd arrived so I asked if I could see you. I only have five minutes."

He nodded, "They haven't told me anything, I've been here almost two hours."

I looked around the candle lit room at the small bed, desk and chair. There were hooks to hang armour and weapons and a small basin for water if one needed a quick wipe down.

"It will be over soon," I said gently, though distracted. "Just another step closer to being together right?"

He nodded again as he lowered his head so our foreheads were together. He took a deep breath, his shoulders slumping,

"When the door opened, I thought you were my father. I don't want to see him."

That made me pause. Sabre had been horrible to me recently but there was something going on with him lately that turned him into *this*.

"Why not?"

I snuck a quick look at the primitive sundial on the wall, while Sabre closed his eyes. They'd positioned it so it could always catch the light from the window that looked out onto the arena floor.

"He makes me…"

I lifted my head so he had to look me in the eye but he shook his head, declining to answer, "You better go. I don't want him to find you down here if he does visit."

I was happy I could leave, but his comment didn't sit well with me.

He kissed me again, more passionately this time and I let him. I quietly wished, for both our sakes, that the his kisses could fill me with as much happiness as they once did. Now all I felt was empty.

I stepped back, wiping the smear of my lipstick from his lips, "I have to go."

He kissed my forehead before I left and hurried down the hall.

Out of breath, but not wanting to look like it, I knocked on Caius' door and waited for him to respond. When he didn't, I knocked again. When he finally answered, my eyes popped out of my head and I almost swallowed my tongue.

He was topless.

He was gorgeously, deliciously, irritatingly topless and I couldn't stop staring at his defined abs and sturdy chest. I was no stranger to a good body considering my adventures with Sabre, but this was something else.

Caius looked *strong*.

There was no way to describe it other than, he didn't have muscles just for show, they actually *did something*. The way extra muscles bulked on the tops of his shoulders and veins lined up his forearms. He wasn't as big as Olcan, but he was close.

How had I never noticed this before?

"Aspen?"

I just stood there, staring like an idiot until the dryness of my eyes forced me to blink.

"Umm, hi. Can I come in?"

He wanted to say no, but for whatever reason, stepped aside so I could walk into the room. It was the same as Sabre's except everything was on the opposite side, just like the maze.

"What are you doing here?" he demanded as I faced him. He'd shut the door and stood with one hand in his pocket, the other was holding a book. He stood glaring at me.

"I needed to see you."

He raised one eyebrow, "Yeah?"

My eyebrows knotted as my eyes followed him across the room to where he threw the book on the bed, then started arranging some of the other things on it. Clothes, socks and a pair of black boots I assumed, he'd be putting on.

"Yes," I said, growing mildly defensive. "I came to apologise and to te—"

"For what?" he continued packing his clothes into a little overnight bag, his back still to me. The muscles in it moved and contracted as he stretched and shoved items in his holdall. I swallowed down my trepidation.

"For the other night. I was meant to meet you but Sabre cam—"

He laughed and finally laid his eyes on me again, "I see. No apologies needed, I know exactly what you were doing. Get out, Aspen."

My eyes widened with disbelief, "What? I'm trying to apologise and te—"

"Well, you've said it. Now leave!" he shouted so unexpectedly, slamming the holdall into the bed, making me jump. My reaction fuelled my anger and embarrassment.

"Why are you yelling at me?" I shouted back at him, desperate not to let tears fall. In the next moment Caius was close to me, his eyes feral as he raged, "I waited for you, for *hours* Aspen"

The continuous use of my name told me enough about how upset he was.

"You told me to meet you and I...I waited for you, knowing...I knew you were with him."

I was quiet for a moment, thinking of Caius pacing outside his cave. Waiting.

For me.

I looked him dead in the eye, "I didn't stand you up. I was on my way to see you." The way he kissed his teeth showed he obviously didn't believe me.

"Sabre turned up just as I was leaving. He wanted to come inside and I couldn't find a reason to stop him, but I didn't in the end... because of you."

He continued to glare, "Because of me?"

"Yes, because he was finally opening up to me, telling me about his plans with Goliath and I knew it could be important to you."

His eyes somehow grew more intense at that, but he didn't immediately respond. The tension was slowly transferring itself to me, making me snap.

"Can you stop looking at me like that?"

"Like what?"

"Like I betrayed you!"

Where he had previously been glaring at me, something suddenly took over Caius and his face morphed into a look of complete indifference. Where his eyes usually blazed with fury or amusement, there was just nothing. It didn't matter that I had information for him. Something had changed between us and I needed to know what it was.

"You're right," he muttered. "You didn't betray me. I just don't like being made a fool of."

"I wasn't trying to make a fool of you. I wanted to see you, I…"

I wasn't ready to admit how much I'd been looking forward to seeing him. I didn't need him knowing that in the last month, he was the only person I ever wanted to be around.

Instead I told him about the march on Boltese and about Goliath using Ulren. He was pleased with the first and shocked by the second bit of information. Whether they were helpful, my work here was done.

"Thank you," he said quietly.

"You're welcome."

I felt deflated. I waited for days to share this with him, to be closer to him because of it but everything was ruined. He felt further away than ever. We stood looking at each other for a long while before I said, "I wanted to be there."

Caius sighed, looking down at his sock covered feet then back up at me and there it was, the fire that I'd been missing.

"I..." he stopped himself.

What was this? Caius Caldoun lost for words? Instinctively, I made to go towards him, ready to tease him but he retreated from me.

"I'm sorry, I—"

"You should go."

Caius was firm but not unkind. I nodded, a little embarrassed at having misread the signals and headed to the door.

"Grey?"

I turned, elated that I was Grey again.

Caius stared over at me a moment, "You look nice."

God help me, I blushed. My cheeks heated and I hung my head in an attempt to hide it,

"Good luck," I mumbled and rushed out of the room, straight into the glaring face of Lady Xana.

CHAPTER TWENTY

Lady Xana stood before me in an elaborate black kaftan, embroidered with white and grey detailing. Wolves, moons, trees and other ancient symbols covered the material and seemed to glow in the faintly lit hallway. Except for the thin cornrowed braids at the front of her head, holding her thick, white hair back from her exceptionally beautiful face, she never bothered with fussing it into any type of hairdo, leaving it unbound and gorgeously unruly.

I hadn't thought much about her since our meeting in town so many weeks ago, but now she was here, her words came rushing back to me.

The choices you make will affect us all.

I was yet to work out what choices she meant.

"Good evening, young Aspen. What, might I ask, are you doing down here?"

I wouldn't let this woman intimidate me, no matter how much she embodied the powers that ruled over our community.

"I came to wish the competitors good luck."

Lady Xana smiled knowingly, "Lie to whomever you wish, just not to me."

I didn't reply. I wasn't going to talk myself into trouble with her. She scared me and I just wanted away from her.

"I should be going," I mumbled, moving to walk around her. As I passed, the smell of the natural products in her hair and the faint scent of the magic that flowed through her veins teased my nostrils.

"Have you thought any more about your choice?"

"If you're talking about Caius or Sabre, I don't *have* a choice," I hissed at her, conscious of the boys in the rooms around us.

Lady Xana smiled clearly amused by admission as much as I was shocked by it. The fact I viewed Caius as a possible choice of partner was apparently a very real thing to me.

"Doing what you want is the easy path, Aspen, but doing what is right is *always* a choice."

I stopped to look at her, "Excuse me?"

Lady Xana turned her whole body to face me and stared dead in my eyes, "Just know that the path you walk will not be an easy one, but you must walk it anyway, to free us and yourself."

Anger flared up at her and I lost my composure, "What does that mean? Why is everything so cryptic with you?"

For the first time, Lady Xana looked apologetic, almost sad, "If I could say or do more, I would."

"Do more for what? What is going on?"

"Miss Anai?" I turned at the sound of Arlo's voice. "Who are you talking to?"

When I turned back to face Lady Xana, the old woman was gone.

I sat in the Beta box with my family, waiting for the challenge to begin.

The Riadnaks had their own gilded box on our left and the Caldouns occupied the one on our right. If I leaned forward on the balcony and turned my head either way, I could easily see them all. The Caldouns were talking among themselves, their attendants fluttering in and out to accommodate them, while the Riadnaks sat in silence. Goliath had the golden circlet of the Alpha on his head, while Celeste and Fern sat on either side of him, the whole family in the eternal white. I couldn't quite feel the awe I once had at their dignity, knowing what I knew, and feeling the hollow left by the missing member of the family.

I missed Tala terribly. Why hadn't I appreciated her more when I had her? Thanks to Caius I knew she was safe, but it wasn't the same as being with her. I found comfort in the fact that she was with Sire, who would undoubtedly protect her.

I reclined in my own seat, my sister on my right and my parents on my left. We listened to the roar of the crowd that now filled the arena around us. Thousands of people from across the country had gathered to watch, and as Arlo stepped into the speaker's box on the opposite end of the arena, a hush fell over all of us.

"Ladies, gentlemen and all *laecan* kind, I am honoured to welcome you to the second challenge of the Mating Games!"

His voice had been magically projected by Lady Xana, so no one had to struggle to hear him. It was also done for any *maejym* in the crowd, as they couldn't amplify their hearing as the *laecan* could.

"Look now upon the Mating Maze. It has taken over a year to construct and it is now ready to put our challengers to the test."

The crowd erupted into elated applause.

"With the help of Invernell's illustrious and beautiful shaman—Lady Xana—we have built this maze so that we all may observe the action within. Understand, that the challengers however, will not be able to see or hear us. Once they enter the maze, they will be in total darkness and completely alone. They must rely on their senses and their speed and agility to succeed."

Dark? It was almost noon! How Lady Xana was doing this, I didn't want to know. Shaman powers were universally enigmatic.

Finally, Arlo raised his arms, "And now, I present to you the first challenger." A murmur of anticipation moved through the crowd as Arlo favoured a dramatic pause before booming: "Caius, of House Caldoun!"

I held my breath, convinced the crowd would boo, hiss or do something to embarrass Caius, but people applauded him. We couldn't see him from our seated position, despite the slant in the seats that allowed us to look down on the action. We wouldn't be permitted to stand until Sabre came out. There were continued cheers and whistling for Caius and I found myself relieved.

"Now, his opponent—the heir to our mighty ruling family and rightful leader of the new age of *Iaecan*..."

Overdoing it a bit there, aren't we Arlo?

"Sabre, of House Riadnak!"

The thunderous applause was deafening as the entire arena gave Sabre a standing ovation. It was a vicious reminder of the difference in support for the two men. From the highest to the lowest tier, hands clapped, feet stomped and voices raised as they celebrated the heir. The sea of colourful faces, clothes and headgear before me exploded into a rumbling chant,

"SABRE! SABRE! SABRE!"

I turned to see my mother smiling and looked to my sister, who was just as enraptured with the scene as she clapped. We all stood, showing our support for Sabre. I didn't have to lean forward at all to be able to see them both as they were standing a few feet below me at their designated entrance to the maze. I stepped closer to edge of the balustrade, readying for my speech. My family flanked me, as required, and faced the crowd.

"And now," Arlo's voice broke through the cheering, making everyone quiet down, "we open the challenge with a word from the Female—Miss Aspen Anai!"

The celebratory screams hadn't died when they clapped for Sabre but rose considerably for me. I smiled and raised my hand to wave at the masses as they continued to cheer and praise. My hands felt clammy. This was the first time I officially addressed the people I was meant to rule and I realised I'd been so caught up in everything that had happened over the past few weeks that I hadn't prepared. I had taken for granted that this would come naturally, but my throat was drying up. They were all looking to me.

My mother gave my lower back a soft pinch and it prompted me to finally draw a breath, surprised at how steady my voice was as I began,

"I, Aspen of House Anai, eldest child of Bracken, stand before you as the Female member of the Triquetra. I hereby give my luck and blessings to the challengers, Caius Caldoun…"

I lowered my head to look down at Caius. He returned my stare and for a brief moment, there was no one else in the arena but us. I struggled to look away, his gaze boring into me like a brand, hot and deep against my skin.

"May the *laecan* laws protect you." I finished my blessing, turning my attention to Sabre.

"And to Sabre Riadnak, may the *laecan* laws protect you."

Sabre looked up at me, topless—the same as Caius—and gave me the briefest of hopeful smiles. I'd been in such a rush to get to Caius that I hadn't lingered on Sabre's worry when I entered his cell. He'd been afraid that I was Goliath. Why was Sabre apprehensive about seeing his father? Despite his actions towards me, there was a vulnerability in that earlier moment. Sabre had always been the unyielding force in my life, he was the one person that made me feel wanted and special, and even though knowing I no longer wanted to be won left a bitter taste in my mouth, it didn't make any of this his fault. He was a Riadnak in the same way I was the Female and we both had our obligations to those titles. There was a bond between us because of our similarities and our shared history, and there was no way around that.

I looked away from him and out onto the maze and the thousands of people surrounding it. Sabre and Caius turned to face their respective entrances and a hush fell over the crowd.

I raised my arm, one hand to the sky, then lowered it, "Begin!"

In seconds, they *turned* and darted into the maze.

They looked like two strokes of black and white paint against a brown and green canvas. They bound up the first path at roughly the same speed before Sabre was forced to turn right and Caius to turn left.

As they hurtled around their respective corners, fire exploded from the hedges that lined their path.

"Ahh!" a shocked gasp escaped the crowd as both wolves, taken by surprise, tumbled away from the flames.

"A little fire never hurt anyone…much!" Arlo commented cheerily. The crowd screamed at the commentary, excited by the obstacle.

My eyes darted between the wolves, trying to keep an eye on their progress, but I found my focus pulled to Caius. He was hunched on his front legs, watching the fires that burst out in front of him. I turned to look at Sabre who was trying to crawl under the first bout of flame, but got caught when another burst singed the top of his head. While I couldn't hear it, I knew he had yelped by the way he cowered on the floor once it touched him. Unable to do anything about it, I focused on Caius. He was staying perfectly still, focusing intently on the flames. I soon realised they came in a sequence, and Caius was counting the intervals of the fire bursts.

"It seems the Gamma heir has figured it out, ladies and gentlemen, that the bursts are in fact, timed. Figure out the sequence and you can get through unscathed!"

Caius took off, executing what had just been revealed. He leapt over the first blast and crouched low to duck the second. He scrambled forward before jumping quickly over the third and crashing into the left side of the hedge to avoid the burst that came out again on the right. He raced along the left hedge before he dropped to the ground, rolled to the right and allowed the second burst from the right side to shoot out over his head. He kept his tail low as he quickly raced forward, and with a final leap over a lower fire that burst from his left, he cleared the path.

The crowd exploded with cheers.

I gripped the marble balustrade, my knuckles straining under the pressure of my hold as I watched Caius catch his breath against the hedge before racing on. I returned to follow Sabre's progress, who now understood the sequence himself and was on the second to last fire burst. He cleared it, leaping over it just as Caius had and crashed into the hedge in front of him. He didn't bother stopping to catch his breath before scrambling onto his feet and bolting down the path.

Once again, the wolves were neck and neck as the crowd watched them mirror each other from above. Sabre turned left while Caius turned right, both racing with such speed and strength, the ground beneath broke away, torn to muddy shreds. Arlo said they were in the dark so their wolf sight would be at its peak.

The wolves turned again, heading north to us but really a right turn to Sabre and a left one to Caius. They carried on, blazing through the hedges when a blade shot out through the tightly grown foliage in front of them.

Both wolves were hit this time, although Sabre was a little short of the blade. It sliced across his face, making him fall back.

Caius was less fortunate.

As he had been further ahead, the blade caught him directly in his right side, slicing between his ribs.

"Ooh!" the crowd cried, as we all saw him take the hit. I raised my hand to my mouth in horror as I watched both wolves gather themselves.

"Blades can be very dangerous, ladies and gentlemen. Don't be caught unaware with these fine pieces of Agmantian iron! Not quite the same durability as our steel, but all the deadlier."

Arlo's voice was beginning to grate. His commentary an idle observation, repeating things I already knew. It didn't help that iron was more deadly to *laecan* than anything. Cuts from iron blades didn't heal as fast, if at all. They scarred. And receiving one, stung like fiery piss.

Not that I'd ever experienced fiery piss of course.

Again, my eyes went to Caius as once again, he observed the blades. I couldn't see the severity of his wound from above, but he seemed okay for the moment. He was crouched low in anticipation of more blades coming out, but this time nothing happened. The blades that had cut them, long, thick and protruding menacingly from the hedges, suddenly withdrew. Caius made to go past his but it shot out again, slicing him almost directly in the same spot. This time I *turned* my eyes and with my heightened vision saw blood on the blade. Caius fell to the floor, in pain.

"Be careful!" Arlo called out. "The same tricks won't be played twice!"

These blades weren't timed like the flames. I watched Caius stumble back and onto his side before clambering to his feet.

Come on, Caius...

He crouched, and I couldn't bare to watch, so I turned my eyes on Sabre.

He wasn't having any more luck than Caius, and when the first blade receded after his second attempt at getting past it, Sabre simply barrelled through. The first blade shot out, triggered by his movement, and he skidded to the right on his belly to avoid it. He jumped to the left to avoid the second blade that shot out from the hedges. As he continued on, countless blades shot out in front of him so that he had to weave his way through them. The problem was that he'd been running so fast, he'd gained momentum, and found it difficult to slow down.

But this was the agility challenge, designed to have them prove their dexterity with their bodies. Sabre continued to charge through the blades, expertly weaving through them so fast he was a streak of snow on mud.

I'd barely taken a breath since they were both cut by the first blade, but as Sabre cleared the shards of metal, I let out a tortured exhale. There were blatant cuts on him, glaring against his white coat, but nothing life threatening.

"A smooth path delivered by our prized and most respected heir, Sabre Riadnak!"

The crowd went wild at his name, but I decided to divert my attention back to Caius. He was now racing down his own path. To my horror, I saw blood on the trail behind him. My heart quickened at the sight, but I had to remain calm.

There were no obstructions for either of them for a few yards, but as the wolves slowed infinitesimally, I realised the path ahead of them was narrowing. The hedges continued closing in on them, with added sharp, seemingly unending turns, so that the stretch of their path looked like designs on the edge of a mosaic: a cluster of small squares they had to pierce through until forced to jump over the last, as the path wasn't wide enough.

"As wolves, one must be adaptable, swift and agile to get through the smallest of areas!"

Both wolves jumped out of their narrowing paths and raced on ahead, Sabre now in the lead by a small distance. I heard a sharp cry of triumph from my sister, but ignored her.

The wolves ran and the crowd cheered while I perspired. I could barely take a breath as I darted my attention between them praying that none of them would get seriously hurt. It seemed our God wasn't listening or I should have kept my prayers to myself, because at the same time, both Caius and Sabre dropped to the ground.

"Oooh!" the crowd raised their voices in shock, as the wolves fell.

They collapsed, writhing in the dirt as they tried to dislodge something that had pierced their sides but the movement proved futile. It only served in Caius' case to push the projectile further into his side, into the wound from the blade, already bleeding. Sabre had abandoned his attempt to dislodge the shot and scrambled to get upright instead. He raced ahead, but even I could see that he wasn't steady on his paws.

I looked to my right, to Caius' family. Regina Caldoun was watching her son intently, her eyes focused on where he was now running labouredly down his path. Maximus was holding her hand on the top of the balustrade and Asher stood beside her. His hand rested gently on her shoulder as she watched in fear for her eldest son.

The crowd continued to cheer and clap and stomp their feet, heightening the tension as the wolves were both clearly struggling to even remain standing.

"The infamous wolfsbane, everybody!" Arlo called out, making the crowd hiss with disagreement. "Large doses can render any wolf immobile and cause serious harm, even death as we all know. Let's see what a few shots of it will do to our challengers!"

I looked toward the Riadnak family, where Goliath and Celeste stood peering down at Sabre. Neither looked tearful or afraid and they weren't holding hands or supporting one another in any way. Fern stood by her mother's side, watching her brother, but her face looked tortured. It was clear she was trying not to look afraid, but the way she gripped the balustrade was telling a different story.

I returned my attention to the wolves and watched in horror as the ground began to open up in front of them. I couldn't feel any movement, but the ground receded into itself, revealing a pit of blazing hot coals.

The wolves continued to run as fast as the wolfsbane and injuries would allow, with no idea what lay just around the next corner.

"No," the breathy rejection came out of me as I watched the wolves race towards the perilous obstacle ahead of them. My eyes darted between the streaks of white and black as they both saw the gaping hole at the same time.

Caius was on unsteady feet.

He wouldn't make it.

Both wolves leapt into the air across the coals. Both missed the edge by mere inches, their hind quarters fell towards the heated coals and the crowd roared with excitement.

"OOOH!"

"CAIUS!"

His name ripped from my throat before I could stop it and I was leaning over the balustrade as if I could reach him from my high position a breath later. I watched fearfully as his back legs struggled to gain some momentum against the wall in front of him, using his front paws and jaw to scramble up.

My body physically shook, terrified for him if he fell into that heat. No amount of healing ability would stop the pain he would go through. The tender pads of his paws and his thick fur would be scorched and ruined. Caius' coat gleamed from the light of the coals, the black as pure as death.

He was gripping with his claws, digging them deep into the dirt, keeping himself from sliding into the glowering pit. My hand went to the base of my throat, clenching there as if in prayer. Time was slowing, my pulse was hard in my veins, I couldn't breathe…

…until finally he pulled himself over the precarious ledge.

He'd made it.

Barely.

He lay there for a moment, panting, trying to catch his breath as he struggled against the effects of the wolfsbane and his wound. I could see the blood on the floor beside him as he tried to gather himself. Now I knew Caius was relatively safe, I turned my attention to Sabre who had thankfully cleared the coal pit but was now running erratically down a meandering path. The wolfsbane was getting to him too and he was slowing, even as he neared the finish line. Sabre was going to be Alpha. He only needed this win and it would all be over.

I felt a hand on my bare shoulder and I turned to Rogue, who let her hand fall, catching my eyes with hers—her expression unreadable— before tilting her head behind me. I turned to my left and met my mother's murderous gaze. I realised belatedly that my family had heard me scream Caius' name.

I knew trouble was coming my way, but I couldn't find it in me to care.

"And now, ladies and gentlemen, the final stretch towards victory!" Arlo's voice rang out and we watched in amazement as a wall at the end of the course began to rise out of the ground.

If either of them had been along the final stretch already, they could have raced and simply leapt over it, but the longer they faltered on the path to the end, the higher the wall became.

Soon, it would be too high for them to jump over at all.

Both Caius and Sabre were stumbling now, the wolfsbane decelerating them even as they pushed on.

I watched in anticipation, fear and surprising longing as the wolves came close to one another, a simple hedge between them, then separated as their mirroring paths took them away from one another over and over.

They both finally reached the long path towards the exit and set eyes on the rising wall at the same time. With clear determination, Sabre and Caius darted for the wall as fast as the circumstances would allow. I leaned forward on the balustrade, my heart thumping rapidly as I watched them run. My palms were hot against the cool marble, sweat pooled under my breasts and my jaw tensed. I panted, unable to take a deeper breath as my gaze followed Caius. He came up to the wall and leapt for... the hedges.

Caius bound onto the right hedge, then the left and back again, propelling himself higher and higher until his front paws grabbed hold of the rising wall.

He held on with all his strength, using his back legs to leverage himself up the wall and finally, over the other side, his blood trailing down the wall as he disappeared.

I turned to see what happened to Sabre and watched the exact moment he plummeted from the wall just as it locked into its highest position. He'd seemingly tried to leap for it in one bound and missed.

Sabre fell to the floor, his body collapsing onto itself before he set himself right. Sabre looked up at the wall that was now too high to climb, lifted his head and howled, although we couldn't hear it.

The obstacle course was over.

Caius had won.

CHAPTER TWENTY-ONE

Hours after the challenge, I stood before my mother in our living room and found myself trembling with real, unfiltered fear.

The Riadnaks left the arena almost immediately, but a messenger had approached us, saying my presence would be expected at the Manor once Sabre had recovered. I was not looking forward to that particular meet-up, but the message had come straight from Goliath. The only reason we hadn't gone to the Manor right after, was because he would be in no mood for visitors.

Sabre had lost.

His rage would palpable.

It wasn't lost on me that although Caius was the winner, the Female was being restrained from congratulating him: a clear denunciation of his victory.

My mother said nothing to me on the carriage ride back to the manor. She'd barely looked at me. My father and sister were no help, both knowing that I was in a world of trouble for my outburst, my father not having nearly enough authority in matters concerning the Female to stop it.

When we'd entered our home, my mother ordered the maids to get her bath running as she would retire in a moment. Without losing her stride, she'd walked into the main living room and we'd all followed without question.

I stood now on our Cotaini rug, my hands clasped before me and my head down, waiting for her to yell at me. I'd been staring at the rug for so long, I knew there were exactly thirteen petals on the flowers that bordered the design and thirteen flowers on the vines they extended from. My sister was sitting on an armchair to my right, my father on the long couch beside her. Both silent, both expectant as I was.

I didn't lift my head until I saw the tips of my mother's shoes approach me and with a readying intake of breath, I looked up at her. Before I was able to set my eyes on her face, my mother slapped me.

The sound echoed around the room like a clap as my head whipped to the right and I stumbled back. I lifted my head, my vision blurred, when she slapped me again. This time, I felt my lip split from the impact. I brought my trembling fingers to my mouth and they came away with the dark red of my blood on their tips.

Shaking, I looked up at my mother, tears dripping down my face in anger, frustration and hate. I was breathing heavily, desperate not to make a sound as Ianthe glared at me. My face was on fire, it felt like it was itching. I tried to blow the pain away through my nostrils, but it just kept stinging. I felt my healing start to work as my skin cooled, but just as the sensation began to soothe me, my mother reached out and slapped me once more, rattling my jaw.

"Ianthe," my father finally said. "Enough."

I didn't look back at my mother this time. I left my face hanging, looking again at the thirteen petals on the thirteen flowers. This time, one of the petals was tainted with a drop of my blood.

"Have you given yourself to him?"

What?

Slowly, I lifted my head as a single tear trailed down my bruising cheek.

"Answer me, Aspen."

"Just because I care whether he's hurt doesn't mea—"

"Answer me."

"Mother, he's not a bad person."

"ANSWER ME."

My mother used her wolf voice and practically roared at me. The house shook with the force of her words and when I looked at my father, desperate for his intervention, he ignored me. I would get no salvation from him. I turned back to my mother, loathing in my eyes.

"No," I growled, furious at her for embarrassing me like this. "I have not had sex with Caius Caldoun."

The breath that escaped her was utter relief.

I was just a vessel to her.

The pure Female that she wanted an Alpha—*the* Alpha—to pluck because it made her special. She didn't care about me.

None of them did.

I was a pawn to be used in everyone else's games.

"I have never given you any reason to think I wouldn't do my duty to this family," I looked up at my mother, a ring of gold now blazing in my eyes as my rage took hold of me. Her own golden rings flared back.

"You've done nothing but cause trouble for the last few weeks."

"I've done *everything* you've ever asked of me."

"Out all hours of the day and night, not showing your face at the Manor?"

"I would never betray my kind, why do you think I will?" I screamed at her.

"Get out of my sight," my mother commanded, but I wasn't going anywhere. I was far from done.

"Tell me why I'm not allowed to see him?"

"Aspen, stop this," my father cut in, standing from his chair.

"He's a Triquetrian," I continued as she turned her back to me, ignoring me completely. "After today, he might even win. I might have to mate with him, so why are we being kept apart?"

The fourth blow to my face sent me crashing to the floor, blood spurting from my mouth and I coughed feebly. I spit out blood onto our hundred thousand gold coin carpet and nodded to myself, with conviction and clear understanding. No one in this house gave a shit about me when I was constantly battling with how my choices would affect them.

"You're being kept from him because I will not allow you to destroy this family with your stupid decisions. I've worked too hard and for too long to see you fuck this up now."

Tears trickled down my face, my heart aching with my realisations.

"Stay away from him, do you hear me, little girl? Stay away from him!"

I didn't bother answering, my tears choking me. It didn't matter that I didn't confirm I would obey, because she knew that I would do my duty. I always had. This display was nothing more than her taking her fury out on me. I wasn't Aspen. I was the Female; a symbol, a tool, to keep tradition alive, to keep our society intact. That was my purpose.

I curled in on myself on the carpet, listening to the swish of her gown as she sauntered out of the room, my father and sister following close behind her.

An hour later, I stood outside the Caldoun manor and knocked the door before I lost my nerve. It was so quiet under the moonless night that my knock on the door sounded like thunder to my ears. I had the echoing sting of my mother's hand still on my cheek to remind me why I shouldn't be there, but I couldn't have stayed away. I was almost fully healed, but she had put her wolf strength into the final blow and it would take a moment for the bruises to truly disappear.

I hadn't bothered to change and had snuck out of the house once my mother retired. I had to know if Caius was okay and there was no one I could ask except him or his family.

The manor was silent, which while I'd realised it was normal for them, was unthinkable after the win Caius had managed to secure today.

The Caldoun manor should be lit up with decoration and heaving with people trying to get a piece of the newest champion. Instead, the grounds were as silent as the grave. The Riadnak manor would have been ready to welcome Sabre as champion, but this house had never even prepared for it. People should be here, applauding him and raising him up, but instead they stayed away so not to offend the Alpha. No one would be seen to support the Gamma heir. Everyone was too loyal to Goliath.

Or too scared of him.

I swallowed my apprehension, unable to turn back now, and waited for the door to open.

When it eventually did, Regina Caldoun stood there. The hallway behind her was softly lit, candles dotting the walls and mantles intermittently, but I could see she was still in her outfit from the challenge as well.

"Aspen?"

"Good evening, Mrs Caldoun," my voice shook with nerves.

"My goodness, Aspen, what happened to your face?" I looked away embarrassed.

"I'm sorry to bother you, Mrs Caldoun, but I wanted to... I needed to see if..."

Regina shook her head, "Ianthe," she cursed. I could tell she wanted to say more, but didn't. Instead she smiled warmly and something in that smile made me ashamed to look at her. I looked down at my feet again.

"He's in his room," she replied. "I don't think he wants to see anyone."

I looked back up at her, wide eyed, "Please, I... please?" I didn't have anything to say. I didn't know how to say it. I wasn't even entirely sure what was happening.

Yes, the obvious: my feelings for Caius were changing, but now that he had won and could very well win the third challenge, everything was different. Now there was a chance that Caius would beat Sabre, everyone else wouldn't be able to ignore Caius any longer. Bound by their own laws and prejudice, I could be allowed to want Caius because if he won the final challenge, I wouldn't be doing anything wrong.

"I just need to see that he's okay."

Regina was silent for a moment before she stepped aside and allowed me into her home. She closed the front door softly behind me and lead up the sweeping staircase in front us onto the next landing. I heard Maximus and Asher in an adjacent room and a maid passed us in the hall.

The Caldoun manor looked a lot like my own with its seemingly endless rooms. Crystal chandeliers hung above our heads while golden doorknobs glistened under candlelight. Tapestries adorned the walls, as well as portraits of ancestors, showing an array of brown faces. It was customary to have one's wolf form in a portrait beside them and so, walking down the hall of the Caldoun home, I saw finely dressed lords with their own image laying regally at their feet. Mainly black or a combination of black and other colours, the coats of the Caldoun ancestors stared back at me.

As we approached what I knew was Caius' room, there was a large portrait of a handsome man in black robes with a jet-black wolf by his feet. He was stunning to look at and I couldn't help but stare,

"Caius Caldoun."

"Sorry?" I blinked to tear myself away from the portrait.

Regina inclined her head to the picture, "That's who I named my son after. The first Gamma Caldoun to ever become Alpha."

I turned back to the portrait and saw the determination and hunger in those ancient brown eyes.

"Caius read everything about him when he was little," Regina explained. "Idolised him, wanted to be just like him."

"He wanted to become Alpha?"

Regina took a moment before saying, "He wanted something that only being Alpha could get him."

When I tore my eyes away from Caius the Elder and back to Regina, she was watching me closely. She said nothing for the moment and with a brief touch on my arm, she retreated back the way we came. I knocked once, but this time I didn't wait for a reply and simply opened the door.

When I entered, Caius was standing at the foot of his bed in only a pair of loose fitting trousers, attempting to apply something to the most hideous wound I had ever seen, cutting along his bare right side.

He looked up as I entered, so shocked to see me that he dropped the jar he was holding. It landed directly onto his foot and he cried out before falling back against his bedpost. The way he twisted his torso to regain his balance clearly angered his wound because he bellowed again and hopped on one foot around the side of the bed, lowering himself onto it, clutching his side.

"Caius!" I charged into the room, slamming the door shut behind me. "Are you all right?" I asked stupidly.

"Do I look all right? Fuck!" he hissed, holding his side where blood was seeping through his fingers.

"What should I do?" I panicked, reaching out to touch him but he backed away from me.

"Go away, that's what!"

"No," I snapped. "I'm here now and I want to help."

He snarled at me, literally making a gravelling sound as he bore his teeth at me and in a display of dominance, I growled back.

"Fuck," he rolled his eyes before slumping back onto his bed. "I'm in too much pain to fight you right now. Get the cream I just dropped."

Quickly, I retrieved the glass jar of cream from the floor. It had rolled a little under his bed. Thankfully it hadn't smashed on its way down and been blocked by the carpet and Caius' toe.

I brought it over and handed it back to him. He took it from me and went to apply it to the gash in his side.

I tilted my head like a bird, "Aren't you going to clean it?"

His fingers stopped inches from his skin, but he didn't look at me. I huffed, "Don't touch it."

I kicked off my heels and went into his adjoining bathroom, situated just off the side of his bedroom. It took me a while to find everything, but I soon had a bowl of warmed water, a washcloth and some cloth for bandages. Why he wasn't already bandaged, I didn't understand and asked him when I returned to the room.

"I had to bathe, didn't I?"

I held up my palms, "All right, I was just asking."

He had positioned himself in the middle of his bed and was leaning against his large wooden headboard. He was topless, his incredible body was on display, his muscled stomach crunched in the middle where he was bent. He was leaning slightly to his left, trying to get a good look at the wound down the right side of his rib cage. I climbed onto the mattress, placing the bowl of water in front of my now bent knees.

"Lift your arm," I said, dipping the cloth into the water.

"I can do it my—"

"Lift..." I dropped my green gaze onto him and let it clash with the fire of his "...your arm."

He continued to stare at me before slowly lifting his right arm and resting it above his head. I swallowed, wet my lips and leaned forward to clean the wound. He winced as the cloth touched him but I continued to wipe and dab gently around the bleeding.

"Sorry."

We continued like that, in silence. As I worked, I stole glances around his room. His books, his haphazardly thrown clothes, the maps and sketches on his walls were glimpses of a side of Caius I would love to know. The room felt cosy and safe, in tones of burgundy, brown and taupe warmed from the fireplace to the right.

Once the worst of the blood was away, it didn't actually look that bad, even though the wolfsbane and iron were delaying the healing. The Arena staff would have given him something to offset infection and delirium but because of the iron, the scars would remain. Our natural weaknesses, the poisons were in his blood and would take time to leave.

When the wound was clean, I applied a different cream made of tree sap that I found in the bathroom. He winced again. It stung.

"Sorry," I said.

"It's okay," he murmured.

Our legs were touching and when he spoke, I felt the vibrations through my body.

He flinched when I worked the sap into the wound, but soon I felt him start to relax. I tried to ignore the feel of his skin beneath my fingertips, but felt myself grow increasingly aware of his proximity until my own skin felt like it was humming.

I hurriedly finished, but knew I was far from done. Clenching my jaws briefly I reached over his legs to pick up the cream he was attempting to put on before.

"What do I do with this?"

"Thick layer all over and seal under the bandages."

I scooped my first two fingers into the container and proceeded to slather the mixture all over the wound, watching as he closed his eyes blissfully. I may have taken longer than I needed to and he may not have mentioned it. Once done, I climbed off the bed and urged him to follow.

"We need to get the bandage around you."

He didn't argue and shuffled off the bed to stand in front of me. Hurriedly, I unravelled the bandage strips and began to walk around him to tighten them. With his hands above his head, Caius asked,

"What happened to your face?"

I glanced up at him, met his eyes briefly, but looked away, focusing on tightening the bandage as I replied, "Ianthe felt it should get acquainted with her hand."

"Why?"

My fingers didn't seem to want to cooperate as I tried to secure the now tautly wound bandage with the appropriate pins. I'd forgotten he and Sabre couldn't hear anything in the arena. He had no idea that I'd called out his name.

"It doesn't matter why."

The bruise and cut would be gone by tomorrow, even if the internal scars would linger.

When I finished, I gently patted his stomach, but didn't completely remove my hand from it. Caius took a deep breath and I watched his chest rise and fall, feeling his eyes looking down at the top of my head, neither of us saying anything.

"You were incredible today," I murmured as I allowed my fingers to walk slowly up and down his bandaged mid-section, but never where his skin was bare. My head still hung low, "When you got hurt," I mumbled. "I... I was so scared."

I lifted my head then and rested my eyes in his. The look he gave me was purposeful and so inviting that I stepped into him, our chests touching. My legs began to tremble, the heat between them pulsing as I licked my lips, daring him to kiss me.

Dear God. I wanted him to kiss me.

Caius peered down at me, never balking from the intent that was suddenly so clear in my eyes, on my face and...

We both jumped back at the same time as the evidence of our attraction to each other almost suffocated the room.

He did want me.

I could *smell* it.

His desire exuded from him like smoke from a campfire. If I could smell him, then I knew he could smell me. The musk and heat of my desire for him, suddenly too obvious to ignore or dismiss with clever words.

"Sabre will win," Caius said.

I blinked, shocked at the mention of Sabre's name, "What?"

"Sabre will win and then what?"

I searched his eyes for the want that was there only moments ago, "But you won. You beat him, you—"

Caius stepped away, releasing my fingers from the little contact they had with him. He stared back at me like I'd grown a second head.

"And he'll beat me in a month's time and then what. You'll go to him—after this?" he gestured into the space between us.

"If you hadn't thrown the first challenge you would have *already* beat him!" I snapped.

"And if you hadn't come to see me at the arena today, I wouldn't have wanted to!"

I froze.

He wanted something that only being Alpha could get him, his mother had said only ten minutes before.

He'd tried to win today… for me. It seemed Caius was interested in the prize afterall.

"Caius…" I reached out to him, but he backed away from me.

"You're his." He shook his head dismissively. "You've always been his…and you always will be." He shook his head, angry now, as he marched over to his door, "Today was a mistake."

"A mistake?" I spun around to face him but, he'd retched the door open and gestured to the hallway beyond.

"I shouldn't have entertained the farce of you being pruned and bred like that's all you're good for. You have Sabre for that."

I started blinking rapidly, hurt and confused and so overwhelmed by the change occurring between us.

"Caius."

"Just leave."

"Stop this," I cried out. Everything had been going so well, why was he ruining it? I stormed up to him, "Why are you fighting this? You can't deny what just happened."

"Why not, when you have been for the past six years?"

Six years? What was he talking about?

Caius grabbed my arm and shoved me out his bedroom door, "I almost forgot what you are," he looked me up and down. "I won't forget again."

Tears stung my eyes, "Oh, and what is that?"

"*Prized flesh*," he spat at me and slammed the door in my face.

CHAPTER TWENTY-TWO

In the wake of Caius' victory, my mother was losing her mind. No one had expected Caius to win and so there were no measures taken for a celebration for him in the immediate days after the challenge. Food, drink and general merriment had all been cancelled at the Riadnak Manor, as Goliath refused to host anything for a loss.

I shuddered to think how he was treating Sabre, but knew I would eventually have to show my face. It had been requested.

Prized flesh.

Caius' words had stung because they were true. Everything he said was true, which only made my wanting him that much harder. I wasn't fooling myself into thinking that I was in love with Caius. Spending half an hour in his room had shown me that I barely knew him, and I couldn't seem to figure him out, or get him to open up to me, not entirely. But I did want him. I wanted him with a ferocious and carnal intent that I could no longer hide, now that I had smelled the same feelings in him.

The solution to everyone's – my – issues was simple enough: Caius had to see reason and win the Mating Games. If he won, he would become Alpha, he could continue his mission to stop Goliath and I wouldn't have to sleep with Sabre. Now, all I had to do was convince Caius of my little plan and going off his attitude last night I knew I had my work cut out for me.

I sat at breakfast with my family the following morning. My mother was in a fit of rage as her plans for the month up to the final challenge had been ruined.

"Where did that strength even come from?" She stabbed at an innocent sausage on her breakfast plate hard enough to break the porcelain. "That amount of wolfsbane should have paralysed him."

I lifted my eyes to look over at my sister and even Rogue's eyebrows knotted,

"Don't you mean *them?*" she asked.

"What?" my mother spat, cutting into her sausage and finally putting it in her mouth.

"The wolfsbane," Rogue replied. "Don't you mean the wolfsbane should have paralysed both of them?"

My mother fanned her fork in the air dismissively as she chewed, "Yes, of course, both of them, but with his wound from the blades the boy shouldn't have been able to walk, much less scale a fifteen-foot wall!"

My jaw clenched at what my mother had all but admitted.

"Caius displayed excellent form yesterday, Ianthe. He should be praised as the champion he is." My father offered, bringing his coffee cup to his lips, slurping deeply. He only drank the Mortanian brand because, as he put it, it was 'richer'. I had no idea what he was talking about. I would stick with tea, thank you very much.

Ianthe sucked her teeth at my father's words, "Champion, my hide. He's a lecherous little beast that has ruined the upcoming festivities. Do you know how much those embroidered emblems cost, Bracken?"

"Yes," my father replied drily. "I paid for them."

I remained silent, in no mood to goad my mother into slapping me again. My bruise had faded, but it didn't stop the shame and hurt from having been physically abused by her. My mother growled at my father, the sound rumbling from the base of her throat, but she stopped as Noa walked in.

Noa had been in our employ longer than I could remember, an older *maejym* who lived in a small cottage at the back of our estate. He was from Mortania—like Lydia, and a lot of the other household staff—but was married to an Agmantian, Grace, who managed the laundresses and other female attendants in our home.

Noa approached my father and handed him a stack of letters, informing him that further correspondence were in his study. He handed another pile to my mother, and as he walked around the table to my side he dropped something by my feet. Annoyed, I bent to pick it up, but saw it had my name on the front. I looked up to Noa, astonished,

"My apologies, Miss," he said gently as we both straightened at the same time, but I snuck the note onto my lap. Noa walked away without another word.

"You are expected at the Riadnak Manor after breakfast, Aspen."

My father's tone was conversational and should relax me, but all I could focus on was the paper, feeling like a stone against the fabric of my pants.

"Yes, Daddy."

After a few forced bites of food, I finally excused myself from the table, saying I needed to change to go to the Manor. I left the breakfast room, the paper secured in the pocket of my pants and went upstairs.

Safely in my room, I leant against the door and fished the note out. It hadn't been mailed, there was no postage, it was just a small, folded piece of paper with my name in capital letters. It smelled like coconut and sugar. I opened it and read the strong and decisive hand:

Cave. 9pm.

Before I could meet Caius, I had to see Sabre. I arrived at the Riadnak Manor a few hours after breakfast and was shown to his room. I knocked and after a few moments with no response, I gingerly opened the door and admitted myself. The curtains were drawn and a lone candle, burnt almost to the base, was on a side table by his bed. The low glow it emitted showed me there was a lump under the covers that I could only assume was Sabre.

I walked over, dressed in loose fitting cropped trousers and short sleeved shirt, my braids loose around my face. I sat on the bed closest to the lump and gently called out his name,

"Sabre?"

The lump shuffled and seconds later, amber eyes peered at me from beneath the covers, "Aspen?"

I gave him a quick smile as he removed the covers from around his head. When his face came into view, my smile dropped and a gasp escaped my lips.

"What happened?"

Sabre had been beaten. His face was swollen and coloured with bruises made worse by the wolfsbane still in his system.

"My father doesn't like losing."

When I'd gone to see him before the agility challenge, he'd been terrified that I was Goliath and now I knew why.

"What did he do to you?"

His voice low with the effort it took to talk. "He laced his fists with wolfsbane so they're taking longer to heal, that's all."

"That's all?" I replied sarcastically. "*That's all!*"

Sabre said nothing as he awkwardly got out of his bed. He hissed as he straightened himself and I could see that he was in indescribable pain.

"Sabre, he can't be allowed to get away with this!"

"Who's going to stop him, you?"

I remained silent as Sabre finally made it out of bed and staggered toward a dressing table where a pitcher and glass were situated. He went to pour himself a drink, but I quickly rushed over and did it for him. He thanked me with a nod and collapsed onto the nearby couch, where Olcan and Fenrir had been sitting the last time I was here. I handed him his water and watched him take an unsteady sip.

"Does he do this often?" I asked quietly.

Sabre shrugged, "Depends how often I disappoint him." He laughed, mocking himself but nothing about this was funny. Sabre lowered his glass and just stared off into the distance.

"Everything I do is for him," he finally said, still staring at nothing. "Everything I do and try to be is for him, but it's never enough."

I was horrified as tears dropped down Sabre's cheeks. I had never seen Sabre cry, not once. He was always so strong and sure of himself. Cocky and arrogant sure, but I'd never seen him broken.

"This is all I am, all I have," he continued as more tears fell. "If I lose the challenges—what then?"

I was stunned by the power that laced my next words, "This is not all you are Sabre. You have a choice to be anything you want to be. You *always* have a choice."

"How, Aspen?" Sabre glared at me with disbelief, like I was insane. I couldn't very well tell him to throw the competition. I knew he would never willingly lose.

"My father is the most powerful Alpha our kind has ever seen and I am his son, his only heir. Do you know what that means, what's expected of me?"

"Of course I know but that doesn't mean you have to let him beat you like this!"

I reached out to take his hand, but he shook the touch off him and got to his feet. He regretted that move soon after, as he winced at the pain and looked down at me irritably.

"My father's word is law and I have to obey him."

"Losing the challenge shouldn't count as disobeying him."

"Of course it does," he exclaimed. "My Alpha told me to win and I didn't deliver. I deserve this."

He gestured to his bruised face, his cut-up torso, a look in his eyes that showed his determination to believe this to be the truth.

"No," I said with emphasis, keeping from raising my voice in order to keep anyone from coming to check on us. I rushed to him, taking his face tenderly in my hands. "No one deserves to be beaten for failing. It's only human."

Sabre took hold of my hands and gently peeled them away from his battered face. The sadness and acceptance in his eyes were as damning as his words,

"That's just it," his voice croaked as tears fell. "We're not human Aspen—we're *laecan*."

I had nothing to say, nothing to comfort him with, and so I stood in silence, hoping to comfort him with my presence, while my heart was tearing for him.

And for what I still knew I wanted to do.

Sabre and I had more in common than I'd realised. We were both expected to do our duty to our kind at the cost of our own feelings. While it was great that I'd found something to draw me back to the man I'd loved for so long, it only highlighted that I now wanted to steal his purpose from him.

If Caius beat Sabre and freed us from the bonds of our duty, Sabre would be hurt for *our* choices and no one deserved that.

I looked at Sabre with unflinching clarity and knew that we couldn't both do our duty, serve our purpose and come out the other side unscathed.

I arrived at Caius' cave just before nine. I didn't see him outside but for the first time I saw a faint light coming from inside. Nervous that I was breaking his one rule, I approached and barked into the dark opening. My bark echoed into the cave and moments later, amber eyes and a black hide appeared in front of me.

...*you got my note*...

...*obviously*...

He *turned* and I did the same in response. I looked at him, unwilling to start the conversation, considering he'd invited me here, and so I waited.

"I'm sorry about what I said yesterday." He shifted his feet in the dirt. "It was cruel and unfair and I didn't mean it," he smiled cheekily. "At least not all of it."

I shrugged, but couldn't keep a smile down. He was always handsome, but when he smiled his eyes warmed in ways that I felt somewhere deep within me, something recognisable. It felt like it belonged to me, and only me.

"Would you like to come in?" he gestured to the cave and my eyes widened, smile broadening.

"Are you sure?"

He nodded and without needing any more convincing, I followed him inside. The tunnel was fairly dark, but there was a light source somewhere up ahead, which turned out to be a lantern, hanging by a nail punched into the rock, the candle inside fairly new. I understood that he'd lit it for me to know he was in here. We turned left, walking further into the cave, another lantern lighting the way until we finally emerged into a large space that completely surprised me.

Caius had made a den, but the large cavern had been furnished to suit him as both a wolf and a man. He'd covered the cavern floor with dirt and bark that smelled fresh, so he must change it regularly; in contrast, an indescribably large canopy bed stood against the curved back wall and underneath it was an ornate carpet, deep and soft, to place his human feet. I could judge even from the doorway that the bed could accommodate a full-sized wolf, but what took my breath away was the mountain of pillows and cushions that adorned it. The pillows were a mixture of dusky grey and gold, but the sheets and furs were black as night.

I moved my eyes from the bed to the large fire pit in the middle of the room, where logs crackled, warming the space. Three large cushioned chairs were placed around it and the rest of the room showed off a writing desk and chair, a small ornately carved table with two chairs, various cupboards and two large dressers, the latter two flanking either side of the bed. To my astonishment, there was a small area in the corner where water streamed directly out of the rock. It disappeared into a slightly raised platform on the floor.

As I continued to look around, I was amazed to see, cut into the cave walls on almost every side were shelves lined with books and scrolls as well as containers of who knew what. Moveable ladders were attached in order to get to the higher shelves and lanterns lined the highest ones so that the titles would be easily readable. The ceiling was so high above our heads I felt dwarfed just looking at it.

"Caius...this is...this is..."

"Garish?" he said, self-deprecatingly.

"Beautiful!" I gasped as I turned in a small circle, staring above us. "How high does it go?" I couldn't see the top.

"High," he laughed.

I lowered my head to look at him, but my eyes went to an opening cut into the wall behind him, "Where does it lead?"

"Well," a mischievous grin came onto his face. "I can't tell you all my secrets just yet."

He winked at me and I smiled, quickly averting my eyes. I ventured further into Caius' haven, toward the chairs by the fire, taking a seat.

"I come here to get away from everything," he said as I ran my fingers along the cushioned arm of the chair. "Sometimes it gets a little too much."

I nodded my agreement,

"I wanted to show you as a peace offering. I've never brought anybody here."

"Then what's with the chairs?" I joked as I cautiously took a seat in one.

Caius laughed good naturedly, but his answer wiped the smile off my face, "Hope, I guess."

Hope that someone would share it with him.

He was fidgeting, looking from me to his space in quick succession. I'd never seen him so uncertain and it was endearing. I tried to lighten the mood, "So, now that you have me here—what will you do with me?"

As soon as I said the words, I knew they were the wrong ones. I'd meant to tease, but it just sounded awkward and suggestive. I stood up and slowly walked over to him, watching his face set into a reluctant scowl.

"Caius."

"Yeah, we need to talk… about that."

"Fine. But I don't want to fight. Okay? We'll just… talk."

He nodded agreeably and walked back over to the chairs by the fire, gesturing me to take a seat beside him. I obliged and faced him expectantly. Caius took a deep breath. I could see the top of his chest peeking from underneath the loose cotton shirt he was wearing, and had to lick my lips. I struggled to push down my scent and so looked down at my intertwining fingers.

"Now that we know that… that we… that…" he stammered.

"That we want to have sex."

I kept my face as straight as possible, but when his mouth dropped open I couldn't keep the giggle down. Caius growled and stood up again, pacing the floor, "Grey, this isn't funny."

"Why not?"

"Because now you realise what's changed, other people might realise it too."

"What's changed?" I raised my eyebrow, keeping the smile on, unable to not feel mildly smug that he was growing so flustered, but Caius wasn't as amused. He lifted his hands and ran them through his short waves before pulling them down his face in distress, "You still don't know?"

Worry engulfed me as I answered, "Know what?"

Caius finally looked at me, his eyes tortured, "…that I'm your mate."

I didn't immediately answer, unsure what to say or believe. Your mate's soul and body were meant to be linked to yours for eternity.

And Caius was mine.

"How do you know this?" I knew I should have been more shocked by this but I just... wasn't. It felt right.

"Didn't you ever wonder why your mother didn't want you around me?"

"Because she's an elitist bitch who wants me to marry a Riadnak Alpha? It's all she wants."

"Yes, everyone knows what Ianthe Anai is about. Didn't you ever consider why she hated me so much?"

I hadn't. Not until very recently. Thankfully, Caius didn't make me admit that. He continued to watch me as he spoke, "Ianthe is threatened by me because she knows what the bond could make us do."

I can smell your intent all over you!

Have you given yourself to him?

My mother had known Caius was my mate. That's why she'd kept me from him. While the bond didn't mean I would choose Caius over all males, it did mean I would most likely be physically drawn to him more than others. If I'd allowed that to happen in my early teens, I could have easily given Caius my virginity and ruined all her plans. All she'd ever cared about was whether I was pure, because Goliath would never allow me to be with his son and heir if I was tainted. Him denouncing and banishing Tala for sleeping with someone Goliath deemed not worthy, was enough proof of that.

In that instant, I knew exactly how my mother had managed to control my mind: that Godforsaken tea. It had somehow dampened my attraction to Caius so that I wouldn't recognise him as my mate. It had made me physically sick to be around him. It had also inhibited whatever magical eyes Lady Xana had on me because she'd only approached me once I stopped drinking it.

"How long have you known?"

"Since I *turned*."

His confession hit me like a punch. Six years, he'd said. He meant how long I'd suppressed the pull of the bond.

"You thought I knew." It wasn't a question, but the guilt on his face was enough to answer me. I was angry, "You thought I knew and set you aside anyway."

"Would it have mattered if you did know?"

"We'll never know now," I snapped.

Silence once more. I'd meant that I didn't want to fight so I remain silent.

"Even though being mates doesn't obligate us to want each other, *laecan* can still smell it," Caius filled the silence while my mind whirled.

Caius was my mate.

"There are some *laecan* in Invernell who believe in the bond more than others—the Lacostes, Mrs Dune" Rhea's parent's and Susi's mother. "If they found out, then you and I could be seen as a power couple..." he used his fingers as rabbit ears as he said the last two words.

"They wouldn't want Sabre to be Alpha," I finished the sentence for him and Caius nodded, seemingly relieved that I was finally getting it.

At least now I had some clarity as to why I'd been feeling so lusty towards Caius recently. My body was calling out to him after having been denied him for so long. No longer with my Sabre blinders on, I was able to listen to my hormones, my blood, and realise what it wanted.

The wolf in me wanted Caius.

But did I want Caius?

The jury was still out on that one.

"Wait," my brain began to work as I stood up, remembering the reason I'd steered my paws here in the first place. I paced for a moment then turned back to him. "This fixes everything."

His eyebrows raised, "What? How?"

"Easy—you become the Alpha."

I'd thought this already but hadn't had a moment to put the motion to him. Caius stared at me before he burst out laughing, "Are you insane?"

He stormed away, shaking his head violently but I was not to be deterred.

"No, I'm not insane. How does this not make perfect sense to you?"

"Because its lunacy. Grey. I've already told you that I'm not going to become Alpha."

"Why not?" I whined.

"Because I don't want to be the leader of this fucked up society and our fucked up people that grovel and beg for scraps off Goliath's table," he growled at me, getting to his feet. "I don't want anything to do with trying to salvage what little good is left in this shithole. I just want out."

I was shocked at his vitriol, but not surprised, remembering how he'd left the clearing during the first challenge, as though wanting everyone to know how little he thought of them, of us, and our belief in the Triquetra rituals.

Still, I refused to back down, "But if you become Alpha—"

"You make it sound like winning the title immediately makes me Alpha," he cut me off, shaking his head at me. "I only get the title once Goliath dies and how do you think life will be for me and my family until then? You saw what happened after my win. Nobody wants me to be Alpha and they'll only make my life harder to prove it."

He wasn't wrong, of course. The high born Riadnak loyalists of this town were like vultures; scavengers for prime bits of meat and at the moment, that wasn't Caius. If he beat Sabre, they'd ostracise him, rally against his rule despite the shaman's magic. They couldn't stop it of course, but in the hundreds of years that a Riadnak had been crowned Alpha, they wouldn't accept a Gamma's ascension without some resistance.

"You just said some people would back us being mated."

"Do you want to start a civil war for something we don't even want?"

That hurt. That being with me or wanting me outside of the mating bond hadn't even crossed his mind.

"So we just let them win?" I asked softly. "I just let him have me?"

A very small, petty part of me rejoiced at the pain that I saw in Caius' eyes.

The jury were now deliberating…

"I know what I have to do," he said. "You need to walk your own path."

I hung my head, disappointed that my genius plan wasn't so genius. Caius stepped a little closer to me and focused his fiery eyes onto mine.

"I will not beat Sabre in the final challenge."

"Cai—"

"You have to come to terms with what comes after."

I felt the closeness of him like a soft wave of heat across my skin. It was something to get drunk on, intoxicating and highly addictive.

"What if I don't want to?" I murmured.

The jury in my head had reached a verdict but Caius only smiled,

"You'll get over it," he said softly, before reaching out and taking one of my braids between his fingers. "It's only biology after all."

I knew as soon as he said it, that he was so wrong, that this was so much more, and that somewhere along the paths we'd been running together, I had begun falling for him.

"Right," I said, with a soft huff, getting myself away from him as I turned around and headed for the mouth of the cave. "Biology."

In the case of Aspen Anai wanting Caius Caldoun, over Sabre Riadnak, how did I plead?

Guilty.

I returned home, and since I'd rushed dinner to go and see Caius, I was starving. I headed to the kitchen, passing the living, dining and breakfast rooms on my right and the drawing and music rooms on my left. As I approached the back stairs, ready to descend into the kitchen area, I heard a crash, followed by a shriek from my mother.

I hesitated for only a moment before I crept stealthily down the hall, bringing my ear to the door of the drawing room. My mother was always the loudest, but for once my father's voice was raised to match hers.

"How could you?" she yelled.

"*Calm down*, Ianthe."

"I will not calm down when you and that infuriating daughter of yours fight to destroy me with every breath you take."

"Stop being dramatic."

"Dramatic? What of my reputation? Known as the wife of the man who tried to blackmail the Alpha!"

"Don't worry, dear. Just suck Goliath's cock a little harder than usual. I'm sure he'll set you up after he gets rid of me."

I heard the slap through the door so clearly that my own head reared back. There was silence for a long time afterward. I held my breath, desperate not to be caught, but unable to leave.

"You haven't touched me in years. What did you expect?"

My hand was over my mouth and now it pressed even harder as the truth wasn't denied.

"Don't make this about me," my father retorted. "You were with him long before I fell out of love with you." It didn't seem my mother had a reply for that. "I did what was needed to get Lydia back to us, and to save face. I knew Goliath wouldn't take my threat to expose Tala lightly, but I admit, I didn't expect this."

Expect what?

"What are we going to do?" my mother asked.

"I am going to handle this and you are going to continue fucking Goliath. Stay in his good graces, *wife*. And keep us there with you."

I didn't stay to hear the rest. I was no longer hungry and ran upstairs to my room.

CHAPTER TWENTY-THREE

The girls were at my house again for training. Ulren was still unavailable so we had another elder filling in for him. After an intense run-through of the combative routine, we'd changed our staffs for swords, and I welcomed the lesson as a much-needed distraction.

After warming up with Koda, I paired with my sister. I'd had no inclination to speak to her recently. We stood before each other, swords in hand and I swiped at her first. Rogue blocked the blow, swinging out of it easily. I struck at her, but she parried gracefully and in the back of my mind I hated her for her skill. My sister was beautiful and graceful without having to try. I'd always been well aware of it, even if I never told her so. Everything was always so easy for her and in these tumultuous times it seemed I was finally the one stuck in feelings of envy.

I wondered then whether Rogue was privy to the dealings of our community, and whether she'd known about Goliath and Ianthe. She was always too secretive for me to know where her allegiances lay. I wanted to ask her, but I still wasn't sure how I felt, so kept that little nugget to myself for the moment. My mother could have done no wrong in my eyes only a few months ago and now I despised everything about her. She was a vindictive, spiteful, adulterous bitch and I couldn't trust her.

My sister and I continued our dance of swords, sweat dripping profusely. I was panting with the exhaustion from the training, but my anger over my mother's infidelity and how I felt like such a fool for believing everything she had ever told me, was like burning coals inside my ribcage. I wanted to hurt something. Or say something. Speak what I'd heard out loud and share the burden. I charged at my sister. Rogue dodged the attack, her long braid swooshing behind her like a black snake as she moved.

"Have you seen Dad this morning?" I asked as we broke away from each other, twisting the swords to loosen our wrists before she blocked.

"No, why?"

"No reason," I mumbled, gritting my teeth against her following overhead strike.

"Have you seen Caius this morning?" Rogue teased.

I snarled at her, "No, I haven't. Have you seen your *boyfriend*?"

Rogue stopped mid-swing, lowering her staff with a click of the end against the floor, holding it as she cocked an eyebrow, cool as ever, "What did you say?"

"I smell mimosa root on you all the time. Who is he?"

My sister laughed as she gave me a scornful look up and down, "Wouldn't you like to know?"

"Yes, actually,"

"Why? Pissed that I got there before you?"

"*No.*"

It came out too sharp, too telling, and there was nothing my sister missed. She was on me like a dog with a bone, smirking self-assuredly, "Don't worry, Aspen. You'll get to be a big girl soon enough."

Rogue laughed to herself before sauntering away, twirling the sword, apparently deciding lessons were over. As I continued staring at my sister's back, a messenger ran into the yard, heading straight to Koda. I saw her eyes fill with tears reading the note she'd been handed and I rushed over.

"What's going on?" I asked, still out of breath from my fight with my sister.

"It's Fenrir," she sobbed. "He's been hurt."

"Where, what happened?" Rhea asked the question before I could. The other girls looked on, distressed.

"The border. He was attacked. I have to go home."

"Miss, the lesson is not over."

"I think it is," I snapped at our teacher and returned my attention to Koda, "I'm coming with you."

I spent a few hours at Koda's house with the others before heading back home, in desperate need of freshening up, still in training gear from the morning and smelling like it too.

My time spent at the Lamentelle home had been helpful in my understanding of what was going on with the fighting. Goliath had *laecan*—including Fenrir and Olcan—travelling along the borders of Celestia to stop the threat of invasion from Faenym. As Sabre confessed to me, Ulren had been unleashed on a rather large force of Faenymese *laecan* and they'd finally retaliated. Fenrir, Sabre, Olcan and other Invernelli males had all been dispatched at one time or another, as well as *maejym* fighters like Lydia's son, Jacob.

So far, they had been victorious in their attempts to hold the Faenymese forces back, but Goliath's wolves, including Fenrir, had been hurt in their attempt to march on Boltese. I realised instantly that Caius had warned Boltese after I gave him the information. They'd been prepared for the attack and Goliath's wolves had been foiled. I'd helped them get one over on Goliath, but in the process, I'd got Fenrir hurt.

I learned all of this through Sabre, although the details were pulled mainly from Rhea's questioning. It seemed in his shock and upset over Fenrir, he was a lot more forthcoming about giving information. Olcan, enraged by being outsmarted by the Boltesians, was also a lot more talkative.

As we waited for news of Fenrir's recovery, I caught snippets of conversation between Goliath and Fenrir's father, Runan. He was furious that his son had been hurt and I watched intently as Goliath tried to calm him down. He'd refused to be conciliated until Goliath had dragged him into a room and slammed the door shut. Needless to say, I'd no idea what was said behind that particular door. When I'd tried to approach it, Sabre had intervened, blocking my path with a reproachful look. He'd been distant with me since our conversation so I didn't push.

Before leaving, I heard that we'd lost *maejym* lives and countless other *laecan* were injured. Goliath planned on taking his revenge. What I found interesting, was that while it was clear to all who were admitted to the house who we were fighting, no one seemed to question why we were fighting them.

If Faenym were an ally, why were they fighting us and if Boltese had no prior issues with Celestia, then why were they at our door? Noone questioned it, and so it was obvious that most in this room, myself included, were the ones who knew the true nature of Goliath's plans. Whether they all agreed with them was a different story.

Once I'd returned home and washed and changed, I finally had a moment to myself. I would have to speak to Caius about what I'd heard at the Lamentelle's, but I'd also have to approach the subject of him being my mate.

Being his mate didn't mean I was obliged to want him, but I *did* want Caius. There was no denying that. At the very least I wanted to kiss him. At the most I wanted to devour him. There was no other way to describe the lascivious things I wanted to do, to and with him. There was, however, the tiny problem of being intended for Sabre and my mother killing me if she ever got wind of my intentions to jilt him.

As I sat across the table from her that evening at dinner, I battled internally not to glare at Ianthe with intense hatred for her betrayal of me and my father. It didn't matter that my father knew—she was a hypocrite and a whore and I despised her. For keeping me from Caius, making my father a fool and lying to me about her true nature.

I picked at the food on my plate. Usually my favourite, but the curried chicken and fluffy white rice held no appeal as I stewed on how much I hated my mother. She was babbling on about some event or other that she'd attended last night. None of us cared, but she didn't care that we didn't, as long as she got to speak.

I'd had enough.

"I won't be attending any more classes."

I declared, finally looking up from my plate. My father cleared his throat after taking a sip of wine, my mother simply glared at me.

"Excuse me, Aspen, I was speaking."

"I don't care. I won't be going back to classes."

My father continued looking at me while my mother lowered her cutlery to steeple her fingers together. She stared across the table,

"Okay Aspen, I'll bite. How do you intend to pass the required classes without attending?"

"Oh, I don't know. I thought you could talk to Goliath for me and get him to make an exception." I made sure I was looking her straight in the eye. "Since you're both *so* close."

It took a second but I saw the moment she realised what I meant. In an instant, her brown eyes went from dark intent to sheer horror, without even blinking. She looked at my father then back to me.

"Aspen, it's no—"

"Don't," I hissed at her. "Don't you dare lie."

Ianthe's eyes darted around the room at the few servants who waited on us. I didn't remove my focus from her as she tried to find her way out of this.

"Everyone," my father chimed in. "Will you excuse us." It wasn't a request, and immediately, the staff ushered out of the dining room. "You too, Rogue."

"No," my sister said with a laugh, a wine glass in hand beside my mother. "I'm not going anywhere."

My father sighed, but didn't push it. I still hadn't looked away from Ianthe, but she refused to look over at me.

"Aspen, I don't know what you think you know…" my father began but I finally averted my stare and turned my angry eyes on my father, "Don't patronise me. I heard enough."

"I didn't hear anything, do tell," Rogue encouraged.

"Rogue, please." My father looked tired but I didn't pity him. He may have known about Ianthe's infidelity, but he'd allowed it to continue without consequence.

"Rogue," I finally turned to my sister. "Our mother has been fucking Goliath and Dad knows."

"Mum!" Rogue turned wide eyes to Ianthe, wine still in hand. She was having a great time with the revelation, but I didn't fault her for it. If I'd been her, I would have been loving it too.

"Rogue, you don't understand."

"Oh, she understands, we all understand. Goliath has always been the prize for you. Pushing me to be an Alpha bride so you could live out some sordid fantasy through me. Knowing you would never be anything more than Goliath's whore!"

"Aspen!"

Rogue shuddered to hide her laughter behind her wine glass, even as my father tried to reprimand me. I ignored him and stood from my chair.

"I meant what I said about classes. I'm not going and you can't make me. Not anymore."

"What do you expect us to do?" my mother finally cracked and turned her hateful eyes onto me. "You're required by law to complete them."

"You're required by law to remain faithful to your husband, but that didn't stop you!"

A resounded hush fell on the room, "You can't threaten the Alpha, Aspen." I saw the barely perceptible look my mother shot at my father, before returning her face to mine.

"I'm not threatening the Alpha...I'm threatening *you*." I let that sink in for the moment. "Do whatever you need to save face Mother...but you won't be controlling me anymore."

With that, I stood from my chair and strode out of the dining room. I hadn't quite made it to the door when I heard my sister call out my name. I stopped in the hallway but I didn't turn around to face her,

"Aspen, wait."

Rogue caught up, stopping in front of me and looking confused,

"What do you want?"

"How did you find out…about mum?"

"Does it matter?"

She shrugged, "I guess not, but…"

"But what?" I was in no mood for any of this anymore.

Rogue looked uncertain as she cast her eyes down, looking at her feet rather than at me. This was odd. My sister was always so sure of herself and her disdain for me, so what had changed? She finally lifted her head, "Mum may have had her reasons."

"For cheating on Dad?"

"For wanting Goliath."

Something happened between us in that moment that I couldn't readily explain. While I didn't think my sister was justifying my mother's actions, she was attempting to understand them and I didn't agree at all. Our difference in opinion created an even bigger chasm between us that right then, I didn't even want to cross. If Rogue could find common ground with Ianthe for what she had done, then she was worse than her.

"Status isn't everything."

"You can say that since you've always had it," she replied.

"You're a Beta, just like me."

"But I'm *not* just like you. I'm not the Female!"

"Do you want me to apologise for that?"

"No."

"Then what *do* you want?" I screamed, tired of constantly having my title thrown back in my face.

"I want you to understand where mum might be coming from…because I do. Always being in the shadows, always being less. Dad didn't deserve to get cheated on, but mum is entitled to feel wanted."

I sucked my teeth in annoyance, "Wanted? If she needed to feel wanted she could have tried to get back with Dad. Failing that, she could have spread her ass for any other man."

Rogue pursed her lips together defiantly, but I continued.

"Don't kid yourself into thinking this is about being loved. This is about power and Ianthe wanting to feel like she's better than everybody else. She wants to be wanted by Goliath. She wants to be wanted by power. Nothing else matters to her."

I looked my sister up and down, disgusted by her, "If you can understand that…I pity how you see yourself."

I didn't give her the chance to reply. I walked away from her, leaving her looking for some form of understanding I knew I would never be able to give.

CHAPTER TWENTY-FOUR

A while later, I lay on the floor of Caius' den in my wolf form. I'd run all the way, desperate to get away from the hypocrisy and humiliation of my family. It made me feel so ashamed. Of who I'd been, who my mother had tried to turn me into.

Now, I had just over a month to figure out how I was going to spin the situation I was in. I had no idea where to begin, and since getting Caius to be Alpha was out of the question, unless I found a way to get Invernell to defunct hundreds of years of tradition, I was out of the more obvious options.

As if in answer to my thoughts of him, Caius' scent teased the air around me and I lifted my head toward the cave entrance. His scent was everywhere in this place, but the addition of the musky hint of warm rain told me the scent of his coat was new. He bounded into the den and stopped sharply as he saw me lying there, staring over at him. He was wet, tiny droplets of rain falling from his fur, wetting the dirt beneath his paws.

...*hi*... I said, walking over to him, close enough for our noses to touch.

...*hi*...

We both stood watching each other until I moved forward and lightly stroked my head against his. Caius went rigid as stone, unmoving as I made my display of affection. If he rejected this, I would let it go, but I prayed he didn't. I didn't want to put him in an awkward position, but I wanted to let him know that I was happy to see him. I was about to retreat, to give up, when almost indiscernibly, he tilted his head into mine. Relief flooded through me as we rubbed our massive heads against one another until, reluctantly, I took a step away from him.

...*is it okay that i'm here?*...

...*my cave is your cave*... came his sultry voice into my head. If I had been human, I probably would have blushed. ...*come outside with me*...

...*it's raining*...

...*that's why i want you to come with me*...

I was hesitant ...*all right*...

Caius padded away from me to head back out the cave, his large and bushy tail flowing rather elegantly behind him. I followed, unsure what to make of this, until we came to the mouth of the cave. It was pouring down, but in true Agmantian style, the rain was warm, quenching the country of its thirst.

Caius turned to me, ...*try to keep up*...

Without another word, he darted out of the cave and into the showery night, giving me no choice but to follow. Though the moon didn't make us *laecan*, the power she emanated was part of the make-up of wolves and so we held it in high regard. At night, our vision, hearing and sense of smell were always heightened thanks to her influence on us.

As Caius and I ran, she hung in the sky above us, giving the clouds an iridescent glow, even as they pummelled us with raindrops as hard as pebbles, bouncing off our powerful hides as we ran, drenching our coats and the surrounding terrain as we barrelled through. Caius was ahead of me, darting up and over fallen trees and tearing through bushes and mud like a hand through water.

I marvelled at his powerful black hide as my paws pummelled the ground and my claws tore up the earth underneath me to keep up with him. Everything about my body followed him: my eyes, my ears, the thumping of my beating heart as my need for him coursed through my veins.

Caius' powerful frame bounded between trees, then from one raised rock to another as I kept pace. My muscles stretched and ached with the force of running, but I revelled in the activity. I rarely exhausted my lupine form like this and it was exhilarating. My mother didn't encourage it and being with Sabre never gave me any cause. Being *laecan* was something I simply was, but I'd forgotten to feel truly blessed by the power that lived within me.

With a brief look to my changing surroundings, I finally realised we were climbing as Caius took me up the side of a mountain, so high that when I chanced a look down, I saw a misty and dark canopy beneath us. I wasn't afraid. I was a powerful beast, capable of traversing across the terrain of my land, but I was apprehensive as to our destination. Higher we bounded until we arrived on a plateau of rock, overlooking the expansive lands of our home.

With my wolf eyes, I saw for miles. Through the mist and smoke of lower hanging clouds, I made out the top of the Arena. I turned in amazement at the wonder of nature around us and how far we had run in so short a time. I spotted the dim lights of towns in the distance and smoke from homes and businesses hidden beneath the canopy. My large lungs filled with the balmy air up here as I took in the glorious view. Rain continued to fall, but up here, it had lessened somewhat. I turned in awe and fascination until I faced the Ecacia Mountains that ran like a spine through the province of Boltese. Tala was likely there with Sire and for a brief moment, my heart ached from missing her.

...*caius...this is beautiful*...

Reluctantly I tore my attention away from the glorious view to where Caius and I had originally approached. I was startled to find him standing in front of me, as a man. His clothes were soaked through, clinging to every ripple and defined line over his body as he took deep and steadying breaths. My heart was pounding, my lungs trying to slow down from our run, but as I watched him, watching me, my legs began to tremble. Never taking my eyes away from him, I turned and stood before him in my usual tight pants and loose shirt. I'd not planned to see him this evening, even while pining for him in his cave, so I didn't look my best.

The rain continued to beat down, wetting my shirt so that my braless breasts and now peaked nipples were unashamedly on display. Thankfully, my braids were tied securely in a ponytail, so the sodden locs weren't intrusive. Caius and I watched each other for a handful of drawn out moments, his eyes betraying nothing.

They didn't have to.

His scent did.

I felt Caius' want wash over me like a ray of sunlight. It warmed me, thrilled me and had me struggling to draw breath. Leisurely, he took the required steps toward me, raindrops slipping down his face as he approached, until I had to tilt my head to keep my gaze in his. The fire there was so intense, so purposeful, I shook with anticipation. A ring of gold appeared in his eyes and I knew he was holding back something, something powerful.

I reached out, taking his soaked shirt into both hands, crumbling the material in to my fists as I pulled him into me. My nipples brushed against the hard plains of his chest and I felt his erection against my stomach. I made a sound, I didn't know what to call it, but it escaped me anyway, just as I closed my eyes and...Caius kissed me.

Caius placed his large firm hands on my hips, squeezing me against the swell in his pants and *kissed* me.

His lips felt like feathers, as soft as silk and smooth as warmed chocolate, even as we stood in seemingly unending torrential rain.

I didn't care.

I didn't care about anything as I pushed my arms up between us so I could wrap them around his neck, pulling him even closer. His tongue toyed with mine, the slick heat of it, a tether to this glorious moment between us that I never wanted to end. He sucked on my tongue, my lips, leaving small bites as his hands roamed and found the swell of my behind. He squeezed it once, then again and on the third squeeze, he pushed so that his member pressed into me. He moaned then, low in his throat, a deep and sensual sound as my fingers held his head against mine.

Caius sucked on my bottom lip, but when he eventually pulled away, he pressed his forehead against mine. We were both breathing erratically, our chests rising and falling so harshly I could hear our laboured breathing over the rain.

"Let's go back to the ca—"

"No," he cut me off. "...we can't."

My head was still to fuzzy from our kiss; the most amazing kiss of my life. "W-why not? I want to."

If that was in any way unclear, I had to let him know, Sabre and my mother be damned. But, to my horror, Caius slowly let his hand drop from around me before taking my arms down from around him.

"Caius?"

He looked at me then and the anguish that stared at me from those beautiful blazing eyes was disarming, "We can't, Grey. This was a—"

"Don't."

He sighed deeply as he took another step back, as though he were trying to distance himself from the want. Well, I wouldn't let him and stepped into his space again,

"You want this as much as I do," I growled at him, angry that he was spoiling such a perfect moment. Lightning flashed and lit up his dark face.

His tortured look was illuminated for me to see, "Of course I want this!" he called out over the rolling thunder that followed. "It's why I brought you here."

He stretched out his arms at the downpour around us and I quickly understood: the rain would wash his scent away from me and mine from him. We could smell each other because we were practically sharing oxygen a moment ago, but once we left, the scents would fade and no one would be any wiser about what we'd done.

"I wanted this when I shouldn't have and I'm so, sorry, Grey… but it can't happen again."

"Why not? Why can't I choose this for myself, just like you said?"

"Because you're not choosing me," Caius shouted above the rain and the wind. "You're just *not* choosing him."

His accusation landed hard, as his words tended to do, and I was suddenly unsure of myself, my motivations for being here, for kissing him back, for wanting him. Was he nothing but a signpost? An arrow that I expected would point me in the right direction? Toward my way out of my life? He'd told me he couldn't be that for me. He'd told me so many times.

But his pull was magnetic. My first urge was to reach out for him, to mimic the tender greeting we'd shared earlier in wolf form and let him know that there was more here for me. Now I wondered if there was more for him.

As if he'd heard my thoughts he said, "I want you…"

My eyes shot to his, but there was a barrier there now that hadn't been there before.

"...but I won't share you. Not with him."

He expected me to choose. And choosing him meant foregoing the title of Female for good, which meant most likely angering the shaman and having our family's safety severely threatened by our outright disobedience of Goliath.

Caius *turned* and I knew the conversation was over. He turned back the way we came but looked back at me, waiting for me to follow.

CHAPTER TWENTY-FIVE

The journey back to the cave was a tense one.

I had the time to mull things over but as he kept quiet, wanting me to make the choice for myself, it seemed we no longer had anything to say to each other. We'd shared a beautiful moment, but I was growing painfully aware of why it couldn't be repeated. I'd let my emotions run away with me, and there was too much at stake for us to give in to our base feelings for one another. I wanted to see where this thing could go, but there was no room for it.

My duty and my future was as clear as it had ever been: Sabre was going to win the Mating Games and I was promised to the victor.

Caius and I entered the cave and both *turned*. The rain had stopped during our return, but our clothes were still wet and despite my warm *laecan* blood, I felt a little chill.

"I'll get the fire going." Caius murmured without looking back at me.

"Don't bother," I said, then realised the words sounded rather surly. "I mean, the rain was meant to help with the scent. If I dry off here it will come back."

"I doubt you want to explain why you were wet in the first place." Caius knelt by the stone ringed fire and picked up the pieces of flint. "Just dry off and make sure to run through some aloe before you go back."

"Aloe?"

Curious, I moved toward the hearth, watching the first sparks of the flame.

"Yeah, the bitter scent will mask you enough to get to your room, at least."

I smiled, "How do you know that?"

"Ulren. Herbs and Vegetation last year." Caius got the fire started and blew into the rising flame. I smiled at his answer, though this time rather sheepishly.

"I guess I wasn't paying attention that lesson," I admitted.

Caius shook his head as he continued to stoke the fire, "No. You were lip-locked with Sabre at the time, I think."

He was only teasing, but I didn't like it, "Can we not talk about him right now? Please?"

He lifted his eyes to me with an apologetic expression and nodded his agreement.

Once the fire was going strong, he left me standing by it and went to collect some more wood. He placed the pieces strategically and once satisfied, he grabbed the hem of his shirt and lifted it over his head. I tried not to react, but because the movement came without warning I couldn't help the longing that bloomed inside me at the sight of his body. Without paying any attention to me, Caius draped his shirt over the back of one of the chairs, then turned it so the shirt faced the fire.

"Hand me your shirt," he adjusted the other chair before looking over at me. "I can dry you—"

I didn't avert my eyes as I watched him realise how his idea wasn't going to happen. My hands on my hips, I shrugged which lifted my bare breasts through my shirt as I moved.

"Unless you have another shirt…" I said.

We both knew that wouldn't work, his scent would be all over it. I watched Caius swallow down his want, although his eyes couldn't deny the effect the sight of my body had on him.

"Sit as close to the fire as possible then."

He walked away from me, towards his bed. So not to distress him anymore, I went and sat in one of the chairs closest to the fire. My back now to him, I stretched my legs out, listening to him move behind me. It was obvious he was changing his clothes and it took everything inside me not to turn around and look.

Well, I never was that strong willed a person and so I quickly leaned over the arm of my chair to look behind me and caught the profile of Caius' ass cheek just as he was pulling on some pants. I slammed my legs together as the connection between them began to pulse.

Shit! Hopefully he wouldn't smell it.

"It's fine."

I nearly jumped out of my skin as he took a seat in the chair opposite me, his back to the fire.

"What's fine?"

"Your scent doesn't bother me."

I didn't reply. Looking at Caius now, he seemed so much older than his nineteen years. I envied his maturity. We were the same age but I had lived in ignorance for so long, I was still a little girl where Caius was a man.

"Where were you coming from earlier?" I asked, looking into the fire, crackling in front of me. My toes were warming in my boots and I wiggled them against the leather. I didn't look over at Caius, but heard him take a deep breath.

"I was in Faenym. I had a meeting with some people."

"…What kind of people?"

I chanced a look at him and he was looking back. There was a question in his eyes, but it wasn't one that I could answer. He had to trust me on his own. His heated gaze bore into my soul. I had to lick my lips and take a steadying breath to stop myself thinking about how his mouth had felt on mine.

"I met Isaac Akando. He wants to overthrow Goliath."

Well, that brought all sexual thoughts in my head to a screeching halt. My heart began to race, but I tried not to get too excited that he was sharing this with me.

"Overthrow him?"

Isaac was Barbas Akando's son, and if he thought or knew that Goliath killed his father then it was natural for him to want revenge. If he planned to make no secret of his intentions, then it would definitely mean war.

"It won't be easy, but we need to reduce Goliath's power before he takes over the entire country."

"How do you expect to do that? He is the Alpha of all *laecan*."

"All *laecan*, not all Agmantia, which is what he wants: to rule everyone, *maejym* included. If he succeeds, he'll be unstoppable. We can't let that happen."

Goliath really was power mad if he thought he could achieve this. As the enormity of his intent settled within me, I realised that if he did succeed, that put me in his camp of traitors. Sabre was Goliath's heir and I was meant to be with Sabre. If this continued how most wanted, then one day, I could truly be a queen.

"How do you plan to stop it? Goliath is too powerful."

"With the combined forces of Boltese, Aulandri, Voltaire and Faenym we could defeat Goliath."

I was confused, "Then why are Faenym attacking alone? Fenrir got hurt in the fight with Boltese but they could have worked together."

Caius raised an eyebrow and I explained what I knew about the attack and he confirmed the information I'd given, had been advantageous in them being able to defend themselves.

"Isaac has, shall we say, different plans. Despite what Goliath wants people believing, Faenym started out defending themselves, but now it's turned into something else."

After a moment, I asked, "Would you fight?"

"Sabre and I aren't expected to do much since we're Triquetrians. I help where we can, I just don't do a lot of long term harm to the other side. Sabre has his own issues for doing what he does."

He was playing both sides. Being loyal to Celestia while aiding the people who attacked us. I wasn't sure if I should yell at him or praise him. It also never dawned on me how much time Sabre and Caius might have actually spent together, doing whatever Goliath had the males get up to.

"I'm also included in plans to stage a coup, it's why I met Isaac in the first place—to get rid of Goliath once and for all."

My heart stopped. This was… this was huge. If he could actually pull this off, there would be an uproar like I'd never witnessed. How would our community continue without our leader, even if he was a murdering psycho?

"How many of you are there?"

Caius' eyes didn't leave mine as he said, "Two thousand."

"Wolves?" He didn't blink. "Two thousand wolves are going to invade our home?" Invernell in comparison housed almost six thousand standardly and not all of those were able, fighting wolves.

"You wanted to know what was going on—there it is."

I shifted in my seat, confusion and a trickle of fear running through me, "I still don't understand how you expect to get him out of power or who would take his place. Being the Alpha is what he was born into. It's his right."

"He's abusing that right, Aspen. No matter the *laecan* laws or the prophecies. Since he's been in power, Goliath has abused every privilege his position has given him. He's stolen money from other communities, he's made life miserable for the poor and immigrants with raised taxes and extortionate and unnecessary fines. Not to mention, he's murdered a province leader, possibly two."

He meant Barbas Akando and, most recently, Porvi Belau of Amniare. She still hadn't been seen.

"He has to be stopped and the only way to do that is to be stronger than him."

I understood what Caius was saying, but I couldn't get my head around what I'd been told repeatedly my entire life: Goliath was all powerful, there was no one who would ever oppose him. The love for tradition and the fear of him wouldn't allow people to go against him. Caius had said as much when I proposed he be Alpha instead.

Even if his two thousand wolves tore the loyalists to pieces, if we deposed Goliath, what kind of world would we leave behind?

"You have to have more than brute strength."

"Excuse me?"

"I'm not an expert in rebellions, but even I know that you can't win this just by fighting alone. From what I've learned, Goliath is fighting and winning *now*, so why will this be any different?"

Caius finally looked away from me, shoulders slumping. I didn't know what hurt had taken over him, but I watched the energy slip out of him like smoke writhing from a blown-out candle.

"We have more. But it's a wild card."

"What kind of wild card?"

He turned and snarled at me, "One that isn't any of your business."

Caius stood from his chair and marched over to his bed to get away from me. I got to my feet, looking over at him and felt my heart go out to him. I didn't know what burden he bore, but it was a weighty one. He'd been fighting a war longer than I'd known it was going on and in this moment, there was just nothing I could do.

"I don't know if it will help with anything, but my father is somehow threatening Goliath."

I saw his head lift from where he'd been looking down at the floor, and so I told him about what I'd heard my father say—that he was going to take care of Goliath. I also told him about my mother and her nightly activities with the Alpha.

"Maybe you can use that for something. I'm going home."

I made it all the way to the cave entrance before he called out to me, but I didn't turn around to look at him. It hurt too much to look into his beautiful, tortured face and not be able to kiss him. I needed to kiss him. I'd never wanted to stop kissing him, but I knew it wasn't fair to Caius or myself, if that kiss could never be anything more.

"I want to take the easy way," he said from somewhere behind me. "I want to be able to kiss you again, but it won't matter if I can't keep you at the end of it."

"Keep me?" I finally turned to face him and he was right behind me, our chests inches apart as he stared into my emerald green eyes.

"Tell me I can."

His plea was guttural as my breath caught in my throat. I wanted to say the words, more than anything. He was so close now, the heat from him blending with mine. "Tell me that Sabre doesn't matter. That you're going to walk out that door and throw this whole stupid prophecy away. Tell me I can keep you."

I felt an exhilaration at the thought of it, at claiming it, saying it, but I faltered, and retreated from him, too afraid to take that leap.

"…I can't."

He returned his eyes to mine and my heart raced, as a lonely tear fell. I didn't know why I cried except I knew I wouldn't like what Caius was going to say next. For a moment, he kept his eyes in mine and there was still hope, but then he looked away, and my tears spilled over.

"We can't see each other anymore, Grey."

"Caius…don't."

"Don't come back to the cave, my house. Just stop."

"Please…you're my only friend."

"I can't be the one to save you, Grey." He looked at me with an intense sadness and regret in his eyes, "Not anymore."

He walked away from me and headed toward the back of the cave where an opening was cut into the rock. How had our amazing kiss turned into this?

I waited until he disappeared through the dark hole, then, with tears streaming down my face, I *turned*, and made my way home.

When I left my bathroom an hour or so later and sat at my vanity table getting ready for bed, there was a knock on my bedroom door. Without waiting for an answer, it opened, and my father entered, closing the door gently behind him. I continued taking out the damp braids at the front of my head, redoing them one at a time. I would have to get them redone properly since I got them wet, but that could wait.

My father walked quietly around my room, picking up and putting down various items he found on table tops and in half-open drawers, looking for what, I didn't know. When he finished his search of my personal belongings, he came and sat on my bed, directly behind me in the mirror. I didn't acknowledge him, but he spoke anyway.

"I met your mother when I was seventeen and married her only three years later. You came along almost immediately. I was so in love with her."

Thanks for that mental image, Dad.

But he had a wistful look in his eye as he looked down at his hands, resting against his thighs.

"You see, your mother…she'd always had ambitions but because of her previous station, she could never quite make it to where she wanted to be."

My mother never spoke about her family. She'd told us they were all dead, but I suddenly had the sneaky suspicion that wasn't exactly true.

"Your mother and I are mates, Aspen, but as you know, not all mates fall for each other. In our case…I was the one who came up lacking."

I ended my braid and turned to my father. I'd never known my parents were mates.

"I loved her immediately, but Ianthe, she didn't have the same affections for me in the beginning. I thought I could change her, make her see me instead of the title she craved, but she…she could never get over the idea of wanting more."

He finally looked up at me.

"What are you trying to tell me, Dad?"

"I'm trying to tell you that sometimes going after what you want isn't always the right thing to do. You've seen what your mother's lust for Goliath has done to our marriage."

"And what is it you think I want?"

"Caius Caldoun."

Okay, Dad. Two can play this game.

"Well, he is my mate. What difference does it make if I want to be with him?"

My father's eyes steeled against me, but I didn't back down. He wouldn't apologise for keeping it from me and I wouldn't apologise for finding out.

"The difference, young lady, is that if you follow your heart instead of doing your duty, you will start a war that you cannot hope to win."

I swallowed, staring back at my father. Bracken Anai stood from my bed so he towered over me and looked down into my now hateful eyes, "We shouldn't have kept him from you, I tried to rectify that in the beginning, but your mother is right. No matter her shortcomings and the love I no longer have for her, she is right. We all have a part to play in this life, Aspen, and yours is a lot bigger than ours. No matter what you think you feel or know or want, you will do you duty."

It didn't matter that he was right or that I'd decided this for myself. I wouldn't let him dictate to me like this, "I wo—"

"You. Will."

The worlds rumbled in my father's chest and I physically recoiled from the power and rage I felt seeping out of him.

"I tried to give you some freedom, but you leave me no choice."

"Dad?"

"Until Sabre has won the challenge and been announced as Alpha Apparent, you will not leave this house without an escort from now on."

"Dad!"

"You will return to classes, where you will be watched to make sure you spend no time with Caius."

My entire body shook as tears gathered in my eyes, my lips trembled with rage and I glared daggers at my father.

"You will spend more time with Sabre. I won't have you bringing this family any further down then you already have with rumours."

"Daddy," I cried, not sure how to handle my father actually becoming my mother. Why was he doing this? He hated Goliath himself, why wasn't he on my side?

My father shook his head, "When the time comes, you will do your duty and you will give Sabre an heir. Do I make myself clear?"

"Daddy, please, I swear I'm—"

"Do I make myself clear, Aspen?"

My father's voice rumbled through my room, making the few freestanding objects, shake where they stood. I wanted to fight, to reject the unfairness of it all, but as I looked into my father's eyes, I saw the sheen of tears there and understood that there was more at work here then I was ready for. With a trembling heart, my tears continued to fall and I muttered, "Yes, Sir."

As my father left my room, damning me and my impending future I knew that I had picked a side.

I'd been toeing the line with my feelings for Caius and Sabre and where my loyalties truly lay, but, knowing what I knew about the attacking *Iaecan* and choosing not to tell my father to save myself, my line had been drawn, and my family wasn't on my side of it.

CHAPTER TWENTY-SIX

True to his word, my father didn't let me out of the house without an escort. From my room to meals, to classes and even to the Bane, I was not allowed anywhere on my own. The sanctuary of my bedroom had become my prison. I needed an escape and in the current conditions, only the Riadnak Manor could offer that to me. Sabre had suddenly become my refuge and ironically, my father didn't trust me to be the dutiful daughter while in a class of my peers, yet trusted me implicitly behind a closed door with a boy.

It enraged me, being with Sabre, knowing that I wanted to be somewhere else, with *someone* else. Where once I was the one pestering him for intimacy, he was constantly trying to be close to me and I was running out of excuses to avoid it. It wasn't that I was no longer attracted to him, but being with Sabre in a sexual way after kissing Caius just felt wrong. I had to find a way out of this situation before it went too far.

I lay on Sabre's bed, feet bare, reading a book: *The Autobiography of Erina Anai*. He stood at the end of the bed throwing three daggers into a target board at the other end of his large room. He was restless, as was I, but I wouldn't draw his attention to making me his entertainment.

"So," he said, returning from retrieving his daggers and taking aim to throw again. "Are you going to tell me what's wrong or should I just wait for you to reject me again?"

I took a deep, inward sigh as I closed my eyes, ready for the ensuing argument. I didn't want to fight, I just wanted to be out of my house for a while. I lifted my head to look over at Sabre, who threw his first dagger into the target board. It missed the centre by mere inches.

"Nothing's wrong," I reassured.

"I doubt that." He threw the second dagger and while much close to the bullseye, it still wasn't a direct hit. He adjusted himself to throw again, "Whenever you're here, we barely talk, and its only ever about my father. When I try to touch you, there's always some excuse, so…what is it?" Sabre threw the final dagger at the target and missed it entirely.

Since talking with Caius I'd been trying to get information out of Sabre in order to help the cause, but it had all been pretty tame. During our time together, all Sabre had revealed was that Goliath would be away until immediately before the challenge because there was more unrest in Faenym and Boltese. Sabre hadn't mentioned the number of wolves or anything else. Goliath and a hundred of his personal guard had set out to the neighbouring province to quell the threat, but Sabre hadn't told me how or if any more would be joining him.

It didn't matter that I'd got this information, when there was no way I could tell Caius about it. Everywhere I went I was watched. Even in classes, when he was only two feet away from me, it was impossible to communicate with him.

"I just haven't been feeling great," I finally said, knowing Sabre was waiting for an answer. It was a feeble excuse and he knew it. The way he turned his head to glare at me, I could tell he wasn't going to let this rest. He'd let it go too many times already. I put my book down and shifted uncomfortably on the bed. I straightened against his fluffy pillows and stared right back, unwilling to show how nervous he made me. Sabre stalked over and climbed on the bed so he was sat beside me, his legs hanging off the side.

"Aspen, I can't help you if you don't tell me what's wrong."

"I told you what's wrong."

"Well I don't believe you!" he snapped, his eyes flashing with the anger he was holding back. "We're going to be mating in two days and you're more distant with me now than you've ever been."

Three days.

Three days until my birthday and I would mate with Sabre, my womb would quicken with his seed and my duty would be done. It was all pre-ordained that we would mate on our shared birthday and that the event was the only way to sire the next true heir. A few short months from now, I would be a mother.

"I'm not distant," I mumbled. "I just don't want to upset my parents."

"What about upsetting me?"

"Is that all that matters to you?" I sneered at him,

"No, you matter to me. That's why I want to help you and you won't let me in."

When I looked at Sabre then, I felt guilty for making him feel this way. He didn't deserve to be kept in the dark, no matter how much my feelings had changed about him. He had his own pressures and I was only adding to them.

"I don't want my parents to be mad. They really laid into me. Why do you think I'm here? It's the only place they'll let me be alone."

"Exactly—with me. The only place you're allowed to be, is with me."

Shit!

Sabre leaned forward so his arms were either side of my outstretched legs. His new position brought his face a little closer to mine. His blazing gold eyes shimmered with intent as he licked his lips at me, lifting his hand, tracing the pad of his thumb over my plump bottom lip, before gently pushing it into my mouth.

God, please, don't do this to me...

I sucked on his thumb like I would have usually done as he retreated it from between my teeth and wet my lips with my own saliva.

"Three days...why wait?" his voice had grown so husky with want for me. I could smell it on him, and embarrassingly I could smell it on myself. Again, his thumb traced my lip until he pushed his way in and I sucked it once more. He played with my tongue and my lips as I sucked, until he finally removed his thumb from my mouth and leaned forward to kiss me. He moved closer to me on the bed as the kiss deepened, desperate not to break the connection of our hot and tender mouths. He reached between us and began unbuttoning my blouse. In seconds, his hands were inside my clothes, massaging and kneading my breasts as he devoured me in a flurry of sucks, nips and bites.

"S-s-sabre," I panted as he began kissing down my neck and onto my chest. With an expert finger, he popped my left breast out of my bra and brought the hard bud of my nipple between his lips. He continued working one breast with his hand while the other was teased between his teeth.

"We c-can't do this," I panted, gently pushing at him.

He stopped, thankfully, and looked up at me, breath ragged, "Why not?" he demanded,

"Because we don't know what will happen if we do it before then!" I snapped at him, finding the energy to put my breast away and button up my blouse.

"What if I got pregnant?" He shrugged. "What if I can only get pregnant that one time? What if doing it beforehand voids your win?"

That one got him.

I saw the worry kindle in his eyes like a flame so I ran with it before he could think about it too deeply.

"Neither of us can jeopardise this going wrong in any way. There's too much at stake." I continued looking into his eyes, pleading with him to understand. "All the teachings say we can only conceive the rightful heir on our birthday. Sabre, we have to wait."

I saw that he understood, but I also saw that he hated the idea and in an instant, the passion in his eyes turned into something a lot darker. He got up from the bed and walked back over to where he'd left his shoes.

"Where are you going?"

He reached out to a chair where he left a long coat and put it over his loose shirt, tailored pants and dark shoes.

"Out,"

I scampered off the bed, "Out where? Sabre!" I rushed over to him where he had flung open the door and I saw my two bodyguards stood outside it. I tightened my blouse around myself, "Sabre?"

Sabre finally looked at me as he stepped into the hallway outside his bedroom. He looked me over from head to toe, "*You* have to wait until our birthday."

"Excuse me?"

Sabre glared at me spitefully, "The teachings say nothing about me staying abstinent." With that hateful admission, Sabre walked away from me and down the hall.

The following day, I didn't get out of bed for breakfast or lunch or dinner. It was only when my door knocked and I smelt my mother's scent that I even eased open my eyelids.

"Aspen."

I didn't answer. I didn't have to or need to. She'd won—what was the point?

"Aspen, I need to speak with you."

Still I didn't answer. I lay under my covers, missing Caius. I would see him tomorrow, one last time, before he would let Sabre win and I would be given over like a gilded possession.

Prized flesh.

He hadn't been wrong.

"Aspen, I realise you feel betrayed, but I need you to understand that this is for the best and how proud I am of you."

Proud? Was she for real?

"You might hate me now..."

Damn right I do!

"...but when you're married to the Alpha and hold your special first born in your arms, you'll thank me."

That got my attention. I lifted myself up in my bed, eyes and hair wild from the tossing and turning I'd done in my sleep.

"Thank you?"

My mother looked as pristine as ever, but I got images in my head of Goliath undressing her, kissing her, loving her and wanted to scream. For all they preached to us about tradition and loyalty and purity, they were cheating on their spouses and lying to their families.

"Why would I ever thank you?"

"You don't know what it is to be poor, hungry. Alone. You will never have to worry about any of that because of what I've done for you, thanks to everything I've taught you. The Riadnaks are a powerful name, much more so than the Caldouns, and you will thank me for getting you to be a part of that dynasty."

"You're crazy."

I surveyed my mother with disbelief, but she didn't even flinch at my words, "No, child, I'm the farthest from it. I kept you from Caius to protect you. You are my daughter and I love you, no matter what you choose to believe."

I scowled at her, "I choose to believe that you're a selfish bitch, who didn't get the man she wanted and is obsessed with raising me in her own image." She had the decency to look guilty. "If this is how you show your love for me, then I don't want it."

I threw my covers off and scrambled angrily out of my bed towards her, grabbing her by the arm and dragged her towards my door, using my other hand to open it.

"You won, Mother," I screamed at her. "You've succeeded in making my impending marriage as loveless as yours! The only thing I'll take from this is how not to treat my children because I'll be a better mother than you *ever* were!"

I pushed her out of the room, using my wolf strength. She went careening into the wall opposite my bedroom door, the impact splintering the painted brick like she was a spider in the middle of a delicate web.

"*Thank you.* For everything!" I said, biting back my tears—successfully this time—resting my gaze on hers with all the detestation I felt before I retreated and slammed the door in her face.

Mate
Part Three

CHAPTER TWENTY-SEVEN

I lay on my bathroom floor, thankful for the cool marble beneath my face. It was the morning of the final challenge and I had been up for hours, emptying the contents of my stomach. My throat ached, my head pounded and sweat pooled on my brow as I lay on the floor, trying desperately to catch my breath.

It will be over soon.

Caius' voice echoed through my head. Where once before the words had brought me comfort, now they promised the end of my freedom. I was terrified and I was alone.

After today, Sabre would officially be the Alpha Apparent. After today, Sabre would own me and I would have no say in the matter. He could continue cheating on me and I wouldn't be able to stop it. It didn't matter that I didn't want him anymore—his betrayal was still a painful shock to bear, along with all the rest of them. How could I have been so blind? Who had he been sleeping with? Did I know her? Were there multiple hers in the picture? And for how long? For the entire time we were together?

I felt the tremors of a pending eruption in my stomach. As quickly as I could manage, I made it to the rim of the toilet basin and dry heaved into the bowl. I had nothing else to give. Distantly, I heard a knock at my door and groaned against the need to get up and answer it. Shakily, I got to my feet and rinsed my mouth out with some mint water. The knock continued,

"Coming!" I called out, my voice cracking on the word. I wiped my mouth and headed into my bedroom towards the endless pounding. Clutching my arm to my stomach, I staggered over to my door and unlocked it to reveal my mother, Lara the seamstress and two other women. One I recognised as a woman who had done my make-up on some previous occasion.

"It's time to get ready," my mother said, not meeting my eyes.

"Whatever."

I walked away from the door to allow them entry and soon enough they got to work.

When I arrived at the Arena hours later, the spectators already filled the seats. Where the hedge from the agility challenge had once been, there was now an open, sand covered space. The blazing Agmantian sun beat down from overhead, making the sand shimmer like gold, which was an odd sight now that winter was approaching. In the pit lay a large circle of rocks and stones that went perfectly around the entire perimeter. In the space between the arena walls and the ring of stones were *laecan* guards in their wolf form, with coats of varying colours, standing watch around the edge.

I sat in the Beta box with my family, all of us unusually quiet as we waited for the challenge to begin. It was much the same as the agility challenge in that the Riadnaks sat to our left and the Caldouns to our right. What was different was the tension in the air of a third challenge. With a win each, it was a toss-up who would win. I would become an honorary Alpha because until I gave birth to the heir and married Sabre, I wouldn't officially be an Alpha. As shifter tradition dictated, I was meant to give birth before getting married to determine my inclusion into the family. Marriage was secondary to procreation, and an infertile womb would seldom find a family that would welcome them, though they might find a mate that still would. For all intents of purposes, however, the marriage ceremony was utterly inconsequential to our kind.

It was the bond of blood that mattered.

The air crackled with the anxiety that flooded through the veins of everyone present. I continued to feel sick, but with endless cups of iced water and tiny slices of bread, I kept my stomach down. It wouldn't do to ruin the rather expensive dress I was in, a ball gown of shimmering silver that shifted as I moved, catching the light in ways that made me look like the moon on a starless night.

The strapless bodice, a style my mother clearly favoured, was covered by a sheer material that went over my shoulders and down my arms. My nut-brown skin, teased through the diamonds stitched throughout. The skirts were full, so wide my mother and sister had to sit a chair away from me on either side, so not to crease the glorious fabric. Endless tiny diamonds were stitched into the flowing skirt that covered my silver filigree shoes. It was open on the top half of my back, buttons starting at the dip of spine to keep it against my body. The opening allowed some cool air to briefly touch my skin, whenever nature would allow.

My mother had insisted I take out my braids and so my hair was free of their synthetic confinements and now washed, pressed and flowing down my back in ombre waves. I had a middle part but the front of my hair was pressed elegantly behind my ears, keeping the hair out of my face. As was tradition, I wore the Crown of the

Female, but unlike the first time I'd worn it to *Lunaveya*, it felt heavy. It seemed a heavier burden then I ever wished to bear. I also had the dagger Goliath had given me. It rested neatly around my waistline, not as out of place as I'd thought it would, when my mother insist I wear it to please the Alpha.

The crowd swelled, as did their voices when they noticed something I didn't. I brought my wayward thoughts back to the present as Arlo stepped to his podium across the arena and began to speak:

"Welcome, one and all, to the final challenge of the Mating Games!"

The crowd went into a frenzy, screaming and shouting, waving banners with wolves painted on them. Streamers swayed and horns were blown. I said nothing, my hands trembling even as I held them in my lap.

"The final challenge," Arlo was now saying, "is one of strength. Our esteemed heirs will be pit against one another in a display of strength and dominance that will give us our official Alpha Apparent!"

Again, rapture from the crowd as I simply stared ahead, lost in woe. Caius was down there, somewhere. I hadn't been able to get away to try and see him, but even if I could, what difference would it make? I wouldn't begin to assume what Caius really felt for me, but his request the last time I saw him had opened my eyes and ears to how it all rested with me, because Caius had made his choice. He'd made his a long time ago.

Tell me I can keep you.

It was impossible.

"Unlike the other challenges, the final challenge is always competed as human."

A hubbub went through the audience with excitement. If the competing males ever got to the third challenge, they were required to compete in their human form, their weaker form. If the male beat his opponent as a wolf and as a man, then his right to rule could not be denied.

"Both males will enter the ring, and only by defeat or surrender will one be allowed to leave. The remaining male will be declared the winner!"

More noise and applause. I drowned it out, feeling dizzy. My dress was too tight. I wanted out.

"Please, welcome into the ring the champion of our last challenge in this very arena…Caius of House Caldoun!"

Everyone stood as they applauded Caius. Despite their overt snubbing of his win they would not lose face by so publically showing their disdain, so they clapped, and cheered. It made me feel ill.

My family and I stepped to the edge of the box and, finally, I could see him.

He stepped out of the shadows of the holding barracks and walked to the centre of the ring. He wore loose fitting pants that fit snugly around his waist and ankles, other than that, he was topless and armed with two *katana*, a sword I knew hailed from the northern most continent of Coz. The blades would be made of iron to better inflict lasting wounds. It made for a better show.

I placed a hand on my stomach, swallowing to steady myself.

Caius looked straight ahead, his body in profile to us, and simply waited as the crowd continued to cheer. I wanted him to look at me. I wanted to be able to look into his eyes and combust from the flames I would witnessed there.

I missed him.

"And now—his challenger and our Alpha heir—Sabre of House Riadnak!"

Sabre prowled onto the sand, all six feet of him, and took the spot opposite Caius. He wore the same loose pants, his own perfectly muscled, golden skin was on show and he also held two *katana*.

"Our two males have already taken their vow not to cause mortal injury," Arlo reminded us. "The first to be knocked out of the ring, leave the ring, trip over the ring…" Arlo let the rules sink in. "…will lose."

A show of brute strength. How hard could this really be?

The men stood facing one another, glaring into each other's eyes, although Caius was an inch or two taller. There was an agonising breadth of silence across the crowd before…

"*Begin!*"

Arlo amplified his voice and quicker than I could blink, Sabre was on Caius. He leapt forward and sliced at Caius' neck, but missed as Caius slipped out from under the blade, avoiding the attack.

They began to circle one another.

Generally speaking, wolves didn't fight. We were a species of communal creatures who thrived on family and community. We fought to defend and to hunt, not for sport, but this was most definitely a sport, at least for Sabre. I saw immediately that he was playing offense as Caius simply avoided Sabre cutting him. They growled and swiped at each other, cutting at their faces and eyes, but neither was backing down and, as yet, were dancing around the threat of being seriously hit.

The crowd clapped and hissed and roared their pleasure and discomfort when their favourite took a blow, blades clashing against one another as they fought. A collective gasp went through the frenzied crowd when suddenly Caius took a particularly nasty cut to the side. He countered with the same cut to Sabre on the opposite side. Sabre cried out in pain, but didn't back down, even as he backed off for the moment to work through the pain of the blow.

They continued to circle one another again, until Sabre lunged at Caius with first one blade and then the next. What followed was a flurry of blade and skill as Caius and Sabre fought viciously for the win. I'd never seen anyone move as fast as them. The sun glinted off their blades, blinding me at parts so I couldn't follow the rain of thrusts and parries that they threw at one another. Both were incredibly strong and fast, both so evenly matched that the fight looked to go on forever.

My heart was conflicted as I watched them. Desperate for it to be over, but not wanting the outcome that I knew Caius would hand to Sabre. As the devastation of Sabre's impending win took hold of me again, I wondered briefly at Caius' participation.

If he didn't want this, then why was he fighting so hard?

The glimmer of hope my thoughts gave me disappeared almost immediately as I answered the question myself. He was doing this to give people a show, to throw them off the scent that he hadn't tried.

He was doing this for his mother.

On and on, their blades crashed against one another until, in a move I was barely able to register, both their swords were suddenly crossed at the hilt, bearing down on the other in a bid for submission.

Their faces were inches apart, their eyes glowering as they struggled not to let their hold slip. Sweat coursed down their backs as the crowd roared with the adrenaline pumping through them. Feet stomped ferociously as they held on, forcing the other to yield.

It was only as I watched Caius grind his teeth against the pressure of holding those swords up that I realised he was trying. Caius had thrown the first challenge and admitted he'd only tried to win the second one because I had shown up. Maybe our kiss had changed his mind. Maybe he finally wanted to fight for this.

To fight for me.

With a terrifying roar, Caius brought his foot between them and kicked at Sabre's legs. Sabre lost his footing and fell to the sandy ground, losing his hold on one of his weapons as he did so. The crowd went wild at the change in lead and it noticeably angered Sabre. He flipped forward onto his legs and immediately charged at Caius, quickly disarming him of one of his swords. It went crashing to the floor, leaving them both with one *katana* each. The skill that unfolded before our eyes was unlike anything I had ever seen. Constant battering of iron against iron, both still so evenly matched, even after nearly twenty minutes of constant battle, that they could not get another cut on the other.

My fingers tightened around the balustrade of the balcony, willing Caius to be victorious. I wished for it, I prayed for it, but it seemed, once again, my God didn't hear me.

In an artful move, Sabre disarmed Caius and in the split second he held no weapon, Sabre ran Caius through his shoulder with the iron blade.

The crowd lost their minds at the first serious hit of the fight and they drowned out my cry of dismay, watching Sabre pull his sword from Caius' body, seeing blood on the blade.

No no no!

Caius staggered backward as Sabre lifted his sword into the air and riled up the crowd, unable to resist the opportunity to taunt like the bully he was. His pride would cost him. Caius, taking the opportunity of Sabre being unaware, recovered from his shock and charged at Sabre, knocking him to the ground.

"Oooh!" the crowd hissed as the pair fell to the ground in a heap of brown and tan muscle and Caius punched Sabre in the face.

Swords forgotten, the boys began brawling in the middle of the ring.

And Caius was winning.

Even with his wounded shoulder, Caius was pummelling Sabre's face into the ground mercilessly, roaring as he did it. When the opportunity finally presented itself, Sabre got his own punch in and knocked Caius backward. Not missing another opening, Sabre punched Caius in his wounded shoulder, making him cry out in agony. We heard the roar from the box, the guttural pain that went through him, but still, it wasn't over. Until one of them gave up or one left the ring, it wouldn't end.

Dazed, Caius stumbled backward, clutching his shoulder as Sabre stalked up to him. Sabre went to swing for Caius, but Caius ducked and punched Sabre in the stomach, making him double over before punching him in the side of the head.

It was as though I watched it all underwater, slow and altered. Sabre folded over headfirst, his face smashing into the sand. He must have bit his tongue or the inside of his cheek because blood splattered from his mouth onto the sand.

I watched—breathless—as Caius reached down and grabbed Sabre by the throat. A gasp went around the crowd, the applause lessening as Caius, with one hand, dragged Sabre towards the edge of the ring.

He's going to throw Sabre over it.

He's going to win!

My heart beat escalated as I saw my freedom within easy reach. I saw Caius and me, happy, away from all this drama and politics, living together, free.

With a choking Sabre in his clutches, whose golden skin was littered with bleeding scrapes and lacerations, Caius continued dragging Sabre to the edge of the ring. Sabre's hands clutched at Caius' arm, trying to get him to let go.

My palms were sweaty against the balustrade as I pressed down, leaning out farther than I should in order to see. Finally, Caius approached the edge of the ring. He stopped, inches from victory, and slowly looked up—directly at me.

We caught each other's eyes for a brief moment and the longing for him erupted inside me like a volcano. I blinked at him, one slow blink, but he looked away. He turned his attention to my left, to his family, but I couldn't take my eyes off him to follow his gaze. I couldn't look away from him, couldn't stop willing him to seize this moment and save us.

I'm not the one to save you.

My heart plummeted to my stomach as a feeling of wrongness completely overtook me.

Caius...no.

But Caius moved his gaze to stare straight ahead of him as he dropped Sabre to the ground. While Sabre gasped for breath, choking down much needed air, Caius stood at the edge of the ring.

His hand trembled as it fell down by his side, but... he took a step forward, and exited the ring.

CHAPTER TWENTY-EIGHT

There was a sickening silence for a heartbeat or two, then Invernell descended into chaos.

Ianthe grabbed my arm while my father took hold of my sister and we were dragged from the observation booths into the depths of the Arena.

My mind was hazy as I tried to determine whether the boos and hissing were for Sabre's clear loss or Caius' refusal to officially claim his victory. My family and I were rushed through murky hallways, into the contender rooms where we were deposited with the other family heads, all gathered in a small chamber. Goliath was nowhere to be seen.

I trembled, feeling exposed in my beautiful dress, as though it was an identity marker that painted a bullseye on my back. I was terrified of what would happen to Caius. For all intents and purposes, he had proved himself the better wolf and so should be the next Alpha, but judging by the anger surrounding me, Caius had been right in assuming he wouldn't have a whole lot of backing.

Rhea's father, Kade Lacoste, stood with his wife Jasyn, the two of them arguing with Fenrir and Koda's parents Runan and Alyssa Lamentelle. Olcan's father Ezekiel Salvaterre and Susi's mother Paten Dune spoke in more hushed tones, but their expressions were just as heated. It was obvious they were on opposing sides of an argument. I opened my mouth, not entirely sure what I wanted to say but a sharp pinch on my arm from my mother stopped me,

"Not a word out of you."

I swallowed whatever I was going to say and was relieved when Goliath entered the room, followed by Celeste. I needed to know if Caius was okay. The Caldouns weren't present, and as Goliath shut the door it was clear they weren't expected to join.

"There are things to be addressed," he said.

"If it is that Caius handed Sabre that win and by right should be Alpha Apparent, then by all means, address it."

Kade was the first to speak and I saw immediately where Rhea got her fiery nature from.

Goliath glared at the man, but didn't speak. I was impressed when Kade didn't immediately back down, holding Goliath's heated gaze without even blinking.

"Sabre is the victor, no matter the circumstance. He was the last one left inside the ring. He will be Alpha Apparent," Ezekiel said calmly, opposing Kade's outburst.

Caius simply walking out of the arena rather than finishing and claiming the mantle was the same as losing in the eyes of the Riadnak supporters. I got the distinct feeling that Caius had counted on it but if not handled correctly, there would be a divide in Invernell as those opposing Goliath's rule might make a figurehead out of Caius. I wrapped my arms around me, not sure if I wanted to protect myself, or wished I could somehow protect Caius.

It was clear which side Kade and Ezekiel were on. It didn't take a genius to know which side my parents would take, but what of the other families? And what of the shaman? Where was Lady Xana?

"Caius Caldoun has put our way of life into question. By not completing the challenges as our laws prescribe he has jeopardised the succession and for that act of rebellion, he cannot be given the title."

Goliath's voice had made the room go silent, and at his words there was a palpable tension beginning to grow.

"But for the sake of peace, the Gamma has forfeited," Celeste Riadnak added, soft triumph in her tone.

"What are you talking about?" Paten asked, wary.

Celeste stepped forward and produced a small folded piece of paper. She handed it to Paten, who opened it and read for a moment before speaking,

"Caius denounces his right to the title," she said, still scanning the page. "He doesn't *want* to be Alpha."

That was the reason Goliath had been late to join us. He'd been securing the leadership mantle for his son and averting a possible uprising in one fell swoop. It didn't matter what I knew about Caius' intentions—Goliath's foresight, his absolute control of every situation, was terrifying.

"Where are Regina and Maximus?" Rhea's mother asked, her voice sharp. I was thankful she'd asked, because no one else seemed to care.

"They have returned home. They did not wish to be around such...humiliation."

I didn't believe Goliath's words; I didn't think anyone did until I noticed Kade clench his fists by his sides. He said nothing.

"So as to avert any civil unrest, I will announce Sabre's victory and title as Alpha Apparent and we shall hold the victory party as planned."

I saw then that Goliath had won. Despite the obvious reluctance in Kade, Jasyn and Paten's eyes, no one wanted civil war. To protect our community, our families and friends; they would have to agree that Sabre's win was valid. With the addition of Caius' rejection of the leadership, they had no other choice to fall back on. He wasn't asking them to vote on this as he'd made a poor attempt to make it appear earlier. He was telling them and they knew they had no choice.

Ezekiel, Runan and Alyssa joined Goliath and Celeste and bowed to them—their allegiance clear. These were the people I would have to be careful of once I joined the Alpha rank. They could be the difference between a peaceful life and one of turmoil. If the wolf they considered the purest and truest to lead them was in any way threatened, there was nothing they wouldn't do to protect him. I could see it on their faces—utter devotion.

Once the other elders had given their approval, however reluctantly it was bestowed, we were rushed out of the Arena, into our waiting carriages, and taken to the Riadnak Manor for the victory party, where I knew the celebrations must already be underway. The preparations had gone on for weeks.

I said nothing on the ride there, my mother speaking incessantly about how much work there was to do, now that my wedding was on the horizon. My sister was quiet as usual, but there was an anger simmering in her that I didn't bother to comment on. I had enough worries of my own.

When we finally arrived at the manor, the grounds were lit up with countless torches and fireflies caught in jars, but though the festivities were poised to begin, the revellers were being kept at bay, told to patiently wait as the elders deliberated over the decision and delivered a verdict.

Of course, there was no deliberation. The verdict was already in. I saw now the game Goliath was playing, had always been playing. He had to look as though he was being fair, listening to possible opposing views, when he only cared about his own. The result was fixed and all I could do now was brace myself for a long night of congratulations and empty blessings for my fruitful womb.

An hour or so later the party was in full swing and Goliath had his herald make the announcement of Sabre's victory. The Riadnak supporters and those too scared to oppose them were revelling in their continued success, but I felt sick at the weak spines of the conflicted elders. In the same breath, I understood their position as it mirrored my own: doing something you didn't want to do, for the safety of others. I watched the defeated look on the Lacoste's and Dune's faces and felt for them having to agree with this farce.

Once the excitement had died down, my parents and I were asked into a private meeting with Goliath. He stood waiting for us, with Celeste by his side. Sabre stood in front of him, his hands clasped behind his back. He'd changed into his formal attire earlier, but his face was still bruised. I marvelled at the effects of Caius' punches since they should have healed by now. It was a testament to the power that had gone into those punches—a testament to Caius' strength.

All I could think about was those same hands touching me in the gentlest of ways, holding my hand, brushing against my arm…

A servant shut the door behind us as we entered and Goliath gestured for us to approach. We bowed as we got closer to his desk and stopped, lined up, waiting for him to continue.

Goliath wore white and his gold circlet rested comfortably on his brow, as though he'd been born with it there. His amber eyes watched us, glaring from within the harshly alluring features of his dark-skinned face.

"Aspen."

I swallowed my nerves and bowed, approaching the table to stand before him, "Yes, Alpha?"

"My son tells me that you've had some interest in the war against us."

My eyes shot to Sabre, who didn't look at me. My heartbeat quickened. I said nothing for the moment, conscious of my mother's hot glare on the back of my neck and my father's frosty indifference to the whole thing.

"Bracken also tells me that you had some concerns about the rebels that continue to plague our peaceful existence."

Still I said nothing.

"Is there a reason for your daughter's sudden interest in dealings that do not concern her, Ianthe?" Celeste's interruption seemed to have irritated Goliath, but he didn't say anything as my mother stepped forward and bowed.

"Bracken and I have spoken with Aspen repeatedly, my lady. She has been warned about interfering, but we can only apologise for her disrespect."

I knew it burned my mother to have to posture to Celeste like this, but for the first time I saw the pleasure Celeste took in watching my mother do it. It made me uneasy, and so, on shaky legs, I took another step forward and cleared my throat.

"If I am to be a true and devoted consort to Sabre and a member of your esteemed family, Alpha, I merely wished to understand the part I would be required to play." I made sure to address Goliath and thereby reduce Celeste to the secondary character she was. "I apologise for the line I crossed, but I meant no harm in wishing to be a full and complete part of my future husband's life."

I heard my mother exhale and if I'd heard it, Goliath would have too. Exhaling meant she thought I would say something wrong. Saying something wrong meant I had something to hide. I remained silent, anticipating Goliath's response, but the seconds droned on until, finally, a small smile teased the corner of his mouth and his amber eyes shone with amusement,

"Your words move me, Aspen. You are truly a wonder and I am proud to bring you into my family as future consort, now that Sabre has proved victorious."

I bowed graciously, thankful to be out of the firing line as my knees shook beneath my gown and sweat pooled between my breasts.

"You will be delighted to know then, that the Faenymese and Boltesian *laecan* attempting invasion, have been dealt with and many wolves are returning home in a matter of days."

Dealt with?

I shuddered to think what that meant, but I had a pretty good idea. Goliath moved his attention from me and addressed the rest of the room. I stepped back, avoiding any more reason for him to focus on me.

"Fenrir Lamentelle and Ulren Felltree have both recovered wonderfully since that senseless attack, as I'm sure you'll all be glad to hear."

I was. Ulren might be a moody bastard but he had never done anything to anyone for Goliath to have used his affliction so shamelessly. The only positive from his being weakened was that he couldn't be used on any more of Caius' and Sire's resistance friends. How many lives had been saved because Ulren had been out of it?

"I trust, Miss Anai," his attention was on me again, "that no matter how incentivised, you will not question or look into my actions again."

I knew there was only one way to answer and said, "Of course not, Alpha."

I bowed low, as low as I could without falling over, and kept my eyes to the floor.

"Go now. Enjoy the party." Goliath looked at Sabre and all amusement faded. "I must speak with my son."

My parents and I were dismissed and scurried out of the room.

Despite saving myself from any serious fallout, for the duration of the celebrations, I found myself glaring at Goliath whenever he came into view. Luckily there were plenty of distractions to take up his focus and his eyes never met mine. The music, food, alcohol, dancing and all other kinds of merriment mixed in a cauldron of decadence and wealth. I felt like a fraud and longed to *turn*, to run, to find my way to a cave hidden from view, far away from this macabre display.

The smell of *lief*, a plant that lowered ones' inhibitions by relaxing the senses, was floating in the air, and all manner of debauchery slowly unfolded under the Alpha's roof. For the first time, I saw Goliath openly enjoying himself, smoking on a large cigar, Celeste—very uncharacteristically—seated on his lap. She laughed and smiled and kissed her husband, throwing praise on him so shamelessly it bordered on comical.

Sabre had returned to the party, but while he mingled, it looked as though it was through some considerable effort. I saw him clutch his side in pain whenever someone brushed him too closely, and he even gave in to a slight limp on two occasions. Goliath had hurt him in that private room, of that I was sure, but I couldn't find it in myself to care. Not as I once did. His pain was his own. He would have to deal with it, as I would have to learn to live with mine.

Seconds rolled by like hours as I performed my duties and entertained as I would be expected to do once I became lady of this very house. I smiled and laughed and quipped where needed, but with nothing behind my eyes. No joy, no true engagement with those smiling and laughing at me, no peace within a mind that yearned only to be with Caius.

Was he okay?

Now that Sabre had won, there was no reason for me to see Caius. It made my heart ache at the possibility that I would never spend another minute alone with him. Never feel his lips against mine, never seeing his eyes look at me in that way that set my body on fire.

As I observed my family mingle with the members of our community, catching my mother laughing and smiling with my father, I wondered for the first time whether this was worth it. My parents were happy. Invernell was happy. Did it matter that I wasn't, if the greater good had been achieved? I downed another glass of wine, my third in as many hours, and took a seat in my designated chair on the dais. I sat eating small nibbles when offered and sipped to show I wasn't a corpse sitting upright, but I wasn't present. It would officially be my birthday in two hours and I was dreading it.

Soon, I would be twenty years old and I would sleep with a man for the very first time.

A man I didn't love.

A moment I had once ached for, was now the most feared moment of my life and I wasn't prepared for it. I knew what to expect physically, but knowing what it would mean for me on an emotional level was suddenly too much to bear.

It that moment, clarity washed over me and I simply decided that I *wouldn't* bear it. If I was going to live the rest of my life for everyone else, then I was going to make this one decision for myself. My mind made up, I stood from my chair and leaned down to get Sabre's attention. He was sat on the chair next to mine, talking to Fenrir, his speech slurred.

"I'm going home," I said.

"What?" his eyes were glazed over. He was so drunk off his fake success that he couldn't even see straight. The wounds on his face had healed somewhat, but there were still some welts that would take some time to disappear.

"Home, Sabre. I'm leaving."

"Okay," he unabashedly looked down at the rise of my breasts and licked his lips.

"Until tomorrow, then."

He didn't wait for my reply and returned to his conversation. I didn't care. I stepped down from the dais and found my mother. When she set eyes on me, she looked worried,

"Can I go home? I'm tired."

She seemed to accept that too quickly, looking over my shoulder before answering. I didn't bother looking but she nodded, "Sabre has been sworn in, so you can leave."

I nodded and left her. When I was free of the oppressive throng of highborn sycophants, I took a deep breath of the cooling night air, *turned*, and at last darted off into the night.

CHAPTER TWENTY-NINE

I arrived at the mouth of the cave, staring into the endless darkness in front of me. There were no lanterns lit tonight, but I could smell the warm scent of Caius, even from out here, and knew he was inside. I'd *turned*, and stood at the mouth of the cave with the jewels covering my ridiculous dress glinting as they caught the moonlight. Had he been waiting for me, hiding in the darkness, watching me, he might've thought I'd draped myself in a piece of night sky and brought the stars down for him. I was here to be with him, knowing he would be upset that I'd come. Selfishly, I didn't care.

I walked into the cave, my head held high.

He was waiting for me by the hearth.

The fire was blazing, the flames crackling, casting a glorious golden light over him, making his shadow draw out behind him. His amber eyes blazed out of his beautiful face as he watched me approach him.

He was barefoot and topless, his broad, muscular chest, glowing in the hearth firelight. I took note of the scars from the second challenge, as well as the new ones from today—the latter had healed a lot faster than Sabre's—and I could see where he'd been stabbed in the shoulder, only a thin scar visible, rather than the gaping wound it had once been. I saw all this, but was distracted by the loose-fitting black pants he had hanging so low around his hips, that they revealed those delicious hipbones, narrowing into his groin. I followed the thin line of hair that ran down from his belly button and disappeared below the band of the pants.

I stepped forward, suddenly furious at him. I watched him take a deep breath just as I reached out and punched him in the chest. Tears sprung up as my fist connected, my breathing rattled as rage consumed me.

"Why?" I screamed at him, my tears running freely as I saw no use in holding them back. "*WHY?*"

Caius stared back at me, pained and guilty. It wasn't enough. I clenched my fists and started pounding on his chest.

"Why did you give up?" I demanded, crying as I struck on his solid, unyielding body.

Tell me I can keep you.

He knew I couldn't tell him that. Even as I continued my attack on him, tears streaming down my face, my heart cracking. It was because of me, because I hadn't been strong enough. Because I wasn't strong enough to turn my back on my life and everything I'd ever known. I wasn't daring enough to defy the shaman, our Alpha, our laws. I couldn't bring myself to let go of our entire way of life for this newness that Caius seemed to have embraced so fully. Even with him ready to take me by the hand and lead the way, I couldn't turn my back on my duty.

It wasn't him.

It was me.

He suddenly grabbed hold of both my wrists and stopped me hitting him.

I hung my head in defeat, "Why did you give me up?"

I wanted him to take the blame, just as I'd wanted him to make the choice for me by accepting the Alpha title. I would have been his by default, and even if war broke out, at least the shaman wouldn't have been able to curse us for going against their magic.

I felt my heart shrivelling as the seconds drew out between us.

The entire evening, all I could think about was that we had been so close. He had been so close to being Alpha, to freeing me to be with him, and he'd thrown it all away.

Caius released my left wrist to put his index finger underneath my chin. He made me look at him and I hiccupped on my tears.

"It's all a game to them, Aspen, and I will not play it by their rules. Not ever."

Fresh tears filled my eyes because of course he wouldn't. I felt suddenly ashamed that I'd ever expected him to. But what about me? Would he reject me now, send me back to them? The loneliness of that thought made me give a soft sob, clutching at his arms, near desperation. He couldn't send me back there without loving me first.

Caius peered down at me and I knew what I needed to say, what I needed to happen. I swallowed, terrified of the words that had to leave my mouth, the power they held.

"I choose you Caius," I whispered, looking deep into the fiery pits of his eyes. "I choose you."

He was my mate and he would be my first because that's what I wanted. I wanted him.

He released his hold on my other wrist as my arms snaked up and around his neck, pulling me closer into his body. We were as close as we could be to one another, but still I wanted more. My eyes fluttered closed of their own accord as I leaned forward and placed my lips onto his. The sensation that flooded me was almost indescribable. I felt hot yet chilled, terrified but perfectly at peace. Through the uncertainty of my emotions, there was one thing that was constant.

Want.

A voracious and aching want to be consumed by him in every way possible. His tongue was in my mouth, expertly massaging my own against his, filling me with a passion that burned hot in my core. I moaned, pressing into him, wanting to be a part of him, for him to be a part of me. His hands held me firmly around my waist, the flowing material separating the most important parts of us from touching. Reluctantly, I pulled away from our searing kiss and took my arms from around his neck.

"Grey?" I shouldn't have been so turned on by the uncertainty in his eyes, but Caius looked afraid. As though he expected me to change my mind, to stop this roaring need between us. I couldn't have stopped it if I wanted to and I didn't.

I wanted more.

I wanted everything.

I backed away from him, away from the fire and finally turned to walk over to his bed. With my back to him, I pulled my straightened hair over my shoulder so the buttons that kept my dress together were on show. I looked over my shoulder, saying nothing.

Caius approached on long, lithe legs until I could feel the warmth coming from his body. Slowly, he reached out and began to undo the button at the middle of my back. I shivered as his fingers fluttered like feathers on the wind against my bare skin. I tried to steady my breathing but my breaths came in small, sharp pants as I trembled beneath his delicate touch.

One, then two, then endless buttons later, the pressure around my body eased and I felt the warm air of the cave kiss my back. Caius pulled the material away from my shoulders and helped my arms out of the sheer sleeves. When my arms were free, I brought them in front of me to cover my breasts as the fabric of my dress, pooled in a mound at my feet.

I stepped out of my shoes and the dress, one foot and then the other, curling my toes into the thick rug beneath my feet. I felt Caius move so he was directly behind me again. As he lowered his head, I felt his breath on my neck, his lips on my shoulders with a light graze of his teeth. I was aware of the claim that a bite from Caius would make, but it fluttered from my mind in the wake of my pleasure. I felt his hands on my hips and then his manhood pressing into my back.

A mewl escaped me as I shuddered against the feel of it. I wanted to look at him, I was terrified to look at him but I knew I wanted this. I just needed him to show me how. I was under no illusion that Caius was a virgin. I'd have to murder whoever he'd had sex with to stave off the jealousy pouring through me at the mere thought of him touching another, but I knew he could make this special for me and I wanted him to take the lead.

My body trembled underneath his touch, his lips that lowered from my shoulder blades to the top of my spine. As he got lower, so did his hands until his lips kissed first one cheek then the other, while his large hands gripped my thighs.

My entire body was shaking—I simply couldn't control it. My hands quivering, I took them away from my chest and reached behind me to feel him. Caius grabbed my hand and stilled my attempt before gently, he tugged my arm in a motion that told me to turn. Leisurely, I obeyed and looked down to where Caius was now kneeling in front of me.

His eyes were on fire, a ring of gold blazing with his passion. I took in a sharp breath as the carnal intent that bore out at me shook me to my core. He was going to destroy me. I saw it then, in his eyes, the way his brows knotted as he looked up at me. The tension in his muscles and his chest all told me that I would never forget this night for as long as I lived.

Without taking his eyes off me, Caius reached up, hooked his fingers into the delicate panties I wore and pulled them down my legs. He shimmed them down my thighs, but once they got to my calves they fell to the floor around my ankles. I stepped one leg out of them and used the other to kick them aside.

Approval shone in his eyes, but was quickly replaced with a sinful look that had me swallowing. My heart thundered as Caius reached up again, grabbed hold of my behind and pulled me closer to him. His face was now in line with my most intimate place and to my shock, yet undeniable pleasure, Caius closed his eyes, leaned forward and breathed in.

Caius took in my very essence, my scent, my irrefutable want for him and his body shook. When he opened his eyes to look back up at me, Caius leaned even closer and put his mouth on me.

My eyes slammed closed as I bucked against his mouth, grabbing his head to steady myself as his tongue worked magic on my body. His left hand held my behind but he used his right hand to smoothly lift my leg onto his shoulder. One of my hands was holding his head against me, while the other held his shoulder so I wouldn't collapse.

I moaned, I panted, I groaned as Caius pleasured me, giving me the most intimate of kisses. He licked and sucked, finally moving his attention to the bud of nerves that cried out for release. Caius held me there, his mouth on me, sucking, kneading with his tongue until convulsions began racing through me. He continued mercilessly until I gripped my fingers into his head and into the flesh of his bare shoulder. My breathing was patchy and I couldn't find words as my entire body went tight and I simply exploded.

The shudder went from the tips of my toes to the top of my head as I threw my head back and screamed into the night. Caius eased the pressure but continued kissing along the swollen and trembling folds of my sex. He kissed along my inner thigh, my hip and my stomach, slowly rising to his feet.

I couldn't speak, I could barely breathe as Caius backed me further against the bed, purpose in his eyes. The back of my knees felt the bed in seconds and I allowed myself to fall against it. Shaking, but still very much in need of what was to come, I used my weakened arms and legs to push myself onto the incredibly soft bed.

The pillows I'd seen were as soft as I'd imagined and I positioned myself so my back fell against them and my bare feet faced the cave entrance.

Caius climbed onto the bed and moved so he was in front of me rather than at my side. I lay naked before him and when he finally drew his pants down and all the way off, he was naked before me too. His deep brown skin was aglow in the fire light. His powerful thighs and chiselled torso made me ache. His member jut out in front of him, as hard as Agmantian steel and just as impressive. A bead of moisture glistened at the throbbing tip of it and I swallowed at the blatant display of his virility. I clenched my legs together, trying to stop the beat that pulsed between them but he lowered onto his hands and said,

"No," his molten gold eyes locked into my emerald green. "Open them."

Dear God I was going to die.

I was going to look into this man's eyes and combust into complete nothingness.

Trembling, I did as he said, and slowly spread my legs. Caius crawled towards me, every bit the wolf, his eyes practically glowing. He crawled between my legs and finally lowered himself so that our bodies pressed together in an intimate embrace.

His mouth was on mine again and for countless minutes, we kissed. Breathing each other's air, biting, sucking and nipping at each other's lips as we ground our bodies against one another. While we kissed, his member rubbed against my leg but I wanted it somewhere else,

"Now," my plea was husky as Caius sucked on my breasts. He held them both in his hands as he moved, alternating between left and right, my hands on his head, goading him on and my legs wrapped around him. He lifted his head from my chest and looked down at me. I saw the question in his eyes, the final opportunity to stop this but I said nothing.

Caius reached between us and took himself into his hand to guide himself toward my opening. I spread my legs a little more to accommodate him, but jerked as the tip pressed into me. He was partially on his knees, looking right at me and despite my skittish reaction, I didn't look away.

"I can st—"

"No," I cut him off. "Don't."

I knew he would. In an instant, he would stop if I wasn't comfortable but I didn't want him to stop, not ever. Never taking his eyes off me, Caius pushed a little more. I tried to breathe, tried not to panic but a sense of the unknown, of the pain I was told about, reared its ugly head and I tensed.

"I'm here with you," he murmured, as he lowered himself onto my body and pushed. I took my bottom lip between my teeth as he retreated then pushed again, inching himself further this time. I trembled, my breath caught in my throat as he pulled out once more then pushed all the way to the hilt.

The pain was sharp, instant and I felt something within me yield to him, the final barrier of my purity, and made me his.

Caius was inside me, filling me so completely that I forgot to breathe. I'd scrunched my eyes up, my forehead buried in his neck as he withdrew and pushed into me again. I hissed at the still unfamiliar intrusion, but tried to relax myself.

He was so hard yet so very smooth. He was steel encased in silk as he claimed me with every stroke. I released the breath I'd been holding and gripped around his waist to tether myself to the moment. He withdrew again, then pumped, working himself into a rhythm that had him taking sharp breaths in the space above my head. The pain slowly ebbed, very slowly as Caius ground his hips into me and I soon found pleasure in our movements.

My fingernails clawed into his buttocks, pushing him further into me as the heels of my feet mirrored the movement. Caius lifted himself onto his forearms to look down at me as he continued to thrust. We looked into each other's eyes and I felt… whole.

I felt it the moment he did, the rise of my orgasm, building at the point of our connection. I had to look away from him, the moment too personal, too scary to continuing looking at him. I shut my eyes as I began to pant, to scream as I held his powerful biceps.

He consumed me, he destroyed me as I knew he would, as Caius thrust into me so powerfully and completely, I lifted one hand to steady myself against the headboard. His ending approached, I felt him swell even more within my walls, and he picked up the pace.

"Caius," his name escaped me as I breathed erratically. "Caius." I didn't know what I wanted him to say, I didn't know why I was saying it, but the explosion building inside me demanded it.

Caius grabbed hold of my hips, pinning me to the bed and with three mighty thrusts, he released himself. I felt him throbbing against my walls as my own orgasm ripped through me. I felt his member pulsate as he emptied himself, a feeling that made me feel proud and possessive.

My legs shook in the aftermath of our lovemaking and fell helplessly from around his waist. I opened my eyes to find Caius staring down at me with an odd look on his face. He released himself from within me to lay gently on top of my body, my breasts pressed against his chest. He kissed me, softly, lovingly, until I felt the want build again. Our tongues entwined, our bodies warm and supple on top of his covers, everything was perfect.

As we kissed, I felt him harden against me once more and he lifted his head to ask me softly, "Can we?" He looked down, gesturing to where I was admittedly sore. "If you're hurting…"

I shook my head, desperate for him to kiss me again. When his lips were inches from mine, he asked me again, "You're sure?"

I kissed him, my hands cupping his face as I looked into his eyes, "Always."

Caius gave me a warm and tender smile before we kissed and didn't talk again, for the rest of the night.

I awoke to find myself on my stomach, tangled in an assortment of furs and sheets, my cheek resting on the top of my right hand. For a brief moment, I didn't remember where I was, until an all too familiar scent flooded my senses. I closed my eyes, breathing in the smell of coconuts and sugar. From the tingling of air on my toes I knew one leg was hanging outside of the covers, but the rest of me was wrapped up tight, in a cocoon of fur and warmth that smelled of Caius.

Caius.

His name felt like a promise, a brand that had been seared into my skin. My body ached beautifully, letting me know it was real, that it had happened and I regretted nothing.

Well, that was a lie. I regretted that this moment of bliss couldn't last and that when I left this bed, this cave, the reality of my life would be waiting, unblinking and as demanding as ever.

Today was my birthday.

Today was Mating Day.

I had anticipated this one day for most of my life, but now it had arrived I wasn't elated, as I'd always dreamed I'd be—I was terrified.

A chill shuddered through me, but before the fear could take hold, I felt pressure on the bed. The mattress sunk in and a warm presence was behind me.

"Happy birthday, beautiful."

Hesitantly, I lifted my head and turned towards his voice, resting my cheek on my hand. Even at what I assumed was first thing in the morning, Caius was the one who looked beautiful.

"Happy birthday to you, too."

A lazy and charming smile graced his lips just before he licked them, then lowered his head to kiss me. His lips were warm, soft and sweet. Lifting my hand from the bed, I wrapped it around his neck, pulling him towards me as I turned so he was now leaning over me as we kissed. Caius fought to push the covers aside with one hand, refusing to break our connection. In moments, the cover was free and my naked body was once again on show to him.

He placed his large, commanding hands on my stomach, travelling teasingly up until he palmed my breasts. I shuddered as he touched me, moaning into his mouth as I lifted my leg, pulling him into me so we were skin to skin. Well, one very important part was not in me and I fought to keep it that way, focusing instead on the feel of his lips against my own and his hands all over me. I felt beautiful in this moment, unworried about my body or my performance last night. I felt free with him.

Our kissing was unhurried in a way that only highlighted how much time we didn't have together. As I slowed our kisses, preparing to pull away from him, tears were building. Caius noticed.

"Why are you crying?" he whispered.

"You know why."

The look of guilt and complete helplessness in his eyes broke my heart even further. It was time to leave this piece of paradise we'd created for ourselves before it became impossible. I unlocked my legs from around him, "I should go."

I tried to move, but he stayed where he was, his body on mine pinning me to the bed.

"Grey…"

"Please, don't," I cut him off, looking away. "Please, don't make this any harder."

It took him a moment, but he nodded once and rolled away, releasing me. I felt his absence like a missing limb, my body suddenly useless without him next to it.

Minutes later I was fairly presentable, feeling stupid standing in the middle of his den in a silver ball gown while he stood topless and barefoot. He looked more gorgeous than ever simply because I knew I would never see him like this again because for the first time in my privileged and isolated life, I needed to not be selfish.

I would pay for it with the heartache that was tearing me in two, but it would be worth it if it meant I would be doing the right thing by my kind, knowing so few others were. Lady Xana had hinted at this being what my choice came down to and I saw it clearly now:

duty or happiness. I couldn't pursue both and had been driven by duty my whole life.

Caius and I finally stood by the cave opening looking at one another. There was so much that needed to be said, at least from my end, but there would be no point. Delaying the inevitable wouldn't make this any easier.

"I chose you, Caius," I murmured, looking down at my hands as I took a step towards him. "Please, remember that."

I took another step as tears threatened to fall again, but I held them back. I reached out and put my palm against his face. Caius closed his eyes and leant into my touch, revelling in the feel of my skin on his. I choked back a sob and threw myself into him, crashing my lips onto his. I loved him so much it burned, but I couldn't tell him. Not when I was leaving him to be with another man.

As we kissed, he squeezed me tightly and I squeezed back until, with a sharp push at his shoulders, I ripped myself away from him, *turned* and bounded out of the cave.

The sun had only just risen once I got back to the Anai Manor. I avoided the guards along the front lawn and went around the back to get to my bedroom window. My room was above my father's study, and once I was certain he wasn't in there I gave myself some space to take a running jump and leapt into the air toward my room.

Just as my wolf form reached the ledge, I *turned* and grabbed it with hands instead of paws. Using my lupine strength, I climbed onto the protruding ledge of my window, poked a finger through the lock, smashing it and jumped into my room. Cleaning up the shards of the broken lock, I rushed into the bathroom to wash off Caius' scent.

CHAPTER THIRTY

After an unusual and awkwardly silent breakfast with my family— considering my birthday and my loss of my supposed virginity were one and the same—I received my birthday gifts. A diamond necklace, bracelet and earrings from my father along with the emerald earrings I had asked for. A pearl necklace from my mother that had once belonged to my grandmother and great grandmother before her, a priceless gift considering what I'd learned about my mother's humble beginnings. My sister gave me a journal engraved with my name.

I thanked them all unenthusiastically while my other cards and presents were sent up to my room. I had no care for any of them and said nothing until it was time to leave the breakfast table and wait for the day to really begin.

When the bell downstairs chimed seven o'clock, I finally left my room. I wore a white shift dress and flat sandals to meet, my mother at the bottom of the stairs, ready to go to the temple.

The Laecan Temple was our most sacred place. While we worshipped one God and believed him to be the creator of all things, Agmantians also believed in other mystic abilities that were accessed through other forms, where shamanism and *laecan* were those closest at hand. We didn't think our God gave us these abilities, as Mortanians believed about their Everlasting, but we did believe that he put those possibilities in the world for others to discover.

We worshipped our God for human things, such as good health, decent marriages and wealth. We praised the gift of *laecan* and the moon that aided us for our traditions and abilities.

It was in this temple that Sabre and I would conceive our child. It was on a hill so that the moon, when highest in our sky, would bathe it in a wondrous glow of white light. I'd always thought of it as an extraordinary place.

It was built of stark white marble, with large columns around the perimeter. Torches were lit in large bowl shaped braziers. The fires within them stretched toward the sky, free to breathe in the fresh air of this high point. The temple was square shaped, the smooth columns holding up a roof that peaked into a triangle, with a mural of wolves and humans etched into the front. The history of our kind, frozen in time by much more learned people than myself, had made this place for us to praise our true strength. I stared up at the mural from the window of our carriage, and even though I couldn't understand the ancient language used to tell our history, I felt connected to this place.

The outer columns were for decoration while the inner building, as wide and as long as the façade, was split into various chambers. My mother and I, once we stepped out of our carriage, wearing hooded robes, ascended the marble steps and walked reverently into the entrance chamber. It was a wide, open space, filled with more braziers along the walls, the fire in them putting a warm orange tint over everything. At either side of us were pews facing walls lined with candles; offerings for blessings or blessings for *laecan* dead.

At the far end was the reception chamber, a small room where you congregated until being allowed entry into the main chamber.

We were led into this room by a sweet faced female shaman. She had a large afro against night-dark skin. Her white robes, as white as the robes my mother and I wore, was a beautiful contrast. She walked silently, as all temple workers did, into the main chamber. There were more pews here, rows of them facing the altar. Wolves carved of marble, leaping with open, snarling mouths, stood either side of the podium that held up the *laecan* texts. A series of traditions, histories and prophecies that stemmed too far back for anyone to remember. It was encased in a magically protected glass case for all to look upon it, but only a trained and trusted shaman could actually touch and read from it.

Silently we walked until we came to the back of the main chamber where there were three doors. One in the centre of the room behind the altar, one to our left and the other to our right. The shaman asked us to wait before leaving us, returning the way we entered. Moments later, Lady Xana appeared from the door to our left.

I hadn't seen her since the final challenge and I wasn't particularly happy about seeing her now. She smiled warmly at me, but I saw the frosty tint in the smile she gave my mother. Lady Xana also wore a white robe, but laced with gold to mark her as the leader of this holy place.

She eyed me for a moment, the look questioning, before she gestured to the door she'd appeared from, "Through this door you will find a corridor leading to the Female's quarters. There is a bathing pool and a preparation room."

Lady Xana pointed to the door in the centre, "Through that door is the Mating Room. Your quarters will lead to this room on the other side, as do the Male's quarters." She indicated to the final door on the right. "When Mating is complete, you will exit from the door behind me and return here for the ritual to determine that you have conceived."

I nodded my understanding and with what I thought was a sympathetic smile, she ushered my mother and I toward the Female quarters. I took steps gingerly towards the door and when Lady Xana pushed it open and bid me quietly to enter, I took a deep breath and obeyed.

My carefully applied face was washed away, as though I wasn't expected to be able to decide on a mask for myself, but should let others do that as well. I was scrubbed and buffed for hours until I was considered ready. If it wasn't for the impending coupling that followed, I could have been at a spa. I'd been waxed and creamed until my skin shone like bronze. My hair had been washed, dried and curled into loose waves down my back; my face painted so I looked as natural, *virginal* as possible. Even without saying it out loud, the word stuck in my throat. Everything they did to me was a declaration of my innocence and it was all a lie I was taking soft pleasure in knowing, but keeping to myself.

I was to be presented and I was to be claimed, but my body belonged to Caius, as *I* had chosen, and my mind, heart and soul rested with him in that cave. No matter what happened tonight, they couldn't take that away from me.

The temple maids dressed me in white silk that draped over my breasts and down between my legs and over my behind. It was held together by a thick sash of gold. I had gold sandals on my feet and on the skin that was exposed—my legs, my sides, my arms, neck, throat, my deep cleavage—gold dust had been sprinkled so that I shimmered when I moved.

Prized flesh.

I closed my eyes at that statement, for a moment, and thought of his warm gaze, his fingertips along my spine, that sense of being home…

Tell me I can keep you.

Perhaps he loved me. For a second I regretted not telling him how much I loved him.

My mother had watched my transformation with tears swimming in the pools of her eyes— all her dreams had come true. It was a shame I didn't have the same reverence for the evening.

As I looked in the mirror at the flurry of silk and gold, I hated that I'd allowed things to get this far. I may have only come around to the displeasure of my duty very recently, but I'd always known what it would involve. I'd let myself be manipulated by the conviction of my family, because a small part of me – let's be real, a big part of me – enjoyed being the chosen one.

I had enjoyed being envied.

I wasn't enviable now. No matter how pretty I looked, I was being handed over like some kind of trophy for Sabre's fake win.

As the attendants massaged my hands and feet while I sat in a large cushioned gold chair, the door leading to the Mating Room opened and Lady Xana came in.

"All is ready?" Xana looked to the attendants for confirmation and they nodded, rising from where they sat on the floor. "Then please follow me."

I stood from my chair to follow, but before I got to the door, my mother stopped me with a soft call of my name. I looked at her, my eyes cold.

"Aspen…" she hesitated. "Thank you."

I didn't reply before turning away and following Lady Xana into the Mating Room. Almost at the same time, from a door opposite the one I had entered, a male shaman appeared and Sabre was behind him.

He was dressed in white too, although that was no different to his usual obnoxious attire. If it was meant to indicate his purity, then I wasn't the only fraud in the room.

"We will leave you for as long as you need," Lady Xana said. "When you are ready, please pull the rope by the side of the bed. We will both retrieve you for the ritual."

Sabre and I nodded and with a final respectful bow, they exited through the door that led back to the main chamber.

I took a moment to look around. It was bright, the entire room washed in luminescent moonlight. I looked up and saw that the ceiling was glass, looking up at a beautiful night sky with the moon directly above us. This was truly a spectacular place, built on this designated sacred hill in King Hill, for nights exactly like this. This was the room countless Females had done their duty for better or worse, and I would be no different. I thought then of Erina Anai, who fought to be here, fought for the man she loved. I thought how I was unable to do the same and felt ashamed.

I looked away from the ceiling and other than the large bed that dominated the far end of the room, it was pretty bare. White and gold murals marked the walls and sparse furnishing that held refreshments. There was a sheer gossamer canopy over the bed and lush white rugs on the floor beneath our feet but not much else. The gold rope hung from the bed looking more and more like a noose. Considering we got dressed and prepped in the adjoining spaces, I guess it didn't need much else.

I finally looked at Sabre and found him watching me with challenging, heated eyes. He was in loose white trousers with a gold band around his waist, much like his challenge outfit, with a long white robe over his bare chest. His golden eyes weren't out of place in this palatial and regal setting and I found myself wondering how someone so good looking, could be so poisonous.

"You look beautiful," he said walking towards me, a somewhat tender smile on his lips.

"Thank you. Happy birthday."

My words came out breathless and I hated it. Sabre seemed to like it, the narcissistic bastard that he was and reached out to stroke my heavily painted face.

"Happy Birthday," he murmured, running his thumb gently along my cheek. "You don't have to be nervous. It'll be just like before, only better."

I looked away from him, angry tears threatening to surface. He wasn't even sorry for how he'd spoken to me before, admitting that he'd been sleeping with other females. He felt perfectly vindicated in his selfish decision and I hated him for it.

Sabre took hold of my chin with his index finger and turned my head back to his, "Let's start over."

"What?"

"Everything I said before, what I did…let's put it behind us and start over. Deal?"

It wasn't an apology but at this point, I didn't even need one—it wouldn't change anything. Still, I knew a peace offering when I saw one and I wouldn't refuse out of spite.

"All right."

He smiled then, genuinely, before running his thumb over my bottom lip, "Good… I'll make it good for you."

Disgusted, I moved my head out of his grip and went over to the bed, desperate to get this over and done with. It was a horrible thought, but it was the truth. I walked around to the left side of the bed and, never taking his eyes off me, Sabre made his way to the right. We both got into bed and without any preamble, I undressed. He did the same and before long, piles of gold and white fluttered to the floor either side of the bed.

I shuffled over to him, holding the thinner sheet underneath the duvet against my chest, not out of modesty—he'd seen me naked too many times for me to feel the need, even now—but because I wanted a barrier. Something that I could tell myself I'd done to not simply give in to him, something that was decidedly different to Caius.

Everything about this was different to last night.

Sabre came towards me and started kissing the inside of my neck. I scrunched my fists into the covers, and closed my eyes, trying to think of Caius to keep from seizing up every time Sabre's fingers brushed the softness of my body. It wasn't hard. I'd only been in his arms this morning and I could still feel his mouth on me.

Sabre continued to kiss me, nibbling and sucking on my neck until he began to lower those kisses onto my chest.

"Don't worry," he reassured me as he took the soft flesh above my breast and gently bit it. Sabre edged closer to me, reaching down as he kissed me, and gently spreading my delicate folds until I felt him at my opening. I winced as I felt the tip of his finger graze me.

"I said it'll be good," he whispered as he teased my soft flesh. I closed my eyes against his invasion and focused on my determination to do my duty, to be the daughter my father wanted and the Female my kind needed. I'd had my dream with Caius, a beautiful moment in time that I would cherish for the rest of my life, but I had an obligation to all *Iaecan* to see this through.

My hands tightened into fists at my sides as Sabre continued kissing me and opening me up to him until finally he settled himself between my legs and I felt him against me. A lone tear left my eye and Sabre gently wiped it away, "You don't have to be scared."

The fact he thought this was fear of sex shook me.

See me! I wanted to scream. *See me and know I don't want this!*

I knew he wouldn't.

He thought we'd made peace as well as being bound by the same responsibilities as me. He was here to do his duty.

And so was I.

Sabre kissed me once, so tenderly that when he entered me, my eyes shot open as I drew in a sharp breath. Sabre buried his face between my neck and my shoulder and kissed there gently, his lips light and cool against my heated skin. I said nothing as more tears trickled from my eye onto the pillow case, biting my lip so he wouldn't hear me cry. I closed my eyes against the shame coursing through me while Sabre murmured caressing words against my skin and I lost what remained of my dignity.

CHAPTER THIRTY-ONE

An eternity later, under the watchful eye of both mine and Sabre's parents, Lady Xana confirmed that we had conceived.

My duty was done.

I stood before the *laecan* altar, my eyes vacant as I stared at the now closed door of the Mating Room. As the tendrils of patchouli and sage smoke snaked around my head, under undecipherable ancient words that foretold my future and that of the child inside me, I couldn't take my eyes off that door.

I'd destroyed any semblance of self-respect I had behind that door, the moment I allowed Sabre to…

I crushed the images before they threatened to drive me insane and brought myself into the present. I smiled and nodded where appropriate, my parents looking on as they congratulated themselves on my successful enslavement. Sabre remained by my side, a solid and cold reminder of what we'd done, what I'd let him do…

I made a sound. Something between a choke and a sob as my stomach threatened to empty its contents in the middle of this sacred building.

"Aspen, are you all right?"

Surprisingly, it was my mother who asked. My head was spinning, I just needed to lie down for a moment. I told her so.

"Rest in the Mating Room, I'm sure it's been clea—"

"No!"

My decline came sharp and hot off my tongue. I would never set foot in that room again. I shook my head, closing my eyes against the rush of nausea that coiled through me, "I want to go home."

I didn't understand or care why she did, but my mother nodded and put her arms around me, squeezing my shoulders almost comfortingly. Exhausted and hurt, I let my head fall onto her shoulder and closed my eyes.

"Bracken," I heard my mother's voice as though it were coming through water. "We have to get her home."

I fell then. I fell into an abyss of shame, regret and fear of the future. As I closed my eyes and let myself descend into the darkness of my despair, I saw a pair of amber eyes peering back at me. Amber eyes that looked sad, broken…and betrayed.

Now that I was with child, my duty as the Female was almost over. All that remained was the Fight of the Female and then I would finally be free of my prophesied obligations. Well, until my baby was born.

I lay on my bed the night after the conception, one hand resting on my flat stomach the other playing absentmindedly with my dagger. It was incredible to believe that there was a child inside me; a tiny little baby that would be all mine.

Not exactly.

This child was, of course, half Riadnak…half Sabre…and as such, I was tied to him, forever. I was too tired, too depressed, too everything to think about what life would mean for me now. As I lay there stewing in my own self-pity, my door opened without any knock and my sister stood looking over at me. My eyes moved to look at her, but I didn't bother moving my head.

"What do you want, Rogue?"

My sister stood glaring at me, a look of satisfaction spread across her exquisite face. Rogue took a moment before she sneered at me,

"Do you know how frustrating it was to watch you strutting around here like you owned the place? Like you actually had Sabre's heart, when it's me keeping him satisfied?"

I sat up straight, discarding the dagger and swinging my legs over the side of my bed, planting my bare feet firmly on the carpeted floor.

"Excuse me?"

I barely had the words. They were stuck behind the confusion and betrayal that threatened to choke me to death.

Rogue and Sabre?

How had I not seen this?

"Every day having to hide our love for the sake of what you are, what you mean to everyone." Rogue was seething, practically foaming at the mouth. I watched her knuckles tighten around the door handle as she struggled to keep herself together. Clearly she'd been holding this in for a while.

"Well, it's over now and Sabre and I can finally be together!"

"How could you?" My words didn't come out nearly as strong as I would have hoped. They came out broken, defeated and void of life as tears gathered in my eyes.

Rogue smiled as though my tears delighted her.

"How could you do this to me?" I screamed at her from my bed. "I'm your sister!"

Rogue finally stepped into my room and growled at me, actually growled from the base of her throat.

"You…" she spat, "…are my competition. You, Aspen, are the stupid little bitch who thought she could have everything without paying the price for it, but I'm here to tell you that you were wrong."

Rogue glared at me, hatred in her eyes so intense I actually leaned back. My sister had always loathed me, but this was something different. One of my hands went to my stomach, an instinctively protective move.

Rogue finally turned away and headed out of my room.

"I'll tell Sabre you said hi," she called over her shoulder. "He'll be excited to hear I won't need to use mimosa root anymore." The sound of my sister's laughter echoed in my head.

As the door clicked shut behind her, I sank into my bed, drawing a deep and ragged breath. Rogue had betrayed me with Sabre. I'd known my sister was jealous of me, but I hadn't realised how much. No matter her jealousy, I would have never imagined she could do this to me, to our family. What if mum found out? As I stared into the space before me, I swallowed my pain and came to a decision.

Fight of the Female was tonight and my sister was going to get a confrontation she wouldn't forget.

As the Fight of the Female was only symbolic, it was held in the rearranged ballroom of the Riadnak Manor. Where there had been an orchestra and artfully placed chairs for those taking breaks from dancing, now there was an open, gold edged space with a platform at one end and endless cushions and low tables along the perimeter. The cushions were for reclining and when I entered the ballroom on Sabre's arm, the special guests who'd been invited to witness the fight were already in their plush seats being served delicacies from around the world. Mini patties filled with spicy beef and marinated chicken. Shredded duck and small savoury pancakes from Coz.

Now that the continued reign of Riadnak was set in stone, the theme of the evening was white and gold.

Thankfully, for my own embarrassment and broken heart, the Caldouns were not required to attend. This event was just another reason to exclude anyone who the Alphas did not deem worthy of their time or attention. So, dotted around me in various shades of sycophant and degenerate, were ambassadors and defunct chiefs and their closets allies. The Alphas and my parents were already there, talking among themselves about who-gave-a-shit-what.

I entered barefoot, as we all were, in a long robe that covered practically nothing. It was sheer, displaying the expensive and embroidered gold bralette and shorts underneath. My body had been painted with whirls of gold and white paint that apparently told the story of Erina's victory in some accent pictorial language. My hair was pulled back from my face in a severe ponytail with a long train of jet black hair that had gold ribbon braided into it. My make-up was full of gold accents, from the dust on my eyes to the glitter on my cheeks, to the paint on my lips. I knew the staffs we'd be using would be white, a bright contrast against the light of all this gold.

Music played as we entered, a soothing melody that seemed to blend effortlessly into the strands of *lief* smoke, that clouded in the air. The fight would begin soon, so as not to have the fighters affected too much by the smoke, but it was pleasant none the less. It did its job in easing the nerves that continued to course through me as I walked arm in arm with Sabre.

After bowing to the Alpha, we took our seats on the large cushions that had been designated to us. Sabre, once he'd reclined and positioned himself comfortably, leaned back to whisper in my ear, "You look amazing."

I didn't say anything. He was quiet for a moment before tilting his head questioningly, "Is something wrong? You've been quiet since the mating."

The fact he saw no issue with how we'd slept together was a problem in itself, but what could I really say?

I hated that I allowed you to violate me for the sake of my duty to Iaecan.

I hate that I betrayed the man I'm in love with by sullying myself with you.

It didn't exactly roll off the tongue. There was also the tiny issue of him sleeping with my sister.

"I'm just tired."

A lame excuse, but I had nothing left to give. To his credit, Sabre didn't look convinced, but let it go,

"I know you're pissed about what I said about other women, but I thought we were passed that now?"

He was sleeping with my sister and was trying to act like I had the problem? I didn't have the energy for this.

"It's fine. Like I said—I'm just tired."

A servant interrupted us just as he was about to respond, forcing him to drop it. He let go of my hand and reclined against his pillow, watching me as I took a glass of juice from the waiter's outstretched tray. Shaking, I positioned myself against my own cushion, trying to remain calm and look at ease with the whole situation until it was time for the fight to begin.

Once everything was ready, Balton stepped to the centre of the room and called out.

"Welcome, to our most special and honoured guests! As we all know, House Riadnak has officially held the Alpha title, undisputed, for the last three hundred years…"

Relax Balton. Considering we live a little longer than maejym*, that only means the last three Alphas*, I thought to myself, sipping my juice innocently. Balton went on for a while longer until…

"…now, the final event, for your entertainment…the Fight, of the Female!"

The room exploded into thunderous applause as my friends filed into the room from the large double doors. The choreography played out the Erina legend and so Rhea, Susi, Koda, Fern and one other girl, who should have been Tala, came in dressed as Females representing their own families. They were in outfits exactly the same as mine, although where I had gold paint and make up, the girls had blue, red, purple, green and yellow respectively. Rogue would be wearing silver, representing Orlagh Caldoun, the Fallen Female. Despite Orlagh having died first, I would fight Rogue last to display my final triumph over her.

The other girls paraded themselves in a sensual dance that spoke of aggression, determination and pride. They twirled their staffs and twisted their bodies in fluid and sexual ways that had the eyes of the males in the audience practically bursting out of their heads.

When my part arrived, I rose from my recline and engaged them in battle. As we had rehearsed, I fought first Rhea, then Koda, before moving on to Fern, Susi and then the other girl – Piper – until they were all figuratively dead. They all lay artfully in two lines either side of me to be clear of Rogue's entry path. I twirled my staff above my head before bringing the end of it crashing to the floor in a display of dominance that was a little on the dramatic side.

No one could say I didn't commit to my craft.

"Who will challenge the Female?" I cried out, knowing full well my sister's line would come from behind me.

"I will."

I looked behind me and when I finally laid eyes on my sister, my heart stopped beating for a brief moment. As ever, Rogue was devastatingly beautiful and from the collective gasp and mumble that echoed around the room, everyone else knew it too. She looked breath-taking in her silver bralette and shorts, her thick thighs, the same as mine, on display for all to see. She stalked toward me, her head held high as I turned my body completely to hold out my staff to her, horizontally. Rogue didn't bother with the theatrics and launched into the routine. I obliged and danced with her, our eyes never leaving each other's as we battled.

I hated her.

I wanted to rip my sister's face off, tear her limbs from her body and beat her with them, but I couldn't do any of those things. So, embarrassing her would have to be enough... for now.

Realising I was not playing by the rules, my sister engaged me and went on the attack. She came at me with all the rage that had been built up inside her, all the resentment and jealously that she'd been forced to keep inside. She roared at me as she swung her staff above her head and brought it crashing down over mine. I blocked with my own staff before using the end of it to ram at her head. In order to avoid a hit to the face, Rogue danced out of the hold. I didn't give her time to recuperate and lunged at her with the staff in a barrage of thrusts and hits that she struggled to keep up with.

Rogue came at me again, a feigned swipe at my left before actually hitting me on my right and as the staff connected and pain laced up my right thigh, I growled and spun on my tiptoes. Staff twirling, I spun out of the offensive position, grabbed the higher end of my staff with both hands and rammed the end of it into her stomach.

Rogue's eyes bulged, her staff fell from her grip as she coughed and spittle came out of her mouth from being winded. The crowd gasped as Rogue stumbled back, clutching her stomach. I stalked toward my sister and without hesitation struck my staff clear across her face.

Rogue fell to the floor, smacking her head on the marble, her mouth bleeding from where I'd hit her, her jaw broken.

I didn't care.

I threw my staff down beside her and stormed out of the room.

Not caring about the Riadnaks or my parents, I *turned* as soon as I left the ballroom and went home. I'd been sitting in the rear gardens for hours, alone, when I smelled my sister. She'd probably smelled me, which would explain how she knew I was out here. It seemed our standoff had arrived.

"You *bitch*!"

I stood. Rogue stopped in front of me, her eyes burning with rings of gold.

"You're one to talk."

Her jaw had healed, but her face was horrifically bruised. Already a dark blueish purple as she was healing faster than most, the bruise crawled up the side of her face, going over her blood shot eye. Rogue sneered, not even remotely sorry for what she had done.

"Stop whining because I finally let you in on what almost everyone knows! It's not my fault you were too dumb to notice!"

I wished I had something more vicious to say to her, but the fact that my friends had known about them and said nothing? The hurt was too much.

"Did you really think he loved you?" Rogue continued with her hate tirade. "Did you really think that he wanted you for more than what you can give him?"

"How are you any different?" I spat at her, my eyes blazing with my own fury, not because I *had* believed that, but because how did she think her situation wasn't the same?

"Excuse me?"

"Answer me, Rogue!" I stepped forward and pushed her, making her stumble. "Why do you think that Sabre wants you anymore than he wanted me? It might be status with me, but it's just physical with you!"

"He loves me!"

"I thought so too and yet here we are!"

We stared at each other, anger and resentment in both our eyes, but I knew I was the only one sorry for it. No matter what Rogue had done, I pitied her. No matter what Sabre did or didn't feel for her, he'd used her and she couldn't even see it.

"You're just trying to get into my head, like always."

I rolled my eyes at her, "Rogue, I don't care enough about you to get into your head. Your jealousy did that, not me."

Rogue narrowed her eyes at me, "You never thought I was good enough. You never considered me."

"Considered you for what?" I laughed, genuinely amused. "No, wait. Maybe I should have been considering you when I was being drugged by mum, or pressured by dad or manipulated by Sabre? Maybe I should have considered that my only sister would fuck my boyfriend, because of her own delusions of grandeur!"

I went to walk away, to be done with the conversation and her but her next words stopped my exit, "You're a hypocrite!"

I looked back at her, her face morphing back into perfection in front of my very eyes as her healing accelerated, "Oh really?"

"Yes, really. You talk about delusions of grandeur when you walked around here like you owned the place, like everyone was beneath you and you couldn't be bothered to give them the time of day."

I'd had enough of this pathetic excuse of a reasoning for her betrayal.

"I might be a hypocrite, little sister, but I'd rather be that than a consolation prize."

My head rocked and my vision blurred when she slapped me. I stumbled back, dizzy from the unexpected connect as I held my hand to my stinging face. My sister watched me, her chest heaving with her resentment and her wish to do more, but I saw her change her mind. I saw her look down at my stomach then back up and knew she'd weighed up her options for hurting the Female and none of them ended well for her.

In an instant, she *turned* and the thick brown and grey coat of my sister's wolf form stood in front of me. I lifted my head to look into the eyes of the beast who snarled at me. Her teeth bared, I continued to stare at her, daring her to do something that would end this for both of us.

She took a snap at me, so close I felt spittle land on my face, before she darted away past me towards the front of the house. Slowly, my eyes followed the path Rogue had taken to escape the garden, her mighty paws imprinted in the grass. I sank to my knees, suddenly too weak to stand, and while cradling my bruising face, I cried into the seemingly endless night.

CHAPTER THIRTY-TWO

Our family dinner that evening was tense. The smoke of burning words left unspoken clouded the air, choking the civility out of us.

Rogue, seemingly unfazed by her betrayal, ate her meal in triumphant silence while my mother, ever forthcoming in her disappointment in me, had nothing to say about my latest outburst. It seemed I would be forgiven any and all transgressions now that I carried the Alpha heir. My father, at the head of the table, also ate in silence, shooting me random looks of concern. He would move his lips as if to say something, then quickly decide against it. I didn't know if my parents knew about Rogue and Sabre, but really it didn't matter either way. I'd not received any backlash after my fight with Rogue, but even if I had, I wouldn't have cared.

Once I'd finished my meal, I pushed my empty plate forward and my seat back, desperate to get away from my family.

"Where are you going?" my mother asked, worried.

"I'm going to see Sabre."

I was out the door before I could see my sister's reaction.

When I arrived at the Riadnak Manor, I was greeted warmly by the house guards. I'd chosen to walk to the manor on human feet, which gave me some time to think about all that would change now that I carried an Alpha heir.

The new familial lines had been drawn and once Goliath passed away, everyone would take their places in the new world order, with Caius and his family as the new Betas. In just over two months—once my child was born—Sabre and I would be married and any connection I wanted with Caius would be gone.

It felt like a lifetime ago since I'd seen him, how could it have been only yesterday when I'd lain in his arms, breathed in his scent and felt his smooth and powerful body beneath my fingertips? It was only yesterday that I'd felt his lips on my neck, his fingers teasing my skin with the memory of his intimate touch.

I wanted to go to him, to run to the cave and never leave, but it wouldn't change how dirty I felt at having been with Sabre, hours after being with Caius. I couldn't look Caius in the eye, knowing what I'd allowed to happen. I'd rather not see the look on his face as he tried to ignore what we both knew stood between us. Our perfect and beautiful time together had been soiled. I wanted to remember Caius the way he'd been looking at me before, with what I tentatively hoped was love.

I'd said my goodbyes and that was how it would have to stay, even as we grew and I watched him marry, have children and be happy with someone else. I choked back the tears of despair threatening to choke me as I marched up the stairs of the manor towards Sabre's room. I was about to push the door open without knocking when I heard voices coming from within. I froze as the unmistakeable bass of Goliath's voice rumbled through the open doorway.

"...to defend us. I've sent Olcan to the front to check on things, but I need to get the others in line so we can cut the Faenymese out by the root."

"I can't do that with the wolves I have, it's not enough," Sabre argued, a strain in his voice that I'd never heard before.

"Make it enough! I didn't make sure you won the title just to let the power slip through your fingers, Sabre!"

"If I'm such a disappointment, then why not do it yourself?" Sabre hissed at his father. I heard the responsive punch as much as I smelt the blood that escaped from its connection when it misted the air.

"If you did as you were told, you wouldn't be a disappointment!" The rage that brewed in his tone was sickening, "After your embarrassing defeat in the second challenge, despite my interference, I should have known you weren't good enough. He handed you that third win! Perhaps I should have backed the Gamma; God knows he's stronger than you. Was I wrong to put my faith in you, Sabre?"

"No, Sir," came Sabre's muffled reply before I heard shuffling and staggered footsteps. My mind reeled from Goliath's words, realising that I had been right in suspecting that my mother had sabotaged Caius in the second challenge, giving him a higher dose of wolfsbane than they had Sabre. I hadn't thought Goliath was involved as well.

"Deal with Isaac and his pathetic excuse of an uprising, and do it quickly, or I promise you won't like what happens to you."

Realising Goliath was about to leave, I stepped slightly away from the door and raised my fist as if I were about to knock. When Goliath opened the door, he was more than a little shocked to see me standing there. I mirrored his expression before quickly bowing, "Apologies, Alpha. I came by to see Sabre."

As I straightened, my head still bowed, Goliath cleared his throat and I raised my eyes to look at him.

"No need for all that, Aspen, you are family now. I hope you're taking care of yourself and my grandson?"

He reached out and palmed my still flat stomach. I jumped at the unexpected connection, having never touched the Alpha before, or had him touch me. His large hand covered my entire stomach. The power in that one hand had a shiver of trepidation rush through me.

I nodded, answering his question, "I begin taking my tonics tomorrow."

"Good, see to it you do everything you can to birth a strong and healthy son."

I nodded with a smile, ever complacent and accommodating, until he smiled once more and strode down the hallway to his bedroom. My body shook with anger but I swallowed it down and entered Sabre's room.

"What are you doing here?" Sabre asked, already annoyed from his confrontation with his father, but I didn't care. There was a fresh though fading bruise on his face.

"You're sleeping with Rogue."

He froze for a moment, words on his lips that he decided against and shrugged. Actually, shrugged. He walked over to his desk to rifle through the papers and roughly written notes that littered the surface, "So what?"

"You're not even going to deny it?"

"Why should I? You know, and now that you're pregnant I don't have to hide it."

My fists clenched by my side, "Sabre, she's my sister. How could you do this to me?"

His eyes were suddenly vicious and cruel as he stared back at me, all evidence of the man who'd kissed me and told me he loved me for the past few years gone.

"Don't start your bullshit, all right? I'm not in the mood."

"My bullshit?"

Sabre rolled his eyes, clearly tired of me and this conversation, "All you do is complain and now that the Mating is over, I don't have to pretend to want to deal with your issues anymore."

I tried to find something to say, but the words were stuck.

"You had a role to play and you played it. Just continue in the same way, stay quiet and we'll get along just fine. Like we always have. Right?"

"My role?" I parroted him again, my chest ached with the intensity of my rage.

"Yes," he said, impatience flaring though he still wasn't giving me his full attention, occupying himself with looking through the papers. "Your role, as my beautiful, devoted and most importantly *silent* wife. Who does whatever the fuck I tell her to do and doesn't complain about my extramarital affairs."

"You can't expect to continue with her after we're married. Goliath won't let you!"

Sabre laughed then, a harsh and jubilant laugh that told me I wouldn't like what he was going to say next. He lay his hands on the desk in front of him and looked up at me,

"Do you really think he'll care, considering what he's doing with Ianthe?"

How long had he known? My face heated and my jaws clenched while rage burned in my eyes,

"Just continue doing what's expected of you and everyone wins. Don't you get that by now?"

Obviously, I didn't. It seemed I was the only one who was doing any of this for the right reasons and I was the only one it had cost anything. I'd been made to lose Caius because I was desperate to do what was right for my people, to stop conflict. All the time, everyone else around me got what they wanted. Sabre became Alpha Apparent, Goliath grew more powerful, my mother claimed status through me and my sister got to play this cruel and unusual joke against me.

I was completely alone.

"I won't let you treat me like shit, Sabre!"

Sabre came around the desk, reached out and grabbed hold of my face, squeezing my cheeks so tightly my lips puckered.

"You won't have a choice, you never have. You are nothing without me and my name. Now go and be nothing somewhere else." Sabre pushed me away from him, looking at me in disgust.

With tears threatening to fall and nothing else to say, I scurried out of the room and into the hallway, desperate to get away from him. Sabre's words cut me to my core as I replayed them over and over in my head. They cut deeper when I acknowledged not only that he was right, but that I believed him.

Two nights later, my presence was required at the Riadnak Manor for a celebratory dinner. I'd had it with the endless dinners and parties and celebrations, but Celeste Riadnak apparently wanted to shower her son in further praise for simply impregnating me. Not like I had anything to do with half the biology of it, of course.

The main families and elders had been invited and now, after four courses and sufficient entertainment, the young people were in the lounge, talking. At his less than cordial request, I sat by Sabre's side, his arm draped over my shoulder as he sipped tentatively from a glass tumbler. The tips of his fingers were able to brush lightly against the bare skin of my thin-strapped dress and it made my skin crawl every time he did it. His fingers were cold and spindly, like spider's legs, and I just wanted away from him. He didn't even want me, he just wanted to make me suffer. I hated that he was succeeding.

Rogue sat on his other side, quietly observing everything around her, but for once not shooting poisonous looks in my direction. Even she could see I didn't want to be there as much as she didn't want me there. Where I once would have been the life and soul of any gathering, I sat beside Sabre offering nothing to the conversation.

"Are you all right, Aspen?" Olcan enquired suddenly as he poured himself a drink from the side table. I smiled immediately, not wanting to anger Sabre by letting on that I was nowhere near all right.

"I'm fine, why do you ask?"

"You just look a little pale, that's all."

"She's pregnant, stupid," Fern giggled, accepting one of the drinks Olcan had brought over as he took a leisurely seat beside her. Olcan nuzzled his lips into Fern's neck and a smile bloomed on her face. I averted my eyes, jealous at how happy she looked.

"Yeah, he's growing quickly." I placed my hand on my stomach. It had only been a few days but my body had already started to change, my diet, my sleeping patterns, everything. Sabre put his hand over the top of mine,

"My boy is going to be strong, that's why!"

I snatched my hand away, clearing my throat as I did so. I didn't look at Sabre, trying not to acknowledge his anger at my rebuttal.

"When are you going to have a baby, Fern?" I asked instead, but she just burst out laughing.

"To ruin my figure and have this one look elsewhere? Half past never!" Fern launched herself at Olcan, their drinks forgotten as they began to kiss.

He's already looked elsewhere, I thought. I shot a look in Rhea and Susi's direction, but while Susi avoided my eyes, Rhea stared back defiantly. Knowing they were a part of the resistance in some way, I found I no longer cared why they'd done what they did. I'd done far worse for less.

"No one in their right mind or not bound by *laecan* tradition would have a child now," Fenrir jumped in. "Not with this fighting going on."

Everyone agreed.

"I don't see why it's still going on," Susi moaned as she downed another drink. I watched how effortlessly she played her part, knowing that she was involved in more than she let on. "Just give Isaac what he wants and be done with all the killing."

"War is necessary to keep peace, Susi," Fenrir responded.

"Only to those that are winning."

"So, you want us to give in to his demands? Roll over and let him do what he wants?" Fenrir snapped.

"That's not what I'm saying,"

"Then what are you saying?" Sabre's stern voice cut through the room and everyone waited for Susi's response. I gave her credit for not recoiling from the stare that would've had me quaking in my boots, but then, I now knew what a demon Sabre was, maybe she didn't.

"I'm saying, that innocents shouldn't have to die for the sake of a few. Goliath didn't have to raze Andrix just because their countrymen were fighting hundreds of miles away. They have a right to want to make their own rules."

Either she was talking about the fight where Ulren had been used to eradicate countless *laecan* or another attack had taken place since. Either didn't sound good, and if it was the latter, I wondered if Caius knew.

"It was a message, Susi, that we're not to be underestimated or undermined," Rogue chimed in and it angered me, realising that she may have discussed this with Sabre. Could it be that, as they lay in bed together, laughing at me, he discussed his battle plans with her, while whispering nothing but fake platitudes to me?

I wanted to scream.

"You can send a message without killing innocent people," Susi snapped.

Finally, Rhea stepped in to defend her, "Susi's right. Armies should fight other armies, not butcher women and children in their beds."

"It's a means to an end. My father does what he must."

"He must rape and pillage a town of his own kind? I doubt that!"

"You can doubt it all you want—it doesn't stop it being true," Sabre growled and the room went silent. "My father is a king even when the choices to remain as such are hard ones. Faenym will understand that soon enough, as will Boltese eventually, and anyone else who wants to come against us."

Olcan and Fenrir were firmly on Sabre's side, nodding in fast agreement. Rhea stood from where she had lounged next to Susi, the rest of us looking on as her mate followed in her footsteps.

"You can keep telling yourself that this is okay because it has your shiny wolf logo on it Sabre…but it's still murder. Let's go Suze."

The girls marched out of the room, leaving the rest of us in a deafening silence. I searched around the room, looking at the faces left behind, and realised that no one was upset by Rhea and Susi's departure. Every single one of them were on Sabre's and therefore Goliath's side, the side of war and vengeance.

Was this the world I was marrying into? A world that I would have to sit and pretend didn't sicken me?

More than ever I wished I was with Caius, on the side he'd chosen, but I was stuck here, and all the choices I'd made for what I hoped was the right thing, were turning out wrong. I held my hand to my stomach and sighed deeply, praying the child inside me would be worth all this pain.

A week later, I was shaken awake by my mother holding a candle, the only light in my otherwise dark bedroom. My eyes adjusted to as I brushed my hair away from in front of my eyes.

"What time is it, what's wrong?"

"It's Goliath," my mother's voice trembled, as did the flame in her hand. "He's dead."

CHAPTER THIRTY-THREE

To keep the unfathomable news from touching wider ears, the main families were essentially dragged from our homes under the cover of darkness and brought to the Riadnak Manor.

Our leader, our protector, the all-powerful Alpha, was dead—and the Council, I had no doubt, was out for blood.

My mother was distraught as we sat in the back of the carriage on the way to the Manor. My sister's eyes were bloodshot and my father's face was devoid of any emotion. I remained silent, my own fears building in the pit of my stomach. I had to calm myself, knowing for once this wasn't about me and that a world of discord was about to descend on Invernell.

My first thought was: who had done it? There were more than enough suspects for me, including my own father, who I'd heard say he was going to take care of Goliath. There was Caius, who had expressed he could never broker any real peace while Goliath was alive, and Sabre, who was constantly beaten by his domineering hand. Even Tala, before leaving, had threatened to kill him. Any one of them could have been the culprit, but how would we find out?

When the carriage came to a stop outside the manor gates, we were ushered inside under hooded robes to shelter from the cold night air. It was officially winter and even Agmantia felt the chills of winter winds. In the north, thick layers of snow would cover the mountains and the winding trails that lead into the northern cities. Roads would be difficult to travel as wolf or man and leaves had fallen from trees.

For some unknown reason, my mind wandered to Caius' cave and wondered how warm it would be in the harsh weather. What I wouldn't give to be bundled in that bed of furs with him, away from the torture of my new existence. Holding him, kissing him, loving him.

Before tears could build and fall, I wiped at my face and stepped into the manor behind the rest of my family. Balton was there to meet us and rushed us into Goliath's study.

It was a large room decorated in dark wood with gold furnishings. Three of the four walls were lined with books and ledgers, a small open sided bar with decanters of whisky, brandy and bottles of wine. A fire was roaring in the large stone fireplace to the right, warming the room, and at the far end, sat behind his father's desk in a high-backed leather chair, was Sabre.

His mother and sister stood to his left, Fenrir and Olcan to his right, while the other heads of families stood together on the left-hand side of the room. My mother took a seat, straight backed on a chaise lounge at the front of the room with my father stood dutifully behind her. Everyone was here except…

All eyes turned to the door as it opened once more and the Caldouns entered.

I took in a sharp breath as I laid eyes on Caius for the first time since our night together, but quickly swallowed the ache that lodged itself in my throat. Caius was the most beautiful thing I'd ever seen and if I thought I'd missed him before, it was nothing to how I felt seeing him now. He wore black, a loose hooded top over trousers and boots. His thick eyebrows peaked out from under his hood but as he walked into the room and took a place beside his family in front of the fire place, he didn't even look over at me.

I needed to see his eyes.

I needed to know he still cared for me.

Please, look at me.

My will alone didn't change anything and Caius looked down at the floor, waiting for the meeting to begin. Heartbroken, I looked away from him, turning to look towards Sabre and his family.

Sabre lowered his troubled eyes and cleared his throat, "You have all been invited here as a courtesy before the news is broken to the rest of Invernell. My amazing and powerful father... your Alpha... was murdered." He lifted his eyes again and began to scan everyone in the room. "He was found upstairs in his bed, his throat slashed. My mother... my mother found him after returning from King Hill with my sist—"

"And where were you?" Rhea's father Kade interrupted. Where I expected Sabre to answer, Celeste Riadnak stepped in for her son. Her eyes were puffy from tears and I could see from where we stood closest to the desk that there was blood on her hands and gown. I felt ill at the sight. Goliath's body, I assumed, was still in the house...

"My son was with Fenrir at his home, Kade. I'd hate to think you were trying to imply Sabre had anything to do with this!"

"I imply nothing, my lady, but if we are all to be questioned at some point, then it's only right that Sabre's whereabouts be made public knowledge. I meant no offense." Kade's tone said otherwise.

"I can vouch for the boys," Runan, Fenrir's father, chimed in, his deep voice rumbling around the tight space. Fenrir looked a lot like his father, both with light skin and steel grey eyes. "I was at home until the messenger came to inform Sabre."

"I bet you were."

"If you have something to say, Kade, then come out and say it!" Runan shot back. Kade stepped forward, fists clenched.

"Enough!" Celeste growled, making the few items on the desk shake. She placed her right hand on her son's shoulder while pulling Fern into a comforting hold with her left. Fern sobbed into her mother's neck as we all looked on, grieved by the sight.

"I have my husband's blood on my hands. Our way of life is on the brink of destruction and you wish to have petty arguments!" Her voice was shrill as she raised her voice, "I don't know who did this and we will get to the bottom of it, but until then…the succession blessing must take place."

The family heads outraged almost immediately, saying Sabre wasn't ready, that he was too green to take the role so soon.

"The boy's too young," Kade protested and I saw a slight nod of Maximus' head, he was in agreement. Celeste let who would do so object, then she raised her hand.

"I am aware Sabre is still in his minority until he turns twenty-one…" Celeste stated. If Goliath were still alive, Sabre would continue his training with him, learning from him how to seamlessly take the title upon his death which should have been many, many years from now.

"…but it is imperative we showcase a united Alpha family now that the Faenymese are practically at our gates."

Celeste let her eyes roam the room, daring one of us to deny her. "Sabre won the challenges, he impregnated the Female…" my eyes went to Caius, but he was still looking at the floor. "…he is the rightful heir by law and blood."

She wasn't wrong and everyone knew it, "So, I put to you that before the vigorous investigation into my husband's murder and the approaching chaos that will undoubtedly ensue, we bless Sabre in as Alpha. Agreed?"

There was a tense moment of silence before Runan spoke, "Agreed."

My father was the next to follow until the room came alight with approval of Sabre's leadership. Last to speak was Kade, but it wasn't to acquiesce.

"Where is Lady Xana? She is to make the blessing. Surely she should bear witness to this expedited change?"

I'd forgotten about Lady Xana but Kade was right, she should be present if she were to bless his reign.

"I agree," Maximus Caldoun finally joined in. "I have no objection to Sabre being, Alpha Celeste, but the shaman should be here."

Celeste's usually warm eyes were now calculating and petty as she stared Maximus down.

"Very well," Celeste agreed. "I will send for Lady Xana in the morning, once you agree—"

"Or I could do it now."

There was a collective rush of heads as we all turned to face the door where Lady Xana now stood. No one had heard her enter. I swallowed, suddenly terrified at seeing her again, her presence never leaning toward anything good. The old woman walked to the front of the room, the family heads parting for her without question as her staff thudded on the carpeted floor. The sound seemed to vibrate throughout the whole room and again I found myself with my hand protectively on my stomach. There was power in this woman, magic in everything she did and I felt it humming through me.

I looked up again to where Caius stood watching Xana cross the room. My breath caught as I realised he would finally turn to face me, but when he'd turned enough to actually see me, he looked away. My heart sank as I hid my disappointment and looked to the shaman instead. Surprisingly, she stopped directly in front of me and looked down to where I held my hand against my stomach.

Lady Xana moved away from me, her jewellery jingling as she moved until she stood in front of Sabre, who still had not spoken. He eyed the shaman with unfiltered contempt, but when Celeste squeezed his shoulder, his expression softened.

"Do I have your blessing, Lady Xana?" Sabre asked smoothly. Lady Xana stared into Sabre's eyes and the atmosphere in the room thickened.

"I know this boy's heart," she finally said, easing the tension that choked the life out of us. "I know that this ruling will bring about much needed change… when the right choices are made."

Choices. It was always about choices with her.

My eyes found Caius once more and my heart ached for the choice I'd made about him. I'd chosen him to be my first, but it hadn't been enough. What good were choices if you always made the wrong ones?

"I give my blessing." Lady Xana confirmed although her words seemed strained. With a few choice words chanted over Sabre's head, the deed was apparently done. Lady Xana stamped her staff onto the floor with one thunderous bang, and then she was gone.

"Investigations will be carried out by the Riadnak guards so until we have my husband's murderer in chains, you will all do well to be helpful in their search." Celeste now said. "Now, if you will excuse us. My children and I wish to be alone."

Before filing out of the room, everyone bowed their heads to Sabre, now officially the Alpha. I watched as Caius bowed dutifully to him and Sabre's face morphed into a picture of sadistic glee. Caius still didn't look at me, leaving the room without ever turning in my direction. When my family and I finally left the Riadnak

Manor, guards traipsing up and down the stairs, I was completely and utterly defeated.

Goliath was gone.

Someone had killed him and now there was nothing standing between Sabre and absolute power over *laecan*... and me.

CHAPTER THIRTY-FOUR

Another two weeks went by without seeing Caius in the streets of Invernell or across the bar at the Bane and Goliath's murderer has still not been found. The Riadnak and wider Invernelli guards had questioned everyone in town and come up with nothing.

Goliath was last seen at an event near the Celestia coast with a few members of the war council that he had stationed there. After a night of festivities, Goliath returned home to an empty manor, but for the staff, and retired to bed in the early evening. Sometime between his arrival and Celeste and Fern's return later that night, someone had slit Goliath's throat while he slept, and left him to bleed out. The only lead they had was that the blade had been made of iron and laced with a lethal dose of wolfsbane.

If the sliced artery hadn't killed him, the metal and poison would have, paralysing him so he couldn't have called or moved for any kind of help. It was a coward's way of killing, my father said, while my mother reasoned that poison was a woman's weapon.

Whatever the case, Invernell had fallen into mayhem. My father had been called away to the Riadnak Manor more than once, for meetings with heads of families and ambassadors from all over the country. The Voltairi ambassador hadn't stayed long, claiming the *maejym* war that King Ridian fought against the Coznians took up enough of his time.

And while Invernell struggled to fill the hole of power that Goliath had left behind, Sabre thrived in it.

After the traditional Nine Nights of mourning before Goliath's pyre burning, that consisted of celebrations over his life and declarations of his successes, Sabre took to being Alpha as quickly as he'd taken to bedding my sister. In the short weeks since his ascension, Invernell had turned into a battleground. Where any fighting had once been hidden away—at least from my immediate knowledge—it was now at the forefront of everything. There were petty power struggles among the social elite and brawls broke out at the Bane because of constant civil unrest. I was told to stay inside as much as possible and when I did venture out, I had guards. War had come upon Invernell and not just among the privileged elite who made money from it, or were privy to the information beforehand. We were given curfews and told not to travel to neighbouring cities. We were forced into a lockdown that kept us from our family and friends in an attempt to protect us from a threat we couldn't yet see.

Despite these events, Sabre held an endless stream of parties and gatherings. He claimed they highlighted the prosperity of his newly anointed reign, but I saw it for what it really was: a court jester had been given a crown and believed himself a king.

Almost every night, despite the restrictions he'd placed on the town, there was some pompous soiree he wanted me to attend on his arm. I tired easily because of the baby and I had no inclination for his childish and petty behaviour.

I sat on an ornately decorated chair beside Sabre at his most recent party and decided I'd had enough. Celeste sat on the throne the other side of him, while Rogue sat in his lap for all to see. My mother, despite venomous words in an attempt to discipline Rogue, could do nothing about their affectionate displays, now that Sabre reigned. Rogue's antics with the father of my child would go on unpunished because now Sabre made the rules. Anyone who discussed him, me or my sister in a less than favourable manner was swiftly dealt with. Sabre was turning into a carbon copy of his father, and I saw in the eyes of the elders who watched him that they were terrified of what they'd allowed to be unleashed into the world because they hadn't fought Celeste.

Sabre's antics with my sister, embarrassing as they were, broached the subject of Celeste's involvement in Sabre's actions. She either didn't care or couldn't do anything about their affair, and hadn't relinquished her authority of Alpha Consort to me.

It wouldn't be official until Sabre and I were married, but it didn't make the slight any less severe. Celeste didn't respect me as the Female or as her future daughter-in-law. Her less than pleasing nature was a shock, to say the least, as she'd never treated me unkindly before.

I stood from my chair, hating everything about my current existence, and made for the door.

"Where are you going?" Sabre grabbed hold of my wrist.

"Bed. I'm tired."

His eyes narrowed into slits as he pushed Rogue off his lap and came to stand in front of me. I refused to back down, now or ever again, considering what he was putting me through.

"Don't lie to me."

"I'm not lying, your child makes me tired, so, I'm going to bed."

He had no response for that and released my wrist. I curtseyed to him for the benefit of onlookers and marched out of the room. When I was safely outside and was sure no one had followed me, I *turned* and headed towards the woods.

I found myself outside Caius' cave some time later. Even though *turning* took a lot more effort than it used to because of my pregnancy, I did it happily to get to him as fast as I could. I raced down the dark opening, my heart pounding when I saw no torches were lit.

"Caius!" I called out, hurtling around the corner into the doorway of his den and approaching nothing but darkness. "Caius?"

There were embers in the ashes of the hearth and as I *turned*, looking around the wide shadowy space, my heart plummeted.

"Caius, are you here?"

Please be here, please be here!

There was no sign of him. His bed was made, there were no clothes thrown about anywhere and it was just too quiet.

He wasn't here.

Defeated, I took a deep trembling sigh as tears filled my eyes. I tried to stop them falling, biting my lip and scrunching my eyes up, but soon, my face was wet. I hiccupped with the force of holding in my cries and so, not knowing what else to do, I walked over to the bed, kicked off my shoes and climbed on. I burrowed my face and my hands into the sheets, into the smell of him and cried. I missed him so much. There were no fancy words for the simple and undeniable ache of wanting him.

As I lay on Caius' bed, breathing him in, drowning myself in him, I cried inconsolably. I curled into a ball, clawing at the sheets as I wept, my heart threatening to break out of my chest.

"Grey?"

I shot up off the bed, eyes wide to see Caius standing in the cave doorway. His golden eyes stared back, confused. With no care for my puffy, tear stained face, I leapt from the bed and launched myself at him, wrapping my arms around his neck and planting my lips onto his. He resisted at first, his arms held out as he tried not to wrap them around me but he soon gave in and pressed me into his body as my lips plundered his. I moaned as he deepened the kiss, his tongue pushing between my lips and sucking until my knees were weak. I pulled back to look up at him, amber eyes blazing like steel in a blacksmith's forge. The heat from them coursed through me, warming me from the inside out.

"I won't give you up," I said. "I can't."

"Grey, we can't—"

"We can. Everything we were fighting for is crumbling down around us so why do we have to suffer? Why can't we be together?"

He didn't have a response and so I pushed, locking my green eyes deep into his amber ones.

"Tell me you don't want this and I'll leave." I licked my lips, suddenly nervous and unsure despite the evidence of his desire pushing against my stomach. "Tell me you don't want me."

I tried to press myself further into him, but he resisted once more and pushed me away, taking a decisive step back and I felt the rejection like a punch to the gut.

"Grey, please... just leave."

"I'm trying to," my voice croaked. "I'm trying so hard, but I can't *just leave*. Not from you."

I watched as his eyes glazed over. I took a tentative step closer again and this time he didn't move. I reached out and placed my hand on his chest, feeling the solid wall of it beneath his shirt. He was warm, despite the weather, the heat of him radiating through my trembling fingers.

"Caius, I lo—"

"Stop," he backed further away.

My hand froze mid-air at the disconnect and I wilted with hopelessness.

"Caius..."

"Stop it."

Knowing I couldn't force him, I accepted the choice he was making.

"I know I shouldn't have come but… at the Manor… you didn't even look at me," I said. He sighed, eyes on the fire. "I just needed to see you… to know if the other night was real and that it meant to you what it did to me."

"Grey…"

"It's fine if it didn't," I put on my bravest smile and gave a small shrug as I turned away from him. I rushed towards the entrance of the cave but was stopped by a firm grip on my wrist.

I didn't want him to see me cry again so I didn't turn around. He seemed to understand and slowly let go of me. I felt him, his chest against my back a moment before his hands snaked around me and pulled me into him. I tilted my neck to the side and rested my head against him. I closed my eyes as the tip of his nose brushed my skin and he breathed me in. My hands were clasped over his, willing him to pull me tighter and to never let go.

"It meant everything to me," he whispered, the rumble of his voice sending a warm tingly sensation over my body. "*You* mean everything to me, Grey."

We stood there, my chest to his back for a while,

"Grey, please," he sounded defeated, even as he took the sting out of his words with my nickname. I knew I would have to go. "Just be happy that we got our night."

"How can I be happy with just a night when I want forever?"

I felt his body stiffen behind me, his breath stopped just as mine did. Within moments, he released the breath and slowly turned me around. He didn't answer me. Instead, he lowered himself to take hold of the backs of my thighs and lifted me up. I wrapped my legs around his waist and kissed him as he carried me over to his bed.

Caius and I lay in each other's arms a long while later, just… looking.

I looked at the mess I'd made of his waves while dragging my nails through them as he'd pleasured me. He looked and trailed a finger over the faint bite mark he'd left on top of my breast. I looked at his insanely long coal black eyelashes and traced my finger over his thick eyebrows. Caius lowered his eyes and for a brief moment, he looked at my slightly protruding stomach. As I'd said to Goliath, I'd begun taking the required tonics to promote a healthy pregnancy and child, but I still felt like it wasn't real. There was a child inside me and because of everything that had happened, I wasn't focusing on it the way I should have been. It was just something that was happening to me. My eyes averted from his, ashamed. I knew my little issue would present itself eventually, but I hadn't had a second to care. Not when I was palming his chest as I rode him or when I'd held his hands over my breasts as he'd entered me while we spooned.

"Do you hate me?" my voice was hushed as I spoke into the small space between our bodies.

"No, Grey. I don't hate you." His voice was soothing and reassuring which only made me feel worse.

"Does it bother you?"

"Yes."

I didn't say anything, afraid to look at him, my shame stopping me. Caius reached out and lifted my face to his so he could lean forward to kiss me. His hand rested on my still straightened hair. I hadn't had a chance to put my braids back in.

"It doesn't change how I feel about you," he said gently, and I wanted so much to believe him. "I'm going to get some water. You want anything?"

I shook my head with a small smile. Caius turned to climb out of the bed. He sat on the edge of his mattress and bent to pick up his underwear and trousers. As he pushed his feet into them, my eyes focused on a blemish on the top of his right ass cheek. It was such a small thing. I don't know why I even noticed it except it didn't fit with the rest of his skin. I'd never studied his back at much length and never his naked rear end.

Caius stood and pulled his underwear over his behind, but the mark was still visible above the band around his hips. My heart began to beat faster, my breath short as I leaned closer and angled my head to get a better look at the distinct *A* etched into his skin.

The Alpha mark was on Caius, which only meant one thing: Goliath was Caius' father.

CHAPTER THIRTY-FIVE

My heart pounded and I couldn't catch my breath as I stared at the birthmark on Caius' skin. He stood up, heading toward the kitchen area.

"He's your father."

The words came out in a disbelieving breath but Caius stopped, looking over at me still in his bed.

"You say something?"

My eyes stung as bile threatened to rise. I watched Caius, pulling the bed sheet around my naked chest, "He's your father."

In a matter of seconds, his eyebrows transitioned from knotted, to disappearing into his hairline completely. He looked down to his right hip and sighed, "Fuck."

He ran a hand over his face, before returning his gaze to me, "Grey, let me explain—"

"You *knew*!"

In the seconds, it took me to learn this devastating revelation, it hadn't occurred to me that Caius would have already known. It was stupid of me of course, because everyone knew what that birthmark meant, but if he'd known all along then...

"Grey, please."

"You knew and you didn't tell me?" I yelled at him, feeling sick. He'd known and let me go to Sabre, *knowing* they were... brothers.

"I have to get out of here." I rushed to get out of the bed, mortified.

"Grey, wait!"

Caius reached out to me as I bent to put on my underwear. When his fingers touched me, I recoiled aggressively, "Don't touch me, Caius!"

"Grey, will you just let me explain?"

His eyes were frantic as he searched my face, looking for a sign that he might get through to me.

"Explain what? How you lied to me? Or why you let me go off to have sex with your brother?"

Caius' entire body went rigid as he growled at me. I wasn't sure what he was mad at; my honesty or the fact that Sabre was his brother.

"Sabre is *not* my brother."

That answered that question.

I snorted as I continued getting dressed. I wasn't about to get into semantics with him. My own revulsion and shame aside, Caius had kept this from me and it was no small thing. How had no one known this for so long? Why was his coat black when Goliath's was white? Did Maximus know? Who else knew?

"Grey, I wanted to tell you, but I didn't see the point."

I spun on him once I had my dress on and rammed my finger into his chest.

"The point would have been to stop me making the biggest mistake of my life!"

"That's not fair," he protested. "You slept with Sabre after sleeping with me, because you chose to. You think knowing we have the same father would have stopped you?"

I slapped him with every ounce of strength I could muster. The sound echoed like an explosion in the silence of the room. Caius licked the corner of his lip where I'd split it open and worked the pain out of his jaw. When he turned his head to look back at me, both of us were seething, but he had the sense to stay quiet.

I finally said, "You betrayed me, just like everyone else."

I searched the floor frantically for my shoes. I was so embarrassed about my night with Sabre, the fact I hadn't been strong enough not to go through with it, and now Caius had just thrown that fact in my face. My responsibility, my choice—but knowing they were related could have changed everything.

"Grey, I didn't betray you," Caius insisted. "Do you realise what people knowing about this would mean?"

He stood behind me as I searched on my hands and knees. I found my shoes under his bed and rammed my feet into them. I was feeling lightheaded and needed to get out of there, but his words stopped me. I got up from the floor to face him and his eyes were pleading.

"I didn't tell you to protect you, to protect my mother."

I hadn't thought about Regina's position in all this, but it didn't stop the implication of his earlier words.

"If Goliath is your father, you would have a blood claim to being Alpha, just like Sabre." Guilty, Caius looked away from me and it was then I understood. "That's the wild card, isn't it?"

He lifted his eyes to me again and didn't deny it. I almost laughed. I would have if I didn't feel like clawing his eyes out with my bare hands.

"That's why the resistance includes you. If they win, you'll be a leader of their choosing and you'll still have a blood claim to the title."

"Grey, it's not just about that. We have to rip Goliath's evil out from the root, start afresh. He's manipulated everything from the beginning and I didn't want to be a part of it. I didn't want him to win!"

I know what it feels like to be betrayed by your family... by your father. I thought he'd meant Maximus, but he'd meant Goliath.

"Goliath forced himself on my mother," Caius confessed, imploring me for understanding. "He found a way to manipulate the shaman's prophecy so that he could father both males." My mouth went dry. "He wouldn't allow his legacy to go to chance and so he influenced the outcome so that whoever won would still be *his* heir."

None of this made any sense. The shaman law had been steadfast for centuries—how could someone manipulate it? And how was it even possible for Goliath to impregnate them physically at the same time?

"He infiltrated the House of Gifts and has shaman there in his pocket. It's why Amniare was the first to be taken over," Caius said, reading my mind.

The House of Gifts was a school in Amniare, southern Agmantia. It was where learned people went to train in the mystic arts. Shamans from Agmantia, Gifted in Mortania, Mages in Coz and Cotai and Witch Doctors in Yitesh. All of them travelled to the large melting pot of magical education to better their powers and bring new knowledge to service their native lands.

"He had help manipulating the prophecy so he would know when to..."

I knew what Caius meant and so I saved him having to continue, interrupting him with a question of my own:

"You knew all this, knew that the prophecy was a lie, and you didn't tell me—why?"

Caius sighed, "I wanted you to make the choice on your own. If you couldn't, I knew you weren't ready."

"But you could have stopped *this*," I pointed at my stomach. "Fuck choices and fuck free will, we could have been together! I'm tied to Sabre now, forever!"

I knew I shouldn't feel like my baby was a mistake, but the way in which it had been conceived was wrong. Knowing it could have been avoided, that Caius could have saved me that pain, hurt me more than I could have ever realised.

"This is about more than us being together!" he raised his voice and I felt sorry for him then, as his voice cracked and his eyes pleaded with me, because I saw the battle he'd been fighting nearly his entire life. This battle of wills, secrets and betrayals had only been my world for the last few months, but Caius had been fighting this war forever.

"Goliath looked me in the eye when I was twelve years old and told me he would only acknowledge I was his son if I won the Mating Games."

I tried to hide my surprise, but I wasn't sure it worked. Caius' eyes shuttered in a way that told me he wasn't exactly here as he spoke.

"He came to my house and in one breath told me he was my father, but that I would never be good enough for him unless I won the Games. Even then, I knew I didn't want his approval that way. I didn't want his *love* that way. As I got older, I realised I didn't want it at all."

Despite his strength, Caius had a softness to him that I hadn't seen in many wolves. I had no idea what hearing that from his father must have felt like. Caius lifted his head and his smouldering gaze was on me once more, "Then there was you."

He stepped closer to me and like a fool I didn't move away. "I *turned* for the first time and suddenly I couldn't stay away from you. I told my dad, then he told my mum and they explained about the mating bond. Your parents came over one night, I heard them arguing and I knew I'd done something wrong, that wanting you was... wrong somehow."

I was breathless again, but for completely different reasons. While he had been struggling with his new feelings and his father's dismissal, I had been living in ignorance.

"They stopped us seeing each other and I missed you so much, but the longer they kept us apart, and you started hating me, I started to hate you too. I forgot about being your mate and made myself loathe you with everything inside me, for being so blind and allowing them to do this to you. I told myself my feelings didn't matter, that *you* didn't matter, and when I discovered the resistance and an opportunity to try and get rid of Goliath; it made even more sense. Just to let you continue on your path, the way I had to continue on mine."

He took another step toward me and I could smell him. I could smell myself *on* him as he reached out and cradled my face, peering deep into my eyes and my heart.

"Then you started asking questions and everything I'd told myself about you went out the window. You came to me before the second challenge and I wanted you so much Aspen, that I won that challenge. I won it so I could be a step closer to having you for myself, but if I did..."

"You'd be playing into Goliath's hand."

There was a pressured silence between us as I lifted my hand, placing it on top of his that clasped my face. I finally understood why he'd been pushing me away, but it didn't make his betrayal any easier to accept. Caius hadn't told me about Goliath being his father because he'd hoped it wouldn't matter. That I would marry Sabre and take his choice about me, away from him.

He'd been just as much a coward as I was. He couldn't stay away from me, so he'd tried to make me stay away from him.

Gently, I took his hand away from my face and stepped back, closer to the door.

"Grey?"

I continued stepping back. I couldn't do this. I couldn't keep pining for him, knowing he was fighting battles I couldn't be a part of. Now that Goliath was dead; I didn't even know what Caius' plan was and there was no indication he was going to share it with me. Invernell was falling into ruin and we were on opposite sides of the fight. I was pregnant with Sabre's child and I had a duty to that child, if not to anyone else, to make sure it was kept safe.

"I'll make the decision easy for you," I said. "Maybe I should have been stronger, but I made my choice, and now I have to live with that. You should do the same."

I turned toward the door, knowing this would be the last time I would see him like this.

"Grey…" he tried, and when I didn't react he cried out, "Aspen!"

I stopped, waiting for what, I wasn't quite sure.

"I just…" his words failed him but the ones he found held nothing back. "It shouldn't be this hard to love you."

His words cut me so sharply, my chest jolted forward as I swallowed down my cry of anguish. I looked at him over my shoulder, tears in my eyes. That his admission of loving me came in the same breath as saying I wasn't worth fighting for, was more than I could take.

"Then I won't make it any harder."

Before I lost my nerve, I walked away from him and out of the cave. I didn't *turn* until I got to the mouth of the entrance, but just as I did, I heard a tremendous crash come from behind me. It was followed by a gut-wrenching howl that tore my heart to pieces. I wanted to go back, to take back everything and just be with him, but nothing had changed.

We had both made our choices. Caius and I were over before we'd ever really begun.

I bound away from the cave toward home, leaving Caius behind for good.

Our backyard was a magical place at night. Filled with endless light provided by torches, with billowing flames that lit up the trees from a safe distance. As winter settled, the branches stood bare and the wind took a chillier note as it whipped through my hair and stung at my face.

I'd re-done my braids a few days ago and the icy wind was harsh against my exposed scalp. I barely had time to register it though, as I stared into the dark trenches of our garden. I sat on the same stone bench I'd been on when Rogue fought me, what felt like an age ago. I'd wrapped myself in a large fur blanket, and the sturdy carved wolf legs of the bench kept me a few inches off the ground. Truth was, I wanted to fall into the earth and let it swallow me whole.

I'd ended things with Caius over a week ago and everyone had continued with their lives as though my world hadn't ended. I had nothing and no one to lean on and so I sat, existing, waiting to give birth, hands resting on a visibly protruding stomach. With only a few short weeks to go before it was due to arrive, I both felt and looked pregnant.

My mother fussed around me, my father asked after my health constantly and my sister, as expected, hated everything about it. She scorned me with her eyes and scoffed at any mention of the baby's arrival. Through it all, I remained silent, reserved and hating her just as much in return. Both of us, openly and privately hating that she hadn't been born the Female instead.

As I sat on the bench, wallowing in my own self-pity, I thought of Tala. I missed her so much, needing her strength and honesty now more than ever. Somewhere my best friend was safe with the man she loved. Tala had made her choice, the *right* choice, and now, I assumed, was happy.

Why couldn't I have been as brave?

Knowing what I did now about the prophecy and the part Goliath had played in manipulating all our lives, my supposed sacrifice for the greater good felt more superficial than ever. His murderer still hadn't been found, despite the endless interrogations going on in Invernell. The Riadnak guards had decided that it wasn't anyone in our immediate community, disregarding the nature of his murder, which had been intimate and brutal and most likely done by someone with a high level of access. Despite his many enemies, most of which were still storming our borders, there was no real evidence to support that Goliath had been killed by an outsider. I had my own suspicions about who had taken Goliath's life, but without proof or, let's be real, an actual care to find out, it didn't change anything.

Goliath was dead, Sabre ruled and he did so with a cruelty and iron will that none of us would have ever seen coming. In the few gatherings of elders I was permitted to attend, Kade and Paten continued to oppose him in little ways, but it was clear that power was corrupting Sabre to the core. I was truly worried when my mother mentioned one night that if Sabre's position was questioned, then surely mine would be too. While Ianthe was focused on Sabre's antics for the wrong reasons, she wasn't wrong.

If the *Iaecan* community found the means to really oppose Sabre, where would that leave me?

I continued playing my part by presenting myself at the Riadnak Manor for whatever farcical parade Sabre had put on. On more formal occasions, when trying to impress foreigners who tried to undermine him, Sabre was good to me. He showered me with affection and praise as the exulted mother of his child and soon to be wife.

When Invernelli residents were in attendance and knew him for the conniving and vindictive bastard he was, Sabre tormented me. He paraded Rogue in front of me and his court with no regard to how it shamed us. They disappeared for hours at a time during his incessant parties and returned smelling of one another so potently, it left little to the imagination of what they had been up to.

Amidst his child's play and fornicating, Sabre was running our military forces into the ground. Now that Goliath was dead, the Faenymese *Iaecan* were out for Sabre's blood. Only Amniare remained on his side and Voltaire hadn't joined any side, focusing their attention on their own war with Coz. We'd not heard anything about Aulandri.

As the days went on, the casualties rose, and in the few snippets of conversation that I was privy to I understood that it would only get worse. We were losing and if Sabre didn't do something soon, he would lose his crown before he'd even begun to wear it. If Sabre was after the Agmantian crown as his father was, he was steadily undoing everything his father had achieved by not being able to maintain his own borders, much less take over others. I didn't want him to succeed, of course. I no more wanted Sabre to remain Alpha than I wanted to be his wife, but I had to think about my baby. If all the other provinces invaded and overthrew him, where would that leave me and his child?

"Aspen?"

I was startled by my mother's voice as she approached. Her boots made the icy blades of grass crunch as she walked and came to a stop in front of me.

"Are you ready?"

I nodded and stood from the stone bench. My mother was dressed in a dark hooded robe with black fur trim. She was here to escort me to the Riadnak Manor where I was to move in for the rest of my pregnancy. Attacks on Invernell had increased substantially, so for my safety, Sabre wanted me within the Riadnak Manor walls where he could better protect me. All my belongings had been packed and sent over to the manor over the last few days and the day to pack myself off had finally arrived.

I walked, silent, by my mother's side, through the backdoor and into the open hall of my home, where I discarded the blanket on a nearby bureau. I'd grown up here. Laughed and cried and fought with my sister over things that all seemed so petty now.

"You don't say much anymore."

I didn't bother to look at her, "I don't have much to say anymore."

There was silence before she said, "I didn't know about them."

We approached the front door and Noa was there with my own hooded robe and helped me into it. When it was buttoned and I was sufficiently shielded against the cold, Noa bowed to me and left the entrance hall.

My mother turned to me, her eyes tortured and dark, "I shouldn't have ignored her the way I did…"

I realised she was talking about Rogue and her involvement with Sabre, but I no longer cared. I knew then my mother wanted something from me. Forgiveness maybe. She wasn't going to get it.

"You still wouldn't have stopped her. You would have just made her be discrete about it." I knew that for a fact, and as she took a steadying breath I knew she acknowledged the truth of it.

"Did you know Goliath was his father?"

She didn't bother to pretend not to know what I was talking about, "Yes."

"Then... why?"

Why did it matter? Why couldn't I be with Caius, if he was a Riadnak when all was said and done?

My mother looked down at my stomach then back up at me, her eyes resolute in her coming conviction.

"Love makes you do silly things."

I took her to mean that she would have backed any horse Goliath did. Is Goliath had chosen Caius as his heir, my mother would have forced him on instead, just to please him.

"Goliath made choices that affected all of us, and when you become a mother, you'll understand that you'd do anything to keep your child safe."

Tears suddenly appeared in my mother's eyes, "I went about it terribly, Aspen, I see that now, but I kept you from Caius to protect you."

"Protect me from what?"

If Goliath had made sure that the Alpha would be his heir, what difference did I make?

"You are too important, Aspen, I had to make sure you wouldn't do anything to betray them."

"The jokes on you because I never would have thought twice about it if you hadn't interfered with my life."

I saw a hint of shame in her eyes, but she didn't back down, "I won't apologise for doing what I needed to keep you safe. You'll do the same when the time comes!"

"What do you mean?"

"No matter the circumstances, you're not stupid. That child…" she stabbed the air with her index finger at my stomach. "…is a Riadnak. His father is now the most powerful *laecan* in the country and he will be raised in his image. You think you can stop that without some kind of cost?"

My hands trembled at my sides at the force and truth of her words. My jaw clenched so hard I thought my teeth would crack.

"They'll use the baby to control you, Aspen," my mother said, defeated. "And you won't be able to stop it."

CHAPTER THIRTY-SIX

They'd converted Tala's old suite for my use, since Sabre was still using his bedroom until Celeste moved out of the Alpha Suite. Personally, I wouldn't have wanted to be in the room my husband had been killed, but in the month, I'd been living there, I learned Celeste would do anything to assert her power over me and the household. She flaunted herself around the grounds—when she could bother to be in attendance—scolding maids and ordering guards around. When she wasn't in the house torturing the staff, or belittling me, she was arranging Sabre's parties and, of course, our wedding. I had no say in any of those preparations, but unlike my confrontation with my mother, there would be no barking at Celeste.

I'd never known the woman to be so harsh and the longer I saw her and her son together, I realised that maybe Goliath hadn't been Sabre's only negative influence. She was constantly in Sabre's ear, influencing every move he made and the more I observed, the more certain I was that Celeste had something to do with Goliath's death. She'd mourned him as was appropriate, but the way she ruled the manor was as though *she* were the Alpha. I tried to stay well away from her whenever I could, despite the forced dinners and familial social obligations.

I lay in bed one night, my hand on my stomach. The midwives had seen me only this morning and said that my time was near. My stomach, according to them, was rather large and they expected an easy if not long birth, reassuring me that the child was healthy and in no immediate danger.

I felt thirsty and so, on slightly swollen ankles, I got out of bed to get myself a drink. The water pitcher sat on a dresser on the other side of the room, closest to the door. Once I'd waddled to it and poured myself a drink, I heard voices in the hallway. Having no interest in the affairs of others outside of keeping myself and my unborn child safe from the snakes in our home, I drained my glass and proceeded to go back to bed when I heard my name. Startled, I inched closer to the door and gently pressed my ear against it.

"...then you should do the same!"

"I've done everything you've asked, but I *won't* do this."

Celeste and Sabre. Their voices were muffled as I realised they were walking toward Celeste's rooms that were at the farthest end of the hall. I *turned* my ears to listen better.

"Sabre, everything is within our grasp. You just have to reach out and take it!"

"I can't...it's too much...not after Dad..."

There was a moment of silence in which I assumed she was comforting him over his grief, but Celeste's next words cancelled that notion.

"Your father was necessary, Sabre. It was the only way we could be free to do what we want."

I staggered back from the door, almost tripping over myself as understanding rocked me. I staggered over to my bed, trying to catch my breath. As I dropped to my knees, one hand held to my belly and trying desperately not to throw up, I felt someone behind me. I jerked around to find Lady Xana standing there. I cried out in alarm, but the sound was cut off with a swipe of her hand as she looked down at me from the darkened corner of my room. My hand flew to my throat, terrified at my missing vocals.

"I am not here to harm you, but you will need to be quiet."

Her voice was commanding, a force of strength in the suddenly terrifying darkness. She stepped closer to me so the lights from the garden illuminated her a little more. She wore dark robes, embroidered with black thread so the designs weren't immediately clear. Her usual white curls were hidden in a black head wrap that rose high above her head, making her look bald in the darkness behind her.

"W-what are you doing here?" I stammered, getting up from the floor and steadying myself against one of the bedposts.

"I've come to see if you're ready to make your choice?"

A sharp pain cut into my belly, making me jump, but it disappeared almost as soon as it came, "What choice?" I hissed at her.

"What shines brightest: the sun in the day or the moon at night?"

"What?" I couldn't deal with her riddles right now. New shooting pains were suddenly too much.

"Will you choose to walk in the light, or fade into darkness?"

Her words weren't helpful, but her eyes were sad. As I climbed into bed, I watched her mouth move to say something, but no sounds came out. I winced from another pain in my side and blew out a sharp breath of air, unable to answer her even if I did understand what she meant.

"It's time then."

I assumed she was smiling, but in the dark it looked more like a grimace. The sharp pain came again, tingling all the way down to my toes, causing me to cry out.

"The change is coming."

I didn't have a moment to take in what she said as a resounding crash echoed through the house. The foundations shook, the entire room trembling, making furniture move and displacing the items on them. Shouts and screams erupted from outside the window and down the hall.

"W-what's happening?"

Lady Xana rushed to the window and I watched as her eyes widened at whatever she saw out there.

"Invasion." Her voice was low, but I heard her even from across the room.

Invasion. My thoughts went to Caius before I clenched my jaws at another wave of shooting pain. Lady Xana returned from the window and rushed over to me, helping me further onto my bed as a debilitating cramp took over me. I got into the covers just as another boom rocked the room.

"Dear God," Xana mumbled again, mostly to herself.

"Xana, what's going on?"

"You're going into labour, but it looks very much like wolves and men are storming the manor."

"I'm *what?*"

"I have to go," she rushed towards the door. "I will return, but… I must go."

"Please, don't leave me," I whispered just as she disappeared.

I was barely alone for the blink of an eye as the door slammed open and Sabre barged inside with two guards behind him, breathing heavily, as though he'd run here from down the hall.

"Sabre," I said between quick pants, trying to manage the labour cramps the way I'd been taught to. "The baby."

In that moment, I didn't care what had gone on between us—I was scared, I needed someone, and he was there. Two guards remained in the doorway as Sabre approached my bed.

"What's wrong?"

His eyes darted between my face and my stomach as he reached out to me.

"The baby's coming," I got out. "What's happening?"

He looked over his shoulder at the guards before answering me, "The manor is under attack," he admitted. "I came to get you somewhere safe, but…"

If I hadn't witnessed the change that washed over him—from the cruel man who hadn't cared for my feelings for the past weeks, and into a terrified and anxious father-to-be—I wouldn't have believed it. But I saw it, I saw the fear in his eyes matching the terror in my heart and I clasped at the hand that was holding onto mine.

"What do I do?" he asked gently.

"Midwives," I breathed out heavily as another burst of pain had me shaking.

Sabre didn't need more instruction, calling over his shoulder to the guards, "Get my mother and summon the midwives. The Female is going into labour!"

He looked back at me, reaching out and stroking one of my braids away from my face, his expression tender.

"It's going to be okay," he whispered, but whether it was to soothe himself or me, I wasn't sure. "Everything's going to be all right."

I nodded, unable to form the words as the sweat that had been beading on my forehead began to slowly trickle down the side of my face and he helped me settle in bed.

Laecan births weren't the same as *maejym* births, the same way our gestation periods were different. While some women could be in labour for days, my baby could be here in minutes, an hour at the most. Our young also grew differently in that the ageing process doubled in the first year. By the time they were six months old, a child would have the abilities of a one year old. None of that mattered at the moment of course. I was simply terrified and even though Sabre held on my hand, I desperately wished Caius were here.

Moments later, Celeste appeared in the doorway dressed in delicate armour. When in war, *laecan* would armour themselves so that if, for any reason, they couldn't *turn* or were forced to fight as human, they would be ready and equipped to do so. I didn't know whether Celeste had the skill to fight or had any intention of doing so, but she looked the part.

"Mother," Sabre called out, rushing over to her and taking her hand.

Sabre had lit the candles in my room while we waited for the midwives amidst the snarl of *laecan* and screams of *maejym*. Pain that threatened to break me ripped through my body and I cried out again, my cries mingled with the growls and howling that rouse steadily outside my window. They were joined by the clash of steel and the cries of those who wielded them. I tried to drown them out and focus on getting through my own pain.

"The midwives will be here soon," Sabre reassured me as he stood by his mother's side.

"The Faenymese are storming the house, Sabre. You need to be out there with your soldiers."

Sabre looked at his mother in disbelief, "Aspen is in labour!"

"And she must deliver the child quickly, before they get in here!" Celeste growled at him and for a brief moment Sabre and I were allies as we both snarled at her.

"I can't exactly rush this!" I groaned, arching my back and digging my head into the pillows as my body shook with agony.

Another bout of intense throbbing washed over me so unexpectedly, I grit my teeth with the force of it. I almost bit clean through my lip as I tried to brace myself against the feeling. Sabre looked over at me, unsure and afraid.

"What can I do?" he asked, finally coming over to me but I shook my head,

"Get," I breathed out, taking another breath in. "...my mother."

"He will do no such thing," Celeste interrupted and turned to her son. "You will get your armour and you will make sure that those filthy dogs don't make it in here before the child comes."

I needed to be protected, I could see that, but Celeste's lack of empathy was shocking to say the very least. Sabre looked down at me and I knew he didn't want to leave. I appreciated the sentiment, but if he didn't hold the wolves back, it wouldn't matter what was happening to me.

"She needs someone," Sabre finally said and before Celeste could object, Lady Xana appeared by her side.

"She has me." She looked over at me as though she hadn't just left. I didn't care about her reasons for keeping her shenanigans to herself, but when she started giving Sabre orders, I suddenly felt much better.

"I can stay with the Female."

"My guards went to get the midwives," Sabre explained,

"They won't make it in here, not in the middle of an attack."

"This is the Alpha heir!" Sabre snapped.

"Exactly, no midwife is good enough except me."

"I'll be safe with her Sabre. Go and protect our son."

Sabre looked at me for a long moment and something passed between us that I couldn't readily explain. Perhaps a bond between parents but whatever it was, it had him kiss my clammy forehead before backing out of the room, taking Celeste with him.

Lady Xana came over to the bed and immediately began to undress me. I tried to resist but the ongoing pain was just too much.

She pulled off my thick nightdress, exposing my swollen breasts to the cool night air which felt incredible. She reached out and palmed my breasts gently, along with my stomach and when she looked at me, I felt power in her stare that caught my breath.

"W-what's wrong?"

"Do you trust me?"

"W-why?" I squinted my eyes against another sharp shot of pain and quickly began to pant, trying desperately not to cry. Lady Xana gently rubbed my back and the feeling was beautiful. Her hands were so cool against my scorching skin that I slumped against her palms.

"You have no need to fear me, girl. I have told you this, but you do need to trust me. Now more than ever. I am perhaps the only friend you have in this world."

That much was true. Tala was lost to the winds and Caius...Caius was just... gone.

"I trust you."

Lady Xana smiled, though again it was sad. Sad, I realised, for me.

She left my bedside and returned with another nightdress she'd found in my wardrobe that was much lighter than the one I had on. It stuck to the dusking of sweat that had appeared on my skin, but it felt soothing. When I was feeling marginally better, she disappeared into the bathroom and returned with a large bowl and thick towels that she arranged expertly.

"Just keep breathing," she said. "Ignore everything else and just keep breathing steadily."

I tried, but the fighting outside was relentless. The growls and snarls from wolves was merely enhancing the terror of my own pain. As Lady Xana readied her tools, Celeste and Sabre reappeared and this time he was armoured. He hadn't been away long, but I saw there was blood on his hands and wondered whose it was. An enemy? A fallen ally?

"How long will this take?" Celeste asked, barely looking at me.

"As long as it needs to," came Lady Xana's curt reply. I was thankful she was on my side today because I didn't have the strength to give Celeste any more attitude.

My baby was coming in the middle of a war and she was judging me for it taking too long.

"You must leave," Lady Xana commanded. "You must leave and no one is to return until it's done."

"I will remain here."

Though Lady Xana didn't turn her supportive gaze from me, I watched her mouth move a fraction at Celeste's remark, and ancient words escaped from them. My bedroom door flew open with a crash against the wall and it was a direct order for Celeste to exit.

"You have no power over me, woman." Lady Xana warned, still not turning to face Celeste. Although I was concentrating on my breathing and my vision swayed with the onslaught of labour pain, I saw Celeste regard Lady Xana with venom before she sharply exited the room again.

"You too, Sabre. Your child will be here soon enough."

With less resistance, Sabre actually smiled gently at me before leaving the room, closing the door behind him. When it was just the two of us once again, Lady Xana pressed her hand on my stomach, feeling around and muttering words I didn't understand.

"They're coming."

My brain was fuzzy, but I acknowledged the word she'd used as my eyes widened at her.

They?

"*They're* coming?" I was breathless, tensing up at the contraction that coursed through me, sweat dampening my head.

"You're having twins, Aspen," Lady Xana confirmed as she gently pushed me back against the mounted pillows of my bed and lifted the bed sheets above my now raised knees.

"Excuse me?" I couldn't think straight; I couldn't even see straight as my fist clawed into the bedsheets.

Lady Xana ignored me as I heard her washing her hands once she'd rolled up her sleeves.

"Be ready, sweet girl," she said, leaning forward between my knees. Sweat was plastered on my head and my body ached. "Your choice is upon us."

Choice? Was one of my babies not going to survive?

"W-what choi-aargh!"

The urge to push tore through me like a knife. During training, I'd been hurt many times, healing so quickly that I barely bore any scars, but this pain was something else. At the foot of the bed, Lady Xana coaxed me, continually reassuring me I was doing well. When she eventually told me to push, I pushed and when she told me to wait, I desperately tried to do as she asked. Just when I thought I wouldn't survive another moment of this ordeal, I pushed and the pressure I felt eased up. The next moment, Lady Xana held something, *someone* in her hands. I heard no cries, no sounds at all and I immediately began to panic.

"Xana?"

My door rattled, but didn't open. My heart lodged in my throat at the possibility of the enemy getting in when my first baby had just been born. She turned away from me and I heard water splashing, towels rustling and at last I heard the tiniest little sound.

"A boy," Xana called over her shoulder before she moved to show me the swaddling in her arms. "He bares the mark."

Xana brought my baby over to me and placed him in my arms. He was golden skinned, like Sabre, and shockingly, his eyes were open. His silver-grey eyes stared back at me wondrously. She'd not wrapped him too tightly and so I could take one of his tiny little hands between my fingers and see the small patch of fuzzy white fur on the top of his left hand. The inside of his wrist bore the distinct mark of the Alpha.

The sounds of fighting dropped away and all I perceived was my son.

"He's beau—" my admiration of him was cut off as another contraction hit me.

You're having twins…

"Quickly now," Lady Xana took my son from me and I wished she would keep him where I could see him, but the second contraction made me close my eyes anyway. Again, the pain and again the release of pressure until finally, the other baby was out.

"What is it?" I asked, slumping back on the bed, completely exhausted. The door banged again, but I couldn't focus on it.

"Another boy, Aspen. You have two sons."

I smiled lazily as I slumped on the pillows waiting for Xana to bring him to me, but as she did so, the look on her face was pained. The hairs all over my body rose up in preparation for danger and when she finally handed him to me, I learned why. He was brown skinned like me, if not a little darker. His eyes were also open and the molten gold of them made me smile immediately. I reached for his right hand, but where there should have been a patch of white fur, it was as black as the darkest night. My smile dropped from my face, my heart pounding as I looked up at Lady Xana.

"No," I shook my head, desperate for her to tell me this wasn't true. "It can't be."

"He doesn't bear the mark." Xana confirmed regretfully. "I checked."

But I didn't need her to tell me. I already knew, I could feel the truth of it to the very marrow of my bones: my second son was not born to the Alpha.

My second son, belonged to Caius.

CHAPTER THIRTY-SEVEN

I held the twins in my arms once Lady Xana had cleaned up the bed and me. She'd helped me into some fresh clothes after padding me up against any prolonged bleeding, and had given me a tonic for the post-labour pains. The pain of my contractions was all but forgotten as I locked into the mesmerising eyes of my beautiful sons.

Pups fathered by different males was possible, but it was incredibly rare. A female didn't usually find herself in such a predicament once choosing a mate. For *laecan*—just as for wild wolves—the pack and those closest were paramount to our way of life. Family was everything. And now I was left feeling uncertain of what family I had helped create.

What I was not uncertain of, however, was the love I had for both of them in equal measure.

They were miraculous.

I'd named my eldest Silver, the patch of white fur and the mark of the Alpha on his wrist confirming his status within our community, while I'd chosen Canon for my youngest. The walls of my room were illuminated by moonlight and as war raged outside my window, I confessed to Lady Xana that I knew Goliath was Caius' father. She in turn confessed that she was unable to tell me the truth as she'd been restricted magically from doing so but she couldn't tell me by who.

"Goliath deceived us all, and he did it, to the great shame of all my kind, with help from some of our most powerful. We are not all plucked from the same garden, Aspen. The choices of others are not for us to decide."

Sabre entered before we could talk further and his face was a picture of anticipation and pride, "Where's my son?"

I ignored my fear, ready for whatever came next. It didn't matter who their fathers were, these were my children and I wouldn't let anyone hurt them. Even if wolves that would, were not only outside my window, but standing before me.

Sabre's eyes filled with tears as he looked at the two babies in my arms. He walked over to the bed, his face beaming with excitement, "Two of them?"

I nodded, unsure how to approach what needed to be said, sooner rather than later. Interestingly, he walked around to the right side of the bed where I currently held Silver. Both Silver and Canon's furred hands were on display and once Sabre stroked the small patch of Silver's tiny clenched fist, he went to do the same to Canon. I watched Sabre's hand, rather than his face and saw his finger still, then curl into his palm until it created a solid fist. His bluish veins popped out of the top of his hand, stark against the golden yellow of his skin as realisation dawned on him.

"Is it mine?"

It. He knew and was already turning my child into something less.

"Sabr—"

"Does it bare the mark?"

I growled in the base of my throat, "*His* name is Canon and no, he does not bear the Alpha mark. Only Silver does."

The mention of his son's name put a stopper in his anger for a brief moment. A *very* brief moment, before I finally lifted my head to observe the fury that flamed in his toxic gaze. I saw a ring of golden light flash around his eyes and knew the rage that was building up inside of him. He moved toward me, his fist clenched as he drew it back…

"Sabre," Lady Xana called out and he stopped. As sure as the sky was blue, Sabre had been going to punch me. He loosened his hand and backed away from the bed, from me and my boys until he was by his mother's side. I hadn't realised Celeste had entered, but there she stood, glaring at me.

From the blood on her armour and the dripping sword in her hand, it seemed she did have fighting skill.

"What did she do?" she gasped as she looked at me, seated in the large bed holding my children.

"There are two of them…" Sabre explained, staring at the children in my arms. "…only one of them is mine."

"Who on earth could the…?" Celeste was slow to the party, but she soon caught on. Sabre smirked, his eyes clouded but hateful,

"It seems Aspen and the Gamma are closer than anyone would have any cause to suspect."

Celeste was a picture of darkness, her shadowy eyes glowering with fury as she looked over at me. I got the distinct impression I was now no more to her than the dirt on her shoe.

"Who is the elder child?" she asked.

"What?" I looked to Lady Xana for help, but while she continued to give me a reassuring smile, she didn't offer me any help with the answer.

"It's a simple enough question, Aspen. Which one of them did you spit out first?"

Celeste's rage was barely contained as I slowly caught on to her meaning and the revelation hit me like an arrow. I furrowed my brows, for some reason beginning to sense that this was important.

"What does it matter?" I asked. "Only one of them bears the mark."

She stared at me, looking as though she wanted to rip my head off of my shoulders, and I was struggling to understand why.

"So Sabre's child is the eldest?" Celeste pushed for an answer and Sabre started to look guilty.

What was the issue with who was the eldest...?

I stared back at Celeste and I could tell that she realised I was beginning to put two and two together, slowly, but surely. I looked over at Lady Xana, who was smiling encouragingly. Why wasn't she speaking? It was as though she couldn't. As though there was an invisible gag over her mouth.

Are you ready to make your choice?

All the riddles, all the half-spoken sentences, all the hinting—it had lead into this moment.

Oh, God, how idiotic had I been, how spineless and naïve at what was going on around me? The prophecy—my *purpose*, everything in my life—had been based on a lie.

Prized flesh...

Yes, that's what I had been taught: to submit but... I was the Female.

Like Erina Anai before me, I was descended from women who fought for what they wanted because they had the blood of the rulers running through their veins. The Female was special, not because she was the *prize* at the end of the challenges, but because the challenges secured *her* an heir.

The right to be Alpha was *mine*, as was the power to provide the heir to take my place.

That was the true heart of the prophecy: the Female Alpha.

Whichever child was the eldest would be the rightful heir because I was his mother. Sabre would have no claim to the Alpha mantle if that eldest child *wasn't* his.

As I looked in Celeste's eyes, I saw her realise that I now understood.

I saw how the history of *laecan* had been so systematically patriarchal that no one in living memory had ever even heard of a matriarchal origin. Celeste knew, so Goliath must have. How far back did the corruption of the prophecy go? How much of our history had been completely rewritten?

If I told them Canon was the elder child, everything they'd schemed for, everything they had killed Goliath for, would be ruined.

This was my choice.

I kept my eyes in Celeste's as I said, "I don't know."

Sabre finally stepped forward, enraged, "What do you mean you don't know?"

"Lady Xana delivered them." I was strong in my conviction, knowing I would never tell them that Silver was the first born. "I'm sorry, but I can't tell you which came first."

"You will do this now. Tell me!" Sabre roared and the room shook with the force of his wolf voice. The boys wailed in my arms,

"That is enough!" Lady Xana stepped in as I lowered Silver to my lap and tried to silence Canon, who seemed a little more riled up. I only had two hands—I couldn't do this by myself.

The commotion outside made itself known through a resounding boom. No matter the back and forth between us, the blood on the hands of both Sabre and Celeste was a clear indication that we were all in very real danger.

"Aspen and the children need to get to safety. Now the babies are here, she can't stay here any longer!"

Sabre spun on the old woman, "Tell me who's the elder child, witch, or I swear on my father's grave I will skin the flesh from your bones and burn you alive."

Everyone in the room went still, even the babies stopped fussing as the vicious intent of Sabre's words echoed through the room. I held my children to my chest, for the first time genuinely afraid of what Sabre might do. Lady Xana walked steadily toward him, stopping before him with no fear in her eyes.

"I'd love to see you try," she said, voice gentle, but her look was steeling against his as they glared at each other, both refusing to back down when suddenly, a helmeted guard barrelled through the open door.

"Alpha!" the guard exclaimed.

"What?" Sabre snapped, turning to him.

"The Faenymese have breached the lower halls and are flooding in through the servant's quarters. We need you at the front!"

He turned his attention to me and I wilted under his frosty glare. He growled as he looked between Lady Xana and me, then backed toward the door, pointing his finger at me, his eyes clear and focused as he promised, "I'm not done with you."

Sabre rushed into the hallway and I heard him barking orders to get his mother, me and the children to safety. Celeste was dragged from the room, reluctantly, as it was clear she would rather remain to hurl abuse at me now that her son could no longer do so. Another guard appeared, entering hurriedly and beginning to pack for me, since the maids had all gone.

Lady Xana rushed over to me and began to wrap up the children.

"I made my choice," I said as I pushed to get out of the bed, my legs shaking with weakness.

"I told you it would affect us all."

I said nothing, conscious of the guard in the walk-in closet ruffling through my things.

"Why not tell them Canon was the elder twin?"

I sighed, keeping my voice low, still wary of the guard. "I couldn't put him in that position without his father knowing about it. He'd... I don't think he'd ever forgive me for putting a target on Canon's back."

Lady Xana nodded with understanding as she placed a now snugly wrapped Canon back on the bed beside me. Once Silver was dressed appropriately, Lady Xana stood up, looking over at me with a sombre look on her face.

"What am I going to do, Lady Xana?"

She sighed heavily as she ran her hand in the air above the twins and muttered what sounded like a prayer.

"Live, my child. You're going to live."

She vanished almost immediately, cutting off any response I would have offered.

"Are they ready?"

I almost choked on the breath caught in my throat as my head snapped in the direction of the voice. The guard now stood in the doorway of the walk-in closet with the strap of the packed satchel in one hand...smelling like coconuts and sugar.

He dropped it unceremoniously to the floor, took off his helmet, and made my heart threaten to tear through my rib cage with the shocked relief that flooded it, at the mere sight of him.

"Caius!"

CHAPTER THIRTY-EIGHT

A tremendous crash outside my bedroom door wasn't enough to take my attention from Caius, and I watched with a soft thrill of hope as he stepped out of the shadows toward me.

"Are they ready, Aspen?" he asked again, looking briefly at the children on the bed. I nodded vigorously, wanting to reach for him, but holding the urge back, "Yes, but—"

"Get dressed," he cut me off, moving up to the door, poking his head outside. "Rhea and Susi will be here soon."

Rhea and Susi?

He closed the door again before starting to undress, "Can you walk?"

My thoughts about Susi and Rhea's involvement was cut off as I watched him discard the Riadnak guard uniform to reveal his own black armour underneath.

"Y-yes, but—"

"Good. Then get dressed. Quickly!"

It was clear, I wasn't going to get any answers out of him right now and so I got off the bed and walked into the closet to find something that didn't require much effort since I was still a little sore. I saw immediately that he'd left a few warm items out for me: wool breeches, thick socks and some boots: travelling clothes.

His thoughtfulness filled me with warmth that I almost started crying with relief that he was here. I managed to get a hold of myself, and to find a warm, softly knitted sweater and a cloak to go with what he'd already presented me with.

When I returned to him, Caius was once again by the door, peering out. I went to check on my children.

On our son...

Both of the boys had fallen asleep, even with all the turmoil. I wondered how long the snooze would last. They looked so peaceful and my heart swelled. No harm would ever come to them—I would make sure of it.

"Caius, please," I said, turning to him, "What is happening?"

He finally looked at me, really looked at me, and it may have been better if he hadn't. The warmth that usually came from him when looking at me was gone and a cold determination had replaced it. Whether this was because of the fighting or his feelings about seeing me as a mother of Sabre's child, I couldn't tell. Caius walked over to me and the twins.

"Grey, do you trust me?"

Grey.

"With my life."

As the words left my lips, the door burst open and Susi and Rhea were standing there, both armed and splattered with blood. Caius looked back at me, my eyes wide, "Please, just do as I ask."

I nodded, watching as the women approached us.

"We have to leave now, before he gets back," Susi said, breathless. "We came up the back way, but the front stairs are heaving with the assassins. We might have to kill them."

Assassins?

As Susi finished speaking, footsteps thundered on the stairs and battle cries rung out in the air. Rhea sighed and twirled her dripping sword in her hand, "Sounds like we *will*, have to kill them."

Caius rushed over to where he'd left the satchel by my closet door and threw the strap over his head. Susi and Rhea ran back out the door and the sound of clashing steel met my ears almost instantly.

"Get the babies and stay close to me!" Caius called out. I rushed to the side of my bed and briefly looked at my dagger resting on its stand on my side table. I thought about taking it, it might be useful but what could I really do now that I had the boys. I left my dagger there and picked up the boys, cradling them to me. As instructed, I kept close to Caius and we finally left my room.

The hallway was destroyed. The crashing sounds I'd heard earlier must have been some kind of explosion as pieces of the walls had fallen to the floor, cracked from their foundations. It was a miracle my bedroom door hadn't been blown off. As I held my children to my chest, terrified beyond reason, I watched Rhea, Susi and Caius crouch into battle stances and my blood went cold. The three of them proceeded to take out the approaching hoard as I kept as close as I could without getting myself or my babies in the way.

There was blood everywhere.

Blood splattered against the walls and stained on the thick, expensive carpets as Riadnak guards fell to the floor. Some had their throats slit while others had been run through the gut. I watched men I had known, die at my feet and hated that this was happening. The house wasn't built for any *laecan* in the homely quarters and so I watched the light die out of human eyes.

Caius remained in front of me as we travelled down the carpeted hallways, Susi and Rhea in front of him, taking on the first wave of guards. They seemed to come in a never-ending charge, but finally we reached the stairs and descended, leaving a pile of dead and dying behind us. I pulled the twins tighter to my chest, so tight that Silver fussed, but thankfully remained asleep. As Rhea and Susi rushed on ahead, Caius turned to me and grabbed my arm.

"Are you all right?"

I nodded, shaken but trusting that he would get us out. We continued through the house towards the back rooms, Rhea and Susi momentarily missing, probably killing some unseen threat. So far I had only seen dead human bodies, but increasingly I could hear the snarls and growling coming from outside. As I ran past the ballroom, I spotted the first dead wolf and my heart lurched at the sight.

The moment we emerged onto the grounds from the lower level kitchens, I saw more dead wolves as well as live ones. Fighting in the house had been limited to human forms, but out here, a *laecan* war was raging. Piles of fur, broken limbs and snapped necks lay scattered on the grounds we passed, some of whom I knew. I saw the brown mottled fur of Elias Dremyr, a boy I'd crushed on briefly when I was younger. I saw the half-white, half-brown coat of Taya Aminez, my music teacher's daughter, laying on the ground with her entrails spilling onto the ice touched grass beneath us.

Caius pulled me along, away from the carnage. I could only assume that the majority of the fighting was taking place elsewhere, because I could hear it but this was all I could see. As we ran across the back of the estate, Rhea and Susi appeared again,

"Asher has the wagon ready! Quickly!" Susi cried out and Caius followed her back through the grounds and through the trees from where they'd appeared.

Within moments, we emerged into a small clearing where a wagon and Asher Caldoun awaited us. It was covered with a stretched leather canopy and had a large black horse strapped securely to the front of it.

"Quickly, Aspen," Susi's voice shocked me out of my daze and I rushed towards the wagon. Asher smiled at me as Caius climbed up onto the small bench that served as the driver's seat, behind which, was the opening to the wagon. He pulled back the canvas and threw the satchel inside. From where he stood, one foot inside the wagon and the other on the small bench, Caius reached down, gesturing for me to pass the babies to him. I handed Silver to him and he disappeared inside the wagon with him before returning for Canon. I noted that he had held his son for the first time, however briefly and my heart ached. I wanted to say something but I knew it wasn't the right moment.

Asher reached out for my hand, "Let's get you inside, Aspen," he said gently and I smiled, appreciative of his help.

"Thank you, Asher," I said, letting him pull me up and I kissed his cheek before entering the wagon.

Caius was arranging the twins on a pile of cushions, creating a makeshift cradle, with furs and blankets to protect against the cold. He stepped aside in the small space but I still had to drop to my knees and crawl so I could be beside my sons. They were still sleeping, but my breasts felt heavy and instinctively I knew I'd have to feed them soon. Once I'd settled myself beside the boys, Caius turned to me, "We're going to be riding hard and fast so I won't be able to come back here for a while."

"I understand. Just tell me where we're going, please."

"I will, but you just need to trust me for a little bit longer, okay?"

He could barely look at me and I felt the stab of that rejection sharply. He resented me because of the babies, I knew it but in the same breath, I knew I couldn't expect him to be okay with this.

"I'll explain everything soon," he assured me, a brief glance my way. I nodded once more as he turned away from me, dodging getting tangled in the blankets as best he could and going to the opening. I settled into a groove created between the thick boards of the wagon's walls, the boys in the crook of each arm, when Caius called out to me,

"Aspen?"

I looked up at him, hurt that he'd called me by my name and not Grey. For a second it looked like he was going to say something, but stopped himself. After a moment, he shook his head, "Keep warm."

He disappeared through the opening before I could reply, leaving me confused, disappointed and suddenly terrified about what the future would hold for Caius and me. I could see his shadow against the canopy as he jumped down to hug his brother before climbing back onto the driver's bench. He flicked the reins and set the wagon in motion. I watched through an opening between the leather canopy and the boards as not only Asher, but Rhea and Susi as well, *turned*. Two of the shadows ran alongside us and I realised with soft elation that Rhea and Susi would be coming with us.

I had no idea where we were going, but I'd have a lot of explaining to do and choices to face once I got there.

The mantle of Alpha was rightfully mine, and I had to decide whether I was going to claim it and, if I was, how to even go about it.

The twins began to fuss, forcing my thoughts away from rebellion and so I readied myself to feed them. In the sway of the wagon, with two she-wolves keeping pace beside us and the father of one of my sons taking us to safety, I fed my children until they were peaceful once more.

Whether I would ever find peace on the run from Sabre and the wrath he was sure to bring down on me, I wasn't so sure.

CHAPTER THIRTY-NINE

SABRE

Hours after the fighting had ceased and wolves and men lay dead on my land, I stood by Aspen's bedroom door as Fenrir and Olcan stepped out of the room.

"They're gone, Sabre," Fenrir confirmed and I clenched my fists by my sides.

"And the traitor?"

"The guard who distracted you has been dealt with."

My mother stepped out of the shadows from where she'd knelt to inspect the body of one of our many dead guards. We had taken a massive hit tonight, but still managed to beat back the Faenymese, hindering their attempted takeover of the manor.

"You should have done it immediately. As soon as you found out what that little whore was up to!"

My mother growled at me, but I simply rolled my eyes at her. I'd had enough of her badgering for one night.

"Sorry, Mother. I was only trying to keep your head on your neck."

I'd killed dozens of wolves today to keep her on her soon to be redacted throne and this was the thanks I got. She could be in the hands of Isaac Akando's men by now—tortured, raped or worse—and all she had were complaints about how I'd handled Aspen.

"You couldn't do one little thing, Sabre!"

"Little thing?" I couldn't believe the audacity of this woman. "Killing women and babies is not a little thing!"

"Even when one woman and one baby could ruin us? Everything we've worked toward? Everything we've yet to accomplish?"

I didn't reply, knowing she was right. I should have done what was required as soon as Aspen refused to obey me and confirm my son as her firstborn, but I'd hesitated. Just like I had the moment I'd seen Aspen with the twins and thought that maybe there could have been a chance for us now that we were parents.

Except they weren't both mine. I wouldn't hesitate again.

"I'll get it done," I said, leaning up from the wall and looking at my mother, still seething.

"How will you—?"

"I said," I snapped, silencing her, "I'll get it done!"

I turned to my friends and soldiers, "Have ten of our best on the hunt for Aspen and the twins. I want her found and I want her dead."

"And the children, Sabre?" Olcan asked.

"Silver is my blood. He's to be returned to me, unharmed."

I went to walk away, to find Rogue and do things that would take my mind completely off her duplicitous sister.

"And the other child?"

I didn't look back at Fenrir's question as I descended the broken stairs of my childhood home, replying, "I have no use for my brother's seed," I looked over my shoulder at them to underline my order, "Kill the mutt."

Acknowledgements

Writing this book was the first time I understood the term: a labour of love. Writing *Duty* has been one of the most enjoyable things I've done in a while and a big reason for that, was my Beta readers and friends, who engaged with the story before, during and after its conception.

A massive thank you to Victoria for answering all my questions. Your brain is an amazing tool; thanks for letting me borrow it! To Katrina for her enthusiasm and the genius idea to make Caius give Aspen a nickname. To Sara for being an amazing critique partner and to Silra, Luke, Lily and Cam for their Beta feedback that helped shape the story. A huge thank you to Nicole, Charis and countless other readers and followers who have invested so much time and effort into my stories, you are appreciated to no end.

Endless thanks go to my editor Annelie, who polished the plot and highlighted the inconsistencies. Your input has been invaluable and I cannot thank you enough for helping me with such professionalism as well as fun throughout the process.

Thank you to my mum and my boyfriend who have supported my writing and listened to my endless random comments about wolves and their questionable mating habits.

Also, a huge thank you to the writing community on Instagram who have shared and liked and promoted *Wolves* from the very beginning. You are truly an amazing tribe to have.

Lastly, a big thank you to you for reading this novel and hope you're ready for the sequel...

About the Author

Charlotte Murphy is the South London born author of the #EverVerse series. The YA Fantasy trilogy, *The Antonides Legacy* and its Dark Fantasy prequel *Genesis of Dragons,* all of which debuted in 2020.

Following the lives, legends and loves of a mighty dynasty, the #EverVerse is a series which now includes *Wolves of Duty,* has something for everyone.

An English with Creative Writing graduate from Brunel University, Charlotte has been writing and reading since a young age and can usually be found at home with her partner and daughter and their large collection of collectable Funko Pops and special edition books that she will probably never have the time to read!

You can follow her on Instagram, TikTok, Twitter and Facebook: @CharliAuthor

Printed in Great Britain
by Amazon

28521300R00235